Concentrate, damn it

Jake repeated the silent mantra, hoping it would stick, hoping it would stop the parade of sinful images marching through his mind.

Then Maggie turned her earnest gaze on him. "Is there anything you need me to do for you?"

Her business-like tone should have doused the crazy feelings. But his traitorous body found another meaning to the innocent question, responding in a way that would have shocked her down to her covered toes.

Jake looked up at the mirrored ceiling, with its etched-gold crown motif, and tried to calm the heat caused by her unintentionally provocative words with thoughts of ice. A great big sheet of ice.

What the hell is wrong with you? Nervous, mousy brunettes weren't his type, even with a sexy accent— he preferred cool, confident blondes. Plus he'd decided less than ten minutes ago to cut women from his life until he'd won the cup. His focus had to be on hockey. No distractions. No exceptions.

His body obviously hadn't got the memo.

Dear Reader,

Thank you for buying my first book! I've wanted to write romance novels since I read my first Mills & Boon at age nine, so having this book published by Harlequin is a dream come true.

Of course, in those days, my stories were a little simpler and usually involved Barbie and Action Man—I thought Ken was a drip!

But perhaps I misjudged Ken. Appearances can be deceptive, after all, and preconceptions can be dangerous.

Think about the famous comedian who suffers from depression when he's off-stage. The confident businesswoman who is really painfully shy. All those nerdy people who turn out to be superheroes.

Hockey players have a reputation for being violent thugs because people can't separate what happens on the ice, from the person on skates. In reality, hockey players are among the most humble, gentlemanly and kind-hearted people I've ever met.

This dichotomy intrigued me and that's how Jake's story was born. Who better to challenge Jake than a woman who believes she's weak, yet had the strength to survive abuse? A woman who thinks she knows the truth about sports stars.

I hope you enjoy the journey of discovery that Maggie and Jake take. I love to hear from readers, so please drop me a line at anna@annasugden.com or Box 174, Regis House, 23 King Street, Cambridge. CB1 1AH. England.

Happy reading!

Anna Sugden

A Perfect Distraction

———

Anna Sugden

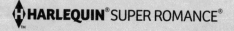
HARLEQUIN® SUPER ROMANCE®

ISBN-13: 978-0-373-60798-3

A PERFECT DISTRACTION

Printed in U.S.A.

ABOUT THE AUTHOR

Three-time Golden Heart finalist, Anna Sugden, is as avid a fan of romance novels and happy endings, as she is of hockey. Her office is filled with overflowing bookcases, treasured trinkets and some pretty awesome hockey memorabilia. When not reading or watching hockey, Anna enjoys cooking, making simple cross-stitch projects and shopping for great shoes. Anna lives in Cambridge, England, with her wonderful husband and two bossy black cats. You can find out more about Anna by visiting her website, www.annasugden.com.

For Keith, my hero, my inspiration—I love you.
For Eileen Sugden (1924–2008)—this is your book.

Acknowledgments

With a first book, there are so many people to thank,
especially when the journey to
publication was a long one.

I couldn't have survived the journey without the writing
advice, support, laughs and love of my best buddies—
Beth Andrews, Terri Garey, Kathleen Long,
Janice Lynn and Tawny Weber. You ladies rock!

Special thanks to:

My agent, Jill Marsal, and my editor, Wanda Ottewell—
you made my dream come true!

Kate Lutter, Maria Imbalzano and Nancy Northcott for
their critiques, support and friendship.

Jeff Vanderbeek for giving me access to the
New Jersey Devils organization.

Ken Daneyko for answering my questions and for
sharing his experiences as a world-class hockey player.

Tom Ferreri, VP of Arena Operations,
Izod Center (Continental Airlines Arena) for taking me
behind the scenes at the arena and
giving me great insights into how it all works.
Thanks, too, for the Zamboni ride!

Caitlin Knighton for sharing her legal expertise and
helping me plot and resolve Maggie's custody issues.

CHAPTER ONE

"You DIDN'T tell me there would be paparazzi!" Maggie Goodman muttered into her phone.

As if she wasn't nervous enough. She ducked behind the trees, out of sight of the snap-happy vultures with their powerful cameras and long-range lenses. Thankfully, they hadn't spotted her; their attention remained focused hungrily on the front entrance of Trump Place.

"Relax, sis," Tracy soothed. "They'll be watching for Manhattan's glitterati. They won't care about the ex-wife of a jack-the-lad footballer. Soccer isn't as popular in the States as it is back home in England."

"Everyone here seems to know David Beckham and Posh Spice."

"Sure, but how many have heard of Wayne Rooney and Colleen, let alone know what they look like? They won't know Lee Goodman." Her voice softened. "Or you."

Anonymity was one of the reasons Maggie had leaped at Tracy's offer to come to the United States. She'd been tired of having the details of her messy divorce splashed across the tabloids and of being asked questions by the gossip media every time her ex was seen with a new woman. He could date who he pleased as long as he left Maggie and her seven-year-old daughter, Emily, alone. They'd suffered enough.

"They won't recognize you," Tracy added. "You look completely different now."

Maggie smoothed her dark brown hair, recently restored to her natural color from bleached blond, then checked the café au lait linen dress and matching jacket she'd worn for this evening's meeting. Understated, professional and elegant, it was as far from tarty footballer's wife as she could get. Not what she was used to wearing—she'd thrown away every bling-covered, barely there outfit as soon as her divorce had been finalized—but it felt normal.

Lee would hate it. Despite the heat, a shiver went through her as she recalled the repercussions of his disapproval. She shook her head to clear the brutal images. She didn't have to worry about what her ex thought anymore. She didn't have to worry what any man thought. Maggie would never give anyone the chance to control her life that way again.

"You're right." She wished the nervous fluttering in her stomach would settle. "I just don't want to let you down. I know how important this meeting is for Making Your Move. What if I mess it up?"

Bad enough that Tracy was flat on her back in a hospital bed after emergency surgery for a ruptured appendix and that her assistant had run off with a minor-league baseball player, one of the relocation business's clients. Maggie would never forgive herself if she ruined her sister's chance of winning the contract with the New Jersey Ice Cats, the local professional hockey team.

"I doubt you could make things worse. What could go wrong?"

"Jake Badoletti's a professional sportsman with a bad-boy reputation. We both know how temperamental they can be." Her gut twisted at the thought of the one she'd divorced nearly a year ago. She touched a finger to the fading scar on her cheek.

"Jake at his worst is a million times better than your snake of an ex. When I dealt with Bad Boy, he was charming—not what I'd expected given the media stories about him."

Maggie had read the client file about the popular hockey player. Jake "Bad Boy" Badoletti was a top defenseman who played as hard off the ice as on it. Clippings from the society pages and celebrity magazines, as well as excerpts from internet sites like TMZ, had shown him dating a staggering array of beautiful women and attending countless parties and celebrity events.

Admittedly, there had been a shift in the stories after the horrific car accident that had taken the life of his good friend. Jake had been injured badly enough that there were fears he'd never skate again, let alone play professionally. Once he'd recovered, the media coverage had focused on his charity work and fan-appreciation events.

Had he really changed, or was he as good at playing the PR game as he was hockey? In her experience, leopards didn't change their spots.

Either way, it made no difference; she had a job to do. "I'd better go or I'll be late."

"I really appreciate you doing this for me, sis."

"Let's see if you still feel like that after I've spoken with Jake."

"You'll be fine. It's a straightforward meeting."

"Get him to sign the paperwork that says everything went okay with his move from Chicago." Maggie tapped her briefcase. "And check if he needs anything else."

"See, piece of cake. You'll be in and out of there in no time. Then I promise you can focus on helping me with the admin side of the business instead of taking client meetings."

"Sounds good." Maggie kept her voice light. "By the time I finish here and collect Emily from your neighbor's house, we'll have missed visiting hours. We'll see you tomorrow."

"I'm glad Emily hit it off with Janice's daughter, Amy. It'll do both of you single mothers a favor." Tracy swore and lowered her voice. "Nurse Attila is outside my room. She'll give me hell if she catches me on my cell. She's already confiscated my laptop."

"That's because you're supposed to be resting, not working."

"Working helps me feel better." Tracy's sharp intake of breath said moving was still painful.

"So would following the doctor's orders."

"You always were the bossy big sister. Oops, got to go. See you tomorrow."

Maggie shook her head indulgently as she snapped

her phone shut. Not much kept her sister down. She'd do well to take a leaf out of Tracy's book.

Helping Tracy was a small way to thank her for giving Maggie the chance to provide a safe, secure life for Emily, far away from Lee. It was also an opportunity to rebuild the self-confidence and independence her ex had stolen from her. This meeting was an important first step. Admittedly, she hadn't done anything yet, but from the smallest acorns...

"Okay. I can do this." She squared her shoulders, then strode purposefully toward the brass-and-glass entrance.

Tracy was right. The paparazzi paid no attention to Maggie, giving her only a brief, dismissive glance as she walked past them and through the doors into the lobby.

Relieved at having made it past the first hurdle unscathed, she stepped into a waiting elevator and jabbed the button for the fortieth floor. She checked her appearance in the mirrored wall and grimaced. The ferry ride from Weehawken, along with the summer heat and humidity, had reddened her cheeks and frizzed her hair. Grateful for the air-conditioning, she tried to fix the damage, then turned her mind to the upcoming meeting.

Jake Badoletti was New Jersey's prodigal son. Recently transferred from Chicago, the Ice Cats management and fans believed he'd bring the ultimate hockey prize, the Stanley Cup, back to his home state. Keen to ensure their star player's transition went smoothly, the Ice Cats had given Tracy carte blanche in managing Jake's relocation. They'd promised to put her on retainer for all their player moves if she delivered for Bad Boy.

With Jake settled into his new place, all Tracy needed was for him to sign off the move. She hadn't wanted to wait until she was out of hospital and had begged a favor.

Maggie swallowed hard. She'd never done anything like this before; she'd been a secretary, then a sports star's wife, not a businesswoman. Talk about a baptism of fire.

Taking in a deep breath, she tried to calm her jittery pulse. It was only one meeting, and Tracy was depending on her to give it her best shot. *I won't let her down.*

The soft digital voice announcing the fortieth floor made her heart thump heavily.

"Showtime." Stiffening her spine, she strode out of the lift.

Her steps faltered. Noise spilled out of the open apartment doors. Voices and laughter, underscored with a heavy bass beat. The air was thick with a mix of expensive perfume and potent aftershave.

Jake had arranged their meeting during a party? That didn't reassure her about the kind of man he was.

Several enormous men headed past her toward the elevator. Built like tanks, with thick necks and tattoos, she guessed they were American footballers. A couple of tanned women wearing microminis, crop tops and skyscraper heels hung off each player's arm.

Maggie couldn't help a pang of envy when she saw one of the women wearing a sexy pair of Giuseppe Zanotti studded sandals. Her toes curled in her sling-

backs. Even though they were Chanel—she hadn't
given up the designer shoes she loved—the sedate pair
didn't have the same feel she knew those strappy sti-
lettos would.

Once, she would have loved being at a party like
this. She would have delighted in rubbing shoulders
with those richer and more famous than she and Lee
were, hoping some of their glitz would come her way.
Back then, she would have found a way to be the center of attention.

"Get your butt over here, Cindy," one of the men
growled impatiently at a blonde tottering unsteadily
behind the group.

Maggie's stomach twisted as darker memories filled
her mind. She turned away, desperate to escape both
her thoughts and the building as fast as possible. Before she could take a step, an inner voice reminded her
that wasn't an option.

She brushed her damp palms against her linen dress
and forced the memories aside. Her heels clicked on the
marble floor as she walked along the hallway.

Her sense of dread grew as she progressed through
the apartment. Aside from the flamboyantly garish
decor, this could have been the house she'd left behind
in England. From the leather, steel and glass furniture
to the top-of-the-range boys' toys in every room, the
place reeked of money and testosterone overload.

She'd expected to find Jake at the heart of the party,
but he wasn't among the crowd in the living room.
There were some fit blokes, probably teammates, and
a couple of actors she recognized from one of the New

York cop dramas, as well as a bunch of fresh-faced clones in buttoned-down shirts and chinos who could be Wall Street whiz kids, lawyers or the wealthy of Upper Manhattan. The women were all tall, thin and tanned with long, shiny hair and the latest designer fashions.

Jake wasn't among the thick necks doing body shots off a giggling redhead sprawled across the long, shiny table in the dining room. Nor in the den, where another group of men sprawled on leather couches alongside yet more tanned, scantily clad women, watching a baseball game on a giant plasma screen.

Where the heck was he? How could she make a good impression on him when she couldn't find him? Biting back a sigh, she headed in a different direction.

Near the master suite, she noticed a pair of handsome, well-built men coming toward her. Clearly brothers, they looked like athletes. Hockey players? Maybe they knew where Jake was hiding.

"Excuse me. Have you seen Jake Badoletti?"

"Honey, whatever you want from Jake, I can do better," the taller man said with a twinkle in his eye.

Though she normally ignored such blatant flirtation, the man's grin was infectious. Maggie couldn't help smiling back.

"Behave, Tru." The stockier bloke frowned, then glanced through the open door behind them. "Jake's kind of busy."

Maggie's smile faded. Great. Her client was holed up in his bedroom with a groupie. She was tempted to leave and make him reschedule, but she didn't want to get Tracy into trouble. "I'll wait for him in the living room. Thank you."

"Don't rush off. Have a drink with us." The friendlier brother stuck out his hand. "Tru Jelinek. I play with Jake on the Ice Cats. This is my brother, Ike."

They seemed harmless enough, and it would be better than waiting alone. "Nice to meet you. Maggie Goodman."

"You're English?" Ike studied her carefully. "I didn't think you Brits were hockey fans."

"I'm not a fan. I'm with Making Your Move. I have an appointment with Jake."

"Tracy's company?"

"I'm her sister. I'm helping her out until she's back on her feet."

"We heard about her busted appendix." He sounded concerned. "Is she doing okay?"

"Yes, thank you. She's recovering nicely, but frustrated she's not healing faster."

"I bet," he muttered.

"Do you know her well?" She was curious about his reaction.

"She helped me find my town house last summer."

From his tone, there was more to that story than the single, bald sentence, but she didn't have time to explore it, as Tru motioned her toward the open bedroom door.

"Since you're here on business, you should go on in."

When Maggie hesitated, he urged her on. "You're not interrupting anything important. Besides, the sooner you're done, the sooner you can join us for a drink."

Swallowing her apprehension over what she'd see

within, she gripped her briefcase tightly and stepped into the doorway.

In the large sitting area of the suite, by the floor-to-ceiling windows, a group of women fluttered around a tall, dark-haired man like a flock of brightly colored exotic birds. That must be Jake Badoletti.

Her mouth went dry.

None of the photos in Tracy's file had done him justice. She'd known he was good-looking, but that didn't begin to describe the man in person.

Heaven help her, he was gorgeous!

Square jawed and rugged, with piercing blue eyes and a crooked grin. He was clearly a warrior of the ice, but his broken nose and scars somehow added to his appeal and made him more intriguing. Unlike the hulking bodies of the thick necks, Jake had the firm, solid lines of an athlete in peak condition. Lean, corded muscle shaped the snug-fitting black shirt and faded jeans. Exciting and enticing, he brimmed with charm and hints of danger.

No wonder he had that reputation—any woman would have a hard time resisting the pull of this particular bad boy. Once upon a time, she'd have been in that crowd, fighting for his attention. Not anymore. Never again.

Still, she couldn't help feeling a little relieved that she probably wouldn't see him again.

He'd be Tracy's problem, assuming Maggie did what she had to do in this meeting. Pushing aside a last-minute nervous quiver, she donned her polite but reserved media smile and entered the lion's den.

"WHAT CAN I get you, Bad Boy?"

A skinny blonde in a figure-hugging yellow micro-dress and spiked heels offered a champagne flute and a shot glass, but the message in her baby blue eyes said, "Choose me."

Jake held up the beer bottle he'd been nursing for the past hour and forced a smile of regret he didn't feel. "I'm good, thanks."

Her full lips pursed in a disappointed pout that six months ago he would have been tempted to kiss away. Now he couldn't dredge up any interest. He was relieved when she and several of her friends flounced off.

The high-pitched chatter of the women who remained reverberated in his head, making his temples throb. The sickly mix of their perfumes made him yearn for fresh air. He had to get out of here. If it wasn't for the paparazzi camped outside the building, Jake would have gone for a walk. He would take the heat and humidity of the city in August if it meant he got some respite.

This party had been a mistake. He should have been in his element. Instead, he felt dissatisfied. Empty, with a lingering sense his life was incomplete.

He wouldn't even be hosting this shindig if Tru hadn't insisted. His childhood friend had said that the best way to celebrate the transfer from Chicago was to invite Jake's new teammates to one of his famous star-studded bashes. Though he hadn't felt like partying since the accident, Jake had given in. Which was why his apartment was filled with the cream of Manhattan's glitterati mingling with stars from the other pro sports teams in New York.

Jake wished he was somewhere, anywhere, else.

He bit back a sigh. His move home was supposed to be a fresh start. God only knew why he'd been lucky enough to survive that crash, but Jake had promised Adam, at his friend's graveside, that he'd make the most of the second chance he'd been given. He'd change his life. Show the world, and himself, that he was more than his reputation. More than his nickname.

He knew nothing would bring Adam back. Nor erase the guilt that lay heavy and hard, like a frozen puck, in his heart. But he'd sworn to honor his friend by fulfilling the dream they'd both had since peewee hockey. The dream that had died for Adam on that back road in Chicago. Jake would win the Stanley Cup and raise it above his head in his friend's memory.

It wouldn't be easy. Hell, it would be the hardest thing he'd ever done. He'd come close before—even made it to the final, before losing in six games to the Penguins. But this time he had to go all the way. Coming second was not an option.

A husky voice interrupted his thoughts. "Come and dance with me, Bad Boy." The invitation came from a brunette dressed in scarlet with lips painted to match. "They're playing our song in the living room."

He shook his head, softening his rejection with a smile. "You go ahead. I'll catch you up shortly."

She shrugged and waggled her fingers in farewell before leaving with a few friends.

If only the rest would follow her.

Jake swigged his beer, grimacing at the flat, warm brew. Once this party was over, his fresh start could begin. He would have one goal, one focus. No more high-octane living, nothing that could be a distraction. No women, either. Dating was off the cards until next June. He'd find somewhere else to live, too. This Trump Place apartment was pure Bad Boy. The old him, not who he needed to be now.

That reminded him—he was meeting someone from Making Your Move this evening. He was glad he'd deliberately scheduled the follow-up during the party; he had an excuse to duck out of the *fun*.

A movement by the door caught his attention. He glanced over, wondering idly whether the newcomer was a celebrity, a socialite or a puck bunny, and mentally braced himself to switch on the charm.

His attention caught and held.

The woman standing there clearly wasn't a party guest. She wore little makeup and her dark brown hair was scraped back. A few curls had escaped to softly frame her face. Her neatly tailored brown outfit draped nicely over her curves, but there wasn't an inch of skin visible from midcalf to neck. Even her toes were covered.

Instead of turning him off, she had him wondering if those shapely calves meant her legs were gorgeous all the way up. Did she paint her toenails fire-engine red or shell pink? How much smooth, creamy skin would be revealed if he undid one of those large jacket buttons?

Unexpected heat flashed through Jake.

This was crazy. He was surrounded by the most

beautiful women in New York, yet his body chose to spring to attention at Miss Prim and Proper?

Pull yourself together, Badoletti. He shook his head to clear it.

"Is something wrong, Bad Boy?" A model in a hot-pink crop top, which emphasized both her tan and her jutting shoulder and pelvic bones, touched his arm.

Fighting the urge to brush off her hand, he shook his head again. "Excuse me. There's someone I need to see."

She followed his gaze. "Sure," she said, flicking a dismissive glance at the woman in brown before sauntering away with a deliberate swing to her hips.

As Jake walked across the room, Tru appeared beside the intriguing newcomer.

"Hey, bro, this is Tracy's sister, Maggie." Curiosity gleamed in his green eyes. "Apparently, you have a meeting."

"We do." Jake grinned. "Thanks for coming, Maggie. Hope I haven't kept you waiting."

"Not at all." She shook his hand.

Her accent made her sound cool and polite. Yet the instant their fingers touched, tiny sparks of heat danced across his skin. Desire speared through him, even as she pulled her hand away.

"Don't keep her working too long. This is a party." Tru laid his hand on Maggie's shoulder. "Hope to see you again very soon."

"Thank you for your help."

Her soft smile at his friend as he left caused Jake's stomach to tighten.

"Let's find somewhere quieter to talk," he suggested, motioning for her to precede him out of the master suite.

"All right."

Maggie's expression was stony as they walked down the hall, past several laughing, tipsy couples, toward the spare room he'd commandeered as an office. He was surprised by her stiff attitude until he noticed the wariness in her chocolate-brown eyes.

Realization dawned. She thought he wanted to turn their meeting into a private party.

Disappointment twinged. It was his own damn fault. He'd spent too long living up to his image and courting publicity, relishing every column inch and glossy photo.

That would all change after today. And she was here to help.

Jake reached past her to fling open the door. She flinched when it banged against the wall. Jeez, the woman was uptight.

"I'm sorry for the mess." He gathered up folders from the marble-topped coffee table and tossed them into a box. "There's so much paperwork associated with a transfer."

Maggie scanned the room, then joined him. A hint of her light, fresh fragrance teased his nose as she handed him some files.

"I've seen worse. Besides, the boxes help distract you from the—" she waved a hand to indicate the purple-and-gold-flocked wallpaper, the matching curtains and gold-leaf-encrusted furniture "—unusual decorating style." Her lips twitched.

So Miss Buttoned-Up had a sense of humor.

"Yeah, it's kinda over-the-top." He grinned, feeling a kick of pleasure at her answering half smile. "The owner's a young basketball phenom who's moving to Miami. He didn't want to give up his apartment and it suited me to rent from him."

Maggie pulled a folder and pen from her briefcase. "We should get started. I don't want to keep you from your guests."

He didn't bother to correct her assumption that he wanted to return to the party.

"Grab a seat." He shifted some boxes from a pair of purple-and-gold silk-covered armchairs.

As she sat, Maggie's hem hitched higher, momentarily displaying more smooth leg. She quickly straightened her skirt so it covered her knees once more.

The tantalizing glimpse sent a spike of heat through Jake. He brushed it off, annoyed. He wasn't some long-haired dude in those romance novels his mom read, who got turned on by a nice ankle. Then why did his body tighten uncomfortably as he watched her undo those big buttons on her jacket to reveal a demure neckline? He'd been right about the creamy skin.

Focus.

Maggie put on black-framed glasses. They should have made her look worse, but they actually made her look cute. He imagined her removing them and letting down her hair like in those old movies.

Concentrate, damn it.

She turned her earnest gaze on him. "Is there anything you need me to do for you?"

Her businesslike tone should have doused the crazy feelings. But his traitorous body found another meaning to the innocent question, responding in a way that would have shocked her down to her covered toes.

Jake looked up at the mirrored ceiling with its etched gold crown motif, and tried to calm the heat raging in his groin with thoughts of ice. A great big sheet of ice.

What the hell is wrong with you? Nervous, mousy brunettes weren't his type, even with a sexy accent—he preferred cool, confident blondes. Plus less than ten minutes ago he'd reaffirmed his decision to cut women from his life until he'd won the Cup. His focus had to be on hockey. No distractions. No exceptions.

His body obviously hadn't got the memo.

"I want to move," he blurted, desperate to focus on the meeting.

She frowned, surprise evident in her voice. "You just said this suited you."

"I thought it did, but I've changed my mind."

"I see." The surprise turned to concern. "May I ask what's wrong? Is it the location?"

Jake nodded. "Don't get me wrong, I love Manhattan. But it's a long, grueling season—eighty-two games from October to April, half on the road, then a play-off run that will hopefully last through June. It'd be better if I lived closer to the arena and the airport."

"Won't you miss everything the city has to offer?"

How did he explain that that was the point? Staying here would be a mistake. Too much temptation, too easy to get sucked back into his old lifestyle, to be distracted. When he'd rented this place, he'd been sure he could handle it. But tonight was proving otherwise. "I'll still be able to get into the city if I need to."

"Fair enough." Maggie pulled some papers out of her folder. "We should complete this questionnaire. It'll help me figure out the kind of place you're after."

"Okay." He leaned forward and rested his arms on his thighs. "Go for it."

Maggie tensed and scooted way back in her seat.

What the hell? Stunned, he froze.

It took a moment to register that she was uncomfortable with him sitting that close. Carefully, he shifted and eased away. She relaxed visibly, making him wonder why she was so skittish around him.

"So," she said briskly. "You want to be in New Jersey. Do you have an area in mind?"

"Somewhere near where my parents live."

Her brown eyes widened. "You want to go home?"

Her question struck a chord. Was that what he wanted?

Six months ago, he would have laughed at the idea of living in the quiet, leafy-green suburbs alongside the workaholic commuters and the soccer moms. Now it seemed like the perfect solution. He could buy a house with a yard. Have room to breathe, the time and space he needed to cope with the stress of the season. Somewhere to chill or hang out with Tru and Ike. A place to be himself—whatever the hell that meant.

Best of all, there would be no distractions in Jersey.

"Yeah," he said finally. "I want to go home."

CHAPTER TWO

"ANOTHER WEEK of bed rest!"

As her sister slumped against her pillows, Maggie bit her lip to hold back a smile.

"But you're home, Auntie Tracy, and we'll look after you." Emily danced around the room with the boundless energy of a seven-year-old. "We're much nicer than Nurse Attila."

"That's true." Tracy crossed her arms. "I expect the best service in this establishment. You'll have to wait on me hand and foot."

"Will you give me big tips?" Emily widened her eyes innocently. "You said that's how you get the best service."

Maggie swallowed a laugh.

Her sister groaned. "I thought a niece did those things for her favorite aunt out of the goodness of her heart."

"Does that mean *for free?*"

"I don't know where you get that precocious streak from," Tracy grumbled.

"Don't you?" Maggie arched an eyebrow.

The doorbell rang with a familiar double peal.

"That's Amy. Can I go and play with her?" Emily skipped from foot to foot.

"What happened to looking after me?" Tracy whined theatrically.

"Mummy can do that. Besides, Amy's mum is making brownies. With pecans *and everything*." Emily turned to Maggie. "Please."

"You may, but…" Her voice trailed off as her daughter thundered downstairs. "Make sure you're back at noon," she called out.

"Thanks, Mummy. You're the best." The front door opened, then slammed shut.

"Tossed over for brownies," Tracy groused.

"Not just any brownies. They have pecans *and everything*." Maggie tucked the quilt more closely around her sister. "Enjoy the peace and quiet while you can."

Despite her banter with Emily, Tracy was pale, with dark circles under her eyes and a sheen of perspiration on her forehead. The journey from the hospital hadn't been easy, with every bump taking its toll. "I'll have plenty of time to rest, thanks to that doctor."

"At least he agreed you could come home."

"Only if I promised not to work for a week. I bet that's Nurse Attila's proviso."

"She wants you to heal properly," Maggie said.

"She doesn't want me landing back in her ward anytime soon."

"And you, such a model patient." Maggie gathered some magazines and placed them nearby. "Time for more painkillers. Are you hungry? I could make you a snack."

"I'm fine." Tracy waved her hand impatiently. "Grab a chair and tell me what happened at the party."

Maggie hesitated. She'd spent most of last night tossing and turning, her body strangely hot and prickly. Though she'd wanted to blame the heat, she knew full well what, or rather who, had caused her inability to relax and sleep.

Jake Badoletti.

The unwanted attraction that had flared during the meeting had remained with her long into the night. She'd berated herself for being susceptible to his roguish smile and easy charm. After everything she'd been through, she should have been immune to the tall, dark and dangerous sports star. His touch shouldn't have made awareness tingle through her. His deep, rich voice shouldn't have made her pulse skip as if each word was a seductive caress.

Why? She hadn't reacted to a man in ages. She didn't *want* to react to a man like Jake ever again.

Though he hadn't acted like she'd expected—no superstar superiority complex, no outrageous demands or sleazy flirting—Maggie had learned the hard way not to be fooled by a handsome facade. To know a devil-may-care smile could hide darkness. She ran her finger over her cheek, the small scar a visible reminder of her last mistake.

Perhaps she was being unfair to Jake, tarring him with the same brush as Lee. But for Emily's safety and Maggie's peace of mind, she couldn't afford to relax her guard.

Besides, she wouldn't see him again. Tracy would handle all further communication with him. Maggie ignored the twinge in her chest at that thought.

"Was anyone interesting at the party?" Tracy asked.

Safe ground. "I'm sure there were loads of famous people, but I didn't recognize many. I saw that sexy guy from *CSI* who's doing a guest stint with *CSI: New York.*" She sat in the armchair by the bed. "Apparently, that bloke we liked from *Sex and the City* dropped by, but I didn't see him."

"Bloody typical. I miss all the fun."

"Weren't you the one who sat near Tim Robbins at Madison Square Garden? I've lost track of all the stars you've seen at Yankee Stadium."

"But I've never been to a bash like Jake's."

"It wasn't anything special."

"I'm not as blasé as you about hobnobbing with celebrities."

"Jaded, rather than blasé," Maggie said softly.

"Well, you *were* one of them, not long ago."

"Hardly. My only real claim to fame was being a WAG."

"Being one of the footballers' wives and girlfriends makes you a celebrity, too."

"Only because every moment of your life is covered endlessly in the press. What you wear, what you eat, how you look—it's all discussed and analysed. The paparazzi follow you everywhere, watching and waiting. The appeal of having my picture on the cover of all the magazines and being recognized in the supermarket wore off a long time ago."

Much to Lee's displeasure. When she'd first married him, she'd loved the publicity and lifestyle that went with being part of a celebrity couple. It hadn't taken long for the glamour to fade. For her to tire of having every moment of her life controlled by her ex to optimize media opportunities. "Lee still chases the headlines and the column inches. He's desperate to be another David Beckham."

"He's not a good enough footballer. He's never played for one of the top Premier League teams or been picked for England."

Painful memories of what had happened every time Lee hadn't been selected flickered through Maggie's mind. Her now-healed arm twinged.

Her reaction must have shown, because Tracy changed the subject, her tone brisk. "How did the meeting with Jake go?"

"Fine." Maggie pushed the past aside. "He was pleased with the move, but he wants somewhere else."

"Really? I was sure he'd love that apartment."

"Apparently, Manhattan is too *distracting*." Maggie added air quotes. She found it hard to believe an athlete with his reputation wanted a sedate life in the suburbs. "He wants to concentrate on hockey."

"Moving to a new team is quite an upheaval, and it'll be a tough start to the season because he hasn't played in six months. It's hard keeping up with that life when you're healthy, let alone when you've been injured so badly."

"True." She'd struggled to cope after Emily's birth and had wanted desperately to withdraw from the social whirl, but Lee had insisted she continue. It had taken a doctor's intervention to get some respite. "Still, it seems a little sudden."

"He's probably one of those people who makes up his mind to do something and wants it done now, now, now."

"That, I can believe."

"What's he after?"

"A house with at least three bedrooms and a large garden." Maggie explained briefly what she and Jake had discussed. "Honestly, I don't think he's thought through what he really wants. So I'd recommend somewhere with the flexibility to adapt to his needs, like adding a home gym."

"Sounds good." Tracy winced as she straightened. "I should get on this right away."

"You're not up to it." Maggie shook her head. "No business for a week, remember?"

"That was before I knew Bad Boy wanted to buy a house."

"He can wait until you're better."

"Even if he's willing to delay, the Ice Cats won't be happy. This project is a big step up from the ad hoc assignments I've done for them and the clock's ticking. Until Jake signs to say the job's finished to his satisfaction, Making Your Move won't get that retainer." Tracy's words tumbled over each other as her voice rose in pitch. "I can't risk them changing their minds. Becoming their sole contractor for player moves for the next five years would make my business financially secure. Everything has to be perfect."

"I know this project is important, but so is your health. If you rush back to work, your recovery will take even longer."

"I have no choice. There are plenty of firms willing to take my place. Unless..." Tracy's expression became pensive. "I know we agreed you'd only do that one meeting, but would you be willing to help me out again?"

Maggie knew what was coming and hated that she couldn't refuse. Her sister wouldn't rest with this situation nagging her. "What do you need me to do?"

"Manage Jake. Mimi, my favorite real-estate agent, will help you find suitable properties. Also, check his rental papers to see the penalties for early termination and..."

Panic fluttered in her chest at Tracy's list of instructions. It was too much. She couldn't be responsible for all that. "I can't. I have no experience." Lee's sneering voice echoed in her head. *You're useless.* "I'll make a mistake and blow it for you."

"Rubbish!" Her sister smacked the bed. "I hate what that bastard did to you. Bad enough that he controlled every aspect of your life like a modern-day Svengali. His belittling jibes did as much damage as his fists." Her sister softened her tone. "You're a smart, capable woman. You can do this and much more."

Tracy forced Maggie to meet her gaze. "Look what you've achieved in the past few months. When I fell ill, you moved over here, found a summer activity camp for Emily and sorted out a school for the fall. To say nothing of what you've done for me at work."

"But I might make a mess of things and cost you the business."

"You won't. Besides, I'll be right here overseeing

everything." Tracy's smile was wry. "Even if you won't let me use my laptop, I can listen and advise."

This was supposed to be Maggie's fresh start. She'd vowed Emily would never see her as weak and pathetic again. Just because things weren't going smoothly didn't mean she should give up. She owed it to herself to see what she was capable of.

With her sister nearby, what could go wrong? "It's only for the week?"

Tracy nodded eagerly. "Most of the work can be done by phone or email. You probably won't have to see Jake more than once."

See Jake again? Maggie's pulse gave a funny little lurch. It had been one thing to dismiss her reaction to him when she'd thought she wouldn't see him again. Quite another to test her resolve not to be affected by another meeting with him.

Her sister continued, "Then you can return to taking care of the admin, like we agreed. I prom—" She made a wry face. "No promises?"

A smile slipped out. "Okay. I'll do my best."

"Thanks." Tracy settled against the pillows. "So, is Bad Boy as sexy in person?"

"He's nice," Maggie hedged, cursing the heat that filled her cheeks. "Polite, charming."

"You fancied him, I can tell."

Arguing would only fuel her sister's curiosity. "He's better looking than his photos," she conceded. "Why don't I get you a cup of tea?"

"Thanks." Tracy must be tired to accept the distraction so easily. "Bring up Jake's file, too, and let's see what needs to be done."

Maggie had made it to the door when her sister giggled. "You should have the next meeting here, so I can see how hot Jake really is."

Maggie didn't dignify that comment with a response.

As she went downstairs, she wished for a fraction of Tracy's self-confidence. Her sister's bitter divorce from her cheating husband hadn't slowed her down. It had made her stronger.

It was time Maggie followed her example. She'd vowed the night she left Lee to do everything she could to provide her daughter with a happy, safe and secure life. Tracy was giving her the perfect opportunity to make that happen. Maggie needed to dip into the well of strength that had helped her survive her marriage and get on with it.

Maggie made the tea, then went into the office. As she grabbed Jake's file, a picture slid onto the desk. Those killer ice-blue eyes stared up at her. She jammed the photo back into the folder, then put a hand over her pounding heart as if she could slow its runaway pace. The last thing she wanted or needed in her life right now was a man. Least of all, Jake Badoletti.

"He's just a client," she told herself. "Nothing more."

She ignored the inner voice that cackled with disbelief as she went back upstairs.

NOTHING APPEALED TO him.

Jake studied the property sheets spread across his parents' kitchen table and sighed. He'd been excited when Maggie had emailed them ahead of their meeting. An hour later, and with Maggie due to arrive any minute, he had to admit he wasn't jazzed about a single one.

"You don't like these houses?" His mom gave him a glass of lemonade.

"Definitely not these tasteless monsters." He gathered some rejected properties into a pile. "These are too modern, lack soul." He added another group to the stack. "And these…"

"Are you sure you're ready for this change?" she asked softly, concern in her blue eyes. "You've been through so much and this is such a big decision."

"It's because of what I went through that I want to change my life, Ma. I have to."

She didn't look convinced.

His cell rang, and he glanced at the caller ID but didn't answer. The popular starlet's persistence was beginning to tick him off.

"That hasn't changed." His mom smiled. "The girls still call."

"But I don't call them back. I told you, I'm focusing on hockey. Period."

"You're sure?"

"Definitely."

"You're a good boy, Jake. No matter what they call you."

He was glad no one was around to see him choke at his mother's faith in him. It proved he wasn't beyond hope. And reinforced why he couldn't waste this second chance.

He refocused on the property sheets. "These town houses have small yards."

His mom added them to the no pile.

"That leaves these four. I don't really like any of them, but Maggie won't be impressed if I reject everything sight unseen."

"Who's Maggie?" His mom's innocent expression didn't fool him.

He kept his voice casual. "She works for that relocation agency. She'll take me around the places I'm interested in."

"I see." She sighed heavily. "I'd hoped your new life would include settling down, getting married and giving me grandchildren."

"One thing at a time, Ma." He shook his head at her. "Remember, no distractions."

"Since when is a nice girl a distraction?"

An image of Maggie in that mud-brown suit flitted through his mind, followed swiftly by teasing little snapshots: the momentarily hitched skirt, the undone buttons, her smooth, creamy skin. The way she nibbled her full bottom lip when she was thinking. He could swear a hint of her fragrance wafted past him.

His blood heated.

Maggie fit his mom's idea of a nice girl. Given how many erotic dreams he'd had about Maggie since their meeting and how many times she'd popped into his thoughts, the mousy brunette was also one hell of a distraction.

"Nothing but hockey, Ma, until I win the Cup."

"Many players have wives and families and still win

the Cup." She squeezed his hand. "You need balance in your life."

The doorbell rang, saving him from having to reply.

He leaped to his feet. "I'll go."

Maggie stood on the front porch. Today's gray suit was as drab as the brown thing. The demure neckline had a lace collar that would have suited a nun's habit. The itty-bitty heels of her gray sandals looked uncomfortable to walk in. No sign of toenail polish. Not that he was obsessed or anything.

He tamped down his jumping pulse. "How's it going?"

"Fine, thank you." She smiled uncertainly. "I hope I'm not too early. I'm still finding my way around and get lost, even with GPS, so I leave extra time."

"Not a problem."

"Come in." His mom bustled past him. "It's too warm to be standing on the porch. I'm Tina Badoletti." She took Maggie's arm and ushered her down the hall toward the kitchen, chatting a mile a minute about the weather, her garden and the flowers she'd just picked.

Jake followed behind, shaking his head fondly.

As Maggie walked into the kitchen, she turned to give him a slightly shell-shocked smile. His eyes were drawn downward, over her curves to those shapely calves and ankles and back up to…

Buttons. Lace-covered buttons that looked like sugar-dusted candy. In a line, along the side seam of her pencil skirt.

His fingers itched to discover if they were real or just for show. His heart thudded against his ribs at the thought of undoing them, one at a time. His groin tightened at the image of what would be revealed beneath.

Jake slammed to a halt outside the kitchen. This wasn't supposed to happen. This *wasn't* going to happen. He had to focus.

Right after he figured out how to spend the afternoon with Maggie without getting distracted by those damn buttons.

He resisted the urge to knock his head against the wall and entered the kitchen.

Maggie sat at the table with a glass of lemonade. His mom had commandeered the seat next to her and was in the midst of a merciless barrage of questions.

He should intervene. Grown men, even some of the toughest hockey players, had quaked at Tina Badoletti's inquisition. Maggie, the nervous mouse, stood no chance.

Yet as Jake hovered in the doorway, ready to leap to the rescue, he realized she was handling his mom's nosiness just fine. "Of course I have pictures of Emily." Maggie laughed as she pulled out a purse-size photo album.

The tension tightening his shoulders slipped away at the cozy sight of the two of them with their heads together, flipping through family pictures. Funny, he couldn't imagine any of the women in his past being so comfortable with his mom.

Who did that say more about, them or him? He cleared his throat, trying to ease the knot lodged there.

Maggie stiffened. Her wide-eyed gaze shot to him. She closed the album and stuffed it in her purse, then pulled out her notepad. Disappointment tugged his chest at her jerky actions. The nervous mouse was back.

How could he get her to relax again? To replace her stricken expression with the bright smile she'd worn a moment ago.

He said the first thing that popped into his head. "Ma, if you get out my baby pictures, I'll tell Dad about your bingo winnings in the flour canister."

His mom rose, waggling her finger at him. "As if I'd show her your scrawny, naked, six-month-old butt." She turned to Maggie. "He was the skinniest baby."

Maggie bit her lip as if suppressing a giggle.

Jake slid into the chair his mom had vacated, giving Maggie a "what can you do" shrug. "You'll wonder why I wanted to move home when I get so much abuse."

"Pfft," his mom said. "Enough people treat you like a movie star. If I didn't keep you grounded, your head wouldn't fit through the door. Isn't that right, Maggie?"

The giggle escaped, becoming a laugh.

He liked that her laugh was full-bodied, not the squeaky titter so many women had. He also liked how it lit up her face, her eyes.

Clearly torn between siding with his mom and not offending her client, Maggie stuttered an answer, watching him carefully.

"Yeah, you girls stick together." He winked at her

She looked startled for a moment, then smiled tentatively.

His mom slid a plate with a slice of pound cake before Maggie, overriding her objection with a pat on her shoulder. "You'll need the energy to help my son choose a house. He's been as miserable as a wet cat about the ones you sent."

Heat rose up his neck. "Ma, you're killing me. Don't you have something to do?"

"I have to get dinner on." She pulled vegetables out of the refrigerator. "You know your father is starving by seven." She pointed an onion at the pile of papers. "Those are all my son's rejects."

"You didn't like anything?" Maggie frowned as she sifted through the discarded sheets and cross-checked them with her list.

"These four are possibilities." He handed her the details.

"I thought this might have met your needs." She tapped one of the discarded sheets. "It has substantial square footage, a private gym, a master suite with a whirlpool tub and a large yard with trees."

The overblown McMansion *had* appealed to his ego, but only briefly. "Is that the one with a freaking full-size ballroom?"

Her grin caught him off guard. "I thought that would be the clincher. Don't all you hockey players want to be on *Battle of the Blades?*"

"Hell...heck no!" he spluttered. "I don't want to be in any reality show, let alone one that makes me dance or figure skate or whatever you call it." He smiled ruefully at the teasing twinkle in her eyes. There was that sense of humor again. "You got me."

"I'm sorry, I couldn't resist." There was a touch of uncertainty in her eyes, like she'd expected him to be mad. "Back home, lots of sports stars clamor to be on reality shows. I think they're nuts wanting that invasion of privacy. Everyone knowing every intimate detail of their lives."

That had the bitter ring of experience. He wondered what her story was. "Yeah. That can get old pretty quick."

Their gazes met. The click of understanding between them seemed almost physical. What was it about this woman?

A loud "Coo-ee" made them both blink, breaking the connection.

Aunt Karina, his mom's best friend, came in, her gray curls bouncing. "You're home and you haven't been to see me, Jakey?" She shook her finger at him, then hugged him close. "You're too busy with your hockey rabbits to visit an old woman?"

He stifled a grin. Despite being in America for many years, she still muddled her English. "Puck bunnies, Aunt Karina."

"Bunny, rabbit, it's the same, no?" She shrugged.

"Sure. But you're my number-one girl."

She sniffed at his flattery, but her smile was indulgent. "It's good to have you back. Your mother missed you. Me, not so much."

"Mom said you have a new boyfriend."

"At my age, I have gentlemen friends. There's no funny stuff…they're too old." She sighed. "And I'm too old for a toy boy…boy toy."

"You're not too old," he reassured her.

"Correct answer." Her eyes lit up as she spotted

Maggie. "You let me chatter on when you have a girl-friend visiting?"

"I'm not—"

"She's not—" He and Maggie spoke simultaneously, then stopped.

"We're not dating. Maggie's helping me find a house."

"Uh-huh." His mom turned back to her chopping.

"Uh-huh." Aunt Karina sat at the table.

It was as if they could see inside his head. Could see the effect Maggie had on him.

Damn it. If he wanted to convince anyone he wasn't interested in Maggie, he'd have to convince himself. Right. Like that would happen.

He had more of a chance of breaking Wayne Gretzky's scoring records.

Maggie fought envy as she watched the fond banter between Jake and the two women. She could imagine such teasing interplay at family gatherings in the bright, airy kitchen.

So different from the stilted atmosphere in her parents' house, which had lacked any kind of emotional warmth. Where her father dominated, disapproval reigned and opinions from anyone else were not tolerated.

This was the home she and Tracy had yearned for. From the postcards adorning the fridge to the cute curtains framing the large window and the smell of baking that lingered in the air, it felt cozy and welcoming.

No wonder Jake had found the Trump Place apartment lacking.

"I can see why the houses I sent through don't appeal." She picked up the four remaining property sheets. "I suspect these won't be right, either."

Surprise lit Jake's blue eyes. "What's wrong with them?"

Maggie had a momentary pang of unease. He might not like her disagreeing with him. But it was her job to make his move go smoothly. Tracy would expect nothing less. As uncomfortable as it made her, she shouldn't hold back her thoughts.

She fought her nerves, then indicated the first sheet. "This has great square footage, but the rooms look dark and poky. You could knock down walls to make it more open, but it would be a lot of work and upheaval."

"I agree, for sure. I don't need the disruption."

Maggie blinked. He'd listened to her opinion.

She set the property sheet aside, then slid the next one to him. "This one has an unfinished basement. More upheaval. Plus, the house is on a steep slope, with the garage at the bottom. There may be problems with water runoff."

Aunt Karina tsked. "You don't want to worry about flooding."

Jake nodded. "I had reservations about the basement, but hadn't thought about the slope. Good catch."

Heat tinted her cheeks at his praise.

"I'm sure your thoughts about the other two houses will be on the money. Why bother even having a look at them?"

His faith in her judgment gave her confidence a boost. "You might feel differently once you've seen the houses. Also, other things may occur to you as we go round them, which will help guide Mimi and me in finding other properties for you."

"Yeah. It just seems like a waste of time."

Maggie's breath caught in her chest. Had she misjudged his easygoing nature?

"I don't see why it's so hard to choose." Jake's mum chopped herbs with impressive speed. "You travel so much, you won't be around to worry about dark rooms or whatever."

"You and Dad were just as picky before you bought this place, Ma. We saw dozens of houses and you rejected every one."

Tina smiled fondly at her son. "I know you wanted the best for us, but we didn't want to waste the earnings from your first big contract."

Jake bought this place for his parents? Lee wouldn't have been so generous.

"You could have had a house twice this size and I'd have still had money left over." His ears were tinged with pink.

"After that cramped, rented apartment, a house of our own was a dream come true. But we wanted somewhere that felt like home. This house welcomed us."

He rose and hugged his mother. "That's what I want, too, Ma."

Maggie swallowed the lump in her throat. "It's a wonderful home. Jake will have a problem finding anything that's as nice as this."

His half smile sent a glow through her body.

"It's true—this is the perfect house," Aunt Karina

added. "That's why when my boys offered to buy me my own place, I turned them down. I live in the garden house."

"She means the carriage house at the back of the property—in the *garden*." Jake smiled indulgently. "And Aunt Karina isn't really my aunt, she's Mom's best friend."

"But I'm the aunt of your heart, no?"

"Of course."

"Tina and I raised our boys together." Aunt Karina pulled a photo from her apron and passed it across the table. "These four handsome boys are mine."

The two oldest looked familiar. "I met these two at Jake's party."

Jake nodded. "Tru and Ike."

Aunt Karina frowned. "When will you invite me and your mama to your parties?"

"That was the last one. No more parties. I'm focusing on hockey."

The two older women exchanged a worried look. "You'll become a dull boy, Jakey. All work and no fun."

Jake's shoulders tensed. Clearly, this was not a discussion he wanted to have.

Empathy she didn't expect tugged at Maggie. Time for a distraction.

"Is that the time?" She shoved the four property sheets in her bag. "We should get a move on if we're to take a look at these today."

"Good idea." With a grateful look, Jake grabbed the lifeline she'd tossed him.

The two women saw them off at the front door, reminding them to take care in the heat.

The car was halfway down the street before Jake turned to Maggie. "Thanks for the bailout. They're still getting used to the idea that I'm changing things up now I'm home."

"It's nice they care so much. You're lucky." She heard the wistfulness in her voice and cleared her throat to cover it.

For all his reputation, the way he behaved toward the older women said a lot about him. He was fond of them, but he also respected them.

Jake had treated her with respect, too. It had been a long time since anyone other than her sister had treated her like an equal.

For the first time since she'd agreed to help her sister, the knot of tension eased in Maggie's gut. Maybe she'd misjudged how difficult this job would be. If Jake continued to be this easy to work with, it would be a piece of cake.

A couple of days house-hunting, a week tops, and she would have completed her first contract. Then, who knew what else she could achieve?

"YOU'VE NEVER SEEN *The Godfather?*"

Jake's shocked expression made Maggie smile as she followed the GPS's instructions to turn right, the following afternoon. "What is it with blokes and that film?"

"*The Godfather* is an iconic piece of modern culture."

"You sound like Tom Hanks in *You've Got Mail.*"

"Isn't that a chick flick?" He frowned.

"You've never seen *You've Got Mail?*" She widened her eyes.

Jake hitched an eyebrow.

"He calls *The Godfather* the I-Ching and quotes it to Meg Ryan as lessons for life."

The GPS interrupted his reply. "Your destination is ahead, on the right."

The relaxed atmosphere vanished as she pulled up to the last property on the day's list.

"I hope this house is better than the other five we've seen today." Jake got out of the car.

Maggie tried to quell the flutter in her stomach at his disappointed tone.

Yesterday's visits had gone well, even though, as expected, the four properties hadn't been appropriate. They'd spent the rest of the afternoon driving around the area to fine-tune Jake's housing likes and dislikes. He'd been open and frank, while listening to her suggestions. Driving between houses, they'd chatted about other things—a real conversation, rather than the self-centered monologue she'd expected.

This morning, after a good-natured argument about who would drive, they'd set off to look at some new properties that she and Mimi had selected. Though the first house hadn't been bad, the places had gone steadily downhill after that.

With each rejected house, Jake's enthusiasm had waned and turned to frustration.

Turning off the engine, Maggie fought the urge to run away. What kind of example would that set for

Emily? If she wanted her daughter to be proud of her, she'd have to brave it out. Besides, she wouldn't let Tracy down.

A wall of heat and humidity hit her as she got out of the car. The silk underskirt stuck to her legs, making her wish she'd gone for comfort and cool. Could she get rid of her jacket?

She glanced at her outfit. Even without the matching jacket, the beige linen dress was smart. No fancy frippery, apart from the column of bow-shaped buttons down her back. Lee wouldn't have allowed her out of the house wearing the simple, knee-length style with its modest neckline, but then he hadn't wanted her to look understated and professional.

Though she'd have preferred a brighter color and a less severe cut, Maggie was still trying to find a style she felt comfortable with. All she knew for sure was it wouldn't be anything Lee found suitable. She shrugged off her jacket and laid it across the backseat, then gathered her bag and turned.

Jake stood behind her. His rigid stance said he was glaring at her behind his Ray-Bans. "This one doesn't feel right, either."

Resisting the unexpected urge to snap at him, she forced a polite smile. "Shall we take a quick look, anyway? We've learned a lot from the other places we've seen, and it's all helping us narrow down what you're after."

"Let's get this done." He nodded sharply, then strode up the path to where Mimi waited by the front door.

How on earth did the older woman maintain her immaculate appearance? Not a silver hair out of place nor a wrinkle in her mint-green pantsuit. Even her smile looked as fresh as it had first thing this morning.

You can do this, Maggie told herself fiercely as she followed him. Inside the foyer, she stopped. Her stomach dropped to her midheeled Marc Jacobs sandals.

Jake was right. The house was awful.

Though normal on the outside, the Dutch Colonial was a nightmare of rooms painted in eye-popping acid colors. Any original features had long since been stripped out. Someone must have doctored the pictures on the property sheet.

"They've ruined a great old house." Mimi shook her head sadly as she led them past the sunken fishpond in the living room to the narrow kitchen with lime-green appliances. "No wonder they dropped the price."

Maggie stopped by the rear stairs. "Let's call it a day. We can meet again in the morning when we'll have other properties for you to look at."

Jake fixed his ice-blue gaze on her. "This isn't working. We're getting nowhere."

Did that mean he was going to fire her? The internal voice sneered again. *Useless.*

She injected a cheeriness she didn't feel into her voice. "I know today's been disappointing, but there are plenty of other available houses. I'm sure we'll see something suitable tomorrow."

"We said at the beginning it would take time to find the perfect place," Mimi added.

Jake ignored the real-estate agent. "We're chasing our tails. Nothing we've seen has come close to being right."

Maggie tamped down her irritation. He made it sound like they hadn't tried, when he was the one who was so hard to please. The mocking internal voice grew louder.

"We understand your frustration," she said soothingly. "But we've come a long way in a day and a half. Give us a bit longer."

"How much longer?" He crossed his arms over his broad chest and glared at her. "Training camp is around the corner. Once that starts, I need to focus on my play, not where I'll be living."

"You will," she promised calmly, even as desperation clawed at her insides.

His arched eyebrow said he doubted it.

She couldn't lose this contract. He had to give them another chance. "Why don't we meet tomorrow and go through the properties on the system together? That'll speed up the process."

"Great idea. I'll head to the office and get started." Mimi shepherded them toward the front of the house.

Jake shrugged, then indicated Maggie should go first.

She walked ahead of him down the hallway, aware of his brooding presence behind her. Far too aware. Her body clearly wasn't on the same page as her brain. His attitude should have had the same effect as the proverbial bucket of cold water. Why hadn't it?

Jake's arm brushed hers as he reached past her to hold open the door.

Maggie's pulse skipped. She willed her body to toe the line. A few more steps and they would be out of this monstrosity.

There was still the drive to his parents' place. Enclosed in the confines of the car. Inches away from a pissed-off athlete.

Maggie shivered, then told herself to stop worrying. He'd done nothing to suggest he couldn't control his temper. Still, when his hand touched the small of her back, she flinched.

Jake dropped his hand, his expression stony.

She waved goodbye to Mimi, then got into the car. He joined her and instantly the interior seemed to shrink as his scent—raw, male and hot—filled her nose. His lean, powerful body crowded her, putting his muscular thigh mere inches from hers.

Neither of them said anything. Forget cutting the tension with a knife, an axe would barely make a dent.

They'd almost reached his parents' place when nerves got the better of her.

"Look—"

"You know—" They both spoke at once.

They stopped, then glanced at each other. The implacable set of his jaw said he'd reached a decision. One she wouldn't like.

"Go on." She licked her suddenly dry lips.

"Ladies first."

She tried to clear the tightness in her throat, but it sounded like a squeak. "I'm sorry we haven't found anything suitable yet. I'd be grateful, if you'd give us one more chance."

"Knock yourself out."

Maybe it was his patronizing tone that sparked off a long overdue show of defiance. Maybe it was that incessant internal voice that had reached deafening levels. Maybe she was just sick of taking arrogant behavior on the chin for the sake of a quiet life. Regardless, before she could censor her words, she snapped, "Grow up."

"Excuse me?" The chill in his voice sent a shiver skating down her spine.

Instead of being frozen into submission, she seemed unable to stem the flow of angry words. "You're as bad as my seven-year-old. 'I want it and I want it now.'" She mimicked one of Emily's rare tantrums. "I know sports stars are used to instant gratification, but that's not how this works. If you genuinely want a place to call home, you'll have to be patient."

She didn't know who was more shocked by her outburst.

His eyes widened a fraction. If his jaw hadn't been so tight, she was sure it would have dropped. "I see."

Maggie tried to get her runaway mouth to apologize, to say anything that would rescue the situation. But, having done the damage, it seemed her lips were glued shut. The heat of anger gave way to the pain of misery and defeat.

She'd just cost Tracy the Ice Cats' contract.

CHAPTER THREE

IT WAS THOSE damn buttons.

Why else would he be behaving like a complete jack-ass?

Jake knew he'd been out of line all day. He'd never been a prima donna; his parents hadn't tolerated that kind of behavior and the Jelinek brothers had kept his ego in check.

He was frustrated because the day had been a bust and he was ticked off by the lies in the property sheets. He felt cheated. That last place had been the worst, but every house they'd seen had sugarcoated the truth. He hated liars and cheats.

Jake was also nervous about tonight, when he and Tru would start skating and working out at the Cats' practice rink. The countdown to training camp had kicked up a notch and for the first time since his rookie season, he was nervous. Questions had buzzed around his brain all last night. What if he'd lost it? What if he was no longer good enough to stay in the NHL?

He'd been giving himself a lecture about working harder and sticking to his plan of no distractions when the biggest damn distraction had walked up his parents' path.

Today's ridiculously dull dress was beige. Or biscuit. Or whatever the hell they called pale brown. Her short-sleeved jacket left the lightly tanned skin of her arms bare and emphasized her trim figure. Matching beige-slash-biscuit sling-backs covered her toes.

His pulse had raced faster than a player trying to beat an icing call.

He'd managed to greet her without sounding like an idiot. Then she'd turned and he'd seen them.

Buttons.

Bow-shaped buttons that begged to be undone. Starting at her knees, going up over the curve of her bottom and disappearing under her jacket. He imagined them continuing up her back, tracing her spine like a caress.

His tongue had stuck to the roof of his mouth.

The journey to the first house had been torture. Her fresh, clean scent had filled the car. His gaze had slipped constantly to that tantalizing place where her skirt hitched up, showing the smooth skin above her knees. It had gotten worse as the day had progressed, not helped by the fact that she was good company. He'd enjoyed talking with her, even arguing with her.

He'd also wanted to taste those tantalizing lips.

Damn it. That kind of behavior was vintage Bad Boy and exactly what he had to cut out if he wanted to have the best season of his career. Furious, he'd tried to focus on the house-hunting. Easier said than done.

The fire in him had been raging dangerously close to out of control by the time they'd got to the last house. When she'd taken off the jacket, he'd known he was going down for the count. Even the sunken fishpond hadn't snapped him out of it.

He'd been shocked when Maggie had flinched at his touch and lost it. Her tongue-lashing, though deserved, had surprised the hell out of him. Who knew Miss Prim had so much passion lurking beneath those drab outfits? He gritted his teeth, trying to wipe all thoughts of passion from his brain. As if he wasn't having a hard enough time…literally.

He owed her an apology. "Maggie?"

She wouldn't meet his gaze.

"I'm sorry."

"I beg your pardon?" Her frosty tone made her cute English accent sharp enough to slice a puck in half.

"I've been a jerk."

She lifted her head and studied him carefully, distrust in the depths of her gaze.

Why? His reputation might not be great but it didn't warrant her lack of faith in him. Whatever other failings he had, Jake had always prided himself on being a man of his word. He didn't let people down.

Except for Adam.

His gut twisted as images from the accident flashed through his mind. He'd tried with Adam. *Not as hard as you could have.* He forced the dark thoughts away.

"I've got stuff going on right now, and I was wrong to take out my frustrations on you."

She said nothing, her expression hard to read.

"These next few weeks are big for me." He explained about tonight's practice but played down his fears, afraid if he voiced them he'd jinx himself. Instead, he focused on the challenge ahead. "All the skating I've done since the accident has been part of the healing process. Exercises to break down the scar tissue and tone up my leg. Drills to build my fitness levels. Now I'll see how I hold up to training with contact."

As if she sensed the nervousness behind his words, concern shimmered in her eyes.

"The docs have given me the green light, so physically I'm good to go." He rubbed his thigh, feeling the ridges of scars through the denim. "But I have to be one hundred percent up here." He tapped his temple. "I can't afford to be hesitant or duck plays. The coach needs to believe I can deliver my A-game from day one and my teammates need to know they can rely on me to do my job."

Her expression softened. "That's a lot of pressure." She bit her lip. "I'm sorry, too. I was unprofessional. It won't happen again."

Relief whisked through him. "So we're okay."

She paused, then nodded. "You're not going to fire me, even after what I said?"

"You're right—I *was* behaving like a child." While he was clearing the air, he should explain the rest of it. Well, not about the buttons. "I don't get why folks can't tell the truth on those property sheets. We'll find out anyway. I know what to expect now. I'll look at tomorrow's houses with a different mind-set."

The wariness didn't disappear, but she seemed less tense as she pulled up in front of his parents' house. "I'll see you at Mimi's tomorrow. Will late morning be okay?"

He grinned. "Sure. I need to pick up some new equipment at nine."

"How about eleven o'clock, then?"

"Perfect." He opened the door. "Look forward to it."

"Me, too." Her soft smile sent a tiny crack through the ice that had encased his heart since Adam's death.

As she drove off, Jake walked up the path, whistling.

Tru met him at the door. "You ready to skate?"

"Give me five to get changed and grab my stuff."

Tru was waiting in the kitchen with the two moms when he returned. "Good day?"

"Nightmare." Jake told them about the places he'd seen.

"It takes time to find a home." Aunt Karina patted his arm.

"That's what Maggie says."

"She's a sensible girl." His mom nodded, her expression serious.

"Pretty as a photo, too," Aunt Karina added.

"Picture, Mom," Tru corrected, smiling. "Pretty as a picture,"

Aunt Karina shrugged. "Picture, photo. Is the same, no?"

"Sure." Before either mom could expand on the subject of Maggie, Jake said, "Gotta hit the road."

They tossed their gear in the back of Tru's Range Rover and set off. They'd barely gone a mile before his friend asked, "How's it going with the lovely Maggie?"

"Okay. It's harder than I thought to find the right place."

"That wasn't what I meant. Have you asked her out yet?"

"Why would I do that?"

Tru quirked an eyebrow. "Why wouldn't you?"

"How many more times do I have to say it? No more women."

"Yeah, yeah. But Maggie isn't like your other women."

"She's still a distraction I don't need." No way he was telling Tru how much of a distraction. "Besides, she looks like the type who wants a serious relationship. And she has a kid." He stopped, not wanting to overcook his objections. "I sure as hell can't deal with that now. Maybe next June, after we've won the Cup."

His friend shook his head sadly. "You're throwing out the baby with the bathwater."

"What do you mean?"

"You're cutting everything but hockey out of your life. Why? Most NHL players have a life outside hockey."

Jake glared at him.

"You can't keep punishing yourself over the crash," his friend said quietly. "Adam's death wasn't your fault. He couldn't handle that new Porsche. There was nothing you could have done."

The pain that sliced through Jake's gut was as acute as if the accident had been last night, not six months ago. "That's the point—I did nothing. I was more interested in getting to that party and the twin puck bunnies than finding out what was wrong with Adam."

The truth was he hadn't *wanted* to do anything. He'd been fed up with his friend's volatile, irrational behavior—laughing and joking one minute and erupting angrily the next. Been annoyed that it had affected

Adam's play, making him unreliable. Instead of trying to get to the bottom of his friend's problems, especially when the media and the fans had been brutal about Adam's inconsistency, Jake had ignored them, hoping they'd go away.

Some friend he'd been. And Adam had paid the price.

"You weren't the only one. The whole team, even his roommate, had lost patience with him." Tru punched his arm. "You aren't in the cape-and-tights league, bro."

Jake's bitter laugh was humorless. "Adam's funeral made that damn clear."

He recalled that miserable day. Mrs. Stewart weeping over her son's coffin. Mr. Stewart looking bewildered. Adam's roommate, Nick, avoiding Jake, like he blamed him for Adam's death. Those damn display boards, cataloging every year of Adam's too-short life and every stage of his too-short hockey career. Each one a heartrending reminder of what a good man Adam had been.

And how worthless Jake was.

"There, but for the grace of God and a seat belt," he muttered.

"You're not giving me that crap about how it should have been you?"

"Nah. Haven't you heard? Only the good die young."

"Don't turn Adam into a saint. He was human, with faults like the rest of us. He nearly killed you in that accident."

"If it'd been me—" Jake held up a hand to forestall

Tru's objection "—what kind of tributes would I have had? Nothing to make anyone proud of me." His chest tightened.

Tru snorted with disgust. "Can the pity party. To paraphrase Saint Adam, most guys would give a left nut to have one night in your shoes. You're always the same—all or nothing. When you set yourself a goal, it's impossible to get you to veer from the path." Tru calmed his tone. "Single-minded determination is great, but not for your personal life. There has to be a middle ground."

Jake couldn't imagine what that would be. "Like what?"

"Ditching the parties and other wild stuff is fine, but what's wrong with dating a nice woman?"

"I told you, it'll be a distraction." Despite himself, however, a hint of doubt crept into Jake's mind.

He'd always had women skating in and out of his life like players on a shift change. Women who'd relished his lifestyle as much as he had. He'd never dated one woman steadily, let alone someone ordinary, like Maggie. How would that even work?

Tru continued, "Having a good woman in your life and in your bed is a great way to balance out the stress. Hell, if I found someone like that I'd grab her in a heartbeat."

Jake frowned at the hint of wistfulness in his friend's voice, but their arrival at the rink ended the conversation. As they skated drills, he mulled over Tru's suggestion.

Would dating the right woman be so bad?

In the past, Jake would have shuddered at the thought of making a commitment. He would have been horrified at the quiet life he planned to have now.

Yet neither prospect filled him with the dread they once would have. Maybe because he knew nothing could be worse than the alternative he'd escaped. He still had a choice about how to live his life. Adam sure as hell didn't.

He pulled up sharply, his angled skates created a showering arc of ice. Maggie was nothing like the women in his past. For sure, she wouldn't tempt him into his old ways.

Taking a pass from Tru, Jake fired a puck at the practice net, pumping his stick in the air in celebration when he scored. Maybe he should give dating Maggie a shot.

What did he have to lose?

"HOW ARE THINGS going with Jake?"

Though Tracy's question was, on the surface, innocent enough, Maggie fought to control a blush. "Fine."

She focused on her notes, hoping her sister wouldn't notice, though it was hard to avoid Tracy's curious gaze when sitting beside her bed.

There were still two days left of the promised week of bed rest, and allowing Tracy to work for a few hours each day was the only way to stop her from going stir-crazy. Twice-daily update sessions were the only way, short of handcuffing Tracy to the bed, to keep her from going downstairs.

This morning's review had gone smoothly. Until now.

"No more problems after that little bust up?" Tracy put aside her laptop.

"Not really." Maggie wasn't about to admit how much her growing attraction to Jake troubled her. No matter how many times she talked sternly to herself, one sniff of his clean, masculine scent or the warm brush of his hand against the small of her back and her pulse danced. As often as she reminded herself of how wrong he was for her, temptation would try to override her caution. Tantalizing her to relax her guard against this bad boy.

What harm could it do?

Too bloody much. Didn't she have the physical and emotional scars to prove it? No way could Maggie consider taking that dangerous path again.

Tracy cut into her thoughts. "I sense a *but.*"

"The house hunt is going in circles." Her lips twisted. "I'm letting you down."

"It's not your fault the right place isn't out there. Give it a little longer. You never know when the ideal house will be listed."

"But training camp is imminent. The Ice Cats won't be happy if I don't deliver on time."

"Actually, the Cats are very pleased with how you're managing Jake's requirements. They've even asked me to take on another player, a guy they're bringing in from the Swedish Elite League. Thanks to your efforts to bring my admin stuff up to date, too, I was able to say yes." Tracy leaned against the pillows with a satisfied smile. "I can almost taste that retainer."

"That's great. Are you sure you don't want to take over with Jake?"

"I'll have my hands full with this Swedish guy. Bringing in an overseas player is complicated because he hasn't got a credit history. Signing him up for basics like electricity is a nightmare. Besides, like I said, you're doing a good job." Tracy's gaze sharpened. "Is Jake giving you a hard time?"

"No. He's lived up to his promise." She paused, then admitted, "He's not what I expected. He's actually pretty good company."

"Really?" Her sister arched an eyebrow.

"He talks about something other than sports, for a start. He's not patronizing and he doesn't mind if my opinion differs from his. I can say what I think and he'll listen."

"He's hot, too." Tracy grinned.

"He's a client." Maggie kept her voice steady. "All he's interested in is finding a house, and all I'm interested in is ensuring he's happy with our service, so you get that contract."

"Once that's done, you could still have a little fun with him."

"I had my fun and suffered for it. Worse, so did Emily."

Though she'd fiercely protected her daughter from Lee's physical abuse, the emotional strain had taken a toll on Emily. Maggie's throat tightened as she recalled how her bright, bubbly daughter had grown more withdrawn every time Lee had gone on a rampage. How she'd clung to Maggie, never wanting her to be out of sight. As if she'd known he wouldn't hit her mother if she was there. At least until that final, awful night. "I won't let her suffer again."

"Sweetie, I know how much you both suffered. The last thing I want is for you ever to be in that situation again." Tracy took hold of Maggie's hand. "But you can't let that stop you from ever going out with another guy."

"I won't." Maggie squeezed her sister's hand. "I'm just not ready yet. Even if I was, Jake's totally the wrong guy for me."

"There's a wrong guy for having fun with?"

"There is for me. No more sports stars. No more rich and famous. It took a long time to learn the lesson, but I've learned it well."

"I've never heard even a hint of anything bad about Jake. Women tend to gush about how wonderful he is."

"Still, he's not for me. He's a hockey hard man who makes his living fighting and hitting." She doubted anyone who displayed the cold-blooded aggression she'd seen in the video clips online—okay, so she'd done a Google search—could turn it off in other areas of his life. Lee certainly couldn't.

No matter how much she liked Jake or how her body reacted to him, Maggie couldn't afford to take a risk on him. Not just for her sake, but for Emily's.

"When the time is right, I'll start dating again. Assuming I can find the right kind of man."

Tracy studied her carefully. "All right," she said finally. "In the meantime, can you at least get rid of those dreary outfits?"

Maggie stiffened. "They might be plain, but they're smart. You hardly want me in full WAG gear when I'm dealing with your clients."

"You don't need to dress like a dowager duchess, either."

Though her sister was right, the comment still stung. "It's not perfect, but it feels better than the way I used to dress."

"You mean the way Lee insisted you dress—everything short, low cut and clinging, showing as much skin as possible and covered in bling."

"You know, I loved it in the beginning. I had no clue how to dress, and he bought me stuff most girls dreamed of having." Especially the naive eighteen-year-old she had been. He'd showered her with the latest fashions, the most expensive designers. The media lapped it up. "He made sure my picture was always in the press. It was all good…until I wanted to change. To be less flashy and outrageous. Less…"

Tracy sniffed derisively. "Tarty."

Maggie half shrugged sadly. "I didn't want to give up the designer clothes. Just find my own style, something more modest. He disagreed. And it was…easier…to give in."

Tracy's description of Maggie's ex was coarse and pointed.

"Anyway, Lee doesn't dictate my wardrobe now."

"He may not handpick your outfits, but he's still influencing the way you dress. You've gone to the opposite extreme. Other than your shoes, there's not a high-end label in sight. The styles are fine, but the colors are *boring*."

"Thanks a lot."

"I'm not being mean," her sister said gently. "I just think you could find something that's more you. Don't you miss wearing designer clothes?"

"Of course," she admitted reluctantly.

"You sound like you're confessing to a terrible crime. Who doesn't like wearing nice things?" Tracy grinned. "With matching shoes, naturally."

Maggie's answering smile faded. "But it's a slippery slope."

It would be so easy to slide into that life again. First the clothes, then the glamorous parties and events. But the price to be paid was one she couldn't afford.

"One step at a time. Let's change some outfits before we start worrying about the red carpet and the paparazzi. I'll help you keep your feet on the ground."

It *would* be nice to spread her wings a little, fashion-wise. Maybe simply wearing what she liked would be enough that the rest of that seductive lifestyle wouldn't call to her. "I could give it a try."

"Great. You can start by ditching anything beige, gray or brown. Try flowers, polka dots, stripes—anything but plain. What about those pretty summer dresses you brought with you?"

"I thought they'd be too casual, but if you're sure they're okay, I'll wear them. They'll definitely be more comfortable in this heat. Speaking of which—" Maggie checked her watch "—I'm meeting Jake at Mimi's office in an hour for another trawl through the listings."

"I bet he'll find those dresses more attractive, too."

"I won't dress to impress Jake." Maggie frowned. "Worrying about his reaction is no different to worrying about Lee's."

"All right. Point made." Tracy held her hands up in mock surrender. "Then wear it to impress yourself. Now shoo and get changed. That's an order."

"Yes, boss."

Maggie had to admit, half an hour later, the cheerful, pink flowers all over her cotton summer dress made her feel brighter, putting a spring in her step as she headed next door to say goodbye to Emily.

Though her daughter was more interested in the fort she was building with Amy, she stopped long enough to pass comment on what Maggie was wearing.

"You look really pretty, Mummy." She hugged Maggie, then dashed off.

It warmed her heart to see Emily back to her normal, sunny self. Walking to her car, Maggie marveled at how easily her daughter had adjusted to her new life. Time for her to take a page from Emily's book—get on with living her life, her way.

She just had to work out what her way was.

When she arrived at Mimi's office, Jake was leaning against his SUV, talking on his cell. Maggie waved cheerfully.

Her smile faded as he scowled, then shook his head sharply. Her heart pinched, even as she told herself this wasn't the past. Jake wouldn't take his anger out on her. She ignored the tiny voice inside that reminded her of his behavior at the house with the fishpond.

"Damn it. I don't have time for this." *Smack!*

Maggie tried not to flinch as he slammed his palm against the side of his SUV. She tried to tamp down the flutters of panic in her stomach as she backed away slowly, inching toward the door of Mimi's office building.

"I said no." *Smack!*

She froze, her pulse skittering. Memories of that last night with Lee flashed through her mind. The past merged with the present.

Jake paced. Her eyes followed his angry movements, watching for the first sign that his ire had switched to her.

He turned and stepped toward her. Fury blazed in his ice-blue eyes. He said nothing, but his clenched fist was message enough.

CHAPTER FOUR

"I DON'T care how much money Adam owed you, I won't let you cash in on his death."

Jake's grip on his cell phone tightened as he pounded his other fist on his thigh. Nick's plan disgusted him.

"Come on, man," Adam's former roommate whined. "Fans pay crazy money on eBay for hockey memorabilia. His stuff is just lying around the apartment in boxes."

"Give it all to charity, like the Stewarts wanted."

"That was only a suggestion. Adam's parents said I could do what I wanted with it."

"I don't think an online yard sale was what they had in mind." Jake pinched the bridge of his nose, trying not to lose what little remained of his temper. "If you don't want to take the boxes with you to L.A., have them sent to me."

"So you can keep all the money for yourself."

"No, damn it. I've told you, I don't want any part of your sick scheme."

"Your loss. I only offered you a chance to get in on the deal because I felt sorry for you."

There was no reasoning with the guy. Though Jake hated to resort to threats, he knew it was the only language Nick would understand. "You touch anything in those boxes and I'll tell the Hawks and the Kings what you're doing."

"You wouldn't dare." Despite the bravado in Nick's voice, there was an underlying thread of nervousness. "Besides, they wouldn't believe you. Not when I tell them you're having a breakdown because of your guilt over Adam's death."

The malicious jab stole Jake's breath as effectively as if Nick had speared him in the gut with his stick. He rode the pain for a few moments, then used it to fuel his determination. No way he'd let Nick auction off Adam's memory for a few lousy bucks.

"I'm warning you, if you try to sell even one item, I will personally see to it your career is over. You won't even be able to ride a bus in the minors."

Nick's laugh had a desperate ring. "You don't have that kind of influence."

"You'd be surprised how quickly I could spread the word. Guys get mad when they think someone is taking advantage. Do you really want to be the target of their anger?"

Jake's words hung menacingly in the air.

Nick swore. "Fine. You want his stuff so badly, you come and collect it. You've got one week. After that, everything goes in the nearest Dumpster."

The last thing Jake wanted was to have to deal with Adam's things. He didn't need to be reminded that he was a pale shadow of the man his friend had been. He sure as hell didn't need to be reminded of how he'd let Adam down.

It had been bad enough living in Chicago, surrounded by memories of coming up from the minors together, being drafted together, winning and losing together. Since he'd moved home, he'd finally begun to come to terms with what had happened. Not a day passed that he didn't remember and regret, but he'd managed some semblance of peace.

Nick's demand had shattered that fragile peace and ripped open still-raw wounds.

Jake had no choice. He owed Adam that much. "You make damn sure everything is still there—every last sock, button and scrap of paper. Screw with me and you'll regret it."

He hung up and jammed his cell into the front pocket of his jeans, then smacked the flat of his hand against his M-Class.

Damn Nick. Jake had never understood why Nick and Adam had been so close. Adam was a good, honest, hardworking guy. Nick took shortcuts, looked for the easy way. This was a new low.

Jake scrubbed his hand over his jaw and tried to calm his anger.

A flutter of pink reminded him Maggie was here. He forced himself to shove the problem to the back of his mind—he didn't want to spoil the afternoon.

The thought of huddling around Mimi's computer, the warmth of Maggie's soft skin so close, was enough to make his pulse pound with frustration of a different kind.

Where would the buttons be today? His groin tightened as he recalled yesterday's Chinese-style gray dress. The knotted silk buttons had started at the base of her throat and trailed their way across her left breast. *Enough!*

He turned toward Maggie.

What the hell...?

She stood by the door to the building, staring at him, her hand across her mouth. Her ashen skin made her brown eyes look even darker.

She looked scared.

Confused, he stepped toward her.

He halted abruptly when she pressed herself against the door.

"Maggie?"

Her lips trembled, even as her chin tilted defiantly.

What was her problem? Like a slow-mo replay, he reviewed the past few minutes—his anger, his threats, his actions—then swore silently, as he realized Maggie *was* scared.

Of *him.*

She probably believed that clichéd crap about hockey players being violent because they played a physical game. Sure, he'd fought off the ice in the past, but only because some knucklehead had thrown a punch to prove how tough he was. Jake hadn't fought in anger since he was a kid. And he'd never, ever, hit a woman.

Maggie wouldn't know that. He had to put her at ease. Slowly, he raised his hands, palm out, to show he meant no harm.

"Are you okay?" He kept his voice calm and low.

She stilled, nodding sharply. Her dark brown eyes never left him.

Perhaps he should explain. "That was a former teammate on the Blackhawks—Nick. He used to share an apartment with Adam. I guess you know I was injured in a car accident?"

She nodded again, watching him warily.

"My friend Adam…it was Adam's car. He was driving. He lost control and—" he coughed to clear the lump in his throat "—was killed."

The bald statement left a bitter taste, but Maggie didn't need to know about Adam's weird behavior on that drive. His trembling fingers on the gearshift, the sweat beading on his forehead. How he'd veered between moods as wildly as he'd swerved between lanes.

She also didn't need to know Jake had deliberately ignored the signs Adam was troubled because he'd cared more about getting to the party than finding out what was wrong.

Maggie's expression softened slightly. The sadness in her eyes hardened his emotions. Jake didn't want, or deserve, her sympathy.

He stepped closer. Her body remained tense but she didn't flinch.

"Nick's been traded to L.A." He quickly explained the bastard's demands to Maggie. "With house-hunting and training camp about to start, the timing sucks. But I have to rescue Adam's stuff."

Maggie's shoulders had loosened a little as she'd listened to him. When he was done, she said quietly, "May I make a suggestion?"

Damn, the way she bit her lip like that said she was still nervous about him. "Sure."

"I could arrange for a packer to go in and collect

Adam's boxes, then have them delivered when you find a house." Her voice grew stronger. "It'll save you the trip."

Adam's things would be safely out of Nick's reach and he wouldn't have to deal with them until he was ready. A huge weight lifted off his shoulders.

He smiled. "You're a lifesaver. Thanks, Maggie."

"All part of the service." She reached in her bag for her ever-present pad. "If you write down the necessary information, I'll sort it out."

Jake was returning her pad when Mimi pushed through the door.

"There you are. Come in out of this heat."

"Be right there." Maggie slipped the pad into her purse and joined the real-estate agent.

As he followed her to Mimi's office, Maggie's stiff body language reminded him of what had happened earlier, her fearful reaction to his anger. His mind began to whir with images of other incidents—her jittery behavior at their first meeting, her defensiveness when he'd challenged her, the way she'd flinched when he'd touched her in that damn house with the fishpond. Were her reactions more than concern about an aggressive hockey player? Was something in her past coloring her judgment? Had someone treated her badly?

It made a strange kind of sense.

Fury surged within him at the thought of anyone mistreating her, but he tamped it down. That wouldn't help either of them. He'd just have to be careful how he acted with her.

No sooner had the thought crossed his mind than guilt twisted Jake's stomach.

Who was he kidding? He'd let Adam down, a guy he'd been friends with nearly all his life. What the hell made him think he could do better with a woman he'd known for a few weeks and whose past could involve problems more serious than the pressures of the NHL?

On the surface, Maggie appeared to be the perfect woman for him to date. But if he was right, what lay beneath made things a whole lot more complicated. Despite the sizzling attraction, complicated was a distraction he didn't need.

More importantly, he wasn't the right man for Maggie. She didn't need a man she'd always doubt because of his career. A man whose emotions were still too raw, as his argument with Nick had shown. Maggie needed someone she could count on to be there for her. Not one who doubted himself.

"Are you ready, Jake?" Mimi's voice cut through the tumult inside him.

Realizing he still stood in the doorway, he cleared his head, then went to sit in a chair in front of Mimi's computer.

Maggie kept her distance, leaning against the desk instead of sitting beside him, as she usually did. A new tension hummed in the air between them.

"What have you got?" he asked.

"There are two new properties." Mimi clicked on the local listings. "The split-level is nice, but nothing special. I think you'll like the other one, though."

She was right about the first house. He leaned forward to check out the second. His pulse quickened at the picture of the elegant Victorian. Jake hoped the on-screen details weren't exaggerated. From the wrap-around porch and the dark green shutters to the white picket fence and the large yard full of old trees, this house was everything he'd hoped for.

This one felt right.

Before he could stop himself, he looked up to see what Maggie thought. Their eyes locked. His heart stuttered. Excitement zinged through his veins.

Then the hesitance in her gaze registered, making his body stiffen.

Deliberately, he turned away.

"Looks great, Mimi." He grinned at the agent. "I have a real good feeling about this one. I want to go and see it ASAP. When can you fix something up?"

"I'll make an appointment for tomorrow morning. Is that okay?"

"Sure. Thanks."

"Tomorrow morning's good for me, too." Maggie leaned over to direct his attention to the large den.

Heat rushed through him as her scent teased his nostrils. Sparks shot up his arm where her fingertips brushed him.

Damn it. He had to get out of here.

He pushed back the chair and stood. "Are we done?"

Both women looked startled by his abrupt tone.

"Uh, yes." Mimi sent a questioning look at Maggie, who nodded.

Jake's goodbye skated the edges of politeness. He

didn't draw a steady breath until he pulled into his parents' drive.

Turning off the ignition, he slumped in his seat. Back to square one. Well, maybe square one and a half—the house did look perfect. That, and hockey, was enough for now.

Finding the perfect woman would just have to wait.

BY THE TIME Maggie pulled into Tracy's driveway, she was drained and weary.

The afternoon's emotional roller coaster had left her as wrung out as a damp dishcloth. The throb over her left eye warned of a looming tension headache. She rested her head on the steering wheel, trying to summon up the energy to get out of the car and go into the house.

If she'd needed any more reasons for why Jake Badoletti was wrong for her, the incident at Mimi's office had provided plenty.

She wasn't a fool. She knew Jake wasn't Lee. There was something about him, his character and his values, that set him apart from her ex. She'd barely known him a week, had hardly scratched the surface of who he was, yet the differences were clearly visible.

Sadly, the similarities were clearly visible, too. His quick temper when things didn't go his way, the sudden switches from charming to furious to cold indifference and back again.

Patterns of behavior that, this time, she wouldn't… couldn't ignore.

Tap, tap.

She jerked upright. Emily stood next to the car.

Maggie opened the car door and gave her daughter a tired smile.

"You're too old to have a nap, Mummy." As usual, Emily looked like she'd been through the wars. A bandage on one knee and mud stains on her shorts.

"You're never too old to need a nap." Maggie plucked a leaf out of one loose braid. "When you get to be as old as me, you'll look forward to an afternoon snooze."

"I don't want to be that old, ever." Emily grinned. "I want to show you the fort Amy and me made."

Maggie allowed her daughter to pull her out of the car. If only they could bottle Emily's energy—her ancient body could use the boost. She massaged her aching temple, then plastered a cheery expression on her face.

Emily wasn't fooled. "Are you all right, Mummy?" Her wide-eyed gaze swept Maggie from head to toe. "Did that Mr. Bad Boy hurt you?"

Her shaky words drove a dagger into Maggie's heart. "No one hurt me. I had a busy afternoon and probably did too much in this horrid heat."

Concern furrowed Emily's brow, making her look older than her years.

Maggie damned herself for not having had the courage to leave her marriage sooner. For not realizing the emotional damage Lee had done to their daughter. Though he hadn't laid a hand on his daughter until that final night, she'd borne witness to too much. Maggie would never let that kind of ugliness touch Emily's life again.

That's why a relationship with Jake wasn't worth it. Ensuring her daughter was happy, healthy and safe was far more important than whatever fun she could have with him.

She hugged Emily. "I'm okay." She tried to sound normal, but her voice came out reedy.

Emily's arms tightened around her. "Don't worry, Mummy." She looked up, her expression fierce. "I'll take care of you. I won't let anyone hurt you."

Maggie's eyes burned. "I won't let anyone hurt you, either."

For several moments, they stood there silently. Maggie drew comfort from her daughter's warm, slight frame and her strength and courage. Emily was coping with this mess far better than she was.

That had to change. Starting now.

Pulling herself together, Maggie straightened. "Let's see your wonderful fort."

Emily shook her head. "Later. Right now, you need chocolate."

"You're right. Chocolate will make me feel good as new."

Holding hands, they skipped to the house. They burst into the kitchen, laughing.

"We need chocolate, Auntie Tracy." Emily dashed to the fridge, delved beneath the lettuce in the salad drawer and brandished a half bar in its distinctive purple wrapper.

Tracy looked up from her laptop, as Maggie sank into a chair opposite her at the kitchen table. "Why do you need some of *my* chocolate?"

"Mummy had a tiring day." Emily lowered her voice conspiratorially as she doled out the Cadbury bar. "I think Mr. Bad Boy wasn't very nice to her."

Tracy's eyes narrowed. "Really?"

"Emily's exaggerating."

"I bet Mummy sorted him out."

"I hope so."

Emily read the tension humming in the air and sighed. "Can I go back to Amy's?"

Before Maggie had finished nodding, Emily had raced out the door. She was probably as keen to miss the rest of the conversation as her mother.

Maggie tried to preempt the storm brewing in her sister's expression. "Jake didn't do anything to me. He was cross about something. I misunderstood and over-reacted."

"Are you sure that's all there was to it? You look terrible."

"He was arguing with a former teammate." She paused, trying to be honest. "I was scared he'd take that anger out on me. But he didn't."

She explained about Nick wanting to auction off Adam's things and her suggestion to resolve the issue.

Tracy relaxed. "Okay. But if Jake ever scares you, I'll make a formal complaint to the Cats. No contract is worth that kind of behavior."

"Thanks, but this was more my fault than his."

"Isn't that what they all say?"

Maggie winced as her sister's point jabbed home. "I suppose if I say this is different, you'll repeat that comment."

"Too bloody right. I was too far away to help you with Lee, but I won't let anything happen to you here."

"There was nothing you could have done. I had to decide to leave and find the strength and courage to follow through."

"I know, but if I'd only…"

"No point rehashing the ifs and buts, sis. I have enough guilt of my own. Let's not add yours into the mix, too."

Tracy gave a shaky laugh. "All bets are off if Jake or anyone else tries to hurt you."

"Same goes." Maggie squeezed her sister's hand.

"That reminds me—Samantha called."

"My solicitor? Did she say what she wanted?" Whatever it was, it couldn't be good. Samantha rarely called unless something important had come up.

"Lee wants to speak to you."

"What? But why?" Maggie hated that she sounded small and weak.

"She didn't say, just asked you to call in the morning, as she's in court today."

Maggie tried to figure out what her ex could want. "It doesn't make sense. He moved on the minute the ink was dry on our divorce decree." In truth, he'd moved on long before that.

"I'll say. According to the press, it's been a nonstop parade of it girls for the past nine months. I hear his latest is an actress from one of the afternoon soaps, Patty something."

A terrifying thought occurred. "What if he's changed his mind about Emily?"

Tracy dismissed her words with a flick of her hand. "He's always said he didn't want the responsibility. That having a child around would ruin his social life. He didn't blink about signing the letter of consent for her to come to the U.S."

"But the custody agreement gives him the right to see her three times a year." A shiver ran through her. "I knew this would be a problem. I didn't want to agree, but Samantha said it would work in my favor if I showed I wasn't trying to keep Emily from him. The courts are very keen for a child to have contact with both parents." Her throat closed, so her voice was barely a whisper. "I can't stop him from seeing her."

"He's made no effort to see Emily in nearly a year. I can't imagine why he'd suddenly feel the need to play daddy dearest." Tracy passed her a chunk of chocolate. "I'm sure it's just another stupid mind game. Don't give him that power over you."

Maggie inhaled deeply, trying to steady herself. "You're right. I'm probably worrying over nothing. I'll wait and see what Samantha has to say tomorrow."

"That's the Maggie we know and love." Tracy smiled.

"I'm glad you're on my side."

"Hey, it's you and me against the world." Her sister got up to make some tea. "Speaking of which, are we any closer to finding what Bad Boy wants?"

"I'm hopeful we have a winner." Maggie explained about the newly listed Victorian and their appointment the following morning. "He seemed pleased."

Her heart jolted as she recalled the moment when her eyes had met Jake's as they'd read the online property sheet. For that instant, the connection between them had felt almost tangible. Seconds later, he'd blanked her—the fire in his eyes extinguished. She should have been relieved, but his obvious desire to get away had left her feeling oddly disappointed.

Her complicated reaction to Jake made her glad this project was nearly over. If he liked the house, the number of times she'd see him again would be limited. The rest of their business could be conducted by phone or email. And, though the house was in the same town, the chances of them running into each other would be small.

Her life could return to the simpler plan she'd intended. She'd focus on her daughter and her role at Making Your Move and forget about Bad Boy.

Maggie's chest twinged. Must be indigestion. It certainly wasn't anything to do with the thought of not seeing Jake again.

She ignored the laughing voice inside her, which disagreed.

"IT'S ALL RIGHT," Maggie reassured her friend Janice the following morning. "I can make other arrangements for Emily. Your mum needs you. I hope she gets better soon."

Unfortunately, finding another babysitter wasn't as simple as she'd thought, and there was no activity camp. Tracy was meeting the new Swedish player, so Maggie had no choice but to take Emily with her.

Her stomach twisted nervously. Jake wouldn't mind. Would he?

The house visit wouldn't take long. She'd keep Emily out of his way. Besides, Mimi would be there, too.

The real-estate agent was on her phone, dealing with a client, when they arrived. Maggie was surprised to see Mimi fighting to keep her cool. Though her lemon pantsuit and elegant hairdo were still immaculate, the older woman's lips were pinched and her cheeks flushed. How did she manage to sound polite when her client was giving her a horrid time? Maggie would have lost patience long ago.

Rolling her eyes, Mimi mouthed an apology and waved her inside.

As Maggie and Emily toured the house, her daughter's attention was caught by the turret bedroom that reminded her of a princess room. She begged to be allowed to stay there and play with the black cat lounging on the four-poster bed. With strict instructions not to go wandering while Jake was being shown around, Maggie left Emily there and continued to check out the house.

The gorgeous Victorian more than lived up to its billing. The bright, spacious rooms were filled with charming period features: gleaming parquet floors, carved ceiling roses with brass chandeliers and stunning fireplaces with oak mantels.

"Not a fishpond in sight." Mimi laughed, as she joined Maggie in the master bedroom. "Sorry about that call. Some clients can't stand not being in control of every stage of a negotiation. Hopefully I stopped him from making an ass of himself."

"I don't know how you keep your cool with people yelling at you like that."

"Years of experience."

While they walked around the house making notes, Mimi regaled her with tales of some of her worst clients. Even as Maggie laughed, she was relieved she wouldn't have any more client contact once she got Jake sorted out.

The real-estate agent's phone rang again as Jake's SUV pulled up in front of the house.

Mimi checked the display, raised her eyes heavenward and muttered, "Give me strength." She gave Maggie an apologetic smile. "I have to take this. I'll join you shortly."

"No problem." Maggie tried to calm her jittery pulse. "Jake's looking around outside, so you have time."

As Mimi left the room to return her call, Maggie watched as Jake walked down the driveway, taking in the large front yard, complete with requisite trees. Even from up here, she could tell he liked what he saw. She let out a silent sigh of relief.

"Kitty!" Feet thundered down the stairs.

"Not outside," Maggie called out.

The screen door slammed. Too late. Turning toward the window, she saw Jake stop and face the noise. She tried to move, to go after Emily, but her feet were frozen in place.

This time, the hitch in her pulse had nothing to do with the appeal of the bad-boy hockey player. It was pure dread of how he'd react to the seven-year-old charging toward him. Interrupting him. Being there without his permission.

Memories of another time, another place, hammered into her brain. She had to get to Emily. To protect her. She would not let him lay a hand on her daughter.

Her nails bit into her palms as she forced her body to get past the foreboding that chilled her inside. She broke free of the grip her fear had on her and raced out of the room.

Please, God, keep my daughter safe!

CHAPTER FIVE

THE OLD VICTORIAN was perfect.

Jake stood on the sidewalk looking at the house. Strong and solid, its elegance was a proud testament to its history and a promise for its future. Not just somewhere to live, but a home.

The neighborhood was quiet. The big yard was mainly grass, with flower-filled borders and lots of mature trees. Dark green shutters and gingerbread trim offset the white siding and the multipaned windows. Who could resist that wraparound porch? If the inside was half as good as the outside, this would be the perfect base for his new life.

A shadow in an upstairs window reminded him that Maggie was waiting.

His heart jumped. Despite his determination not to think about her, she'd been on his mind and in his dreams all night. He may have decided Maggie wouldn't be a distraction anymore, but his brain and body seemed to have other ideas. It hadn't helped that his mom had badgered him this morning to invite Maggie to their annual Labor Day barbecue.

"Kitty! Come back." A child's voice cut into his thoughts.

A little girl barreled down the front steps, a determined expression on her face. A flash of black streaked past him and over the road. The kid followed as fast as her short legs could carry her.

At the edge of his vision, a silver Lexus turned into the street. He frowned. The driver was on her cell phone.

The little girl hurried past. Fear shot through him as he realized she hadn't spotted the car; her attention was fixed on the elusive cat.

In a move that would have made a goaltender proud, Jake turned and scooped her off her feet as she was about to step off the curb. "Whoa, Short Stuff."

The driver sped by.

The curly-haired imp kicked him. "Let me go. Kitty's getting away."

As he set her down, keeping a watchful eye in case she darted onto the road, he noticed the English accent. His pulse gave an odd little skip as he recognized her dark eyes and the shape of her nose. This must be Maggie's daughter.

Despite her frown, there was a precocious glint in the girl's eye. "Mummy doesn't let me talk to strangers."

"I'll bet she doesn't allow you onto the street by yourself, either." He bit back a smile at her pout. "You nearly got run over because you weren't looking where you were going."

Maggie came rushing out of the house. The bodice of her flowery cotton-and-lace dress clung to her curves, while the skirt floated around her long legs. Unlike the prim outfits she'd been wearing, the soft fabric enhanced her shapely figure. The roses on the material matched the heightened color in her cheeks.

His mouth went dry at the blue flower-shaped buttons running down the front, from the scooped neckline to the hem of her skirt. Undo them and the dress would likely fall open. Jake swallowed hard, forcing aside the image of creamy skin that flashed in his head.

"Emily Marie Goodman, I told you to stay in the house." Maggie's glossy braid bounced as she hurried toward them. "If it wasn't for Mr. Badoletti, you could have been hurt."

"But Kitty went over the road. I had to save her." She batted her eyes at her mother.

The "innocent" expression didn't work. "Rules are rules. We have them to keep you safe. Say thank you to Mr. Badoletti and go back inside."

The little girl looked as if she might argue, but thought better of it. "Thank you, Mister…" She paused, glaring at him suspiciously. "Are you Mr. Bad Boy?"

Unsure how to respond to her sudden antagonism, he smiled. "You can call me Jake."

"Are you the one who was mean to Mummy?"

His smile faded. How the heck was he supposed to answer that? It was like that old no-win question: Are you still beating your wife? Why would Emily think he'd been mean to her mother anyway?

"Um, no. Not…" He faltered, recalling the incident at Mimi's office.

Maggie fixed her daughter with a stern look. "Emily!"

"Thank you, Mr. Bad Boy." The imp's tone was grudging. She trotted up the path and went into the house. He and Maggie winced in unison as the screen door slammed.

As she turned back, Jake noticed the same wariness in her expression as he'd seen after his argument with Nick. The same hint of fear in her dark brown eyes. The same rigid tension in her body. What was she worried about?

"Cute kid." He smiled, trying to put her at ease.

His smile had as little effect on Maggie as it had on her daughter. She watched him cautiously, her gaze assessing, as if she didn't trust his reaction.

"I'm so sorry. Emily usually does as she's told. The arrangements I'd made for her fell through this morning. Medical emergency." Her words quickened and her voice rose in pitch. "I thought it would be okay to bring her with me."

"No problem," Jake interjected before she wound herself up any further. "Shi…stuff happens. Any kid would be distracted by a cat."

"Thank you for catching her. I promise she won't be any further bother."

"It's okay. Really."

She studied him carefully. After a couple of moments, she nodded sharply. "We should get started. Shall we go inside?"

As Maggie opened the door, the fickle Kitty reappeared, slipping past her and brushing her skirt against the shapely legs he'd been trying not to stare at.

"After you." He gestured for her to precede him.

In the front hall, Emily sat pouting on the bottom step of the double-back staircase.

"I promise to behave. I won't touch anything." She shot a belligerent look at him. "Please may I go back up to the princess room?"

"Is that all right?" Maggie asked Jake.

He hadn't a clue where that was, but said, "Sure, go ahead, Short Stuff."

Without waiting for further instructions, Emily charged up the stairs. On the first landing, she came to an abrupt halt when the knob on the stair rail came off in her hands. Immediately, she and Maggie turned to him with identical expressions of fear, their faces pale, their eyes wide.

"I'm sorry." Emily's voice trembled. "I didn't mean to break it." She tried repeatedly to slot the knob back, but it wouldn't stay put. Tears welled, tugging at his heartstrings. "I can't fix it."

Maggie hurried upstairs and wrapped her arms around her daughter, her pose both defensive and protective. "I'm sorry. I'll inform the owners and pay for someone to come in and repair it straight away."

Jake was startled by their terrified reaction to a simple accident. Images from the past few days began to slot together like pieces of a jigsaw. They formed a picture of the kind of baggage Maggie and Emily carried from their past. Anger roiled within him, but he knew he couldn't show it.

Keeping his tone easy, he said, "No worries. This is an old house—you expect things to go wrong."

Emily regarded him suspiciously, like she was waiting for a catch. A nasty catch. The dread in her eyes was like a punch to his gut.

"The owners probably meant to fix that knob for years. They'd have probably forgotten to let me know about it, so you've done me a favor, Short Stuff. Thanks."

He went upstairs and joined them on the landing. They stiffened, but didn't back away.

"I'll take care of that." He indicated the knob in her hand.

"Thank you, Mr. Jake." Her half smile wrenched his heart.

The imp affected him almost as much as her mother.

"I can't believe that call took so long." Mimi walked onto the landing. "I'm sorry, but…" She broke off as she saw them standing uneasily at the top of the stairs. "Is everything all right?"

"Fine." Jake said quickly. "Emily's going to check out that princess room so her mom and I can do our tour of the house. Isn't that right, Maggie?"

"Uh…yes."

Emily waited for her mother's nod before rushing off.

Mimi looked at Maggie. "Are you sure?"

Maggie's uncertain gaze flicked to him. He could see she wanted to believe he wasn't mad, but something held her back.

"She's worried because this came off the banister." He tossed the knob from hand to hand. "I'm trying to convince her it tells me the house has been well loved and lived in."

"You're absolutely right." Mimi took the knob from him. "If only all clients understood such things. We'll add it to the list of items that'll need fixing, if you're interested enough in the house to put in an offer."

"Works for me."

"Speaking of troublesome clients—" she held up her phone "—I'm sorry, but I really need to sort this one out before he blows his sale. You're in capable hands with Maggie."

"For sure. We can manage without you. Right, Maggie?"

Maggie nodded.

"Great." Mimi headed downstairs. "Any problems and I'm only a phone call away," she added wryly.

As the front door closed, Maggie cleared her throat. "Thank you," she said softly.

Jake shrugged off her gratitude. "Shall we get on with the tour?"

"Certainly." Her smile was tremulous but genuinely warm. "We can start up here."

His excitement was tinged with sadness. While the incident had reinforced his feelings about the house, it had also reinforced why dating Maggie could never work.

Her defiant support for her daughter convinced him that someone had definitely mistreated them both. No wonder she was nervous, scared to trust him.

The problem was he didn't know how to handle her or Emily. It had been bad enough screwing up with Adam. Getting it wrong with a vulnerable kid would be a million times worse. No, better to keep things casual. To focus on his game and winning the Cup.

It was a sensible plan. So why did he feel like a loser?

"Do you think the bed's for sale?"

Jake's question made Maggie's heart swan-dive to her stomach.

She'd been trying to avoid looking at the beautiful cherrywood sleigh bed that took up most of the guest bedroom. It was the bed of her dreams.

From the moment she'd seen the bed she'd wanted it. Imagined herself in it. But her brain was playing tricks on her, because in her daydream she wasn't alone. Or sleeping. Worse, Jake was the man who'd tangled the sheets with her in that daydream.

"Maggie?" He stared quizzically at her over the width of the bed.

She hoped he couldn't read her mind. A flush crept up her neck.

"Um," she stammered, trying to regain her composure. "Mimi said the owners were divorcing and pretty much anything can be bought."

"I want this bed and the matching furniture."

Jake walked around the bed to join her. His hand glided over the curved footboard, his fingers caressing the snowflakes carved into the gleaming wood. How could a simple gesture, one she'd done herself only minutes ago, take on such a suggestive feel?

Maggie dipped her head, hoping to mask her blush. "Anything else?"

"Put whatever you think I'll need on the list. I trust your judgment."

"Don't you want a say?"

She'd expected him to be as pedantic about the decor and furniture as he'd been about the house itself. But once he'd decided to buy the Victorian, he'd lost interest in the details. She'd had to insist he take a more thorough look around so they'd know what needed to be done before he took possession.

"Not really." He shrugged. "As long as I can move in and it's livable."

"What about your furniture from Chicago? I don't want you to end up with duplicates."

"There's enough room to accommodate everything in my apartment several times over."

"Okay. I'll make a list, check costs and get your approval before I finalize anything.

"Sounds good." Jake leaned back against the high mattress, crossing his legs at the ankles. "I'd like this bed moved to the master bedroom."

Maggie made a notation on her clipboard. She ignored the twinge in her chest at the thought of someone else sharing her bed...that bed...with him.

Not that it was any of her business. It was just a case of...bed envy.

The silliness of her thoughts made her smile.

"Want to share the joke?"

She looked up. His ice-blue gaze caught hers and held it. The laughter faded to be replaced by heat.

She licked her suddenly dry lips, trying to moisten them.

His eyes dropped to her mouth. She could almost feel his touch on her lips.

Fire raced through her blood, setting her pulse dancing. Her clipboard dropped to the floor. Raising her fingers to the base of her throat, she covered the throbbing that had to be visible to his searching gaze.

A half smile played on his lips, as if he knew what she was doing and why.

The delicate cotton dress, which had seemed appropriate for the humid heat, now seemed flimsy. The thin material clung to her moist skin despite the air-conditioning. It provided little in the way of a barrier, leaving her vulnerable to the flames in those blue eyes and to the desire building within her.

He straightened, bringing his body near enough that his scent teased her nose. If she reached out, just a bit, she'd be able to touch him.

His presence surrounded her.

Overwhelmed, yet thrilled, Maggie began to wonder how he kissed, what he tasted like. No sooner had the thought popped into her head than she yearned to find out.

Now.

She took a half step toward him. He moved closer, too.

He was so tall. So broad.

So intoxicating.

His head lowered as she tilted hers up to meet him.

His mouth was centimeters away.

"Mummy, I'm hungry. Is it lunchtime?"

Emily's voice from the hallway broke the spell.

Maggie stepped away from Jake hurriedly, straightening her clothes with trembling fingers, though he had yet to touch her.

She cleared her throat, then called out, "Just a few more minutes."

Leaning over to pick up her clipboard, she tried to slow her quickened breathing.

Oh, my God! She'd responded to Jake as blindly and urgently as a moth to a flickering flame. She'd been about to make a stupid mistake. Again. Hadn't she learned anything?

Just because he'd treated Emily kindly over the banister knob didn't mean he wouldn't lose his temper the next time something broke. She'd already seen that he could be unpredictable. Even though it hadn't happened, it didn't mean it *wouldn't* happen again.

No matter how attracted she was to Jake, she couldn't risk her daughter's safety.

Maggie straightened slowly, avoiding his gaze. Clutching the clipboard to her chest, she said briskly, "We should get a move on. We still have a few more rooms to go through."

"Maggie?" His voice, huskier than normal, sent a tingle down her spine.

Afraid he wanted to discuss the near kiss, she rushed out into the hall. Thankfully, the next room was a study. She couldn't handle another bedroom.

Why couldn't she be immune to Jake's sexy charm? There was something about him that made him far more enticing, and dangerous, than any other man.

All the more reason not to repeat the same bloody mistake.

"Is everything okay?" Jake stood in the doorway, studying her carefully.

"Fine. Just got lots to do today." Her voice sounded brittle. "So, the study…"

Cool disinterest replaced the heat in his blue eyes. "I've seen all I need. Get me the paperwork and we'll go from there."

As he turned and left, Maggie stared after him. She told herself she was relieved she'd managed to convince him of her indifference so easily.

A little pang in her chest said she was lying.

NICE GOING, JACKASS!

Jake swore silently. What had he been thinking?

His body clearly hadn't got the message that there could be nothing between him and Maggie. One glance at her poised so temptingly beside that bed and his brain had dived into his suddenly too-tight boxer shorts. Hell, without Emily's interruption, they'd probably be testing that mattress right now.

Seeing his own desire mirrored in Maggie's dark eyes had switched off his common sense. All he'd been able to think about was tasting her. Touching her. Undoing every one of those little flower-shaped buttons.

Damn it! He was hard again.

Leaning his forehead against the cool glass of the kitchen window, he willed his erection to subside.

His cell chirped, interrupting his heated thoughts. His mom's number on the caller ID got his body back under control instantly.

"Hey, Ma, what's up?"

"Have you asked Maggie to the Labor Day party?"

He sighed. "I told you, I don't want to complicate things."

"What's complicated? You're inviting her to a barbecue. It's a holiday and she's a nice woman in a new country. You invite your teammates, especially those far from home, so why not Maggie?"

"All right, I'll mention it to her."

He'd just hung up when Maggie entered the kitchen with Emily.

No time like the present. "Mom wants to invite you guys to our annual Labor Day barbecue. It's a fun, relaxed day. Lots of people—neighbors, family and friends."

"Can we, Mummy?" Emily's pleading look was Oscar worthy. "*Ple-e-ease.* I've never been to a Labor Day barbecue. Ever. In my whole life."

"We'll see," Maggie said stiffly.

"That means no." Emily's bottom lip jutted out.

"It means we'll see. Auntie Tracy may have other plans." Maggie turned to him. "Thank your mum and tell her I'll let her know either way as soon as I can." Her closed expression made it clear what that answer would be.

He should have been relieved, not disappointed. Perversely, Maggie's swift dismissal made him determined to convince her to come to the barbecue.

"It'll be a great opportunity for you and Tracy to combine business with pleasure. The Ice Cats will be there, too."

"I'll get back to you." Maggie's frustration said he'd

tipped in a winner. "If you're ready to go, I have another appointment."

"Sure."

The victory felt empty. Maggie's desperation to get away from him was a kick in the ego. Thanks to that almost kiss, the relaxed feeling between them had been replaced by tension. He might as well have stolen a taste.

"If you and Emily wait on the porch, I'll reset the alarm and lock up." Her voice was coolly professional.

"Come on, Short Stuff." Jake held the door open for Emily.

"I'm not short. I was the tallest girl in my class."

He grinned. "You're not as tall as me. Anyway, it's just a nickname. Like Cupcake or Pumpkin or Half Pint."

She wrinkled her nose. "My dad said nicknames are stupid. He didn't like it when Mummy called me Em."

Jeez. What could Jake say to Emily? He could hardly call her father a dumb bastard.

"Almost everybody I know has a nickname. I'm Bad Boy, because it's easier than Badoletti." No point telling her the other reasons. "Then there's my teammates— Blade, Tru, Ike and Mad Dog, among others."

"My dad plays..." Emily paused as Maggie came outside, accompanied by the whine of the alarm, and locked up. "My dad doesn't have a nickname."

As they followed Maggie down the path, he wondered if Emily's father was the one responsible for her fear. It made horrible sense. And reinforced why Maggie and her daughter were a complication he should walk away from.

Yet, it was hard not to respond to Emily. Ahead of him, the breeze caught Maggie's dress, lifting the skirt briefly to reveal almost the full length of those sexy legs. It was even harder, he acknowledged, not to respond to Emily's mother.

When they reached the cars, Emily said, "I suppose it'll be all right for you to give me a nickname." She jammed her fists on her hips. "But not Short Stuff."

Jake pretended to think about it. "How about Babycakes?"

Emily snorted.

"Sugar Pie?"

She rolled her eyes in disgust.

"Choochi Face?"

"Mr. Ja-a-ke."

"I'm out of ideas. What do you suggest?"

"You may call me Princess."

He let out a bark of laughter and bowed. "All right, Your Majesty."

"You're funny, Mr. Jake."

Maggie's lips twitched. "Hop in and fasten your seatbelt, Em."

Emily gave a theatrically royal sigh and did as she was told.

Maggie turned to Jake. "I'll email you the details of what we've discussed, as well as a list of items you may want to purchase."

"Great. Thanks." When she got in the car, he added, "Don't forget Mom's invitation."

"I won't." She closed her door.

Jake watched them drive away. Emily waved enthusiastically until they were out of sight. Grinning, he walked to his M-Class. Cute kid. Just like her mom.

As he got in his SUV and started the engine, he replayed his visit to the house. The near kiss in the bedroom. The tense situation on the stairs. If only Maggie didn't have the baggage of her past, she'd be perfect for him.

He stopped the thought with a shake of his head. The problem wasn't Maggie's baggage.

It was his.

He looked back at the Victorian. Everything was working out fine. The season was right around the corner. He'd found the home he'd been searching for. His new life was pretty much on track. Why, suddenly, did that not seem enough anymore?

CHAPTER SIX

WHEN MAGGIE ACCEPTED Jake's invitation to the Labor Day barbecue, she hadn't imagined the view from the Badoletti's deck would be so spectacular.

A dozen men, half bare chested and half wearing sleeveless vests were embroiled in a game of American football. She'd never seen such a prime collection of six-packs, glutes and pecs.

"Holy cr—"

Maggie cut Tracy off with a stern look. "Little pitchers." She patted Emily's head.

"Sorry." Her sister grinned sheepishly. "But take a look at that."

She followed Tracy's gaze to the tangle of men. "Oh, my."

Jake. Shirtless. Glorious.

Muscles rippled in his broad chest as he scrambled free and leaped to catch the ball. Her heart thudded at the lean, corded strength in his arms and legs.

He must have sensed her watching, because his gaze homed in on her like an ice-blue laser. His triumphant grin turned feral as his eyes skimmed her body from head to toe, lingering on her bare shoulders before dropping to the hem of her sundress and focusing on her legs. Then he winked and turned back to the game.

She exhaled deeply. Jake Badoletti was one hard man to ignore.

"You've been holding back on me," murmured Tracy, as Emily sat on the steps. "What's going on between you and Bad Boy?"

Maggie swallowed. "Nothing."

"Uh-huh. That look made my temperature go up thirty degrees, and he wasn't aiming it at me."

"Jake's all wrong for me." She ignored her body's vehement disagreement.

"I'm not suggesting you marry him. What's the harm in a couple of dates?"

That's how it had started with Lee. The perfect antidote to her father's dictatorial rule, her ex had offered everything a sheltered eighteen-year-old had dreamed of. His charm had thrilled, while his brooding good looks had tempted. But the prison he'd trapped her in had been far worse than the one she'd left behind.

Still, that didn't stop her wondering what a date with Jake would be like. How it would feel to have his attention, his charm focused solely on her. To be the woman in the glamorous dress, on his arm as they went to a smart restaurant or a Broadway show. How the evening might end with...

Stop! She wouldn't let her mind stroll down that dangerous path.

"You could have a short, hot-and-heavy fling."

Maggie ignored the tempting images flitting through

her brain and the twinkle in Tracy's eyes. "That's not why I came to the States."

"I know, but what a nice bonus."

"I want a quiet, normal life. Free from the constant pressure of being in the sights of the paparazzi lenses. From the stress of knowing everything I do will be splashed across the gossip media and analysed to death." She sighed. "It's my only chance to live the way I choose, instead of kowtowing to someone else's rules and expectations. I want to be free to be me— whatever *me* is. A man doesn't figure into that right now. Least of all, one like Jake."

Cheers and groans interrupted their conversation. The vests had the ball again. Good-natured insults flew back and forth.

She turned to check on her daughter. Her heart hitched in her chest. Emily wasn't there.

A moment later, she heard Jake yell, "Whoa, Emily! Wait there until we finish this play."

The blur of yellow racing toward the melee of bodies halted.

Maggie's nails bit into her palm as memories of another time, another game flashed in her brain. A frisson of fear skittered through her as she recalled a furious glare filled with the promise of retribution. She moved toward the steps, toward her vulnerable daughter. Then stopped dead as Jake turned.

His expression was concerned, rather than angry. His querying look asked her permission. Relieved, she nodded.

Jake grinned and returned to the game.

When the play stopped, he waved Emily over. "Hey, Short Stuff. You want to help me beat these bozos?"

Emily nodded. "But you're supposed to call me Princess."

"Sorry." He ruffled her hair. "Take it easy, guys. There's royalty on the field."

Jake explained the rules and showed her where to stand. The teams lined up against each other. Someone yelled "Hup," then threw the ball. Bodies scrambled.

Maggie winced as several thudded to the ground in crunching tackles.

Jake caught the ball, then dodged his opponent and handed it to Emily. She charged toward the goal line, spiking the ball triumphantly as she scored.

Jake swung Emily up onto his shoulders. The shirtless team cheered, then they all high-fived her grinning daughter.

"Yay, Emily!" Maggie clapped.

Tracy leaned against the railing. "Looks like Bad Boy has a soft spot for your daughter, as well." She scowled. "What's *he* doing here?"

Maggie followed her sister's gaze. Ike Jelinek was walking along the path from the cute little carriage house behind the trees, carrying a drinks cooler.

"His mum is friends with Jake's parents. That's her place. Is there a problem?"

"Not really." Her sister's tone suggested otherwise. "Didn't you do some work for him?"

"Yes. Last summer."

"And?"

"And nothing. He's a very old-fashioned guy."

Maggie quirked an eyebrow. "In what way?"

"He believes in traditional roles for women." Tracy's lip curled. "Men drive, men pay, men are gods whom we should worship and serve."

Uh-oh. "Like Dad."

"Totally. Ike doesn't understand the concept of a modern, independent woman. He expects us to be like Mum—subservient and submissive." Tracy flicked her hair. "I'm not going through that again. I had my fill with my marriage."

Before Maggie could delve further, Jake's mum and Aunt Karina appeared, bearing bowls laden with food.

"Can we help?" she offered.

"Thank you." Tina Badoletti handed her two bowls of potato salad and pointed to the picnic tables, covered in red-checked tablecloths. "Put them over there. We have more in the kitchen."

"Gio, we're ready," she called to Jake's father, who was manning the enormous barbecue on the brick patio beside the deck.

The older, shorter version of Jake grinned, blew his wife a kiss then tossed steaks, burgers and hot dogs onto the grill. The sizzle of the meat hitting the hot grate made Maggie's stomach growl.

By the time she and Tracy had finished bringing out the food, the game was over, the guys had cleaned up and everyone was gathered round the barbecue.

Jake was helping Emily fill her plate. Her carefree giggle tugged at Maggie's heart.

Maggie was glad they'd come today. Though, outwardly, her reason for accepting was to help Tracy's business, she'd wanted Emily to experience the warm, welcoming sense of family she felt at the Badoletti's. Something her daughter hadn't got from either set of grandparents.

When they joined the crowd, Tracy linked arms with a tall, blond man with gray eyes. "Maggie, this is Juergen Ingemar. He's moved here from Gothenburg."

The Swede gave her a strange look. "Have we met?"

Maggie shook her head. "I doubt it. I'm not a hockey fan."

"You play hockey in England, no?"

"I think so, but it's not as popular as other sports."

He inclined his head. "Football and rugby, sure."

"Also, that strange game, cricket," a gruff, accented voice added. "Tracy, you're as lovely as ever."

Her sister grinned up at the burly man with the scarred face. "This is Vladimir Ralinkov, aka the Russian Rocket. He joined the Ice Cats last season."

Ralinkov gave Maggie the same strange look as the Swede, but said nothing. He lifted her hand to his lips. She couldn't help being charmed by the twinkle in his eyes.

"You still know how to zero in on the prettiest women, Vlad."

Jake's cool voice over her shoulder made Maggie tense. Though his comment seemed harmless enough, experience had taught her that a calm delivery was more dangerous than shouting. A simple remark—poison delivered with a smile—the prelude to the backhander that inevitably followed.

She knew Jake wouldn't hit her, but she edged away

from him nonetheless, looking anxiously for Emily. Thankfully, her daughter was by the grill, chatting with Gio and Tina.

"We played together for a while on the Hawks." Jake clapped him on the back. "Best damn center in the game. I'm glad we're on the same team now."

The two men laughed and began reminiscing about previous encounters.

Maggie watched Jake carefully. Was the easy camaraderie as genuine as it seemed or was he saving his anger for when they were away from the crowd, like Lee had done? She searched his face for telltale signs but saw nothing untoward. No twitching jaw muscle, no narrowing of his eyes.

Could she trust her own judgment? She'd been wrong about her ex, missed some obvious clues. They said the best way to tell how a man would treat his wife was to see how his father treated his mother. She hadn't met Lee's father until it was far too late, but had known straightaway that history was repeating itself.

Maggie looked across to the grill. Gio planted a smacking kiss on his wife's pink cheek before presenting her with the best steak, cooked just as she liked it. Jake was from good stock. Clearly his reputation wasn't the whole story.

Her pulse skipped at the possibility, even as a cautious inner voice warned there was no smoke without fire.

Maggie had seen enough evidence to know Jake's nickname had been earned. Her eyes traced the white scar on the bridge of his nose and the one bisecting his eyebrow. Could there be something special behind the image? Something different?

Some*one* different?

She was tempted to believe there was. Tempted to find out for sure. Was it time to give Jake the benefit of the doubt?

Maggie thought back over everything that had happened since they'd met. With very few exceptions, he hadn't behaved at all like she'd expected. The way he'd treated people—his mother, Aunt Karina, Emily. Maggie herself.

Jake had surprised her at every turn.

But did she dare take the risk on him?

She looked up at Jake. Their gazes caught and held.

Turquoise fire flared in the depths of his eyes.

Her heart slammed against her ribs. Heat pooled deep within.

Did she dare not to?

"HANDS OFF MY cannoli!"

Jake grinned as Maggie's hand hovered protectively over her dessert.

"But there are none left and you have two." He enjoyed teasing her. "You could share."

She smiled at his hangdog look, then playfully smacked his sneaking fingers. "You've already eaten three. You'll spoil your boyish figure."

His chest caught at the mischief in her dark brown eyes. He shifted to ease the ache in his already tight groin, only to stifle a groan as she nibbled a pastry shell, then slowly, deliberately, sucked cream from its center.

Two could play at that game.

Jake wiped powdered sugar from the corner of her mouth with his thumb. The pulse at the base of her throat fluttered. As he licked his thumb clean, her lips parted on a soft gasp.

He leaned closer.

She watched intently as his mouth neared hers. His lips hovered whisper close, then headed over her cheek to her ear.

"Delicious," he murmured, before snatching the remaining cannoli from her plate.

Maggie blinked, then laughed. "Sneaky. I'll have to keep my eye on you."

His heart kicked. *Yes, please.*

He hadn't meant to spend the whole afternoon with her. This morning, he'd been full of good intentions—he'd introduce her around, then leave her alone. Maybe she'd find a nice, suitable guy there. He'd ignored the wrench in his guts at the thought of her dating someone else; whatever was best for Maggie and Emily was what was important.

Then he'd spotted her in that pink summer dress, looking as delicious as strawberry ice cream. Those daisy-shaped buttons trailing enticingly down her front had blown his noble plan out of the water.

It was only one afternoon. What harm could there be in spending it with her and Emily?

He'd been surprised by how much he'd enjoyed being part of their family unit. It had given him hope for the future. For the new life he would be living. For the changed man he would become.

Now he and Maggie shared a blanket under the trees, watching the party wind down in the graying light. The balmy evening air still held a spicy tang from the barbecue. His mom and Aunt Karina sat on the porch swing, their heads bent over their latest quilt, while Tru, Vlad and Juergen chatted with Tracy at a nearby picnic table. On the other side of the lawn, his dad had set up a street-hockey goal and was coaching Emily as she tried to score on Ike.

A cool breeze rustled the leaves, reminding him summer was ending soon.

Training camp would be starting, followed by the preseason. Then, the craziness of an eighty-two-game run to April. If all went well, he wouldn't catch his breath until June.

The sale of his condo in Chicago had closed a few days ago. Maggie had arranged for his things to be packed, so they were ready to ship when he had the new house. The purchase of the Victorian was progressing smoothly, and he was excited about moving in.

The only downside was that once it was done, he'd lose his excuse to see Maggie regularly. That bothered him a lot more than he'd expected.

Emily's cheer broke into his thoughts.

Ike gave Maggie's daughter an exaggerated glare as he dug the red ball out of his net.

"She shoots, she scores!" His dad whooped.

Maggie clapped. "Great goal."

"She's got a good eye," he said as Emily tried a fancy move, narrowly missing.

"Em didn't get that from me. I'm hopeless at sports."

He seized the chance to find out more about her past. "What about her father?"

Maggie sighed. "Lee plays football—soccer—in the English Premier League."

Her ex was a professional athlete? Jake swore silently. No wonder she was so wary about him. What were the odds the ex had a reputation like Jake's? If the ex was responsible for the baggage that Maggie and Emily carried with them, that put a nasty spin on the situation, too.

"I win." Emily cheered and did a victory dance.

"I bet she'd be hell on skates." Jake smiled at Maggie. "She's got great natural balance."

"You're right. We went to the rink a few times back home and she picked it up easily."

The pride in her voice gave him an idea. "You should sign her up for a Mini Mites hockey team."

"But she's a girl." She frowned.

"Girls play hockey, too. At her age, there's no contact."

"Emily's too young."

Jake ignored her cool tone. Once she understood what fun her daughter would have, she'd be fine. "My dad had me skating at five. The same youth hockey program is still going. The people involved are good. I could get you the details."

"I really don't think it's appropriate for Emily."

As sexy as he found her clipped accent, he knew rejection when he heard it. She wasn't even prepared to listen to him. Frustration churned inside. He'd never recommend anything that would be dangerous for a kid.

Determined not to let her dismiss the idea, he pressed on. "I get why you're nervous, but you can't wrap her in cotton wool forever."

As soon as the words left his mouth, he knew he'd made a tactical error.

Maggie stiffened, her expression as cold and brittle as game-worn ice. "I'm her mother. I know what's best for her."

"But…"

"I said no." Her words echoed around the yard.

As the others turned to look at them, she said quietly, "Drop it, please."

"Is everything all right?" Tracy joined them.

"Fine." He couldn't keep the disappointment out of his voice. "A difference of opinion."

Maggie leaped to her feet. "You must be tiring, sis. I'll get Emily and we can go."

Before he could restore the earlier warmth between them, they were leaving. Emily hugged him, but Maggie kept her distance.

Jake stood on the front porch and watched until the car disappeared.

Way to go. How come with Maggie he always seemed to have his head up his ass?

He ran his hand over the tense cords at the back of his neck. He should stick to hockey. The puck didn't care what kind of man he was. On the ice, the rules were simple.

He walked into the house. Laughter came from the

kitchen as the party moved inside. In no mood to join them, he headed upstairs to his room and flopped onto the bed.

Though he hadn't grown up here, his parents had wanted him to feel at home, so they'd filled the shelves with his awards and put up the life-size picture of the Stanley Cup he'd always had pinned to the wall.

As he did every time he stared at the iconic trophy, he visualized the moment when he'd finally get to lift it over his head. He could almost hear the roar of the crowd, taste the salty tang of sweat, feel the itchy play-off beard and the ache of a body worked beyond its limit.

This year, there would be no soul-destroying loss. He'd do whatever it took to make damn sure he gave Adam that shared moment of glory. It wouldn't make up for Jake's mistakes the night of the accident. Nor would it make up for all the times he'd ducked Adam, putting his frustration at his friend's erratic play and temperamental behavior ahead of helping a troubled man.

No, raising the Cup in Adam's honor wouldn't repay a fraction of the debt Jake owed, but it was all he had. And he wouldn't let anything or anyone interfere with that.

"Arrogant jerk."

Maggie drained her wine. She felt like throwing her glass at Jake's head. "Patronizing, high-handed git."

She'd fumed about his comments since leaving the barbecue. Now, as she and Tracy relaxed in the living room, her anger bubbled over. "How dare he insinu-

ate that I don't know how to bring up my daughter?
What is it about sports stars? Just because they're good
at playing with a ball doesn't make them experts at
everything."

"They play with a puck in hockey," Tracy said
calmly.

"Puck, ball, whatever. The point is the same."

Her sister raised an eyebrow. "What did Jake say to
upset you?"

"I'm a terrible mother because I don't want Emily
to play hockey."

"Really? Are you sure you didn't misunderstand?"

"Okay, he didn't say it quite like that, but it's what
he meant. It didn't cross his narrow mind that I might
have a good reason for not letting her play such a violent sport."

No sooner had she considered letting down her
guard than he'd proved her fears were justified. "He
refused to listen to me, then criticized my parenting
skills. Just like Lee."

"Don't you think you're overreacting?" Tracy asked
softly. "You seemed to be getting on well."

Maggie started to disagree, then stopped. She and
Jake *had* got on well. It had been a wonderful, relaxed
afternoon. Seeing Jake with family and friends had
proved he was more than just a charming facade.

She liked him. Liked being with him, liked spending time with him.

His criticism had stung because it had been unexpected.

Was she being unfair?

"Possibly," she admitted. "But he kept pushing even after I'd told him no."

"He probably got carried away. The man has lived and breathed hockey since he was a kid. You can't blame him for wanting to share his passion."

Unknowingly, her sister hit on the source of Maggie's frustration. She'd been fighting her attraction to him all day. Even now, her pulse skipped as she recalled the tingling brush of his thumb against her lips. The caress of his breath against the sensitive skin of her neck when he'd murmured in her ear.

She frowned. "Why are you taking Jake's side?"

"I'm not. He handled the situation badly." Tracy sipped her wine. "That doesn't mean you should reject his idea out of hand. Hockey's not that bad."

"It's not ideal for a seven-year-old girl, either. I don't want her teeth knocked out."

"They don't play hard at her age and they have decent protection. It's no more dangerous than playing football and she loves that."

"I suppose I could check it out," Maggie said grudgingly. "Em seems really keen. But if I don't think it's appropriate, I won't let her play."

"That's your prerogative and I'll support you one hundred percent." Tracy refilled their wineglasses. "I'm glad to see you standing up for yourself again."

Maggie started at the change of subject. As she considered her sister's words, she realized Tracy was right. She *was* behaving more like the person she used to be before she'd married Lee. A warm glow of pride filled her.

"I wonder why I'm able to stand up to Jake and yet I took everything Lee threw at me?"

"Maybe because Jake treats you properly, most of the time."

"Perhaps." Could it be that simple?

"The point is you're back to being the brave, bold Maggie we know and love. The one who left home at eighteen with only her savings and a typing certificate."

"As opposed to Margaret, Lee's meek mouse of a wife?" She'd hated him using her full name as much as she'd hated the control he'd had over her.

"It wasn't your fault. He was so loving and attentive. No one could have guessed what he was really like."

"You did." Tracy had never liked Lee.

"Don't be so hard on yourself. Lee spun his web around you slowly so that by the time he showed his true colors, you were well and truly trapped."

Maggie felt ashamed. She should have been able to see what was happening. "Still, I shouldn't have put up with him for so long. I put Emily in danger because I wasn't strong enough to leave sooner."

"Luckily, you had enough of your old self in you to be able to walk out on the bastard when you had to."

Her throat tightened; tears welled. She'd never forget the moment of panic when Emily had charged at Lee, trying to protect her mother. Raw fear had torn through Maggie when Lee had turned, fury raging, fist raised to strike their small daughter. "It shouldn't have taken him almost hitting Emily to open my eyes. To act."

"You got in Lee's way, prevented him hurting her and ended up in hospital with a broken arm, two broken ribs and a cracked cheekbone." Tracy came and sat beside Maggie, putting her arm around her. "You've come a long way since that night. Don't revert to being Margaret at the slightest setback."

Pride sparked back to life. Maggie would not let herself regress.

The past year had shown she wasn't incapable or stupid. She'd made small, but significant steps toward becoming the kind of woman she wanted to be. She'd survived the media onslaught of her divorce with dignity, moved to the United States and built a life for herself and Emily and taken on an important role in Tracy's business. Slowly but surely, she was becoming the kind of woman her daughter would be proud of.

Someone she could be proud of.

Yet she was still letting Lee's opinions and actions have power over her and hold her back. That had to stop. It was time to take bigger steps.

Her mind whirred as she thought about how she could do that. She should take a more proactive role in Making Your Move; Tracy wanted her to be a partner. Start living the way she wanted, dressing the way she wanted. Take her hemlines up and let her hair down. She giggled at the old-fashioned phrase.

"You look pleased with yourself." Her sister smiled.

"I am pleased and I want to keep feeling that way."

"That's more like it. Now, what will you do about Bad Boy?"

Her heart hitched. "Nothing."

"You say he's not what you want or need, but he's

sparked more of a reaction from you than any other man, Lee included."

"Irritation is hardly the basis for a relationship."

"A passionate response is better than a lukewarm one."

Whatever was between her and Jake definitely couldn't be described as lukewarm.

"There's no doubt Bad Boy is interested in you—he made that pretty clear this afternoon." Tracy grinned. "I suspect he'll pursue you as determinedly as he plays hockey. I've told you before, you deserve to be happy. Imagine the fun you'll have if you let him catch you."

Maggie tamped down the thrill that skipped through her. "Given the way we left things, I doubt he's still interested in me."

Tracy laughed. "That little disagreement? Trust me…he won't give up on you that easily."

Her sister was probably right. Maggie had experienced enough of Jake's stubborn determination during their hunt for a house. Perhaps it was time for a little leap of faith. What harm could one date do?

"Okay. If you're right and if he apologizes properly, I'll give him a chance."

"Great. I can't wait to see how the revitalized Maggie deals with Bad Boy."

Maggie had to admit, she was looking forward to seeing that herself.

CHAPTER SEVEN

"WHAT THE HELL happened with Maggie yesterday?"

Tru's comment winded Jake as much as the ten minutes of sprints up and down the ice they'd just completed.

He'd hoped to hold off any discussion of the fight with Maggie until after their private practice session at the local rink. They'd planned to grab dinner together at the local diner. He should have known Tru and Ike wouldn't let him get away with that.

"What happened to your legendary charm?" Ike pushed up his mask. "Are you losing your touch?"

Jake ignored the goaltender. He drank water while he tried to figure out what to say, then leaned on his stick. "We had a disagreement."

His words echoed in the nearly empty rink. Even he could hear how unconvincing they sounded. He explained what they'd argued about. "I made a dumb mistake."

"Emily's her kid." Ike shrugged. "It's up to her."

"Couldn't she at least have considered the idea before shooting me down?"

"I bet you pushed too hard. Didn't give her a chance to think about it." Ike wiped his face with a towel.

Tru nodded. "If you'd back off a little, folks might come round to your way of thinking."

Jake didn't want to admit they might be right. "Doesn't matter. I'm moving into the house in a few days. Her job is done. No reason to see each other, even if she wanted to, and she made it pretty freaking clear she doesn't."

"Did you try apologizing?"

Jake shot him a frustrated look. "I called her several times today, but she didn't call me back. She responded to emails about my move, but nothing else."

"So go and see her." Tru reached round him to get another stick.

"She probably wouldn't open the door. She thinks I'm worse than whale crap."

"She thinks you're hot. I saw her checking you out."

His groin tightened at the memory. "Until I screwed it up."

"So, unscrew it." Ike made it sound easy. "You know the drill—flowers, chocolates, grovel, a fancy dinner. If that doesn't work, forget about her." He pushed down his mask. "I'll set up the net so you bozos can work on your shots." He skated to one end of the ice and dragged the practice net into place, then roughed up the crease.

Jake and Tru joined Ike. "I hear the newest Ice Cat, JB Larocque, has a bullet of a shot."

"They're already calling him the next Great One." Tru rolled his eyes. "The kid's stats are amazing. But he's unpredictable—brilliant one game, a liability the next. His off-ice reputation rivals yours, Jake."

"I don't care if the kid's reputation *outstrips* mine—

I sure as hell won't be competing with him for headlines." Jake tipped pucks out of a bucket. "It had better not affect his play. For us to get the Cup, Larocque will need to bring his best game from day one."

"No pressure on the kid, then." Tru grinned. "Better make sure us old guys can keep up."

They began their regular shooting drills. Jake deliberately pushed the intensity and pace to test his healed right arm and reconstructed right leg. His muscles burned, but it was a healthy ache.

A couple of hours later, he was ready to drop. Dripping with sweat, the three of them headed to the locker room to shower and change.

Once they'd cleaned up, Ike pulled a letter out of his bag. "What do you think of the latest missive from management on their new drug-testing policy?"

Jake shrugged as he combed his wet hair. "It was inevitable after all the allegations about those baseball stars. Doesn't bother me—I've got nothing to hide."

Tru nodded, tying up his Nikes. "If it proves the league is clean, I'm okay with it. I know a couple of guys tested positive in recent years, but no player I know would be crazy enough to pump that stuff into their bodies."

"Some guys want an easy route in everything." Ike pulled on a clean team T-shirt. "For them, the promise of an extra edge is hard to resist."

"For sure, but I can't think of anyone dumb enough or desperate enough to take the risk." Jake zipped up his bag. "Not when we've worked so hard to get to the show."

"Me, neither. But I wouldn't be shocked if someone tested positive."

"Let them test away. We're clean and that's all that matters." Tru hefted his bag over his shoulder. "Same time tomorrow?"

They chorused their agreement, then walked out of the rink to the parking lot. Ike got in his Discovery, waved then drove off. Jake tossed his gear in the back of Tru's SUV.

They were pulling onto I-95 when Tru spoke, blind-siding Jake again. "Could Adam have been juicing?"

"No way." Jake leaped to his friend's defense. "He went to church every Sunday, spent his spare time doing charity work and helping disadvantaged kids learn to skate. Even when he partied, he never drank anything stronger than a beer. He wouldn't take drugs."

"That's different to taking steroids, bro. Think about it. Adam was worried about his performance. His play was wildly inconsistent and he was under huge pressure. It might explain why his behavior was yo-yoing all over the place, too."

Jake considered what his friend was saying. Tru's argument made sense, but he couldn't imagine the guy he knew cheating like that.

He shook his head. "Whatever demons Adam was fighting, I can't see him taking such a dumb risk. Then again, I was such a *great* friend, how would I know?"

Before the night of the crash, he'd avoided Adam for weeks. Jake had only accepted the ride to the party because he hadn't wanted to drink and drive. He'd thought it would be okay. Adam had been in a good mood; he'd been excited about being propositioned by the twin puck bunnies.

Unfortunately, the good mood hadn't lasted more than a couple of miles. Jake had finally lost patience with Adam's behavior and had planned to tackle his friend about what the hell his problem was at the party.

Only they'd never made it to the party.

Jake would never know if he could have saved Adam's life if he'd just taken the time in the preceding weeks to ask a couple of simple questions. He'd have to live with the guilt for the rest of his life.

"Adam was a grown man," Tru said quietly. "He could have asked for help if he'd wanted it, from you or Nick or any of his teammates."

"I still should have made more of an effort. I let him down."

Tru sighed. "You didn't, but nothing I say will stop you from beating yourself up over it."

Neither of them spoke for a while, each lost in their own thoughts. Jake replayed the argument with Maggie, turning over in his mind what he'd learned about her past and how he'd mishandled the whole conversation.

As Tru pulled onto the exit ramp, Jake said, "I should have learned from the mess with Adam that I'm no good at dealing with emotional baggage."

"What the hell does that mean?"

"Her ex is a professional soccer player and I think he was also an abusive bastard."

Tru whistled. "No wonder she's wary. But you'd never lay a finger on her or Emily."

"Damn straight." His stomach turned at the thought. "But she doesn't know that. Either way, with my reputation, I'm not the best choice for her to date."

"That's bull. With the amount of time you've spent together lately, she must have seen that you're more than your press."

"Maybe." She'd seemed to enjoy spending time with him until he'd blown it. "But I'm still not the kind of man she needs."

"Because of one little argument?" Tru frowned.

"Because she can't rely on me to take care of her the way she needs. Maggie deserves better than that. Better than me."

"Get over yourself, bro." Tru rolled his eyes. "Don't you think you should let Maggie decide that for herself? Why don't you give her, and yourself, a chance to see if things work out instead of dismissing it out of hand? You like her, right?"

"Yeah."

"You find her hot, too?"

Jake bit back a smile. "Very."

"So, what's the harm in dinner or a movie? Take it slowly for once, instead of rushing things like you usually do."

"But my head needs to be in a good place with the season about to start. This has the makings of being a complication, a distraction I really don't need."

"Seriously? A couple of dates could cause that much angst?"

"It could, if it doesn't work out. Anyway, the timing's all wrong…"

Tru cut him off. "The timing couldn't be better. You've got a few weeks before opening night. Plenty of time to go out together and see whether there's anything there worth pursuing. If it goes belly-up, no harm done."

Jake mulled it over for the rest of the drive home. As the car pulled into his parents' driveway, he asked, "How do I get her to go out with me if she won't answer my calls?"

"You're moving into your new place in a few days. She'll be there to oversee things. Ask her then. Make your famous charm work for you."

Tru was right.

Time for a new strategy. Time to go on the power play.

TOTAL BLOODY CHAOS.

There was no other way to describe Jake's moving-in day.

At least, Maggie thought, it had been organized chaos. But between the movers, his family and friends, various Ice Cats and an assortment of beauties bearing covered dishes, the house had been noisy and crowded since early morning.

She wasn't sure whether her role was to oversee and coordinate or play ringmaster. A crash from another room, followed by swearing, made her sigh. Pass the top hat and whip.

The rich aroma of spaghetti sauce made her stomach rumble. Jake's mom and Aunt Karina were cooking pasta. Maggie hadn't had time to eat since breakfast.

Thankfully, despite the chaos, everything had gone well. The movers had left over an hour ago, as had Jake's teammates and, more reluctantly, the women. Only family and the Jelineks remained.

Her job was finished. Other than tidying up a few loose ends, her professional relationship with Jake was over. Her heart gave a funny little jump in her chest.

Things had returned more or less to normal between them after his apology. Maggie grinned as she recalled the bouquet that had arrived on her doorstep. He hadn't gone for the clichéd red roses or heart-shaped box of chocolates. Jake must have remembered a conversation from when they were looking at houses where she'd mentioned that her favorite flowers were gerbera daisies. He'd organized a glorious arrangement in a vivid array of colors, with chocolate daisies interspersed among the real flowers.

Who could resist such a thoughtful apology?

Maggie certainly couldn't. That, combined with his tenacity, had convinced her it was time to see if this thing between them—this connection, this heat—had legs. What's more, she'd decided to take a leaf out of the old Maggie's book. Instead of waiting for Jake to ask her out, she planned to ask him. Today, if she could ever catch him alone.

Emily's laughter cut into her thoughts. She smiled. Her daughter had begged to be allowed to come along. Since Jake hadn't minded, Maggie had let her. Right now, Emily was helping him and the Jelinek brothers set up his electronic toys.

Perhaps she should go and see how they were doing.

As she walked into the entrance hall, she saw Jake rooting through an open cardboard box by the front door. This was her chance. She checked quickly to see if anyone else was around, but no one was.

You can do this. She wiped her damp palms on her chinos, then squared her shoulders and walked toward Jake.

He was so focused on whatever he was searching for he didn't look up, even when she stood behind him.

"Should be in here," he muttered. "Damn box is marked 'tools.'"

Maggie cleared her throat. "Uh…Jake?"

"Yeah." He turned his head. Stopped rummaging. Grinned. "Hey, Maggie. What's up?"

She swallowed hard. "I was just wondering…um…"

"What?" he asked huskily.

He stood. Suddenly, he seemed very close.

Very tall. Very male.

Her heart thudded against her ribs. Her gaze flew upward. Past the rock-hard abs and broad chest that molded his much-washed Ice Cats T-shirt. The fire smoldering in the depths of his ice-blue eyes captured her. Held her. She couldn't look away.

She moved back half a step. Her shoulders pressed against the front door. Against the coolness of the stained glass.

He edged closer, that same half step. Close enough that his body heat scorched her through her cotton blouse. Close enough for his masculine scent to tease her nostrils.

She swallowed again.

His hands settled on her hips lightly. Firmly.

She couldn't move away. She didn't want to.

The realization wasn't a surprise. More a recognition of the inevitable. An acceptance.

No. This wasn't something over which she had no control. It was something she wanted to pursue. Her decision. Her choice.

Maggie's fingers curled into the softness of his T-shirt, reveling in the contrast between the soft fabric and the solid muscles beneath. The thought of exploring his smooth, tanned skin caused a sharp tug in the depths of her belly.

His fingers tightened on the curve of her hips. Hot. Branding her, despite the layer of fabric between his hand and her skin.

She tilted her head. Lifted her chin.

He lowered his head until barely a breath separated their mouths.

Maggie moistened her suddenly parched lips.

Jake closed the gap. His tongue darted out and followed hers, licking the fullness of her lower lip.

A fiery arrow of desire shot straight to her core, creating a molten pool.

She wanted to taste him. Needed to see if he was as darkly delicious as she'd imagined. She swept her tongue across his firm lips.

Better than ice cream. Better than chocolate.

No wonder all those women were prepared to risk their manicures to make meals for him. Heck, for kisses like this she'd cook for him, and she didn't like cooking.

Jake nibbled her bottom lip. The tip of his tongue teased the corners of her mouth.

More. She had to have more.

Maggie dipped her tongue between his lips.

He captured it, deepening the kiss. His arms wrapped around her, pulling her tightly against him. The length of his body pressed against hers.

Her arms wound around his neck. Her aching breasts were crushed against his solid chest. His hardness brushed her mound, then settled in the cradle at the top of her legs.

Somewhere, a bell rang.

She frowned. She should do something about that. In a minute. Maybe.

His fingers caressed their way up her side to the curve of her breast. She yearned for them to go higher. Instead, he played with the buttons on her blouse, slipping his fingertips between the buttonholes and stroking the sensitive skin beneath.

The bell rang again. "Hello? Delivery for Jake Badoletti."

Those words doused the heat as effectively as the proverbial bucket of cold water.

Maggie pushed against Jake. He let her go, reluctantly.

Desire burned in the depths of his blue eyes. "Come and find me when you're done."

She nodded, then watched as he hefted up the box he'd been rummaging in and walked back to the den. Oh, my. The rear view was just as hot as the front. She fanned herself before opening the door.

A deliveryman in a green uniform thrust his handheld computer at her. Behind him in the open van was a large stack of boxes. Adam's things from Chicago. The last thing Jake wanted to face today.

She smiled sweetly. "Could you help me take them to the basement?"

The man grunted and followed her. It took a dozen trips, but they were finally stacked safely out of sight.

"I really appreciate it." She signed the man's screen and gave him a generous tip.

No sooner had he driven off than the cable guy turned up. With a sigh, she briefed him on the job, then took him upstairs to the master suite.

As she hurried back along the landing to the stairs, the doorbell rang again. Who could that be now?

Her foot had just hit the top step when Jake opened the front door to reveal his visitor.

Tall and slim. Long, straight, glossy blond hair. A skintight cropped T-shirt with the Ice Cats logo stretched across her impressive chest. Skinny-leg black jeans tucked into black suede boots with three-inch heels and gleaming silver buckles.

Instantly, Maggie felt like a frump. Her lip curled at her own modest cotton blouse, her practical khaki chinos and her demure white flats.

"Hey, Bad Boy." The husky voice floated through the air like a caress. "Longest shutout streak by a goaltender?"

Jake grinned and opened his arms. "If it isn't the queen of the puck bunnies. Looking good, babe."

With a throaty laugh, the leggy beauty planted a smacker on his lips.

Maggie wanted to crack Jake over the head with one of his hockey sticks. Only minutes ago, he'd been kissing her.

How could she compete with perfect looks, a perfect body and an intimate knowledge of hockey? She couldn't. What's more, she didn't want to. She'd played that game with Lee and look at the price she had paid—her own identity, Emily's safety. The cost was far too high. She wouldn't make that mistake again.

"Answer the damn question, Bad Boy, or pay the penalty."

Maggie didn't stick around to see what kind of penalty the too-bloody-perfect blonde would extract. She headed back upstairs in search of her daughter.

So much for thinking Jake was different. He may not be abusive, but he was as untrustworthy as Lee when it came to women.

Time to leave. This job was finished.

Emily came without any fuss, excited over the promise of a trip to her favorite pizza parlor. Somehow, they avoided bumping into Jake and the blonde on the way out.

Jake rang as they were being seated at the restaurant but she didn't answer. When she saw his name on the caller ID, she turned her phone off.

Maggie stewed about what had happened all through the pizza dinner and into the long dark hours of the night. By 3:00 a.m., she'd stopped feeling sorry for herself. After all, Jake had kissed *her*. Had wanted *her*.

By 4:00 a.m., she'd worked out how to move forward. She resolved to give the new Maggie a new look. Time to dress like the person she wanted to be.

Long past time.

She finally fell asleep planning her first shoe-shopping trip.

And dreamed of Jake. Delicious, erotic dreams, beyond anything she'd experienced. Dreams that ended just short of fulfillment.

Maggie woke at seven, aching with need and determined to know the truth, even if it wasn't favorable. With trembling fingers, she switched her phone back on.

A dozen voice mails from Jake.

"Where are you?" His deep voice washed over her like a caress. The sexy undertone throbbed with the memory of their kiss, stoking the flames of her already heated blood. "Why'd you leave without saying goodbye? We had unfinished...business."

With each successive message, his tone grew more concerned, until he asked, "Did something happen? Are you okay?"

By the time he left the final message, he sounded bewildered. "Whenever you get this, call me. Please."

She flicked her phone shut. After a few minutes, she replayed his messages. He didn't sound like a man who'd casually tossed her aside for a better offer. Had she misunderstood the incident with the blonde? Had she, once again, judged Jake by Lee's low standards?

There was only one way to find out for sure.

She opened her phone and dialed.

Jake took a while to answer. "Maggie?" His voice sounded husky with sleep.

She got straight to the point. "What's a puck bunny?"

WHAT THE HELL kind of a question was that?

Jake shook his head, trying to jar his tired brain awake. "I'm sorry. I'm still half asleep." He yawned, then sat up. "Are you okay? I was worried."

"What's a puck bunny?" she repeated, ignoring his question.

"Um…a hockey groupie."

"I see." Her tone was knowing, disappointed.

Her jerk of an ex had probably screwed around with soccer groupies. Damn it.

"You saw me with Jenny. Tall, skinny blonde in a Cats T-shirt."

"Yes."

That explained her abrupt departure. One minute her kiss had almost blown his socks off, the next she'd gone. No explanation, no excuse, just gone.

At first, he'd worried something had happened to her sister or Emily. Why else would she have cut out so suddenly?

But as the evening had worn on and she hadn't returned his calls, he'd begun to suspect an altogether different reason for her disappearing act. Now that he knew for sure, he had to figure out how to get things between them back on track.

He decided to cut to the chase. "I'd have introduced Jenny to you if you'd stuck around. She's pretty cool. Got an amazing memory for hockey stats."

"How interesting."

It hurt that she didn't trust him. Did she really think he'd go from kissing her to sleeping with Jenny? He'd never cheated, even at the height of his wildness. For however long he was with a woman, he was monogamous. Some just had shorter shifts than others.

If all Maggie knew about his past was the stuff she'd read, how would she know that? "Jenny and I are just good friends."

"You don't owe me an explanation."

"Maybe not, but I'm telling you anyway. There's nothing between me and Jenny."

"I appreciate the gesture, but it's not necessary. Our relationship is purely professional and now that your move is complete, it's at an end."

Even as her words made his chest tighten, her stiff little speech gave him hope. Maggie was jealous. If she cared enough to be angry, he still had a chance.

He really wanted that chance.

Continuing to insist on his innocence wouldn't cut it. He'd have to try another approach.

"I hope you don't give that kind of goodbye kiss to all your clients."

Her sharp intake of breath was audible. "That was an aberration."

At least she wasn't denying the attraction between them. "What if I'd like to make it more than an aberration?"

"Won't your 'friend' mind?"

"Why would she? I've known Jenny since first

grade. We faced off over the last ice cream at lunch." He grinned at the memory. "She won."

Maggie said nothing for a few moments.

"We never slept together," he added softly. "Kissing her is like kissing a sister."

"You really are just friends." Her words were a statement, not a question.

Yes! Jake wanted to pump his fist but restrained himself. "Nothing more, I promise."

"You don't mind her doing that... Being a groupie?"

"I don't understand why she does it." He shrugged, then realized Maggie couldn't see him. "But it's her choice, her life. It doesn't affect our friendship."

His heart pounded heavily as he waited for her to speak.

"I apologize for jumping to the wrong conclusion. In the past..."

"No need to explain." He cut her short, gently.

"Thank you." She cleared her throat. "Well, I'd better let you go. I'm sure you have a lot to do in your new house."

Jake didn't want the conversation to end without an agreement to see her again, but he sensed her skittishness. If he asked her on a date, would he scare her off? Tru's words about patience and taking it slow echoed in his head. Okay, not a date. Not yet. But what?

"That reminds me, I need your help on another project." His mind whirred as he searched for something, anything, that would fit the bill.

"What can I do for you?" she asked cautiously.

"Um...it's an important project that needs your

expertise." His gaze scanned his room, seeking inspiration. Boxes. Shelves. TV. Nothing helped.

"Doing what?" Now she sounded suspicious.

Suitcases. More boxes. Sports bag. Weights. Hockey gear. Wait…sports bag. Weights.

"I need a new gym," he blurted out. "And my house doesn't have one."

"What's wrong with the one you're using?"

What *was* wrong with it? He pictured the pastel walls and ladies in Lycra. "I want a proper gym. A place to work out, not one where they make me feel guilty for sweating."

Maggie laughed. "All right. I'll pull together a list of suitably sweat-friendly gyms and email them to you."

No way. She wasn't handing him off that easily. "If I switch to another gym, I'm sure a bunch of my teammates will, too. You should come with me to check them out so you can look into negotiating a team rate."

He held his breath, hoping she'd go along with his ridiculously weak plan.

"I'll see what Tracy says and get back to you."

The clipped accent was back, but Jake smiled. She hadn't said no.

The game was still on.

CHAPTER EIGHT

THE PUCK CLANGED off the boards behind the net.

Jake gave chase, beating the other skater. Sweat poured down his face. His leg muscles burned. A few more seconds and he could rest. He turned to pass the puck but a body pounded him into the glass. A player in white glided away with the biscuit as Jake ate ice.

Damn.

The coach blew his whistle. "Reds, you're up."

Jake headed to the bench and grabbed a water bottle. He squirted the cold water across his face, then took a long swig as he climbed over the boards.

"Looking good, bro." Tru nudged him with his padded shoulder. "You've got your speed back."

"I need to get my brain working. Should've seen Vlad." He glared at the Russian.

"You'll be fine once you get a few games under your belt." Tru toweled the sweat from his visor. "Remember, only six months ago you didn't know if you'd ever skate again."

Six months ago, he'd had taped ribs, an arm and a leg in casts and enough stitches to make Frankenstein's monster look like a wuss. Jake's healed ribs twinged. With the endless rounds of rehab before he'd been allowed to train and skate, it had been a lengthy, often painful, road back to health, then fitness. Every day he skated and practiced, he was one step closer to where he needed to be.

"I'll need to be better than fine for opening night."

Two short whistle blasts and everyone gathered around the coach.

"Not bad. Tru, Bad Boy, good work." Max pointed at the rookie, Jean-Baptiste Larocque. "Less flash, more scoring. Think about when to shoot and when to pass."

JB nodded, but his sulky expression said he didn't like criticism.

Jake shook his head. The kid wanted to be the hero on every play. He'd better learn quickly that winning came from teamwork or he'd piss everyone off.

Larocque was a good-looking kid. Pale coffee skin, brown eyes and a grin that would melt the panties off a puck bunny. The dark circles under his eyes were a bad sign.

"He looks tired," Jake muttered. "Someone should tell him to ease off the partying. The pace up here is a killer for new blood. If he burns the candle at both ends, he won't make it."

Tru agreed. "You should talk to him."

"He won't listen to me."

"You've got the right street cred to make him listen."

"I'll see how he goes for a couple of weeks. Maybe it's the excitement of the show and he'll slow down once it gets serious. If there's no change once we're into the preseason schedule, I'll step up."

Max ended practice with a reminder that the team's

new drug-testing program was underway. Jake, Tru and Ike gave their samples, then hit the showers.

"I'm grabbing something to eat." Tru dried off. "You coming?"

"I'm meeting Maggie." Jake tried to sound casual. "She's helping me find a new gym."

"So your grand plan's working?"

"I think so." He pulled on his jeans. "I'll tell you after today's visits."

Truthfully, he wasn't sure. He hadn't seen her for over a week. She'd kept her word and emailed information on suitable local gyms. But between practices, his other team commitments and her schedule, they hadn't been able to meet until this afternoon.

"You planning to take her on an actual date anytime soon?" His friend shrugged into a polo shirt, then combed his damp hair.

"If things work out." Jake zipped up his gym bag and waited impatiently for Ike and Tru to get their stuff. They all walked outside together.

And stopped short.

Who was the sexy babe leaning against his M-Class? Jake did a double take.

Maggie?

She'd cut her hair and left it loose. Glossy, dark curls tumbled across her shoulders, begging to be touched. Instead of those floaty dresses he liked, she wore a slim-fitting red jacket over a matching skirt that ended above her knees. No blouse. Spiked red heels.

As she straightened, her jacket shifted, giving a brief glimpse of lace and shadows beneath. His fingers itched to undo the single large button that held the jacket closed. His heart jolted, then began to pound furiously.

"Is that Maggie?" Tru's voice sounded strangled.

Ike wolf whistled under his breath.

She walked toward them, a confidence in her stride that he'd not seen before.

"Nice day at the office, boys?"

The teasing purr sent a lightning bolt of desire straight to his groin.

Confusion filled him. This wasn't his Maggie.

He managed to unstick his tongue from the roof of his mouth. "What are you wearing?"

Crap. That didn't come out right.

Hurt flashed in her dark brown eyes, quickly followed by anger. Her expression hardened. "A Marc Jacobs suit. The shoes are Chanel. Extravagant, but so comfortable." Her accent could carve ice. "The rest is none of your business."

Tru recovered first. "You look great, Maggie."

"Thank you."

"You looked great before." Jake glared at Ike, who'd just hit him in the back.

"The mumsy look isn't very professional." She glanced at the slim gold watch on her wrist. "We should go. Lots to do."

Tru and Ike made their cowardly escape.

He should apologize. He would apologize. As soon as he got over the change in her. He felt…let down.

That was crazy. He was upset because she looked as hot as she kissed?

No. Because she was dressed like all the other women he'd dated. What had happened to the old Maggie?

He rolled his eyes. It didn't matter what she wore. The person inside was still the same, whether dressed in flowery cotton or in fire-engine red and lace.

Besides, those shoes were sexy. They showed off her great legs and…

"If you're ready?" Maggie's stiff words interrupted a fantasy he had no business having.

Jake cleared his throat. "I'm sorry about what I said."

"You're entitled to your opinion, just as I'm entitled to ignore it."

He winced inwardly. Anything he said right now wouldn't help. He'd give her time to cool off, then try to make things right. First he had to get her to ride with him.

"It's pointless taking two cars. Why don't I drive us to the gyms, then bring you back here when we're done?"

He could see she wanted to refuse but didn't have an excuse.

"Fine." She marched to the passenger door while he dumped his gear in the back.

She'd buckled up and was staring pointedly out the window when he got in. As he turned the key in the ignition, he sighed mentally. This afternoon was going to feel as long as a penalty kill in the waning minutes of a scoreless game.

"WOULD IT HELP if I said I was a jackass?"

Jake's humble-pie tone might work on other women, but Maggie was immune.

Still, as they drove into the parking lot of the final gym on their list a couple of hours later, she was finding it hard to remain cross with him. Not because his puppy-dog eyes were working—such attempts to charm her had long since lost their effect—but because she'd begun to realize there might be another reason for his strange behavior.

One that put a whole different complexion on things.

When she'd left home for their meeting, she'd been thrilled with her new look—it had felt right. Felt like the real Maggie. Tracy and Emily had given her a double thumbs-up.

With one patronizing remark, Jake had made her feel stupid. A failure. Those few words, that horrified tone, had hit right at the heart of her still-fragile self-confidence.

For the first hour, the hurt had blinded her to anything about him. Slowly though, she'd noticed the burning heat in his ice-blue eyes every time he looked at her. He might sound disapproving, but she sensed he found her makeover very appealing indeed.

Maggie sneaked a peek beneath her lashes at him. The rigid set of his jaw, the jerky drumming of his fingers on the steering wheel told her he felt bad.

"That's unkind to jackasses," she said coolly.

Jake acknowledged her jab with a sharp tilt of his head. He parked near the entrance of the single-story building, then turned off the engine. "Since we agree that I'm lower than pond scum, will you accept my apology?"

"Well…" She let her voice trail off. As she leaned

over to collect her bag, she deliberately gave him a glimpse of the lacy camisole beneath her jacket.

Aqua flames flared in his gaze, sending a delicious quiver through her and confirming what she suspected.

She straightened. "Okay."

"Thank you." His shoulders relaxed. "Friends again?"

Friends? Startled by a tug of disappointment, she stammered, "Uh, yes. Sure."

"Great." He grinned. "What prompted this latest change? Not that I'm criticizing, but those floaty dresses were pretty. Made you stand out from other women."

"Oh. Thanks." She hadn't expected a discussion of her fashion sense. "Like I said, a suit makes me feel more professional."

"So you haven't gotten rid of the dresses?"

She shook her head, surprised he was that bothered about some cotton dresses.

"Good. Anyway, red suits you better than pigeon gray or boring beige, or biscuit, or whatever they call it."

Maggie's jaw dropped. "Excuse me?"

He held up his hands. "Just a friendly observation."

"I've been finding my feet, fashionwise." She frowned. "Now I think I've got it right. I feel comfortable." Her direct look challenged him to disagree.

He didn't. "Why did you have to 'find your feet'?"

Though she was nervous about sharing the details of her past, it was only fair. Besides, if they were to be more than "friends," he should know what emotional baggage she carried.

"My ex-husband had definite ideas about what his wife should wear," she began carefully. "At first, I appreciated the guidance. What did I know about dressing to impress? Even if I didn't like what he chose, I loved wearing designer labels and having the latest catwalk fashion. Gradually, I began to have ideas of my own, to develop my own style. He—" she swallowed "—disapproved of my choices."

"Is this a result of his 'disapproval'?" He traced a finger along the scar on her cheek. Her skin tingled, as if his touch was healing the still-red mark.

She nodded.

Jake's jaw turned to granite. "Go on."

"It was easier to give in to his demands than fight them. Especially when Emily came along." She chewed her bottom lip. "Once our divorce was final, I gave every stitch of clothing to the local charity shops. I started from scratch and tried different things until—" she indicated her outfit "—I settled on this."

"Then I shoved my size twelves in my mouth." Disgust colored his tone.

"You didn't help," she agreed. "No matter. Not everyone will approve of what I wear, so I'm learning to focus on my own approval instead."

"Good for you."

Maggie smiled. "Anyway, enough of that. Time to check this place out."

"Sure." Jake undid his seat belt. "If this one isn't suitable, I may consider putting a home gym in the basement."

Maggie batted away a twinge of nervousness. She'd

done her best. He was dissatisfied with the places, not with her.

Jake had been as picky about choosing a new gym as he'd been with the house. He'd found fault with each of the previous places within minutes of entering. Still, she'd saved the best for last. She hoped it lived up to the brochure.

"I can look into that for you, but let's wait until we've seen this gym. It might be exactly what you're looking for," she said cheerily. "From the brochure, it looks perfect."

"Those other places looked great on paper, too. That first gym was disgusting." He got out of the car.

Maggie joined him in front of the building. "The changing rooms were filthy."

"The next couple were too New Age. How can meditating improve my stamina? Aromatherapy sure as hell won't help my puck handling."

"I've heard of several athletes using natural approaches to boost performance."

His lip curled. "No way sniffing lavender could improve my shot."

"I think it was rosemary." She grinned. "Either is better than steroids."

"I guess. I wouldn't take those, either."

No. Maggie couldn't imagine Jake taking any shortcuts to success. "What was wrong with that last place? It was clean, had state-of-the-art equipment and highly qualified trainers."

The muscle in his jaw twitched. "I know the owner. He used to play hockey."

She'd sensed Jake didn't like him. "Doesn't that put the gym at the top of your list?"

"Not a chance." His hard tone brooked no argument.

"Why not? I thought you were all mates off the ice."

"Mostly. Jerks like him, I want nothing to do with."

His vehemence baffled her. "He seemed pleasant enough."

"The guy was dirty. Bush league. He injured some good people."

She quirked an eyebrow. "Isn't that hockey? You hit. You fight. Someone gets hurt."

Jake jammed his hands on his hips. "There's a right and wrong way to do things. That joker's was the wrong way."

"There's a right way to hit a player?"

"Knocking the opposition out of the way is like tackling. Only we can't tackle because our blades are razor sharp."

It made a strange kind of sense.

"That doesn't explain players beating the living daylights out of each other while the crowd bays for blood." Maggie grimaced as she recalled some of the clips she'd seen. "I suppose there's a good reason for fights, too."

"Most of the time they're to inject energy or change momentum. If the team needs a spark, the enforcer will challenge the other team's goon to a fight."

"And the rest of the time?"

"You make a dirty play, you pay the piper. It's part of The Code."

"The Code? Is that like honor among thieves?"

"It's an unwritten set of rules. Helps us keep the game clean and fair."

"You sound like Wyatt Earp." She grinned. "Do the good guys wear white hats?"

"Very funny." Jake's voice was tight.

"I'm sorry." Her grin faded. She'd offended him.

"Forget it. Doesn't matter. Shall we go inside?"

Her pulse jolted nervously at his dismissive tone. "Really, I didn't mean anything by it."

As she studied him more closely, she realized he was sulking. Instantly, her worry eased.

"How long are you going to pout?" She exaggerated a glance at her watch.

"Hockey players don't pout." The tightness vanished.

"Especially not enforcers."

"I'm not an enforcer."

"I've seen the videos of your fights."

"You looked me up on YouTube?" The cocky grin was back.

"Client research," she countered primly.

"Uh-huh." His look said he'd let that slide for now. "Those clips are old. I don't fight anymore, but I still throw clean, hard checks." Jake touched her arm, sending a fizz through her blood. "Why don't you come to a game with me? I can explain everything while we watch."

He wanted to take her out? She stumbled over her

words as she tried not to sound too eager. "Won't you be playing?"

"Not much during preseason. The coach wants to check out the kids, not us old-timers."

"I'm not supposed to date clients." It was a token resistance.

Amusement sparkled in his eyes. "After today, I won't be a client."

"Our contract is with the Ice Cats—technically, you'll still be a client."

"In that case, technically, it won't be a date."

Her pulse skittered. "What will it be?"

"Consider it…research." Jake leaned closer. His clean, masculine scent teased her nose. "Who better to teach you about hockey than a player?"

Her stomach churned with nerves, even as her foolish heart danced with anticipation.

"I'll reserve a suite at the arena." Jake's voice broke into her thoughts. "You can bring Tracy and Emily, and I'll get my folks there, too."

Why not? Her lips tingled with the memory of their kiss; desire stirred within, reminding her of what she could gain. "Thank you. That would be nice."

His grin was jubilant. "Great."

"Then shall we check out this gym?"

As she got out of the car, she hid a smile. Looked like Jake Badoletti was a temptation she couldn't resist, after all.

JAKE WANTED TO strut like a proud rooster.

How could he make the game special? His mind

buzzed as he and Maggie checked out the admittedly top-notch facilities.

"Jake?"

He turned to see a smiling, well-built man come toward him, wiping his face with a towel. A pair of worn boxing gloves hung around his neck and a sheen of sweat covered his dark skin.

"Prince?" The two men slapped each other on the back. "What are you doing here?"

"I run the fitness boxing program."

"No kidding." He introduced his friend to Maggie. "This guy showed me how boxing can help maintain the high level of fitness needed for a long season. He also taught me how to fight." He grinned. "I keep telling him, it's a lot harder throwing punches on skates."

Prince laughed. "A broken nose is a broken nose, Bad Boy. Even if you ice dance first."

"Nice to meet you." Maggie smiled politely.

"Can I interest you in fitness boxing, too?"

"Me?" Her expression was half horrified, half terrified.

"Lots of my clients are women. It's a great way to get in shape."

"But I don't want to hit people."

"You don't have to." Prince told Jake to continue looking around while he took Maggie to meet one of his clients—a petite woman pounding the hell out of a heavy bag.

Jake wandered through the large, airy space filled with equipment. As he pretended to check out the machines, he couldn't take his eyes off Maggie. The way her red suit clung to her curves. The glimpse of scarlet nail polish visible through her peep toes. The way she bit her full lower lip as she listed intently to what Prince said.

Damn it. He wanted her attention focused on him. He strode across to interrupt the cozy little gathering.

"Not today, but thanks for the offer."

What offer?

"Call me and we'll arrange a time for you to try it out." Prince gave her his card. "I'll provide the gloves."

"Great." Maggie pocketed the card.

Irritation spiked. She'd barely given him the time of day because of his fighting, but Mr. I-Used-to-Beat-People-Up-for-a-Living was her new pal? "We should go."

Keeping the goodbyes to a minimum, Jake rushed Maggie out of the gym.

"I'm glad that worked out," she said as they walked back to his M-Class. "I'm looking forward to giving his program a try."

Jake bit back a growl as he opened her door. "I thought you didn't like fighting."

"I don't. But fitness boxing doesn't involve hitting anyone."

A snapshot of her in shorts and a tight top, her face moist with the exertion, her skin glowing, flashed through his head. Heat sparked in his groin.

He forced the image away and tried to concentrate on the drive back to the practice facility. Within minutes, though, he was brooding over the changes again.

First the clothes, now the boxing. What next? Why did she need to change?

On the other hand, the new Maggie was very easy on the eyes. His body sure approved of the new look. Did a few outward changes really matter? Instead of worrying about them, he should be figuring out how to win her over at the preseason game.

Now that was something he knew how to do. Jake glanced across at Maggie, who smiled at him. He grinned. He may be reformed, but he had to admit— even a good man needed a touch of bad boy to win.

CHAPTER NINE

"Hurry up, Mummy. We'll be late." Emily hopped impatiently from foot to foot.

"Won't be a minute." Maggie smiled as she pulled on her ski jacket. Emily was as eager to see Jake's parents again as she was to watch her first hockey game.

Maggie checked her lipstick in the rearview mirror, then closed the car door. She'd give that blonde a run for her money. It wasn't a competition, but knowing she could hold her own gave Maggie a warm feeling inside.

Along with a fizz of anticipation at seeing Jake again.

Tracy locked the car, then they joined the throng swarming toward the steel-and-glass arena that was home to the Ice Cats. Maggie was thrilled to see so many fans wearing Badoletti jerseys.

Above the main entrance, a huge screen showed video clips of the players in action. They watched for several minutes.

"There's Mr. Ike." Emily cheered as the goaltender made an acrobatic save.

Maggie had to admit the game looked fast moving and energetic. Captivated by the action, she was caught unawares when Jake's face appeared on the screen.

"Bad Boy has come home and he's taking no prisoners," the voice-over intoned as Jake's picture faded to a video montage.

Around them, fans whooped as he sent players crashing into the boards. To her dismay, Emily joined in as he floored a player in an orange jersey with a single punch.

Maggie swallowed to clear the tightness in her throat. Clearly, neither the Ice Cats nor the fans expected Jake's fighting to be a thing of the past.

Could she trust that the raw aggression wouldn't spill over into normal life? He'd given her no reason to doubt him, but this video had her questioning whether she was being naive.

Jake's face reappeared, his expression fierce and warriorlike. Every scar showed clearly. His ice-blue eyes were as piercing as lasers. Her pulse skipped as he gave his sexy half smile.

"Are you ready for Ice Cats hockey?" he growled. "Are you ready for me?"

The crowd roared in response.

They might be, but Maggie wasn't sure she was.

Tracy laid a hand on her arm. "It's all hype."

She nodded, but uncertainty settled in her stomach like a stone.

Inside the arena, they spotted Jake's parents, wearing Badoletti jerseys. After a quick tour of the arena, they led the way to the suite he'd reserved.

A large crowd was gathered outside. Jake stood in the middle, dashingly handsome in his dark suit, signing autographs. He chatted amiably with everyone and posed for numerous photographs with fans.

Maggie was surprised and pleased. Lee had always complained about the fans' demands, behaving genially only when the media was there.

Jake grinned as he noticed them standing nearby. His gaze met hers—the unspoken promise in the blue depths made her toes curl.

She licked her lips nervously.

He made his excuses to the crowd and joined them. "Great. You're here."

Jake ushered them into the suite, his hand resting against the small of her back. The warmth penetrated her sweater, sensitizing every inch of her body.

Once again, she was surprised. The room was filled with family and friends, rather than celebrities and media. Maggie's tension eased further as she saw that Jake made sure everyone had plenty to eat and drink, instead of expecting people to fuss over him.

He made it clear that she, too, was supposed to enjoy herself. It had been a long time since she'd been allowed to watch a game she'd attended.

One of the reasons she and Lee had got on well in the early days was that she'd genuinely liked watching sport. Sadly, by the end, all she'd been allowed to do was entertain sponsors in the hospitality suite, occasionally making it to the seats when she was needed for a photo op.

Pushing aside memories that had no place in her head this evening, Maggie wandered to the front of the suite. She looked out over the arena, focusing on the two machines making their way up and down the ice, refreshing the scratched surface.

"They're called Zambonis, Mummy."

Turning, she saw Emily had acquired a child-size Ice Cats jersey.

"There's one for you." Jake held out a bag, his expression as eager as a schoolboy's. "It's got my name and number on it. Hope that's okay."

Touched, she smiled. "Thank you. That's very kind."

His eyes gleamed with pride as she slipped the large red top over her head. "Perfect."

"Say cheese." Tracy snapped photos of them. "Now, one of you and Bad Boy."

Jake slipped his arm around her waist and pulled her back against his hard body. Even through the layers of clothing, she felt his body heat. His familiar masculine scent surrounded her as his breath teased her temple.

To calm her body's reaction, Maggie reminded herself of the video clips she'd seen outside. But the only replay in her head was of his wide grin when he'd spotted her. Instead of dampening the fire burning within her, it fanned the flames.

"Can I get you anything?" Jake asked.

"A beer would be nice." She hoped that the slight throatiness of her words didn't give away her thoughts.

"Why don't you grab a seat and I'll get them."

She sank into one of the leather seats in the back row as he walked away.

Tracy slipped into the seat beside her. "This suite is amazing."

Maggie grinned. "I should say that you can't beat watching a game from the stands, but I can't deny there's a different kind of pleasure in watching from a posh box when the seats are this close to the action."

"I'm glad you're looking more relaxed. I was worried earlier. I know this is tough for you." Tracy touched her arm. "Are you sure you're okay?"

"I'm fine, thanks." As she probed the automatic reaction, Maggie realized she wasn't just saying it. She really was. "I'm actually looking forward to the hockey game."

"Good. You deserve to have fun. Speaking of which—" Tracy jumped to her feet "—your date is back."

The arena lights dimmed and dramatic music began to play as Jake took the seat Tracy had vacated and handed Maggie a beer. Spotlights flashed and cheers began. In the half-light, he looked every inch the warrior from the video despite his casual attire. This time, it wasn't fear or dread racing through her veins.

It was anticipation, pure and simple.

"The game's about to start." The husky note in his voice made her pulse jump.

He reached for her hand. Their fingers twined together. Her pounding heart kept time with the bass beat of the music.

As the announcer came over the loudspeaker, telling the crowd to stand and show their appreciation for the Ice Cats, Maggie leaned toward Jake and said, "I look forward to seeing what you want to teach me, Bad Boy."

JAKE ALMOST SWALLOWED his tongue.

As the arena lights came up, he studied her face.

Though her expression seemed innocent, the twinkle in her eyes made him wonder if she'd chosen her words deliberately.

With any other woman, Jake would have assumed the double entendre was an invitation and acted before the end of the first period. With Maggie, he couldn't be sure. He didn't want to blow the evening by making a mistake before the game had even begun.

He forced his gaze forward.

Excitement raced through his veins as the Cats took to the ice. Though he still didn't know how his body would cope with playing in a game, instead of scrimmaging, he was keen to get out onto the ice and play for real.

They stood for the national anthem. Jake used the time to study Maggie surreptitiously. Tight-fitting jeans and black over-the-knee boots showcased her long legs while, beneath her jersey, he knew the red sweater hugged her curves. Her shiny, dark hair spilled enticingly over her shoulders.

A primal satisfaction filled him that she wore his name and number. He wanted no doubt in this testosterone-filled building whose woman she was.

So far, so good. The friendly atmosphere had relaxed her. He looked forward to explaining the game and building her appreciation for hockey. As well as building her appreciation for him.

As the players got ready for the opening face-off, Maggie leaned toward him. "Why are there only six from each team on the ice?"

Her scent, fresh with an enticing hint of spice, almost

made him forget the basics of a sport he'd played since he was a kid. He gulped, then explained. She nodded, then turned her attention to the game. A few stray curls brushed his cheek, as soft as a caress. Jake shifted to ease the tightness in his trousers.

The movement brought his knee against hers. He swore silently. Only a minute played and he was hard and aching. How the hell was he going to last one period, let alone three?

When she made no effort to break the contact, he forced himself to relax. As if he could have moved his knee anyway.

"What's going on here?" She leaned close again.

For a moment, Jake wasn't sure how to respond. He felt as awkward as a teenager on his first date. Then he realized she was referring to the game. A quick glance showed Larocque headed to the box as the ref announced the penalty.

"Hooking." He outlined the kid's mistake and what would happen next.

"The team goes down a man for two minutes?" she exclaimed. "That's a massive advantage to Carolina."

"You break the rules in any sport, you have to pay the price. The kid'll learn his lesson."

Sure enough, the Hurricanes scored quickly. While they celebrated, JB skated back to the Cats' bench. He smacked his stick against the boards.

Throughout the period, Maggie's questions came thick and fast. She was a quick study. As her understanding grew, so did her involvement in the game.

Before long, she was cheering the Cats, jeering at the 'Canes and cursing the refs like an old pro.

"What game are you watching?" she yelled after a missed call.

Jake laughed.

Her eyes blazed. "How can you be so blasé? Vlad's cheek's cut because that guy was careless with his stick."

"I'd be mad as hell if the refs had missed a high-sticking call in a game that mattered, for sure. But this is the preseason. A little blood's nothing to worry about," he reassured her.

She turned back to the play with a disgusted har-rumph.

Maggie's reaction sent up a warning flare. If she was pissed about a small cut, how would she react to something worse? The chances of a fight in a preseason game were slim, but he watched time count down with a nervous knot in his gut.

As the last minute of play was announced, the action heated up. The Cats buzzed around Carolina's net. The pace became intense.

Maggie became intense, too, her concentration focused. She edged closer to him, her arm pressed against his.

Jake's pulse began to pound.

Sticks clashed. Blades scraped. Players shouted.

Her fingers curved into his arm, her touch searing him.

The puck slammed into the boards.

His heart slammed against his ribs.

Ten seconds and nine…

Her grip tightened.

His groin tightened.

Two seconds and one…

The blaring horn jolted Jake's mind out of its cloudy haze.

"What a shame they didn't score. Is that halftime?" Maggie's cheeks were flushed, her eyes bright.

"It's the first intermission. We play three periods."

"Of course."

People around them got food and replenished drinks.

"What do you think so far?" he asked, hoping the bulge in his pants wasn't obvious.

"It's fast paced and exciting. Lots of action, but still quite easy to follow."

All right! "Sounds like you're hooked," he said as they rose to get refreshments.

"It's entertaining, but I don't know if I'm a full-fledged fan."

Given how she rushed them back to their seats as the second period was announced, he figured she was kidding herself.

Gradually, Jake began to relax and focus on the game. The only thing missing was an Ice Cats goal. He'd bet Maggie would celebrate enthusiastically.

Sure enough, when Larocque banged in a scorcher from the blue line near the end of the second period, she leaped to her feet, cheering.

Their gazes locked. She moved half a step closer, as if to hug him.

His body tensed, anticipating the feel of her against him. Wanting it.

Instead, she raised her palm for a high-five.

He'd have been disappointed but for the heat smoldering in her eyes.

Jake willed the Cats to score again.

Unfortunately, the period ended with the guys down by one.

Maggie spent most of the second intermission bemoaning missed chances. She was incensed by another blown call on a cheap shot late in the period.

"That bloke smashed Juergen into the boards from behind. That can't be legal."

"It isn't." His stomach roiled. He had to tell her about the repercussion that was coming.

"I was amazed Juergen got straight up. You must be black-and-blue after every game."

"Maggie. There's something you should know."

She turned to him, curious.

Just spit it out. "There'll be a fight next period."

Her expression cooled. "Is this part of that Code?"

He nodded. "The guy who hit Juergen has to know we won't stand for dirty plays."

"If the referee had been watching properly, there wouldn't need to be a fight."

Jake sighed. "Yeah, there would. To tell the opposition we'll defend our players."

"That's vigilante justice." She crossed her arms.

Anger rose as she dismissed his explanation. His sport. "It keeps the game clean and prevents injuries."

"They get injured by fighting instead. That's sensible." Her lip curled.

"Better than breaking some guy's neck."

The announcement for the third period drowned out her muttered reply.

When they took their seats, Maggie held herself stiffly. No chance of accidental contact.

She was probably the only person in the arena not to stand and cheer the fight. As the Cats' player downed his opponent with a well-placed punch, she looked disgusted.

Damn it.

From there, the game and his evening went downhill. Two more Ice Cats penalties led to two more Carolina goals. As time wound down, it was clear they couldn't recoup the loss.

Maggie seemed to lose interest and kept looking at her watch.

Any ground he'd gained tonight had vanished. He'd gambled and lost.

THE HORN SOUNDED for the end of the game.

As the Ice Cats headed off the ice, Maggie reflected on the third period. Stupid macho men with their stupid macho codes.

Around her, people gathered their things. The Badolettis put on their coats. Emily begged Tracy for a trip to the souvenir booth.

Jake sat silently beside her, lost in his own thoughts. She knew her reaction to the fight had disappointed him.

Tough. She was entitled to her opinion and was

damned if she'd be scared of voicing it because she was worried about upsetting him. He'd have to deal with it if he wanted to spend time with her. And if he didn't...? She didn't let the unsettling thought form.

Not wanting the evening to end on a bad note, she said, "I enjoyed the game, Jake. Thanks for inviting me."

Surprise mingled with doubt in his blue eyes.

She leaned closer. "I'm glad I came."

"You don't have to say that for my sake."

She smiled at his stiff tone. For a tough guy, he had a tendency to pout.

"I'm not. I didn't like the fight, but the rest was fun. Emily loved it."

"Yeah? Good." Jake's grin sent flashes of heat skipping through her body. How could a simple curve of those lips be so wicked?

"Mummy, look what Auntie Tracy bought for me." Emily rushed toward them waving a stuffed black-and-white cat in a red Ice Cats jersey. "This is Catty and he has a top like mine." She frowned. "Catty doesn't have Mr. Jake's name on his."

"I could write my name on the back with my Sharpie," Jake offered.

"Yes, please." Her daughter handed over the cat.

Maggie knew Jake hadn't thought about the logistics of his offer when he looked up with panic in his eyes.

"Problem?" She bit back a grin.

"Badoletti is a long name."

"And that is a small jersey."

It warmed her heart to see Jake, who was unfazed

by players slamming his body into Plexiglas, scared of disappointing her little girl.

"You could write *Bad* above the number and *Boy* below."

Emily cheered as Jake did what Maggie suggested, then yawned.

"Time to go," Maggie said reluctantly.

"Why don't I take Emily home?" Tracy offered. "You hang out here a bit longer."

"I can give you a ride home," Jake added.

Loath to end the evening, Maggie's pulse leaped at the thought of spending more time with Jake. "Don't you have to join the team?"

"Come with me. The boys go to a local Tex-Mex place, which is pretty good."

One arched look from her sister was enough. "Sounds great."

After a flurry of goodbyes, silence fell in the empty suite. The muffled sounds of the cleanup crew came from the hallway outside, along with a clattering from the ice where a basketball court was being laid for the following day.

It felt as if they were cocooned in this room.

Jake held her jacket so she could put it on. He didn't remove his hands right away. The warm weight on her shoulders was comforting and a little thrilling.

"We should go." That husky note was back in his voice.

His breath caressed the back of her neck, sending a shiver of pleasure through her.

"Okay." She nodded, but didn't move.

Slowly, Jake turned her to face him.

Her heart started thumping heavily. How could ice-blue burn with such a heated blaze?

The lights in the suite dimmed, startling her.

"Energy-saving timers," Jake murmured, never shifting his gaze from hers.

"Uh-huh." Maggie inched a little closer, tilting her chin. "Good idea."

"Definitely." His mouth covered hers.

Lightning flashed through her as his tongue parted her lips and swept inside.

She met him stroke for stroke, lick for lick. Nibble for nibble.

Jake tasted as wicked and dangerous as he looked. His dark, delicious flavor was addictive. Her pulse pounded. Desire pooled deep within her core.

His hands slipped from her shoulders to her hips, pulling her flush against him from thigh to chest. Heat seared her sensitized skin through the layers of clothing. His hardness pressed against her.

She wanted more.

Her fingertips traced his jaw, slid into his hair then down his neck. As their tongues danced, her knees began to tingle.

His hands stroked the small of her back, the curve of her bottom. His fingers gripped her hips, drawing her tight against his erection. She couldn't help but rub herself against him.

Holding on to his broad shoulders, Maggie allowed herself to be swept away in a maelstrom of sensations.

Cold air at the small of her back, where her sweater

had parted from her jeans, brought her out of the haze of desire. She took a moment to savor the fiery caress of Jake's fingers against her bare skin, then slowly broke the kiss.

Jake didn't lift his head right away. He pressed light kisses along her lips, lingering a little less with each one, until the last was the barest of touches.

A tinny tune echoed through the silent suite.

"Damn it." Keeping one arm around her, Jake reached behind him with his spare hand for his cell phone. "What?"

"Am I interrupting?" she heard Tru tease.

Jake growled, "Yes. What's up?"

"You guys coming or what?"

Maggie voted for "or what." But her blood was already beginning to cool, her pulse to settle. She drew away from Jake and instantly regretted it.

"We'll see you in a few, bro." He hung up, the flames in his eyes banked. "Is that okay?"

"Sure. I'm starving." She flushed.

"Me, too," he said softly.

For a moment, they stood there, gazes locked. If he'd made even the slightest move toward her, she knew she'd have been lost. And they'd have been very late joining the team.

Instead, he opened the door of the suite. As she walked past, he murmured, "Later."

She couldn't wait.

CHAPTER TEN

"ARE YOU SURE I don't know you?"

Juergen's question made Maggie uncomfortable. She'd like to hold on to the anonymity for a little longer. He'd work out where he'd seen her sooner or later; most Europeans followed football and recognized the well-known players, as well as the WAGs. Even if Juergen was too polite to ask questions, she could do without the pity she'd see in his eyes.

"I must have a familiar face." She shrugged, hoping he'd drop the subject.

"Those eyes, the cheekbones." Vlad grinned. "Her face isn't common, is it, Bad Boy?"

"Definitely unique." Jake leaned closer. "Uniquely beautiful."

Unfamiliar with compliments, she wasn't sure what to say. Thankfully, the food arrived, distracting the hungry players.

Talk turned to hockey: scores from the other games, rumors and gossip. No one seemed upset by the evening's loss.

"Preseason games don't count," Jake explained. "They're a chance to see how the team's shaping up, how the young players might fit within the setup."

"Like a 'friendly'?"

Ike grabbed a burrito. "Right. The regular season starts in October."

"Are you coming to opening night?" Tru asked.

That was still a few weeks away. Much as she'd like to see Jake in action, who knew how things would work out between them? Would he even ask her? "I'm not sure."

"Maggie's not convinced yet that hockey is the greatest sport in the world." Jake smiled indulgently. "I'm still working on her."

"Come to more games and you'll be sure," Vlad stated confidently.

"We'll see." She wouldn't let herself be drawn further.

As the bantering conversation continued around her, Maggie settled back, enjoying the comfortable weight of Jake's arm across her shoulders.

His thigh brushed against hers. Her pulse skipped, then raced.

Comfort became something else. Something hotter, building on the need that had simmered within since that kiss. Desire danced through her, making her core ache and throb with moist heat.

Jake's teasing smile died.

Her tongue slipped out to moisten her parched lips. She could still taste him, just a hint. She wanted to taste him again.

He leaned closer. His fingers caressed her shoulder, stoking the fire within.

She edged toward him, her lips parting in anticipation.

"Hello, gentlemen." A throaty voice curled around them, like the tendrils of smoke from a vamp's cigarette in a film noir.

Maggie recognized the blonde—Jenny, queen of the puck bunnies. The players welcomed her with enthusiasm as she walked around the table greeting them.

"Ice Man. Chance. Blade." Each name was accompanied by a touch, a brush against a shoulder, a tap on the arm. "Mad Dog."

Vlad grinned as she reached him. "Remember me, Jenny?"

"Detroit. The natural hat trick." Her eyes twinkled. "You scored the overtime winner with fourteen seconds left."

"A memorable night." From the Russian's tone, he didn't mean the goal.

Jenny laughed. She trailed a French-tipped finger along his shoulder, then moved on. "Juergen Ingemar. I haven't had the pleasure."

"We must put that right." He wasn't talking about hockey, either.

The woman was amazingly self-confident. She spoke easily to the players, alternately teasing and flirting. How would she treat Jake with Maggie there?

Maggie's stomach gave a little twist. She told herself not to be silly. It's not like there was anything between her and Jake. Yet.

Jenny dropped a kiss on Ike's head. "You dropped too early on that wrister."

"I know." He sighed. "I thought he was going five-hole."

"Portnoy can't get his shot off quickly enough to get it through your legs. He always roofs it."

Ike tilted his head. "Really?"

"Watch game tape." There was her supreme confidence again.

"I will. Thanks."

"My pleasure."

"Truman." Clipped, cold. Dismissive.

Maggie was surprised when Jenny moved past Tru with no smile, touch or banter.

"Jenny." The easygoing man shifted in his seat, his attention focused with rigid determination on the burrito platter.

"I hear you're starting next game, Bad Boy." The blonde grinned at Jake.

Maggie was relieved to see he greeted Jenny like the old friend he'd said she was.

"Yeah. I need ice time before the season starts." He then introduced Maggie to Jenny.

She braced herself, but instead of antagonism in the blonde's eyes, there was only mild curiosity. And recognition.

Maggie stiffened.

"Nice to meet you." The blonde smiled. "Hope Bad Boy's treating you right."

"So far, so good."

"If he misbehaves, I've got blackmail info that'll get him back in line."

"You're on." Maggie grinned.

"You're not supposed to gang up on me," Jake grumbled.

"We girls always stick together." Jenny slid a chair in beside Maggie.

As the conversation around them returned to hockey, the two women chatted. It didn't take long for Maggie to discover that she liked the blonde. Jenny seemed different from the hard-edged groupies who'd hung around Lee. She sensed a deeper story lay behind the woman's actions.

"So you were married to that jerk of a soccer player," Jenny said quietly.

"You know who I am," she said flatly.

"I didn't recognize you at first. The hair and everything." She waved a hand at Maggie's outfit. "I'm a sucker for gossip magazines, and the English ones are more lurid than ours."

Maggie softened at the blonde's self-deprecating smile. "As long as they're not writing about me, I can't resist them, either."

Jenny touched her arm. "It took a lot of courage to leave that bastard. Believe me, I know all about abusive bullies. I really wanted to give him a taste of his own medicine when I saw those pictures of you leaving hospital—the bruises, the stitches and your arm in a cast."

"Thank you." Maggie's eyes stung at the unexpected support.

"I cheered the day your divorce was final. I loved that photo of you on the steps outside the court." Jenny grinned. "Great shoes." Her grin faded. "I pity your ex's new girlfriend, now he's got that hamstring problem."

An involuntary shudder rippled through Maggie as memories of other times Lee had been injured flashed through her head. The drinking, the shouting. The hitting. She was glad she and Emily were out of reach. "I hope she realizes her mistake more quickly than I did. I wouldn't wish what I suffered on my worst enemy."

Jenny's smile had a cynical twist. "Doesn't look like it. In her last interview, she said she was keen to settle down with him and start a family."

Though Maggie was pleased Lee had a woman to occupy his attention, the information made her nervous. When he'd been playing the field, he couldn't have cared less about seeing Emily. What if his girlfriend changed his mind? Maggie swallowed a knot of dread. She had to keep Lee away from Emily.

"Hey, Jenny, what did you think of my game tonight?" Jean-Baptiste challenged, frustration in his dark eyes.

The table went quiet.

The only outward sign of Jenny's tension was a fractional narrowing of her eyes. "Not bad, but your shot is unpredictable. You should check your blade. A touch too much curve."

Larocque clenched his jaw. "Yeah, sure."

"If Jenny says to check your blade, then check your damn blade," Tru growled.

JB said nothing for a moment, then mumbled, "Okay."

Maggie's stomach twisted as he glared belligerently

at Jenny and tossed back a whiskey. His actions were scarily familiar. She knew how dangerous a temperamental athlete became when he'd been embarrassed.

Jenny ignored him. She turned to Maggie and began discussing the latest celebrity gossip. Gradually, the tension eased.

As the meal drew to a close, several players left for a local club.

"We should have lunch sometime." Jenny stood.

"I'd like that." Maggie scrawled her numbers on a napkin. "Give me a call."

Jenny nodded and smiled, then made her way toward Juergen.

Larocque leaped to his feet. "You should be with me tonight," he snarled.

Jenny's back snapped straight. "Excuse me?"

"I had a goal and an assist—I deserve to have you." The arrogant rookie swaggered toward her.

"I decide who deserves to have me." Frost coated Jenny's words. "It sure as hell won't be a half-assed kid who gave up three turnovers, made five poor decisions in key scoring situations and took a dumb penalty which led to a goal." She turned on her heel and left.

Juergen followed, glowering at Larocque. Jean-Baptiste stormed out, swearing.

"That boy's a real wild card." Ike shook his head.

"He pulls something like that again and I'll take him out," Tru said through gritted teeth.

The weird ending put a damper on the evening.

Jake apologized as he drove her back to Tracy's house. "The kid's a jerk."

"I'm sure he'll settle down. He's just trying to es-
tablish himself." She didn't know why she was defending Larocque, especially when he reminded her
uncomfortably of Lee. But she'd sensed vulnerability
beneath the bravado.

"The wrong damn way. You never do anything to
hurt the team."

She touched his arm. "You could keep an eye on
him."

"I'm the last person who should be babysitting a
troubled kid," he snapped, then fixed his attention on
the road. From his set jaw, it was clear the subject was
closed.

Startled by his abrupt attitude change, Maggie said
nothing for a few minutes. Where had that come from?

Finally, she broke the tense silence. "I liked Jenny."

"She's great. Got an amazing head for hockey."
Warm affection softened his voice. "She played for a
few years—was better than all of us—but gave it up
to look after her sister."

Maggie recalled Jenny's reference to escaping abuse.
Hopefully, someday, her new friend would trust her
enough to share her story.

Jake shared stories of growing up with Jenny until
he pulled into Tracy's driveway.

When he opened her door, she stepped out of the
car and into the circle of his arms. Her heart skipped
a beat then began to dance.

His voice was a husky murmur. "Have I convinced
you to spend more time with me?"

"Do you mean a real date?" Her gaze focused on lips so tantalizingly close to hers.

"A date. Another game. Whatever." His head dipped.

"Um…I suppose so." Her teasing words sounded breathy.

"Perhaps I can persuade you to make that a definite yes." Jake brushed his lips against hers. Once, twice, three times. Sweet, featherlike touches.

Each sent a fiery trail burning through her body, making her yearn and ache.

"Still not sure," she managed to whisper.

This kiss wasn't sweet or gentle. It was spicy and seductive. Hot and hard.

Bad Boy could be very persuasive indeed.

RUNNING PAST A girl's house, hoping to catch a glimpse of her during his morning workout, was pathetic. That's what teenagers did, not professional hockey players.

What had possessed Jake to change his usual route? He must be nuts, he thought as he turned down the leafy avenue of Victorians.

He hadn't been able to see Maggie since the post-game dinner last week, but she'd been in his thoughts constantly. That last scorcher of a kiss had started fires burning he'd yet to extinguish. And still had the power to make him hard.

Not ideal while running.

The house was up ahead. Feeling foolish, he picked up his pace to sprint past.

"Mr. Jake!" Emily charged down the front steps.

He slowed, wiping the sweat from his forehead with

his T-shirt, and tried to look casual. "Hey, Princess. What's up?"

"Mummy's cooking." She made it sound like a treat. "She's making Bendy Eggs."

Bendy? "Sounds good."

"They're yummy. You should have some." She bounced in her bright pink sneakers.

He hesitated. Tempting, but was a cozy breakfast with Maggie's family smart? He generally avoided anything that gave his dates ideas about commitment. Then again, he'd already spent time with Maggie and her family.

He went for the cautious play. "Thanks, but I have to get home. I'm off to Long Island later, for tomorrow's game."

"Are you playing?"

He nodded.

His first game back. An important milestone. The final stage of his recovery.

"Can I watch?"

"You'll have to check with your mom."

A determined glint lit her eyes. "I could ask while you're having breakfast with us."

Persistent imp.

Maggie opened the screen door. "Is your room tidy, Emily Marie? Remember, no Bendy Eggs until it is."

"Oops." Emily headed toward the steps. "Can Mr. Jake have breakfast with us?"

Maggie came out onto the front porch. "Good morning."

He stood at the bottom of the steps, looking up at

her and those gorgeous legs showcased in khaki shorts. "I hope I didn't keep you out too late the other night."

"Not at all."

Their gazes met and held. The memory of their kiss hovered between them.

Amber fire smoldered in her dark eyes. He wondered how high he could make those flames leap if he kissed her again.

"Can he, Mummy?" Emily's voice was like a spray of ice.

He turned slightly, hoping to mask the erection his shorts couldn't hide.

Maggie bit her lip as if hiding a smile. Luckily, her daughter wasn't as observant.

"Mum-my!" Emily insisted.

The smile broke free. "It's nothing gourmet, but you're welcome to join us."

He basked in the warmth of her smile. Where was the harm in joining her…them…for a home-cooked breakfast?

"Sounds good." He grimaced. "I can't come in like this."

"You have plenty of time to get cleaned up. *Someone* has a job to do." She gave her daughter a pointed look.

Emily flew into the house, letting the screen door slam after her.

Maggie winced. "Luckily these houses were built to withstand punishment."

"One little girl is nothing. Imagine five boys charging around."

"Your mum and Aunt Karina were saints."

"A fact they take great pleasure in reminding us of." A breeze chilled his still-damp skin. "I should go. Can you give me thirty minutes?"

She nodded. "I'll put the eggs on when you return."

Jake sprinted home. Once inside, he stripped while taking the stairs two at a time. He showered and shaved, arriving back at Tracy's house with a minute to spare.

The tantalizing smell of bacon wafted from the open windows. Drawing closer, he heard Emily's excited chatter and Maggie's laughter.

As he rang the doorbell, a cozy image popped into his head of Maggie making breakfast while he read the papers and Emily chased a cat. A chubby-cheeked baby sat in a high chair by the large kitchen table. Hand-drawn pictures and family photos battled for space with hockey magnets on the refrigerator doors.

Whoa! Where had that come from? Marriage, kids and a traditional family life was a hell of a leap from a couple of dates. He wasn't anywhere near ready for that kind of commitment, let alone being responsible for Maggie and Emily.

Jake rolled his shoulders to ease the sudden tightness and to calm the sudden urge to run home. This was just breakfast. Eat, small talk, a few laughs and go. Nothing to get himself bent out of shape about.

He rang the doorbell again, surprised no one had answered yet.

When there was still no response, he opened the screen door and called out, "Hello."

A burning smell filled the air. From the back of the

house, a smoke alarm wailed. Concerned, Jake hurried down the hall, following the sound to its source.

The chaotic scene in the kitchen was nothing like the one he'd imagined only moments ago. Tracy frantically fanned the whining smoke alarm with a newspaper while Emily fed a piece of burned bacon to the black-and-white cat under the table. Hissing steam erupted from the sink as Maggie dumped a sizzling frying pan into some water.

Jake reached up and took the battery out of the smoke alarm.

In the sudden silence, everyone froze.

A moment later, three female heads whipped around to face him. The trepidation in their expressions was unsettling. When that trepidation turned to fear in two pairs of identical brown eyes—the same fear he recalled from that day at his house—he felt like he'd been sucker punched.

Emily abandoned the cat, rushing to her mother's side. The way she slipped her hand into Maggie's tugged at his heart. Tracy frowned and crossed her arms, daring him to make a wrong move.

"Mummy didn't mean to overdo the bacon again." The quiver in Emily's voice added insult to injury. "It was an accident."

What he said next, how he handled the situation, was as crucial as a last-minute face-off in a tied play-off game. He couldn't afford to get it wrong. That urge to run flashed through him again.

Jake forced a light tone. "An accident that conveniently ended up in Catty's stomach. I know his game, one flash of those green eyes and he gets my bacon for his breakfast."

As if playing along, Catty began to wash his whiskers.

Though Maggie's expression didn't change, the tension in her body eased. Tracy gave a half nod; he'd hit the right note.

Emily smiled nervously, but watched him warily. "The bacon was burned, Mr. Jake. You couldn't eat that."

"Princess, I spend nine months of the year eating hotel food, arena food and plane food. I can handle overcooked, undercooked, bland, underseasoned and overspiced." He lowered his voice conspiratorially. "I draw the line at gloopy and mushy, though."

"Me, too." Emily giggled.

He looked at Maggie. "Do you have enough food to try again, or are we going to IHOP?"

"We have plenty, if you're willing to risk it." Maggie smiled softly.

Emily grabbed him by the hand and pulled him toward the kitchen table. "Mummy makes great Bendy Eggs."

"What exactly are Bendy Eggs?"

"A poor man's eggs Benedict, with cream cheese instead of hollandaise. Until today, it was my fail-safe breakfast," Maggie said wryly. "I'm afraid ovens hate me and microwaves and toasters barely tolerate me. The jury's out on kettles."

"You don't scare me. Bring it on."

"In that case, have a seat. This won't take long."

Relieved to have skated cleanly through that little crisis, Jake dropped into a chair at the kitchen table.

Tracy smiled gratefully. She handed him the sports section of the paper before joining him. "Don't worry. You won't starve. Maggie's being modest. She can cook perfectly well."

"I didn't say I couldn't cook." Maggie put fresh bacon strips into a frying pan. "I just don't enjoy cooking."

"Because that jerk you were married to wanted a wife who was Nigella, Martha and the Barefoot Contessa all rolled into one. He expected you to party by night and play chef and housekeeper by day."

"Sis!" Maggie shot her sister a warning look.

Tracy threw up her hands in mock surrender. "All right, I'll shut up." But she muttered under her breath, "Neanderthal."

"Mr. Jake's not like that. You don't care about a little dust and dirt, do you?"

"Uh…no." Startled by Emily's cheerful defense, Jake stammered a response. He then focused on the paper and pretended to study an article on the recent defensive woes of the Giants, though he couldn't concentrate on a word.

What had happened to a cozy breakfast with simple small talk? He'd only been here five minutes and he was already tiptoeing through a conversational minefield.

A timely reminder of why that earlier fantasy had been off base. Why he couldn't be responsible for Maggie and Emily. He was no damn good at tiptoeing.

He was more likely to put his foot squarely where he shouldn't and blow them all up. His stomach churned, dampening his appetite.

"Here you are." Maggie slid a heaped plate in front of him. "The infamous Bendy Eggs. I hope you'll like them."

"They look great." He would say the food was delicious even if it was terrible.

Thankfully, it really was good.

As everyone tucked into their breakfast, the conversation turned to hockey.

"Thanks for the tickets to opening night," Tracy said. "We're looking forward to it."

He glanced anxiously at Maggie, who nodded and smiled. "You're welcome. It's a good matchup. It should be fun."

Emily did a happy little wiggle in her seat. "I can't wait."

"You must be happy about hitting the ice for real tomorrow," Tracy said.

"Yeah, I can't wait to get out there. Even though it's still preseason, the first few shifts won't be easy."

Maggie frowned. "Are you sure you're ready?"

"Playing's the only way to know for sure."

"I hope the other team gives you some leeway."

"They won't." He winked. "I won't give them any, either."

She rolled her eyes. "I might have known."

By the time they'd finished eating, the warm atmosphere and jovial company had begun to relax him.

When Tracy excused herself to make a phone call,

he rose and gathered the plates to take them to the sink. "Can I help clean up?"

"Thanks for offering, but I have it covered. You could do me a favor, though, and look at the brochures I got on youth hockey programs for Emily. I'd appreciate your thoughts on the best one."

Maggie's request lit a spark of pleasure in his chest. Getting her to the game had worked. She was starting to come around. "Be glad to. What changed your mind?"

"I did some research. With the right program, hockey is no worse than soccer camp."

Nice. At least hockey advice was one area he couldn't screw up.

"Here you go." Emily skipped over with the brochures.

He flipped through the leaflets and set two aside. "They all have good skating development programs and under-eight Mites teams, but I think the best two are the Junior Ice Cats and the team I started with, the Ice Blades."

Maggie turned from the sink, her hands still in the soapy water. "Do you know any of the coaches in those programs?"

"Sure. The Mites coach for the Ice Blades was an all-star defenseman back in the day. Got inducted into the Hall of Fame a couple of years ago."

"Yes, but is he a good coach for young children?"

Her sharp tone made him a tad uneasy. Like he'd said the wrong thing. He told himself he was overreacting. "I guess. He'll have a coaching certificate from USA Hockey."

Maggie pursed her lips. "I need to know how good he is before I sign Emily up."

There was that tone again. What was he doing wrong? His unease grew but he kept his voice upbeat. "I'll ask the guys in our locker room which programs their kids are in. Who they recommend."

"That would be useful, thanks."

"Won't you be my coach, Mr. Jake?" Emily's face fell.

"I'll be kind of busy training and playing myself, Princess."

"Oh." She thought for a few seconds, then perked up. "I'll need to get skates and stuff. You can tell me what to get, can't you?"

"I might know a bit about that 'stuff.'" He grinned. "But most programs have specific equipment lists and will help kit you out. It's not worth spending a lot of money on fancy gear that you'll grow out of."

"I have enough money. Emily needs the best to keep her from getting injured." The sharp tone had become defensive.

His grin faded. He was definitely back in that minefield again and not doing so well this time. "It's important to get the best skates and helmets. A youth-hockey expert will ensure everything fits properly."

"But I want you, Mr. Jake. Who's a better expert than you?"

With Emily's steady gaze fixed on him, the pressure of expectation started to make Jake uncomfortable. "Well…"

"Jenny used to play hockey. I'm sure she'd help you." Maggie's intervention was a gratefully received respite.

Jake followed her lead. "Jenny was a great player and, being a girl, she'd be able to help you get things to fit better."

"O-kay." Emily stretched out the word to half a dozen syllables. "But you'll come and watch my games, won't you?"

"When I'm not practicing I'll be there to cheer you on."

"I think Em should start with the development program and see how that goes before committing her to joining a team."

He opened his mouth to disagree, then snapped it shut. His knowledge of youth hockey came from playing, not from the perspective of an anxious parent. "Whatever you think's best," he said carefully.

"But I can skate already and I want to be on the Mites team now," Emily pouted.

Sensing the discussion might become fraught, Jake tried to reassure her. "You'll have fun and they'll make sure you've learned the basics properly. Once the coach sees you can skate well, he'll move you up to one of the teams."

"One step at a time." Maggie's disapproving expression said he'd put his foot in it again.

Jeez. How had giving simple advice become so complicated?

Emily must have realized she'd pushed as far as she

could. She skipped to the back door. "Can I go and tell Amy? Maybe her mum will let her play hockey, too."

Maggie had barely said yes before Emily dashed out.

The atmosphere in the silent kitchen was tense. Unsure what to say to make things better, Jake stacked the discarded leaflets into a neat pile on the table.

Maggie drained the sink and began wiping the countertops.

Perhaps he should ease her mind about youth hockey.

Jake cleared his throat. "I know you're nervous about letting Emily get involved in a sport you don't trust, but she'll be fine. They don't allow hitting and checking at that age and they wear every type of protection imaginable. The biggest problem the kids have is bruises from falling on their ass...backsides so often."

"I appreciate that, but there's no need to rush these things," she said coolly.

"Come on, lighten up." He smiled, trying to get her to reciprocate. "She'll have a blast."

Instead, she shook her head. "There are more important things to worry about than fun. You're not a parent. You're not responsible for anyone but yourself. You don't have to worry about your child being hurt as a result of your decision."

Her words sucker punched him.

Jake clenched his jaw. He knew all about making the wrong decision and someone being hurt as a result. That was hard enough to bear. He wouldn't be able to live with the consequences of hurting someone as vulnerable as Maggie. Or worse, her daughter. That's why it was safer for him not to get involved.

He had to get out of there.

"You're right. I apologize." Before she could respond, he said quickly, "I hate to eat and run, but I have a bunch of stuff to do before I head to Long Island. Thanks for breakfast. The Bendy Eggs lived up to their press."

"You're welcome," Maggie said stiffly.

She dropped the dishcloth in the sink, then led him to the front door. "I hope the game goes well for you tomorrow."

"Me, too." He forced a smile, then jogged down the steps.

"Good luck," she called after him.

He raised a hand, then focused on putting one foot in front of the other. As he pounded the pavement, Maggie's words echoed inside his head.

So much for not screwing up.

Perhaps it was best that this happened before things had gone any further between them. Before he'd done any damage.

Jake trudged up the front steps and into his house. He continued to mull over the situation as he got his gear ready for the trip out to the Island.

Maggie was a good woman who'd already suffered enough. She deserved someone who didn't bear the battle scars of playing sport for a living. Someone who didn't bear the emotional scars of letting his friend down. He should back off and leave her alone. Let her find that decent guy.

He thought about Maggie and some faceless Decent Guy, smiling, laughing, holding hands. When he got to the guy undoing her buttons, Jake's gut twisted sharply. His fist tightened on the handles of his duffel bag.

No damn way.

Okay, so he didn't want to back off. What the hell *was* he going to do? How could he be with Maggie when she deserved so much more?

He was no closer to an answer when Tru's horn tooted outside.

Jake hefted his bag over his shoulder and headed out the front door. He'd have to think about this later. For now, he had to focus on tomorrow's game.

Easier said than done.

He couldn't get the problem out of his head. On the bus ride to Long Island, through the team dinner and long into the night, he kept trying to figure out how he could be with Maggie. He tried to analyze the situation like he did his game. He replayed the scene at breakfast, trying to see if he could have handled things differently.

By dawn, all he knew for sure was…maybe.

The morning skate went badly. Jake was a step off the pace, battling to get his legs under him. His coach and teammates blamed rust for his scrappy play.

Jake knew better.

He had to get Maggie out of his head before the game. He had to focus.

Tru grabbed the seat next to him on the bus back to the hotel. "You'll be fine, bro. Once you're into your pregame routine, the nerves will disappear."

"Yeah." Jake didn't correct his friend's assumption.

"Just keep it simple and stick to your game."

A lightbulb flashed in Jake's head. That was the

answer. Not just to his play, but to the situation with Maggie. He'd go back to what he'd originally planned. A few dates, no commitment, no worrying about a relationship. No complications. Just enjoying each other's company and having a good time.

The perfect game plan.

"ARE YOU LOOKING forward to opening night?"

Jenny's question wasn't a surprise, but Maggie had hoped her new friend would wait until after the cheesecake to ask it.

This dinner was their third get-together since meeting at the postgame meal. Their instant connection had continued; they'd talked and laughed through two lunches and endless texts as if they'd known each other for years.

Other than her sister, Maggie had never had a close female friend. Someone she could share confidences with and "ooh" over shoes or giggle over boys. She was enjoying the experience enormously.

At least, she had been until Jenny had asked the difficult question.

Maggie laid down her fork. "I'm not sure."

Jenny's teasing smile faded. "Is everything okay?"

"Jake and I haven't spoken since he came to breakfast a few days ago, so I'm not sure where things stand."

"What happened?"

"Breakfast had an inauspicious start." As she explained, Maggie relived the emotional turmoil of the morning.

Having burned the bacon, she'd been on edge even

before Jake had walked into the kitchen. She'd steeled herself for the disappointment she'd assumed she'd see in his expression because she'd failed to live up to expectations. Though she'd sworn she wouldn't live in fear of another man's opinions, that the only expectations that mattered were her own, her stomach had jolted sickeningly when she'd seen him standing in the kitchen.

Once again, Jake had surprised her. He'd made light of the whole debacle and, as he had with the banister knob, gone out of his way to reassure Emily.

"After that, everything seemed okay." Maggie frowned. "Until I asked him to recommend a youth hockey program. We disagreed about certain points. Then something changed. It was like a switch had flipped and he couldn't wait to get away."

"Like most men, he doesn't like being told he's wrong." Jenny's husky laugh turned male heads at nearby tables. "Don't worry, he'll come around. He doesn't hold grudges."

"But in the meantime, what do we do with the opening night tickets?"

"Use them. You'll have a great time."

"What if he's changed his mind? We're supposed to sit with his parents. It'll be awkward if he doesn't want us there."

"If he'd had second thoughts, he'd have said. I'd take his silence to mean he wants you to go."

"Are you sure? Maybe he hasn't called because he doesn't want to speak to me."

Jenny shook her head. "It's not personal—he has a

lot on his mind right now. He'll be focused on his game, to the expense of everything else. The season opener will be especially tough for Jake."

"Why? He's already played a couple of games and he did okay."

"Sure, but they were preseason games. It's different when the points matter." Jenny's expression grew somber. "It'll also be his first regular season game since the accident."

"I imagine it'll be hard for him to play without his friend." Maggie's heart ached for what Jake was going through.

"Definitely. It helps that he'll be stepping out onto a different rink, wearing a different sweater. Still, Jake's putting a lot of pressure on himself because he'll be playing to honor Adam's memory."

"No doubt that pressure's compounded by his survivor guilt."

"Definitely." Jenny traced a pattern in the condensation on her glass. "He changed after the accident. I think the realization that he wasn't invincible made him reassess his life."

"That's understandable when his friend died too young."

"Sure." Sadness tinged Jenny's blue eyes. "But I expected Bad Boy to live each minute to the full, not withdraw almost completely."

"Perhaps he was scared. You know, there but for the grace of God."

"I suppose. Especially because after Adam's death

everyone talked continually about lost opportunities and lost potential."

"Including his chance to win the Cup."

"Exactly. Though whether Adam was really good enough is debatable. Definitely not, if he continued to play the way he did last season."

Something in her voice caught Maggie's attention. "Did something happen?"

Her friend sighed. "Not really. But those last few months of his life, Adam was wildly inconsistent. No one knew from one minute to the next if he'd be laughing and joking or snapping and shouting."

"Was he under too much pressure to perform?" The more Lee had been stressed about his play, the more unpredictable he'd been.

"Possibly. Anyway, the point's moot. Jake wants to honor Adam the best way he can. Who am I to judge?"

"But you're concerned about Jake?" This conversation was giving Maggie some useful insights, but also raising more questions.

"A tribute's fine, but changing your whole life is something else. An untimely death can raise a normal guy to near sainthood." Jenny's lips twisted. "Adam wasn't a saint. For sure, he wasn't any better than Bad Boy. He was also envious of Jake—the parties, the women—and always striving to live up to him."

"Jake's penance for surviving was to cut them out of his life."

"I think so. That's why I was pleased when he became interested in you. It was a sign he'd come through the worst and was beginning to look forward instead of back."

"Me?" Maggie's heart skipped with pleasure. "But I'm nothing like the women he used to date."

"Which makes you perfect for him."

Her stomach roiled. "I won't have another relationship where I'm worried about being perfect for a man. Been there, done that and got the bloody T-shirt. I'm just beginning to be who I want to be. It's taken too much heartache to get me this far. I can't go there again."

"Of course not. No one's perfect. You have to be yourself. Don't let anyone interfere with that." Jenny's vehemence suggested she was referring to her own past.

Maggie didn't push—everyone had their secrets. "The thing is, we're hardly dating, let alone anything more serious. I don't even know if he's still interested in me."

"Oh, he is. Are you still interested in him?"

Jake had sneaked past her defenses. Most of the time, she liked him. Liked being with him. There was no denying her attraction to him—the man could spike her temperature with a single look. He was certainly different from Lee, but being with Jake was never going to be plain sailing. Still… "Yes."

"Then hang in there. It'll take time for Jake to work things out. The most important being how to fit you into his life."

"What am I supposed to do in the meantime?"

"Figure out how you want Jake to fit into your life."

Jenny was right.

If Maggie wanted to be in charge of her life, she had some decisions to make. Jake wasn't the only one who got to decide how their relationship would work. Or even if there would be a relationship.

Who was she kidding? She was long past the stage of having flings. Aside from what it would do to Emily, Maggie wasn't interested in getting back on that merry-go-round or in being another piece of Jake's arm candy.

This time, Maggie wanted to be absolutely sure, from the beginning, of what she was getting into. She wanted both sides to be serious about what was involved in a steady relationship. Even if it didn't pan out long-term, she wanted the reassurance of exclusivity and that they'd both work at the relationship. She wanted mutual respect. Compromise, not dictates. Give-and-take, where she wasn't the only one giving.

Maybe it was a lot to ask, but this time, Maggie wouldn't settle for anything less.

OPENING NIGHT HAD finally arrived.

In twenty minutes, Jake would hit the ice for real. Warm-up was over. The Zambonis were preparing the ice. The arena was already buzzing with excited fans. Around him, the chilled air rang with the whine of skates being sharpened and the rip of tape. The sharp tang of glue mingled with the scent of popcorn.

Familiar. Reassuring. Home.

This was what he was. What he lived for.

He walked into the locker room, where his teammates gathered for last-minute instructions. Hip-hop blared from the boom box as he sat in his stall. He'd have preferred the pounding beat of heavy rock to get him pumped up. Hell, he'd take country over this crap.

A sharp click and the room fell silent.

Heads turned to the front, where the coach stood to deliver his pregame talk. The mood was somber, intense. The clock ticked down toward zero and game time.

The coach's words washed over Jake. He couldn't concentrate. Emotions ricocheted through his body. Anticipation. Dread. Determination.

And a burning in his gut to get out there and play.

The weight of Adam's lucky penny—a gift from his friend's mom—hung heavy around his neck beneath his sweater. As the talk ended, players checked their gear and psyched themselves up. Adrenaline gave the air an electric feel.

The clock clicked past three minutes.

This was it.

Jake's pulse kicked up a gear. A familiar roaring filled his ears.

The captain, Scotty Matthews, rose and went to stand by the door, his expression fierce. "Let's go out there and show them the Ice Cats play the best damn hockey in the world."

Ike joined him. The goaltender would lead the team out; Scotty was always the last man. Pride swelled in Jake's chest as he and Tru stood behind Ike.

With 1:59 glowing red on the clock, the doors swung open and Ike strode out. He tapped the door frame with his stick for luck. Tru and Jake did the same, and their teammates followed. They entered the short tunnel. The bright lights of the arena shone like a welcoming beacon, bringing them home to the ice.

"Please welcome your New Jersey Ice Cats." The announcer's voice reverberated around the building as the fans stomped and cheered.

Jake inhaled, letting the crisp air penetrate his lungs, then stepped out onto the ice. Immediately, the noise of the crowd muffled while the scrape of blades amplified.

His heart pounded.

As always, he skated round the net twice anticlockwise, then twice clockwise. Before taking his position on the blue line, he tapped his stick against Ike's goaltender pads.

"Good game, bro."

Ike nodded. "You, too."

Joining the rest of the Cats' starting line, Jake removed his helmet, and since they were playing a Canadian team, waited for the two national anthems to be sung. He moved his skates back and forth, unable to keep still.

"Maggie's here," Tru muttered, beneath "O Canada."

Jake's gaze shot to the glass behind the Cats' goal for his allocated seats. There. Next to his parents. He'd hoped she'd come but hadn't believed she'd show.

He hadn't seen or spoken to her since that breakfast. He could blame having been on the road, but that was a poor excuse. Truth was, he hadn't known what to say to make things right between them.

Her presence had to be a good sign.

As the singer began "The Star-Spangled Banner," Jake's eyes drank in the sight of Maggie.

Her gaze met his. *Good luck,* she mouthed. Joy filled him. A surge of energy charged through his veins. Jake flashed her a grin as cheers drowned out the final notes of the anthem.

"Move it, Romeo," Tru teased as players took their positions for the opening face-off.

Jake replaced his helmet and skated into position.

In the seconds before the puck dropped, time slowed.

His senses went on alert. His muscles tensed.

His gaze focused and narrowed.

The linesman leaned over and released the biscuit. Inch by inch, it dropped to the ice.

Action exploded.

Jake was back.

CHAPTER ELEVEN

"WELCOME BACK, Bad Boy."

Tarkov, Ottawa's high-scoring left-winger grunted as he and Jake clashed in the corner.

Jake crunched him to the boards, swiped the puck and shot it across the ice to Tru. "Good to be back."

Within seconds, the Senators had possession once more and Jake and the Russian resumed their battle.

"I won't take it so easy on you in the second," Tarkov taunted as he hip checked Jake.

"You and which army?"

"Stemgarder."

Jake's response about the opposition's goon was blunt and coarse. Again, he stripped Tarkov of the puck. He passed it to Juergen, whose slap shot rebounded off the crossbar and flew high into the netting, stopping play.

As Jake skated to the bench, he passed Stemgarder. They exchanged glares; they'd never liked each other. While he waited for the TV break to finish, he glanced across at the stands. Maggie was frowning.

He didn't have time to consider why, as his shift was called.

When Tarkov skated toward the Cats' goal, Jake cut him off. They collided and the Russian ate ice. Grinning, Jake skated behind the net ready to start a rush back the other way. As he did, his gaze strayed to Maggie.

She looked annoyed. Why?

During that momentary lapse in concentration, Tarkov took the puck off his blade and chipped it behind Ike for a score.

"Damn it, Jake." Ike was furious. "Concentrate on the game, not your girlfriend."

Jake tapped his friend's pads in apology and skated to the bench.

The horn went for the end of the period. The Cats trooped off toward their locker room, giving him heat for his stupid mistake. While the coach talked tactics for the second period, Jake tried to get his head back in the game.

What the hell was wrong with him? He'd never lost concentration like that before. Fans had been yelling crap at him for years—he'd always blocked it out. Yet one angry look from Maggie and he'd been thrown off balance like a damn rookie.

As the team prepared to take the ice, Jake squared his shoulders. He wouldn't think about Maggie for the rest of the game. *Focus on winning.*

Just before they stepped out, Ike growled, "Keep your mind out of your shorts for the next twenty minutes."

Jake nodded sharply, then skated into position.

The second period was hard fought with possession swinging back and forth. Just before the intermission, Jake tipped the puck to JB, who banged it in the net for his first NHL goal.

"Glad you're back in the game," Tru said as they walked to the locker room.

"Sorry about earlier. It won't happen again."

Tru studied him closely. "Bad memory?"

He shook his head, unwilling to explain.

"Why don't you get laid and do us all a favor?" Ike muttered.

Anger surged. "It's got nothing to do with Maggie," he lied.

"Yeah, right."

Jake glared at Ike. His friend backed off.

He returned to the ice for the final period with renewed determination. His focus was complete, his concentration intent.

The Cats went ahead with a couple of quick goals, making the period even more frenetic. As the Senators tried to claw the score back level, Jake and Tru were pressed into extra shifts.

With seven minutes to go, Jake knew Ottawa needed a change of momentum. "They'll send Stemgarder out soon," he panted to Tru as they climbed back over the boards.

"Yeah. He'll want you to drop the gloves."

"I don't fight. He'll have to pick someone else."

Tru laughed. "Get real."

Jake's gaze flicked to the stands. The last thing he needed was for Maggie to see him fight. But he realized with a sinking feeling it was inevitable.

He'd barely got back on the ice before Stemgarder goaded him to go.

When Jake ignored him, the goon chased him, crashing him into the boards. Jake got up, told Stemgarder to do an anatomically impossible act then skated off.

Back at the bench, he squirted water over his face and rotated his aching shoulder.

Tru groaned. "Stemgarder's calling you a turtle."

"I'm no damn coward!" That challenge left him no choice.

Jake headed back out, his heart heavy.

As the puck dropped, Stemgarder shoved him, sneering.

Gloves dropped. Sticks scattered. Helmets came off. Fists flew.

The referees circled. The crowd was on its feet screaming. Players on both benches banged their sticks against the boards.

A punch bounced harmlessly off his pads. Then one caught him under the chin.

Enough. Time to put this jerk down.

Two sharp punches. Stemgarder wobbled. Tried to retaliate and missed.

Uppercut. Right hook. The goon hit the ice.

Victory.

Jake gave Stemgarder a succinct assessment of his sexual preferences while the refs separated them. He tried to avoid glancing at the stands as he skated to the penalty box but couldn't resist. His heart contracted.

Maggie's seat was empty.

His gaze scanned the section. Movement at the top of the stairs caught his attention.

Maggie was marching up the steps with Emily.

For a moment, he thought they might be going to

the bathroom. But they had their coats on and Emily kept turning back to look at the ice.

They were leaving.

He'd won the skirmish on the ice. But he'd lost Maggie.

AM I THE only sane person in the building?

Maggie was definitely the only one not to take pleasure in the fight, she thought as she pulled her reluctant daughter toward the exit onto the concourse.

The noise level was deafening. Everyone was on their feet screaming. Fans banged their fists on the glass while those in the balconies stamped. There was a raucous cheer as Jake and the other bloke skated toward the Sin Bin.

Then play resumed as if nothing had happened.

"Why aren't we watching the game?" Emily's voice echoed in the near-deserted concourse. "We're going to miss the end."

"I know, Em, but I didn't like the way things were going."

A minor understatement.

Maggie had sworn that Emily would never be exposed to violence again. Though she'd prevented Lee from taking out his "bad moods" on their daughter, it hadn't been possible to shield Emily totally. That final night had been the first time Lee had touched his daughter in anger. The first and last. Thankfully, Emily hadn't been hurt. Maggie had got between them and taken the brunt of the contact. She'd never let anything frighten her daughter again.

Yet she'd let Emily watch Jake beat the hell out of some bloke while everyone around them bayed for blood.

This was worse than the fight during the preseason game. Perhaps because she was in the crowd rather than cocooned inside a luxury box. Perhaps because the fight had been so brutal, with each player intent on hurting the other.

Perhaps because Jake was involved, not some helmeted bloke she didn't know.

It was probably all of those things. One thing was certain—it had been a mistake to bring Emily to the game. An even bigger mistake to let her get close to Jake.

"That's not fair." Emily pouted. "Mr. Jake won."

"Fighting is never a good thing." Maggie took a deep breath. The heavy smell of popcorn and burgers lingering from the closed concessions made her stomach turn.

"But he didn't want to fight. It wasn't his fault."

The thug from the other team *had* been goading Jake.

"Even so, violence doesn't solve anything." She hated that the words sounded prissy.

"I think Mr. Jake was a hero."

Startled by Emily's vehemence and conviction, Maggie stammered, "Wh-why?"

"That man was picking on the Ice Cats. Mr. Jake protected his friends by standing up to the bully. My teacher said standing up to bullies is very brave."

"I see." Maggie studied her daughter carefully as she considered what she'd said.

Rather than being scared about Jake punching the living daylights out of someone, her daughter was defending him. Putting a totally different spin on the situation.

Her heart lifted at the impatience in Emily's face as she bounced from foot to foot. The rosy-cheeked imp trying to sneak glimpses of the game on the concourse TV screens was a far cry from the pale, trembling child she'd been only a few months ago.

Clearly, Emily had listened to what Jake's father had told her earlier, when Gio had explained about The Code. Her daughter had no problem understanding and accepting that aggression on the ice was used to right a wrong, to defend a position, to protect a teammate. She also seemed to have no fears about that aggression spilling over after the game was over.

Unfortunately, Maggie couldn't dismiss her own concerns as readily.

Jake had switched from hard-playing athlete into bloodthirsty fighter in a heartbeat. Though the anger in his expression had been unmistakable when they'd first dropped the gloves, his taunting smirk had grown with each landed punch. A satisfied swagger had accompanied his victory.

How could she ignore his transformation into something she recognized…someone she didn't want to recognize?

A burst of noise roared through the concourse. Chanting and cheering.

Emily grabbed her hand and tugged. "We're missing it, Mummy. Can we go back now?"

Maggie weighed the options. If she stopped her daughter from watching the rest of the game, she'd draw more attention to the fight. She also risked confusing and upsetting Emily. Besides, she didn't want to give her daughter a reason to be scared of Jake. Emily hadn't drawn any comparisons with her father—better it stayed that way.

Maggie would have to work out what to do about Jake and his role in their lives later. Perhaps she should face the problem square on—talk to him about her concerns so they could work it out together.

She nodded. "All right."

"Yay!"

Heading back to their seats, Emily complained loudly about missing an Ice Cats goal.

"Is everything okay?" Tracy asked, as Maggie slipped into the seat next to her.

"Fine." This wasn't the time or place for explanations.

Her heart gave a funny little thunk as she watched Jake skate smoothly to the middle of the ice, ready for the next face-off. It was as if the fight had never happened. Though fiercely intense, his expression had returned to normal. His body was poised for action. His focus was on the game.

Still, as the puck dropped, Maggie couldn't help wondering who would get hurt the next time someone got in his face.

THE LOCKER ROOM was empty.

Jake was ready to leave, yet he lingered. It was crazy. He should be celebrating the win with his family, but he was reluctant to join them.

To face Maggie's disapproving look.

She and Emily had returned to their seats sometime after Ralinkov had tipped in the game winner. Once Jake had seen they were back, he'd avoided looking altogether. He hadn't wanted to see her tense expression.

As it was, the thought of her disappointment had weighed like a damn albatross around his neck, making him second-guess every move. Though he hadn't made any more stupid mistakes, he hadn't played his best.

And that wasn't good enough.

Jake had endured another of Ike's lectures until Tru had told his brother to back off. His tone, rather than his words, had ended the rant. This time.

There wouldn't be a next time.

"Move it, Bad Boy. I've got to lock up," the equipment manager called out.

Looking up, Jake realized how long he'd stood there, delaying. Damn it. His folks must be wondering where he was. He grabbed his gear, then pulled open the door to face the small crowd gathered nearby.

"You did good, Jakey." As she had since his first game, his mom pulled his head down to kiss his forehead.

Aunt Karina pinched his cheek. "You shoulda broken Stemgarder's nose."

His dad slapped him on the back. "You made me

proud. All you boys did. You play like that the rest of the season and you'll win the Cup."

"I'm proud of you, too, Mr. Jake." The grinning seven-year-old choked him up.

"Well done."

His gaze swung to meet Maggie's. Wariness tempered the warm glow in her brown eyes.

His shoulders tensed. "Thanks. So you enjoyed the game?"

Before she could answer, Emily interrupted, "It was awesome."

"Great." He kept his eyes fixed on Maggie, waiting for a response.

"It was entertaining," she allowed. "Much more intense than the last one."

The unspoken message wasn't hard to understand.

"Yeah." He tried to keep his tone casual. "We're playing for real now."

"But it's only the first game of the season."

Her comment irritated him. Like she'd have cared less about a fight in April, than October. "Every win takes you two points closer to guaranteeing a play-off spot."

"I suppose so."

His body's postgame aches and stiffness seemed worse in the silence that followed.

"Are we gonna stand here talking all night or can we go eat?" Tru said loudly. "I'm starving."

A chorus of approval echoed in the empty hall.

"Come on, everyone." Jake's dad began to herd

people toward the exit. "We have a table booked at the boys' favorite restaurant."

"We should be getting home," Maggie said briskly. "Congratulations on the win."

"You aren't coming to the dinner?" He couldn't keep the disappointment from his voice.

"We don't want to intrude. This is your special night—you'll want to celebrate with your family. Thank you for the tickets. We all enjoyed ourselves, especially Emily."

"You won't be intruding. My folks would want you to join us. I want you to join us. Unless you have other plans."

"No. We've no other plans."

"Can't we go, Mummy? Please." Emily turned her big brown eyes on her mother. "I promise I'll go straight to bed when we get home."

"Now, there's an offer I can't refuse." Maggie smiled. "In that case, we'd be happy to join you."

"Yay!" Emily jumped up and down.

"Then let's go." He slung his bag over his shoulder. "I'm starving, too."

He glanced at her as she walked quietly beside him out of the arena toward the parking lot. Her body language was contradictory. Though she held herself stiffly, she wasn't acting like he had the plague. Maybe things weren't as bad as he thought.

The heavy arena door slammed behind them. Maggie shot him a nervous look as the sharp retort of locks being thrown echoed through the chilly night air. Her reaction made him wonder how much ground he'd lost because of the fight.

Her trust had clearly been shaken. Even as irritation pricked him that she didn't seem to know him well enough to separate him from his job, he wondered how to repair the damage. He should explain what had happened. Make it clear he hadn't wanted to fight, but he'd had to protect his honor.

Jake sneaked another peek at her profile, then let his gaze drop down the length of her body. His blood heated. It was definitely worth a shot.

He knew at some point he'd have to think about the effect her disapproval had on his play. Affecting his game was not acceptable. There could be no compromise when it came to winning the Cup. If it came down to a choice, there was only one right answer. His gut twisted. No matter how much he'd hate it, he'd do what he had to.

He owed Adam that much.

Rubbing the lucky penny, he pushed aside the whisper of concern that lingered. He'd worry about that another time.

Tonight was for celebrating. He was back. The Cats had won. Whatever other doubts he had, he was sure about one thing. He wanted to share tonight's triumph with Maggie.

A PROPER FAMILY dinner.

A warm, relaxed atmosphere filled with chattering voices and laughter. No stiff formality, no criticism, no head games. Though Gio sat at the head of the table, with Tina to his right and Karina to his left, he didn't lord it over anyone. Mostly he sat quietly, beaming at the group, his pride obvious to anyone watching.

How different would Maggie's life have been if she'd grown up in a family like Jake's? If she'd been supported and encouraged?

Playing what-if games was pointless—she couldn't change the past. All she could do was ensure things were different for Emily.

"Are you okay?" Jake's breath against the sensitive skin of her neck sent a quiver through her. "You're quiet."

She resisted the urge to lean back against his arm, which rested on her chair. "Just a little tired."

"Too much excitement for one night?" A serious note underlay his teasing.

Maggie lifted her glass and sipped the cool white wine. This was hardly the place to talk about the emotional upheaval of the evening. "Probably."

"Are you pissed at me having to fight that ass…jerk, Stemgarder, in the third?"

Her heart tugged at the uncertainty in his eyes. "A little."

"More than a little?"

"Yes," she admitted softly. "I was concerned about the effect it would have on Emily. I needn't have worried."

The corner of Jake's mouth quirked as she explained her daughter's perspective on what had happened. "Smart girl."

"She's certainly very resilient. She's had so much to deal with, and yet she's bounced back really quickly."

"Thanks to you."

The ever-present guilt over what her daughter had suffered because of her jabbed her in the chest. "I don't know about that."

"I do." He nodded across the table at Emily giggling with his father. "She'll be fine."

"I hope you're right."

He pulled her toward him in a one-armed hug. "Trust me."

Maggie couldn't help flinching. The dilemma of whether or not to trust him had been on her mind ever since she'd agreed to come to dinner with him.

Jake stiffened and withdrew his arm. "That's the real problem, isn't it? Because of the fight, you're not convinced you can."

The hurt in his voice made her want to deny his charge. But she knew that wouldn't help either of them. He deserved her honesty.

"It was pretty brutal—" she began, but he cut her off.

"I'd never hit a woman. I'd never hit a man off the ice unless it was to defend myself or protect someone else. I'm not that kind of guy." He thrust his fingers through his still-damp hair. "Hell, I don't want to fight on the ice anymore, but sometimes you don't get a choice."

She wanted to believe him, but she couldn't quite dismiss the image in her head of the beast that had emerged during the fight. "It's hard to know what you'd do if you felt you were provoked," she said carefully.

"I know exactly what I'd do, and it wouldn't involve hurting someone."

"Yet that's what you did tonight," she snapped, frustrated that he couldn't understand her concerns. "And you enjoyed it."

"Stemgarder is dangerous because he doesn't respect The Code. He likes causing trouble and doesn't care who he injures."

"You took great pleasure in hurting him."

"I took great pleasure in *winning the fight*. A fight I didn't want to have any part of, for the record." He paused, jaw clenched for several seconds. When he continued, his voice was calmer. "Someone had to deal with Stemgarder or he'd have run riot. Not just in that game, but for the rest of the season. I may not have wanted to be involved, but I had no choice. I'm damned if I'm going to apologize for winning the fight."

This wasn't a nonapology, like Lee would have made in similar circumstances. He seemed genuinely frustrated.

"I understand why the goon had to be dealt with. Even I could see the trouble he was causing. But," she added when she saw triumph light Jake's expression, "I don't see why *you* had to fight him."

"Do you know what a turtle is?"

She frowned. "You mean with a shell and flippers?"

"In hockey, you call someone a coward by accusing them of pulling their head into their shell…turtling. I'm no coward."

Maggie recalled his grim expression before the fight.

It all added up. She'd misjudged him. "So you fought him because your pride was hurt?"

"I'd prefer to say I was defending my honor."

His mildly offended tone made the tension ease from her body. This time, she'd give him the benefit of the doubt. But actions spoke louder than words, so she hoped his lived up to his explanation. "In that case, I'd say you wore a white hat tonight."

"Our helmets are black…" His voice faded as he made the connection with their conversation about good guys wearing white hats when they'd toured the gyms. The tips of his ears turned pink. "Yeah."

As the meal segued from entrée to dessert, Jake's arm returned to the back of her chair. When coffee was served, she took the opportunity to lean back. The warmth against her shoulders made her system dance with anticipation. The gentle, circular trail of his fingers on her upper arm teased her heightened senses. The press of his thigh against hers fired her cheeks and made her skin tingle. Desire shimmered within her, like moonbeams caressing the surface of a crystal clear pool.

"You've hardly touched your tiramisu," Jake murmured huskily in her ear.

"I seem to have lost my appetite for dessert."

"I can't tempt you with one bite?"

"Not of tiramisu."

The banked flames in his eyes flared to life, becoming hot enough to melt steel. The air around them seemed charged.

"If you're done, we can leave."

"What about Emily and Tracy?"

His crooked grin made her heart flutter. "Didn't your sister offer to take Emily home if we had other plans?"

"She did." Maggie smiled. "Let's go."

The goodbyes passed in a blur as her attention narrowed to a single point: the heat of Jake's hand on her back. Her pounding pulse picked up speed with each step toward the door. Then they were outside, in the cooling night air.

Alone.

A huge full moon overhung the parking lot, providing a soft light. She could almost hear Dean Martin singing. The giddiness filling her made her believe she, too, was moonstruck.

Jake took her hand in his, entwining their fingers.

The walk to his car was both too long and too short. She wanted to savor the closeness their joined hands created, but she wanted to be with him, too. Away from prying eyes.

The SUV was parked next to a towering oak tree. Jake opened her door, but she didn't make it inside the car.

He pulled her beneath the oak's dark canopy. Hidden by the leaf-laden branches, he leaned back against the rough bark and drew her to him.

Her arms wound around his neck, drawing them closer still. Her breasts were pressed to his solid chest, her thighs trapped between his long, muscled legs. His hardness nestled tantalizingly against her, making her ache and yearn.

Slowly, his head lowered to kiss her.

Too slowly. Maggie thrust her fingers through his thick hair, tugging him toward her. She raised her mouth to meet his descending lips.

Their mouths found each other with unerring accuracy.

Their lips parted; their tongues danced.

Her nerves fizzed. Her pulse raced.

Dangerous, decadent, delicious, he tasted darker than chocolate, bolder than champagne.

What was it about this man who enticed her beyond all reason?

"We should go," Jake murmured against her mouth.

She gave a soft moan of protest.

"I want to see you, touch you, taste you." He nibbled her lower lip. "All of you."

Yes, please.

"Not here." Jake's fingers were unsteady as they brushed a curl from her face.

Why not? "Of course not."

They pulled apart. Slowly. Reluctantly.

The journey to his home was quiet, their silence comfortable. Soft rock played. Jake's thumb caressed the back of her hand.

Yet as his Victorian came into sight, Maggie found herself having second thoughts. Was she really ready to take the next step? To sleep with him.

She should have known doubts would surface, given time to think. Why hadn't she insisted he continue?

"I can hear your mind whirring," Jake teased as he pulled into the driveway. "You're not ready, are you?"

Maggie wasn't sure what surprised her more—that he'd read her mind, or the understanding in his voice.

"It's not that I don't want to. It's just…it's been so quick and I'm not sure…" Her voice trailed off. Pathetic.

"It's okay."

"It is?" She studied his expression in the dim light. Intense. Earnest.

"There's been a lot of change in my life. I'm not ready for a relationship right now, but I don't want a casual fling with you, either. Plus, dating a hockey player is not like dating a nine-to-fiver. The hours, the schedule, the commitment, the travel—it's rough on couples."

Encouraged, Maggie found her voice. "What do you suggest?"

"We take things at a pace you're comfortable with—date, dinner, a movie—and give ourselves a chance to see how it works."

The perfect answer. And yet…

"Okay, what have you done with Bad Boy?"

His grin held just enough wickedness to reassure her. And more than enough to heat her blood all over again. The man was lethal!

"You're sure that's what you want?"

Maggie should have known better than to tweak the tiger's tail. The flames leaping in his ice-blue eyes almost singed her.

"Let's be clear." His voice was low and deep, pulsing with primal heat. "I want to make love to you. Everywhere. Every way possible. Until we both can't move."

Moisture pooled deep within her. Her nipples tight-ened beneath her blouse.

"But I'm prepared to wait until you're ready."

Her body was ready now. Past ready. Her mind wouldn't let her tell him that.

"Um...all right." Her voice was husky and she stum-bled over her words. "We'll date. Until..."

"Good." His interruption was a relief. "The Cats head out on a road trip to Toronto, Ottawa and Buffalo tomorrow, so we can't get together until the weekend. How about dinner Sunday night?"

"That would be lovely."

Jake leaned forward, a predatory gleam in his blue eyes. He captured her chin, tilting her face toward him, then brushed his thumb across her lower lip. "Do you kiss on a first date?"

MAGGIE WOKE WITH a smile, cocooned in a warm, happy glow.

She snuggled deeper in bed as she relived every glorious moment of Jake's kisses.

Who'd have thought she'd be dating again?

A giggle escaped. Dating a bad-boy hockey player, no less.

Her heart gave a nervous kick, but she reminded herself that while Jake might appear to be a bad boy on the surface, he was a good man inside. He'd showed her that in so many ways. Not least, his reaction to her second thoughts last night.

She wasn't fool enough to think everything would be plain sailing for them. There was too much baggage on both sides. But her doubts had been quieted enough to give it a try.

Glancing across at her alarm clock, Maggie allowed herself two more minutes to revel in feelings of contentment before she had to get up. This time, though, her thoughts drifted toward anticipation of Sunday night's date.

The phone rang, its strident chirp interrupting her delicious daydream.

Without thinking, she answered. "Hello?"

"I'm sorry to call so early, Maggie, but we need to talk."

Her solicitor's voice shattered the peace and joy of the morning. There was only one reason Samantha would call instead of emailing.

Lee wanted something.

Emily.

CHAPTER TWELVE

I WON'T LET LEE get his hands on Emily.

Maggie's chest squeezed so tightly, she could hardly breathe.

"What does he want?" she forced out finally. "Is he arguing about how much he pays in child support again?" The question was hopeful, rather than with any conviction.

"You know I wouldn't bother you with that." Samantha's tone was apologetic. "He complains about what he pays you, or rather Emily, every month."

After an initial settlement, Lee paid only child support. Maggie would rather not have taken a penny from him, but she'd wanted to ensure her daughter's future was financially secure. She had the money paid into a separate account, in trust for Emily.

"So what does he want?" She wished she could sound nonchalant, but that was impossible. She dreaded what her ex might be demanding.

"Lee's getting remarried. His fiancée, Patty, is the woman he's been going out with for the past few months."

"Okay." Maggie waited for the other shoe to drop.

It landed like a grenade.

"He wants Emily to come back to England."

Panic wrenched Maggie's stomach. She wanted to scream her refusal, but her lips were numb. To grab Emily and run, but her limbs were frozen.

The sound of her daughter moving around in the room next door broke through the wall of ice that encased Maggie. "She can't. He agreed, in writing, that we could come to the U.S. for twelve months."

"He's still entitled to see Emily three times a year."

"But he hasn't seen her since before the divorce. Why would he change his mind now?"

"I suspect this is Patty's idea. Renewing contact with Emily will show everyone he's changed. She's been gushing to the gossip media about how they want to start a family."

"In other words, it's a nice PR ploy." Lee had loved to parade Emily before the cameras whenever he needed good press. No way would she allow him to use Emily like that ever again. "I don't want Lee anywhere near my daughter."

"We can't actually deny him access." Samantha's voice was steady and calm. "Despite your totally justified feelings about Lee, you have to put Emily's best interests first. Remember, we want to show the court, should he ever decide to challenge the custody agreement, that you've been the reasonable one."

"Is that what this is about?" Maggie felt sick. This couldn't be happening. "He wants custody of Emily?"

"I don't know for certain, but I wouldn't be surprised if that's part of his plan."

"No." She tightened her grip on the phone. "He can't. Never."

"Trust me. It won't get that far."

The hard edge in Samantha's voice cut through Maggie's panic. Her solicitor was a staunch advocate for abused women. Smart, tough and dogged, her record for success was unparalleled. She wouldn't recommend anything that would compromise Emily's safety.

Maggie forced herself to calm down. Closing her eyes, she took in several deep breaths. "What do you think we should do?"

"First, we'll tell him Emily can't travel to England because she can't be pulled out of school. However, if he flies over to New Jersey, he can see her there."

"Lee won't go for that. It's football season. Even though he's injured, he can't afford to spend time jetting back and forth to the States."

"That's what we're banking on. So when he rejects that offer, we'll offer a compromise."

Maggie frowned. "What kind of compromise?"

"We propose that he and Emily talk via Skype. It's a court-approved means of communication which, conveniently, keeps Lee and Emily on opposite sides of the Atlantic. We offer to set up a schedule, saying regular face time is better than a one-off visit."

"What if he doesn't accept the proposal? He could go straight for a custody challenge."

"Lee's solicitor will agree that it's better to take things one step at a time and see how this goes before taking up the court's time with another custody hearing. Especially given Lee's lack of interest in Emily to date. Under the circumstances, this is a more than reasonable offer."

"Okay." Maggie sighed, knowing she had no choice. "Email me the best dates for you and Emily and I'll take it from there."

After she'd hung up, Maggie sat for a few minutes, rubbing her chest and willing her erratic heartbeat to settle down. Though her lawyer's plan was solid, Maggie knew if Lee pushed hard to see Emily, she couldn't refuse. Perhaps she'd get lucky and Patty would see through his charming facade more quickly than Maggie had, preferably before the wedding, making the whole thing moot.

In the meantime, she should get those dates to her lawyer.

Maggie threw back the covers, grabbed her dressing gown off the chair and hurried downstairs to the office. As she clicked on her calendar, her phone rang again.

Bloody hell. Had Lee turned down their offer already?

"Don't tell me he refused," she snapped.

The silence at the other end made her look at the caller ID.

She closed her eyes in embarrassment. Jake. "I'm sorry. I thought you were someone else."

"I wanted to catch you before you started work. Is this a bad time?" She could hear his unspoken question—who else would call her so early in the morning?

"No. It's lovely to hear from you…" Her words faded away.

"But…?"

"It's not you. I just had a phone call from my lawyer. About my ex."

"Oh." That clearly wasn't the answer he'd expected. His tone changed, deepened. "Are you all right? What's going on?"

His concern warmed her, chasing away the chill that had gripped her insides since hearing Samantha's voice.

"It's nothing, really," she demurred.

"If you don't want to tell me, that's fine. But maybe I can help, or at least lend you my shoulder. It's pretty broad."

Her lips curved. "That's sweet." His muffled groan widened her smile. "I'm sorry. I know blokes hate to be called sweet."

"I'd rather hear trash talk than…sweet or cute."

"I reserve my trash-talking for jerk ex-husbands."

"Are you going to tell me how he ruined your morning?"

Maggie grimaced. "He's demanding to see Emily."

Jake said nothing as she explained what had happened. When she finished, he swore.

"There's nothing you can do to stop him, despite what he did to you?"

"Not really. The courts bend over backward to ensure children have access to both parents. My only hope is this dies down as quickly as it blew up. Meanwhile, I have to play along."

"Your plan sounds perfect. It meets his demands and buys you time while you wait to see what happens."

She savored his support. "I hope so."

"Do you need an American lawyer? I could get one for you."

"Thank you, but no. Even though we're over here, Emily's custody is governed by English law."

"If the situation changes, let me know."

"Definitely." Maggie yawned. "Sorry. I don't do well with abrupt starts to the day. I prefer to ease into wakefulness."

"I'll try to remember that." Jake's deep chuckle made her toes curl.

"So…um…why did you call?" She rolled her eyes at her teenager-like stammering.

"I wanted to say good morning." His deep voice slid over her like a caress.

Her heart thunked. "Good morning."

"I also wanted to make sure you haven't changed your mind about our date."

"Definitely not. I'm looking forward to it."

"Me, too. I've got to run. The defensive coach has called an extra practice to go over some plays before we fly out to Ottawa."

"Keep your head up. I'd really like to see you in one piece on Sunday night."

Jake laughed. "No new black eyes, I promise."

Once she'd hung up, Maggie swiveled her office chair slowly from side to side, relishing the return of the warm, happy feeling she'd had when she woke up.

A floorboard creaked overhead, breaking up the reverie and reminding her that she had to get those dates to Samantha. With a sigh, she checked the calendar on her computer screen, grabbed a pen and started to make notes.

"IT'S NOT AS bad as it looks."

Jake wasn't about to admit the fifteen stitches in his right cheek, administered without anesthetic during the second period of last night's game, hurt like hell. Even though the cut was the result of an errant high stick, rather than a fight, he didn't want to give Maggie anything to worry about. He jammed his hands into the back pockets of his jeans and leaned against her front door.

The porch light illuminated Maggie's face. Concern shadowed her dark eyes. "Well, it looks dreadful. I can't believe you carried on playing."

"It's part of the game. Don't let them see they've got to you."

She rolled her eyes. "Have you at least taken some painkillers?" She didn't wait for his answer. "Silly question. It would probably break some part of your precious Code."

"Actually, I ran out of ibuprofen."

Her lovely lips twisted wryly. "Come through to the kitchen, tough guy, and I'll get you some tablets."

As she led the way down the hall, she asked, "Are you okay to go out? We could order some pizza and go to Greg's Steak House another night."

Though that was exactly what he'd prefer, he shook his head. "That's not the special date I'd planned."

"A special date is one we both enjoy. You won't enjoy eating at a fancy restaurant when you don't feel good."

"I'll be fine once I've had those painkillers."

"Uh-huh." She gave him the same look she often gave her daughter. "If it helps, Tracy has taken Emily and her friend to the movies and won't be back for a couple of hours."

He grinned. "A cozy evening in with pizza sounds great. Sure you don't mind?"

"Positive." Maggie tossed him a menu. "I'll get those tablets. Why don't you order a couple of fully loaded pizzas? No anchovies, olives or pineapple on mine."

"Okay." Jake pulled out his phone and put in an order. Once they'd confirmed a delivery time, he snagged a chair and sat at the kitchen table.

He'd been worried about Maggie's reaction to his slashed face. They'd spoken every night while he was on the road, so he knew she'd watched the Cats games on TV. He also knew that she still didn't like the hits or the fights. She'd had plenty to say about the return bout with Stemgarder in Ottawa.

Logically, he knew she didn't equate what he did during a game with the man he was off-ice. But, where Maggie was concerned, Jake's mind wasn't logical. Her disapproving expression popped into his brain at the worst times. The harder he checked, the more aggressive his play, the more she haunted him, causing him to second-guess his actions. Inevitably, he then made mistakes. It had to stop before they became costly mistakes. If he didn't fix this craziness, his season would be a bust. That couldn't happen.

Focus on the positive.

Their growing relationship was one hell of a positive. Not just physically—though the passion between them was hot. He liked the way she made him feel. Maggie was good company; he was able to relax with her, have fun. She was the only one outside of his parents and the Jelineks who could make him laugh at himself.

More than that, he admired and respected her. She was a good person. A good friend. A good mother.

A good woman.

It would take time for her to overcome her past completely, but she was worth the wait. Besides, he wasn't free of his own ghosts.

Maggie walked back into the kitchen and handed him a little white bottle, then poured him a glass of water. "Take the maximum dose while I get out some plates."

"Thanks." He swallowed four pills. "The pizza will be here shortly."

"Good. You'll feel better when you've eaten."

He pulled her onto his lap. "I'll feel better when I've had a proper hello."

She leaned forward to kiss the tip of his nose. "Hello."

"That's not a proper hello." He tilted her back, cradling her in his arms, and covered her mouth with his.

Desire slid through his veins as easily as a blade on fresh ice. His body reacted instantly. The aches from last night's game fled his muscles, leaving fiery heat in their place.

Damn, he wanted her naked.

He needed to be buried deep inside her, almost more than he needed his next breath.

He wanted to lose himself in her until none of their problems mattered. Until nothing mattered but bringing them both to satisfaction.

Her hands moved restlessly over his body. She wanted this as much as he did.

Wanted him.

Triumphant, he pulled her closer, caressing her through her sweater. It wasn't enough. He wanted to sample her delicious curves.

The sweater had to go. And her jeans.

And whatever lay beneath.

His shirt fell open, thanks to Maggie's nimble fingers. Her fingertips traced his collarbone to the hollow at the base of his neck, then dipped lower to stroke his chest.

His hand slid beneath her sweater, encountering only soft, smooth, bare skin. His fingers trailed over her flat stomach. She moaned softly, urging him on, but he lingered only a moment before heading toward the curve of her breasts.

He needed to taste her, every inch of her. He ached to trail his mouth, his tongue, over every mound and valley.

The chair tilted precariously and Maggie grabbed his shoulders. Jake planted his feet on the floor, righting them. The moment passed. They remained wrapped in each other's arms, pulse rates slowing, passion cooling.

The doorbell rang.

Jake swore.

Maggie chuckled softly.

"Don't move. I'll be right back." He set her aside gently and hurried to the door, buttoning his shirt as he went.

Thankfully, the delivery guy wasn't chatty, handing over the pies with barely a grunt. Jake rushed back to the kitchen, tossed the two boxes onto the table, dropped into his chair and settled Maggie back onto his lap. "Now, where were we?"

"Your dinner will get cold." She buried her face against his neck.

"It'll be the only cold thing in this kitchen."

"You have no idea," she murmured huskily, before nipping her way down the corded muscle in his neck.

His pulse jerked as she swiped her tongue delicately across the sensitive hollow behind his collarbone. The banked fire within him flared back to life and roared through his veins.

He caught her chin in his hand, gently turning and tilting her face until her lips were a breath away from his.

She closed the gap. Damn, she was one hell of a kisser.

Flames of desire licked along every nerve in his body until the endings sizzled.

Suddenly, he knew if they continued like this, for even a moment longer, there would be no stopping.

Gently he pulled his mouth away from hers.

Maggie gave a little mewl of protest, which he soothed with a brush of his lips.

Their ragged breathing sounded loud in the silent kitchen.

He had to know how she felt. "Maggie?"

She lifted her gaze, looking him square in the eye.

He stumbled over his words, unsure how to say what he wanted.

Laying a finger across his lips, she silenced him. "I'm ready."

"You are?" His heart contracted.

"Aren't you?"

"Yes. No. I mean…" What the hell did he mean? "I'm not just talking about kissing, though that's uh… great." Damn. He'd never had a problem getting his words out before.

Maybe because it hadn't mattered so much before.

Satisfaction curved her lips. "Oh?"

"I want you to be sure. No pressure."

She shifted on his lap, rekindling his straining erection. "Thank you for being patient. For being prepared to give me more time. I know it seems a sudden about-face, but I did a lot of thinking while you were away. I'm ready."

"Are you sure?"

"Yes. Are you?"

"Hell, yes." *What happened to the smooth Bad Boy?*

"So that's not a puck in your pocket?" She brushed her fingertips gently across his forehead. "What about your face? It must hurt."

Jake wanted to deny it, but mentioning his gashed cheek made his face pulse with pain. He gave a disgruntled shrug.

"It doesn't have to be tonight," Maggie soothed.

"But starting tomorrow we play three games in four nights, then head back out on the road for a week."

"It'll be worth the wait."

"For sure." But he didn't want to wait.

"You're pouting again, Jake."

"I don't pout."

"Of course not." Damn woman was making fun of him.

"When do you get back?"

"The twentieth."

"Then it looks like we have an extra-special date on the twenty-first."

The most important date of his life.

"TONIGHT'S HEADLINES AGAIN...AUTHORITES raided the Arkansas pharmacy allegedly behind an internet steroid ring. It's believed a number of big-name athletes from football, basketball and hockey will be implicated."

Jake set aside his paperback thriller and frowned at the TV in his hotel room. No matter how many times they said it, he couldn't believe any player he knew would take performance-enhancing drugs. Hell, most of them refused to take cold meds and painkillers.

As the anchor signed off, Jake realized that the end of the news meant it was almost midnight. If his roommate—a sophomore defenseman called Taylor "Mad Dog" Madden—wasn't here soon, he'd be in big trouble.

The team had flown into Tampa yesterday to prepare for tomorrow night's game against the Lightning, the last on their road trip. With a strict midnight curfew, most veteran players had opted for a quiet night. But the younger guys had headed out for a little excitement.

A familiar double knock sounded on his door. He rose and answered.

"We've got a problem." Tru strode into the room. "Blake's not back yet."

"Neither's Mad Dog. This isn't like him. He's a good kid."

"Blake, too. I have a bad feeling about this."

Jake did, too. "Were they both with JB?"

"Yeah. Your warning to Larocque to cool it didn't work."

Damn know-it-all rookie. "They miss curfew and Coach will bench them."

His friend paced the room. "Do you know where they went?"

Before Jake could reply, Tru's cell rang.

He answered. "Where the hell are you, Blake?" Tru's expression turned grim as he listened. "We're on our way. Hang tight until we get there." He hung up. "Damn Larocque."

"What the hell has JB done?" Jake put on his Timberland boots, grabbed his leather jacket and followed Tru out.

"Mouthed off at some girl's boyfriend. Got into a fight."

Jake swore as he jabbed the elevator button. "The Cats will suspend him. Worse, if the League finds out."

"The nightclub manager's threatened to call the cops. If he does, the media will be all over it. Let's hope no one's tweeted it yet or put a video on Facebook."

"It'll take some sharp skating to get this to go away quietly. Despite his dumb-ass behavior, the team needs Larocque."

Luckily, there was a cab waiting and traffic was

light. On the way to the trendy nightclub, they hammered out an action plan and checked out the social-media sites. Nothing had shown up yet, but it was only a matter of time.

There was no sign of the media when they arrived. The security guy recognized them and opened the door.

"I hustled them out of there and upstairs to the manager's office as soon as the trouble started. Didn't want a YouTube video of the kid's behavior going viral. Hope you can get this done—I've got money on the Cats for the Cup." The heavyset man lowered his voice. "The other guy's an ass."

They thanked him for his help and promised him tickets for the game.

The scene in the manager's office was tense. Too much drink. Too much testosterone. Mad Dog and Blake had JB pinned to a chair.

"What's the problem here?" Jake asked pleasantly.

An overweight man in a Rangers shirt said, "I've got no beef with you, Bad Boy."

The guy had recognized him. At least Jake's reputation was good for something.

Jake jerked his head toward JB. "His problems are my problems."

"He made a pass at my wife," the man blustered.

"Yeah." A skinny bleached blonde stood. She smoothed her painted-on jeans and adjusted her low-cut top deliberately to give him a prime view of her spray-tanned cleavage. "He called me a bitch when I said no."

Her husband grunted. "He kept saying the Blue

Shirts sucked." He sounded more insulted by JB diss-
ing his team than hitting on his woman.

"Don't you love crosstown rivalry?" Jake ignored
the woman and focused on her husband, keeping his
tone casual. "It's what makes hockey a great sport—
loyal supporters like…" He waited for the guy to give
his name.

"Frank."

"Bet Frank's been a fan since way back when, huh?"

"Damn straight, Bad Boy. Haven't missed a game
in twenty years. I was at the Garden when we raised
the Cup in '94." The barrel chest puffed up with pride,
like he'd been on the ice himself.

"See, Jean-Baptiste, this is the type of loyal fan
hockey needs to nurture." Mad Dog's hand clamped
over JB's mouth. "I'm sure, as lovers of the great game,
we can make this go away. Right, Frank?"

The guy was caught. If he disagreed, he'd look stupid. "Out of respect for you, Bad Boy, I'll make a deal.
But you gotta teach the kid manners."

"Don't worry, we will." Jake heard JB struggling.
"We feel bad about your good lady, so we'll treat you
both to dinner." He pulled out a card. "What's your favorite restaurant, ma'am?" At her response, he scrib-
bled on the back, then handed her the card. "You give
this to the owner and tell him the tab's on me."

The blonde was instantly soothed. "Now, hon, isn't
that nice?"

"Frank, how about on-the-glass seats for the next
Rangers game here?"

The man agreed readily.

Now the hard part. Even though it would cost him personally, Jake had to keep Larocque's name out of this. The kid should suffer the consequences of his mistake, but Jake had to consider the good of the team. Adam's face flashed through his mind, strengthening his resolve.

"I need a favor, Frank." Jake smiled. "If anyone asks about tonight, the only name you mention is mine."

"But…"

"We're both older guys, Frank. We know about youthful mistakes." He sent him a knowing look. "We don't want JB to swing for a stupid, drunken move, do we?"

Reluctantly, Frank agreed, in return for pictures taken with Jake. He also promised not to post anything to the internet until after the game tomorrow night.

"What about my damages?" the manager whined.

Tru stepped in, wallet ready.

By the time Mad Dog and Blake had bundled JB into the back of a cab, it was almost 1:00 a.m. They threatened Larocque with duct tape if he spoke before they got back to the hotel.

Once there, they hurried up to Jake's room.

Sobered up with strong coffee, JB apologized. "I've been a total jerk. I'd have been sent back to the minors forever if I'd ended up in jail."

"Worse, you'd have been branded trouble." Jake didn't pull his punches. The kid had to learn his lesson fast. "One more misstep and you'd have been cut loose. We're not saying you can't have fun, but this kind of crap ends careers."

"And mine has barely started." Jean-Baptiste hung his head. "I know I've made things bad for Mad Dog and Blake when all you guys were doing was trying to keep me out of trouble. I'll shoulder the blame with Max for you missing curfew."

Looked like there was a good streak beneath the arrogance.

"We won't say a word, for their sakes," Tru said solemnly. "For the team's sake. It's just between us, on one condition."

Relief filled JB's dark eyes. "Name it."

Jake inhaled deeply. This was a big commitment. The best plan, but a huge responsibility. Did he have what it took?

If he could prevent Jean-Baptiste from making the same mistakes as he had, the angst would be worth it. His resolve hardened. "For the rest of the season, you're living with me."

CHILDREN PLAYED HOCKEY like seagulls diving for food.

Maggie bit back a smile as the knot of masked and padded skaters swarmed around the puck. She shifted her bum on the cold bench and let her mind wander to tomorrow night.

The twenty-first.

As Tracy was on a date, Maggie had arranged for Emily to stay the night at Amy's, so there'd be no need to rush her time with Jake.

Somehow she didn't think he'd want to rush. Her smile broke free.

The coach blew his whistle for the end of the session, interrupting her heated thoughts.

She rose and headed to the gate to wait for Emily to come off the ice.

"Bad Boy is up to his old tricks."

Maggie started at the comment from the clique of too-rich, too-skinny women who sat near the glass. Her stomach roiled.

"I saw the headlines," another voice said.

What headlines?

A third voice. "He can park his skates under my bed anytime."

What bloody headlines?

"Did you see the piece of trash he fought over?" The first woman again. "A model? Who for? Trailer Park Monthly?"

Shrill laughter, like witches' cackles, set Maggie's teeth on edge.

Woman? Fight? Two words that sounded like history repeating itself.

A chill ran through her.

"I almost got a goal." Emily came off the ice bubbling, unaware of her mother's shock.

"Well done, Em." Dazed, she helped her daughter with her skates.

"I'm starving. Is it lunchtime? Can we go to McDonald's?"

"Okay," she mumbled, desperate to get away from the rink.

"You're the best mum ever."

Lunch passed in a blur. Thankfully, Emily didn't

seem to notice anything amiss. Still, Maggie was relieved to pull into the driveway of Tracy's Victorian, so she could get some space to think.

"Is that Jenny's car?" Emily pointed at the red convertible.

"Yes." Jenny must have heard the news, too.

"It's really cool. When I'm a famous hockey player, like Mr. Jake, I want a car like that."

What if the story was true? Emily was already attached to Jake. What would it do to her daughter to discover he wasn't the hero she'd thought?

What it would do to Maggie didn't bear thinking about.

"Don't forget to spray Lysol in your gloves," she called as Emily rushed inside.

Maggie followed slowly, her bones aching with a familiar gloomy weariness, and headed for the kitchen.

Jenny and Tracy sat at the table, their heads bent over a laptop. Her friend's calm contrasted with her sister's disgusted expression.

"Is the story about Jake that bad?" Maggie leaned against the door frame.

Tracy stood and put the kettle on. "*I* think so."

"We should hear Jake's side. There's more to this than what's on a gossip site." Jenny turned the laptop toward Maggie. "You know him. Do you believe a word of this?"

"What's not to believe?" Tracy sniffed. "The woman? The nightclub? The fight?"

Common sense began to replace the panicked fog in Maggie's brain.

Jenny was right—she did know Jake. "We can't condemn him because of his past." She slipped into a seat. "Let's see what this says."

"Fine. But you'll be disappointed."

Her sister's vehemence surprised her. "Why the about-face? You were his biggest fan."

"I thought he'd changed. That he'd be good for you. I didn't realize he's as bad as your jerk ex-husband."

Tracy's comment chased away the last of the fuzziness. "Whatever that story says, Jake's nothing like Lee. Not even close."

If she hadn't been sure of that, she'd never have agreed to take their relationship to the next stage. She certainly wouldn't have trusted him to be around Emily. Jake wasn't violent or obsessively controlling. He accepted when he was wrong and he apologized. Not because it was expected, but because he meant it. More importantly, he treated her with respect.

True, he could be stubborn and overbearing when he believed he was right. He wasn't perfect, but who was?

Jake deserved a fair hearing.

Her heart thumped heavily as she read the on-screen article and saw the grainy cell-phone pictures. "It looks pretty damning."

"You don't believe that trash, do you?" Jenny looked disappointed. "It's a slow news week with Lindsay Lohan in rehab again and Jennifer Aniston finally married, so they've latched onto something that's nothing."

"I know how the media can take a hint of a story and turn it into a full-length novel." Maggie shook her head. "The whole thing just doesn't add up. What has Jake said?"

"Neither he nor the team have made a public statement. They won't want to give the media more fuel for their fire."

Tracy threw up her hands. "There'd be no story at all unless something happened."

"No one's denying *something* happened," Jenny shot back. "Just not what the media are making out. Even if Jake was interested, which he isn't—" she gave Maggie a pointed look "—he could have any woman he wanted. He sure as hell wouldn't go after one like that, especially as she's married."

"And the fight?" Tracy arched an eyebrow.

Maggie thought for a minute. Then it struck her. The Code. Jake was a "white hat." "If there was an altercation, Jake was defending or protecting someone. A friend. A teammate."

"Okay," Tracy acquiesced. The conviction in Maggie's voice must have got through to her sister. "But I still say there's some truth behind the story."

Though Maggie knew in her heart the story couldn't be true, a tiny part of her—the part honed by too many lies—worried her sister might be right.

There wasn't smoke without fire. She hoped whatever the *fire* was, Jake had a really good explanation for it. Otherwise, she'd put her trust, and her heart, in the hands of the wrong kind of bad boy all over again. This time, she didn't think either would recover.

CHAPTER THIRTEEN

"SCORE A GOAL for *us* next time."

Ike's disgust made Jake pedal harder on the stationary bike.

The postgame cooldown was no haven tonight. They'd lost and he'd played the worst game of his career. It was his own fault. His mind hadn't been on the ice but back in New Jersey, worrying about what would happen when Maggie saw the story of last night's mess.

Tru intervened. "We all have bad games."

"I don't." Jake cleared his throat. "I'm sorry, guys. Coach."

"Wouldn't be linked to these headlines, would it?" Max shoved his iPad onto the handlebars. "I don't mean the crap about some NHL star using steroids. Drugs sure as hell haven't enhanced *your* performance."

The story was all over the hockey websites. Damn. Frank had already begun bragging.

"Uh, Coach…"

Jake cut JB off with a glare. He hadn't protected the kid to have him blow it apart. "The guy was a jerk." He tried to sound cocky. "No way I'd hit on his wife. Look at her."

The coach wasn't fooled. "This little party must have broken curfew."

He couldn't deny that. "It won't happen again."

"Veterans like you should set a good example, not break the rules."

Hell. Was he going to be benched? It was one thing to ride the pine when your play sucked—there was no denying his had tonight—but it was something different when you were taking the blame for someone else's idiocy.

Worse, he hated seeing the coach's disappointment in him. He respected Max. They all did. He'd been a hell of a defenseman in his day and had earned his stripes behind the bench with two Stanley Cup rings to his credit.

Max crooked a finger at Jake and Tru. "You two. Outside. Now."

They exchanged uneasy glances as the coach stalked out.

"Bad Boy?" Concern was etched on Jean-Baptiste's face.

"It'll be cool. His bark's worse than his bite," he reassured the kid. "Never again, right?"

JB nodded. This was a good lesson for the rookie. One that had better stick.

Max stood by the laundry room. "Inside."

Once he'd closed the door, the coach grunted, "You gonna tell me what happened?"

"What do you mean?" Tru asked cautiously.

"I'm not an idiot," Max growled. "This is a bunch of crap. You know why?"

Jake shook his head.

"I checked you out before I agreed to bring you into

the Cats. Wanted to be sure you wouldn't be a problem, given all the press. Know what I found out?"

Unsure how to answer, Jake shook his head again.

"First, *you* don't break curfew. Never have." The coach jabbed his finger in Jake's chest. "Second, *you* don't fight off-ice. On top of that, I know that *you* ordered room service at eight and made a phone call at eleven-thirty. Do I need to continue?"

Stunned, Jake shook his head for a third time, feeling like a damn bobblehead doll.

"Larocque wasn't in his room at curfew. What did he do?"

They had to come clean. "You're right."

He and Tru explained, including how Mad Dog and Blake had risked their own necks to rescue JB. Jake finished by telling him their solution.

The coach raised an eyebrow. "I'm still punishing him. JB needs to know he can't disregard rules."

"Fair enough."

Max pointed to Tru. "Get cleaned up. I need to talk with Bad Boy."

What about? Jake's stomach tightened.

Once Tru had gone, the coach said, "Clear your head of whatever the hell is bugging you by the time we hit the ice again, or you're in the press box. Got it?"

"Definitely."

On the way home, the worries that had plagued Jake throughout the game resurfaced. Would Maggie see beyond the story to the truth? Would she believe in Jake, as Max had, or in Bad Boy's reputation? He wanted to trust her, but deep in his gut he couldn't help doubting.

Dreading Maggie's reaction had made him a step too slow on every move and take a second too long on every decision. He'd played like crap. Again.

Which raised a disturbing question. Would his good woman cost him his dream?

COULD THIS MISERABLE day get any worse?

When they landed in New Jersey, Ike took Jake aside. "If you can't handle a relationship and play hockey, you need to choose which is more important."

Like he didn't know that already. "The problem isn't Maggie—it's me. My focus." Jake glared at him. "I can handle it."

His friend shook his head. "We need you with us one hundred percent. Park this personal junk until after the play-offs."

It wasn't that simple. Maggie was on his mind all the time. In his blood.

But Jake knew something had to change. "Give me a few more games. If it doesn't improve, I'll rethink it. Okay?"

Ike didn't look convinced, but agreed to back off.

As Jake drove home, the goaltender's parting shot echoed in his brain. "You'll end up having to choose."

Sweat trickled down his spine. He didn't want to be forced to make a choice between hockey and Maggie.

Because there could only be one answer.

He pulled into his driveway and turned off the ignition. The dark, empty house loomed ahead of him. For once, it wasn't a welcoming sight but a reminder of what he had to lose if he didn't resolve the situation with Maggie.

It was almost 4:00 a.m. With tiredness tugging at every muscle and sinew in his aching body, he was reluctant to move. Sighing, he lowered his forehead to his crossed arms on the steering wheel and closed his eyes. Just for a moment.

He jolted awake, heart racing. Vestiges of his nightmare filled his sleep-fogged brain. Adam. The accident. Over and over again, like a movie clip stuck on eternal replay. Damn, he hadn't had one of those since he'd come back to Jersey. Had the stress of the past few days triggered something in his brain?

Jake scrubbed his hand over his face. The clock on the dash said 7:05 a.m. Exhausted, but unwilling to risk another nightmare, he threw open the door. Stretching out the kinks in his stiff limbs, he let the rising sun and crisp air chase away his dark thoughts.

As his home came into sharper relief in the gray dawn light, so did his mind. He wouldn't rest easy until he'd faced the music with Maggie. God knew his play wouldn't be worth a damn, either. Good or bad, he had to know where he stood.

His chest squeezed at the thought that this might be the end, but he stalked back to his M-Class, determined to find out.

The lights were on at Tracy's house when he pulled up. Maggie was probably getting Emily ready for school.

Sure enough, as he walked up the steps to the porch, the front door swung open and Emily came charging out. She grinned when she saw him, yelling a greeting before running to join the other children on the corner waiting for the school bus.

He turned and saw Maggie waiting in the doorway. Though she quickly smoothed the surprise from her face, the wariness in her brown eyes made his stomach plummet to his Nikes. This didn't look good.

"Good morning." She gave a half smile but didn't invite him in.

No point tiptoeing around the issue. "I hope it's not too early. I thought I'd stop by and clear the air about what happened in Tampa."

"Okay." Her neutral tone made it impossible to gauge her thoughts.

"I should start at the beginning."

"Good idea."

"It's not what it seems."

"Of course not." She wasn't giving him an inch.

"It's complicated." He paced the porch. "The team has strict rules about curfew."

Her expression remained inscrutable as he told her about JB, but softened when she heard how he and Tru had bailed out the rookie. He finished by saying, "I don't cheat. I wouldn't mess with someone's wife. If you believe nothing else, know I sure as hell wouldn't disrespect you like that."

"I knew you'd have a credible explanation." This time her smile broke free.

"You did?" His pulse kicked. He stopped pacing and stood in front of her.

"I wasn't sure at first," she admitted. "The story and pictures looked pretty convincing."

He grimaced. "For sure."

"But the more I thought about it, the more I realized something was off.

"You did?" Her faith took him by surprise, rekindling the hope in his chest.

"That's not how you operate. You'd never mess with someone else's girlfriend. And though you fight when your Code demands—" she rolled her eyes to show she still thought it dumb "—that kind of fight didn't make sense. What I couldn't work out was why you'd be out clubbing the night before a game. You wouldn't risk jeopardizing your performance. You take your fitness, your readiness to play, too seriously." She shrugged. "Like I said, it didn't add up."

Jake stopped in front of her. Speechless. Maggie had seen through the hype, looked beyond the obvious—his image, his reputation. She'd believed in him.

He shook his head. Was he dreaming? *Don't let me wake up.*

"Is something wrong?" She looked worried.

"No. I just can't get over it."

"Why? You don't believe everything you read?"

He laughed. "If I did, my ego would need to be wheeled into the room ahead of me."

"I'm not touching that comment with a barge pole." Her tone was prim, but the twinkle in her dark eyes was not.

Even if the whole scene seemed surreal, his body's

predictable reaction was genuine. He forced a casual tone. "So are we still on for tonight?"

"Of course." She bit her lip. "Unless you've changed your mind."

"Hell, no. I'll pick you up at eight."

He leaned forward and brushed a kiss across her lips. Without waiting for her response, he turned and jogged down the steps to his M-Class. He couldn't resist sneaking a glance in his rearview mirror as he headed down the drive. Maggie had paused halfway through the door. She fluttered her fingers at him, then disappeared inside.

He couldn't wait for tonight.

What a difference a day makes.

Twenty-four hours ago, Jake had been worried about having to choose between Maggie and hockey. Now his biggest concern was if Maggie would think he was moving too fast if he ordered their dessert to go.

Not that the problems in Tampa had been forgotten. There had been a brief media flurry that afternoon when he and the Ice Cats had put out a carefully worded joint statement that neither confirmed nor denied the story. When there was no further comment from anyone involved, including Frank and his wife, it had all died down.

Still, he'd been nervous picking up Maggie. He'd half expected her to call and cancel but she hadn't. His pulse had jolted when he'd seen her silky red dress, with its shiny black buttons running down the front, and the matching spiked red heels. The conversation on the way to the restaurant had been stilted, nervous, but had eased as they'd ordered their meals. By the time the main course had been served, the atmosphere had warmed considerably.

As the server cleared their dishes, Maggie's gaze caught his. She must have read the message in his eyes because her cheeks tinted a delicate pink. She bit her full bottom lip, sending a spear of desire through his body.

Oh, yeah. Things were definitely heating up.

He shifted to ease the tightness in his pants.

"These all look delicious." She sighed as she closed the dessert menu. "But I couldn't manage another bite."

"We could take dessert with us. Jenny says their tiramisu is to die for."

Amber sparks danced in her dark brown eyes. "Sounds good."

The tension during the drive home was for a whole different reason.

Jake did his best not to break the speed limit, but didn't crawl, either. He didn't want to risk anything changing Maggie's mind. As he pulled up in front of his house and turned off the engine, his heart thundered in his ears. "How about some coffee to go with that tiramisu?"

His voice sounded raw, giving the question a suggestive edge.

The hitch in her breathing told him she understood what he was really asking.

He remained still, waiting for her reply.

"That sounds...lovely." Her husky voice was like a caress.

He grabbed the door handle. "Let's go."

She didn't wait for him to open her door, joining him at the foot of the steps. Hand in hand, they dashed up to the porch. She laughed as he fumbled with the key.

Her laughter faded as the front door closed behind them. Slowly, he pulled her toward him, until they stood toe-to-toe in the dark hallway.

His head dipped until his lips were a breath away from hers. "Last chance to back out."

Her free hand trailed up his chest and neck to rest along his jaw. "There have been an awful lot of rumors about you."

His heart thudded. "Yes," he said cautiously.

"One should never trust the media," she murmured. "One should always go straight to the source." Her thumb danced lightly across his lower lip.

The gentle caress was nearly his undoing. Fire rushed through him, setting his nerve endings alight.

"Yes." He trapped her thumb between his teeth, then flicked it with his tongue. Her soft gasp confirmed her desire for him. As did the pulse that throbbed at the base of her throat. And the subtle scent which rose from her heated skin.

Calling on what vestiges of self-control remained, he waited impatiently for her to answer his original question.

"I think it's time I found out the truth, don't you, Bad Boy?"

"Yes, ma'am."

THE HOCKEY PRESS might rave about Jake's puck handling but, in Maggie's opinion, his mouth was as talented as his hands.

The man could certainly kiss.

She could only imagine what his lovemaking would be like. Actually, that's all she'd been imagining since he'd left on his road trip. Now she was moments from finding out.

Somehow, she suspected her imagination didn't come close.

His mouth savored hers. His lips and tongue explored and tasted. Seduced and teased. Flames of passion flickered urgently in her veins. Wanton desire pooled deep within her.

She shifted restlessly, wanting more yet unable to whisper even the smallest demand. Her tongue danced against his in invitation, full of sultry promise.

He read her need perfectly.

One calloused fingertip traced a heated trail from her flushed cheek, behind her ear, down the sensitized skin of her neck to that spot where her pulse thrummed. Then it dipped lower, along her breastbone to the hollow beneath.

He backed her against the front door and pressed closer. His body heat surrounded her. His musky, masculine scent filled her nostrils. She wrapped one leg around his muscular thigh, aligning her aching core against his erection.

When his mouth left hers to follow the downward journey of his finger, a soft mewl escaped. She felt his lips curve against her throat as she arched to give him better access.

Sparks shot through her as he nibbled on the cords of her neck. Desire rippled through the pools of heat within when his tongue laved the bones of her shoulder. Delicious shivers danced along her spine as his warm breath caressed the shadowy vale between her breasts.

Her buttons melted away. The dress slipped open, draping and framing her body.

Jake's fingers became busy once more, stroking the length of her back, exploring the ridges of her hips. Cupping the curve of her bottom.

Maggie thrust her fingers through his thick hair, savoring the silky feel before heading lower to grip his broad shoulders.

His cotton shirt was an unwelcome barrier. Her fingers fumbled with the buttons, making her groan in frustration. Jake reached up, fisted the material and tugged. The rip echoed in the silent room, followed by the *click-click-click* of buttons showering onto the hardwood floor.

She smiled with satisfaction as the expanse of his chest lay bare, not wasting a second before embarking on a thorough exploration of the sleek skin.

Her heart tightened as she encountered the scarred ridges from the accident. Her lips honored every one. Maggie had barely finished before Jake began his own journey of discovery.

His tongue dipped beneath the lacy edge of her bra, tracing its shape across the upper curve of her breast, down into the valley between and up the other side.

Her dress slipped off her shoulders and down her body, the cool silk whispering over her heated skin like a caress. He dragged down one bra strap, then the other with his teeth. His tongue returned to taste the mounds, edging the lace lower with each pass until it rested on her hardened nipples. The soft, damp fabric rasped against the sensitized buds.

Then, that too had gone.

Maggie started when the hot cavern of his mouth surrounded one taut tip, then the other.

Jagged bolts of white heat speared through her system as he suckled. Wave upon wave of liquid need flooded her molten core as he nipped.

When his tongue flicked out at an aching peak, she gasped at the intense, exquisite sensation. Her grip tightened on his shoulders as he pushed her closer to the edge of sanity.

Not enough. She wanted to feel him buried deep within her.

As one, they sank slowly to the floor. Her thighs cradled him. Her breasts cushioned him. Every inch of her body welcomed him.

His mouth found hers once more. Their tongues danced. Urgency overcame her.

Her fingers tore at unwanted clothing. His palms kneaded her naked flesh.

Hot and hard, his erection strained against her.

Soft and damp, her mound rose to meet him.

Desperate, she rubbed against him. Unbearably delicious friction.

It wasn't enough.

Once again, he understood what she needed.

His hand slipped between them, discovering the sensitive nub hidden in her moist folds. He knew how gently or how hard to stroke, when to tease and when to drive her passion.

Just when she thought she couldn't take any more, his finger slid inside. And nearly drove her over the edge.

Now, Jake!

She barely noticed him pulling a condom from his wallet, though it seemed to take forever for him to rip the packet open with his teeth and put the bloody thing on.

With one swift thrust, he was inside her.

He groaned. She sighed.

They both stilled, their breathing harsh in the silent hallway.

He fit perfectly, as if he'd been made for her and she for him. For the first time, she understood what it meant to be truly joined with a man, as one in body and soul.

Slowly, almost tentatively, they began to move.

Then desire and need overtook them, pushing the pace, the intensity.

Harder. Faster. Hotter.

Her arms wound round his neck, pulling his mouth to hers. His hands slipped beneath her bottom, driving him deeper.

Together, they sped toward completion.

Together, they reached the pinnacle of pleasure.

Maggie arched against Jake as her climax overwhelmed her. She felt him stiffen, holding her tighter still. A kaleidoscope of colors whirled through her brain. Nerve endings fizzed and sparked. Deep within, her core pulsed and throbbed. Deep within, Jake's hardness pulsed and throbbed, too.

She'd been right. Her imagination hadn't even come close.

CHAPTER FOURTEEN

JAKE WAS IN heaven. Correction—heaven was in his arms.

Sunlight streamed through the bedroom window, bathing him and Maggie in its warm glow. Their legs were tangled together. Her lush breast filled his hand, her pebbled nipple pressed against his palm. The curve of her butt fit perfectly against his groin.

His nose was buried in the mass of brown curls spread invitingly across his pillow. He inhaled, drawing in her sweet scent. The nape of her neck enticed him. He couldn't resist. Shifting slightly, he ran his tongue down the soft skin. *Delicious.*

Though he'd tasted every delectable inch of her last night, he couldn't get enough.

Something new for him.

He'd always enjoyed women—their company the perfect antidote to too many hours surrounded by testosterone. The sex was invariably good, but never enough to stay long. Have fun, move on.

Maggie shifted in her sleep, her bottom settling more snugly against his hardness.

He went from sated to insatiable.

Something new, for sure.

He'd never wanted with such ferocity before. He nibbled at her shoulder.

They'd only been together a few hours. After a few days, this urgency to make love with her would surely subside.

Her foot rubbed against his calf. His erection twitched.

Then again, maybe not.

His fingers trailed over her breasts, edging lower to her stomach, her hip and the top of her thighs. Maggie murmured and shifted again.

He teased, played, dipping into her moist heat, not quite reaching her nub of desire.

She moved restlessly, urging him.

He resisted her demands, wanting her to be ready for him.

Her eyes opened, dark pools lit with golden flames.

"Jake." Her voice was husky with arousal.

Slipping his finger into her slick core, he stroked the hidden bud with his thumb.

Maggie arched with pleasure. "I want you. All of you."

And he wanted her. All of her.

Grabbing a condom, he sheathed himself, then sank deep into her hot wetness. Her muscles tightened around him, claiming possession. He was a willing captive.

In moments, Maggie cried out her release. He followed immediately after.

Definitely something new.

Something he could want…for the rest of his life.

JAKE WAS A much nicer wake-up call than a ringing phone, Maggie thought as she surfaced from sleep a second time. She squinted at the clock.

Eleven-thirty!

Well, her sleep had been disturbed. Heat filled her cheeks as she recalled how passionately she'd been disturbed.

Oh, my God. She'd been wanton. She sat up, clutching the sheet to her chest.

Jake raised himself on one elbow and glared at the phone. It stopped ringing. He leaned over, smoothing a curl from her forehead. "Sorry if that woke you."

Her heart skipped. "I can't believe I overslept."

"You had a very late night." Fire smoldered in his gaze. "Or a very early morning."

Heat raced through her body, making it tingle and ache. Her womb tightened with need.

Again? She couldn't believe it. Sex had always been pleasant. Nothing special. Nothing earth-shattering. Until last night, when the earth had definitely shattered.

And she'd discovered an insatiable craving for Jake.

Maggie forced her mind to ignore her need to lick her way down his broad chest…again. "You could have answered."

"They'll call back if it's important." He shrugged. "What are your plans today?"

"Emily's staying with a friend, so I'm free." She paused, not wanting to sound too forward. "Unless you have other plans."

He grinned. "Practice is at two. Until then, I'm yours. What do you want to do?"

Her mind shouted several decadent suggestions. But before she could answer, Jake's stomach rumbled loudly.

"Looks like we're having breakfast." He smiled wryly. "What's your pleasure—in bed or at IHOP?"

She leaned back against the pillows, licking her lips slowly. "Breakfast in bed."

"Your wish is my command." Aqua sparks leaped in his blue eyes.

"Now, there's a thought."

His head dipped toward her lips, only to be halted by his growling stomach.

He moaned. "I'll be back shortly."

He got out of bed. Maggie savored the play of smooth skin over taut muscles as he pulled on a pair of jogging bottoms.

When he'd gone, she rushed to the bathroom to freshen up. She groaned as she looked in the mirror. She'd hoped for sexily sleep tousled, not "dragged through a hedge."

She'd barely hopped back into bed when Jake appeared with a breakfast tray.

He looked chagrined. "It's not a great selection—the refrigerator's bare because I was on the road. I had enough milk for your tea, though."

Maggie wrapped her hands around the steaming mug and sipped. Just how she liked it. She was touched he'd remembered—Lee had never bothered. "Perfect."

Jake drew her attention back to the tray. "Muffins,

peanut butter, cheese, bananas and strawberry jelly. In any combination you like."

The phone rang again.

He frowned. "I'd better get this, in case it's one of the Cats."

"Of course." She nodded, then selected a banana.

Maggie realized pretty quickly that the caller was JB and there was a problem.

Jake's frustration came through as he covered the mouthpiece. "I'm sorry. I forgot I insisted the kid moves in today. I could put him off, but…"

"It's okay," she cut in, smiling. "I understand."

"Are you sure? I'll be done in time for our date, but I had other plans for today."

"You're pouting again." She touched his lower lip. "Why don't I stay and help? We can have our date after."

With a grateful look and a swift, but delicious, kiss, Jake returned to his conversation.

She was impressed by his personal commitment to helping JB and the way he'd taken responsibility for the rookie's future. Jake would claim it was for the good of the team, but she thought it went deeper than that.

"You're doing a good thing," she said as he hung up.

He shrugged. "I can only do so much. The rest is up to him."

"With you guiding him, he can't fail."

Despite her earnest tone, Jake's expression became bleak. "I'm not the best example for him to follow."

"Your experience makes you the perfect person to help him through this."

"I suppose…" His voice trailed off. He shook his head, as if to clear it. "Anyway, this isn't getting you breakfast."

Maggie allowed the change of subject. Then she decided to distract him.

Dipping her finger into the peanut butter, she sucked it into her mouth. She took her time licking her finger clean.

Flames leaped to life again in his eyes.

"Not bad." She swirled her banana in the peanut butter, then bit into the fruit. "Mmm. This is my new favorite."

"Damn it, Maggie." The tray hit the floor with a crash.

It was a while before they ate breakfast.

THE BADOLETTIS AND Jelineks celebrated Thanksgiving the way they did everything—loudly, surrounded by friends and with mountains of food. Jake had rarely been able to return to New Jersey for the holiday; he was usually with the team in a hotel on the road. Dallas last year, Anaheim the year before.

This year was different—they didn't play until Saturday afternoon, at home—and he was relishing every minute. Even the tradition of the men cleaning up after the meal while the women relaxed.

He carried a stack of dishes over to the sink where Tru and Ike were washing up.

"Looks like the kid's being loaded with leftovers." Tru inclined his head at JB, who was packing a couple of grocery bags with foil-wrapped packages.

"The moms love fussing over him." Jake grinned. "Beats eating his own cooking, for sure."

"So it's working out okay?" Ike dried a large baking dish. "I know he's settled down recently, but he hasn't completely lost his arrogance or his quick-fire temper."

"That's what gives JB his edge." Jake slotted knives into the dishwasher's cutlery basket. "He's doing fine."

JB had turned over a new leaf since Tampa. He was also playing better and scoring more consistently.

"Let's hope he can keep it up." From Ike's expression, he wasn't convinced.

Jake shook his head at his friend's cynicism and wandered back to the dining room for more dishes. Maggie's giggle rang out from the next room.

Emotion swelled within his chest. Despite the shaky start, after the Tampa incident they'd spent as much time as they could together, alone and with Emily. Laughter-filled days and passion-filled nights.

Once, spending so much time with one woman would have been his cue to start working on his exit strategy. He'd have already started to feel hemmed in, aware that the relationship had run its course, and begun to pull away.

Not this time. Not with Maggie.

Buoyed by the way his play had improved in parallel with their relationship, he'd found himself wanting to spend more time with her. Instead of shying away from the fact that they were a couple, he wanted to shout it from the rooftops. To make it public knowledge. He wanted everyone to know that he was serious about her.

The holiday had reinforced those feelings. The cozy

atmosphere, the warmth and love, made him determined to take their relationship to the next level.

Thanks to the Ice Cats' PR department, he had the perfect opportunity to do so.

He deposited the last few dishes with the Jelinek brothers, then walked into the living room, where the women were slouched in chairs, engrossed in a holiday movie.

"Do you want to go for a walk, Maggie?" he asked.

"That's a good idea." His mom smiled indulgently.

"We'll look after Emily." Aunt Karina's eyes twinkled. "Don't hurry back."

Jake rolled his eyes at their blatant matchmaking.

"That would be nice." Maggie rose. "Thanks."

They'd barely turned the corner before he pulled her to him. "It's been too long since I tasted you."

"About eight hours." She nipped his bottom lip.

A flash of heat speared his groin. "Way too long."

A car honked as it drove past, making them draw apart. Her reluctance pleased him and gave him the boost he needed.

"I've been thinking." He slung his arm over her shoulders, steering her toward the park.

"Is that allowed under The Code?"

"Funny. Any more wisecracks and I'll resort to tickling."

"No! Anything but that."

They laughed together. It felt good. Right.

They snuggled close on a bench beneath an old maple. The pale, wintry sun did little to warm the damp, chilly air.

He inhaled deeply, enjoying the way Maggie's soft scent added a subtle sweetness to the smell of wood smoke and autumn leaves. "I want you to come to the Ice Cats Gala Charity Evening with me."

He groaned inwardly. *That was really romantic.*

She stiffened. "That's the team's major event of the season."

"You'll love it. They hire out a fancy ballroom and invite season-ticket holders, investors, sponsors and anyone associated with the organization to spend a crazy amount of money per plate to have the team serve their dinner."

"It must get a lot of media coverage."

Surprised by her subdued response, Jake played up the event's glamour. "Yeah. The Cats always manage to get a bunch of celebs to come."

Instead of impressing her, his words seemed to unsettle her more.

"Sounds like a fun evening." She twisted her fingers in her lap. "Perhaps another time."

He frowned. Most women would jump at the chance to go to such an important function with him. He'd never asked anyone before, preferring to go stag than give the wrong idea—it wasn't an event where you brought a casual date.

"Besides, we've only been dating a few weeks."

"And this is the logical next step." *Logical?* What the hell was he saying? "I mean, it's the perfect opportunity to show everyone the wonderful woman I'm dating." Damn. He should have worked out what to say beforehand. "I want people to know how important you are to me."

Why did she look like he'd asked her to sacrifice her firstborn?

"I appreciate the sentiment, but I'm not sure I'm ready for that kind of function yet."

Had he misjudged her feelings about him? "I thought things were good between us."

"It's been wonderful." She raised her eyes to his. The warmth in the dark brown depths was encouraging.

"So what's the problem? You don't want people to know we're together?"

"This isn't about our relationship, Jake."

"What is it about?" He shook his head, confused.

"A high-profile party with massive media exposure. Being thrust back into the public eye, dodging the press and the paparazzi. Having my picture and my life splashed everywhere again."

"It's not that big a deal," he backtracked quickly. "Hockey events don't get the same coverage as the NFL. There'll be plenty of famous faces for the media hounds to salivate over. We'll be lucky if one picture of us makes the cut."

Maggie shot him a disbelieving look. "You're a guaranteed headline. I've seen the media attention you get."

"Used to get. Other than the Tampa thing, I haven't graced their pages in months."

"Which is why they'll focus on your latest bit of arm candy."

"You're way more than that." Irritation sparked within him. "Attending the gala evening with you sends that message loud and clear. Once they know things are serious between us, they'll back off. There's no story in a steady relationship."

"It doesn't work that way, especially for someone like you. It'll whet their appetite for more." She sighed wearily. "I've been through this before. I was the wife of a sports star who loved the glare of the media spotlight. I've only just escaped the circus surrounding my divorce. I'm not sure I'm ready to face it all again."

He'd chosen the wrong tack. He'd have to do some sharp skating if there was to be any chance of her going with him.

"I don't want the attention anymore, either. But this isn't just a social function. It supports the team, and local children's charities benefit. Don't worry. I'll protect you from the piranhas."

"I'm sure you'll try, but you won't be able to keep a low profile."

He hated that she was right. "Once I've fulfilled my commitments for the Cats, I'll make sure we enjoy the rest of the evening undisturbed."

"You know it doesn't work that way."

Frustration bubbled inside. She wasn't giving him anything to work with. "It can if we want it to."

"Something always goes wrong." She shook her head sadly. "Despite the promised good intentions. Whether it's because of the free-flowing booze or the larger-than-life egos or the exclusive-desperate media, there's always trouble and it always escalates until it's blown up out of all proportion."

"I take it you're talking about the jerk again." His lip curled.

Maggie nodded. "In the beginning, I loved those kinds of events. The glitz, the glamour, the famous people, the fabulous clothes, even the publicity. But I grew to dread them." Her eyes darkened at the painful memory. "Lee was always at the center of the trouble and I always bore the brunt of the fallout." Her voice faltered on the last word.

Jake's fingers curled into a fist. He wished he could make her ex suffer. Instead, he smoothed a curl from Maggie's forehead. "From what you've said, he chased publicity. And trouble. This will be different. *I'm* different."

Surely she knew that by now. Doubt twinged his chest.

"I know you're not like him." Maggie laid her hand on his.

Jake twined their fingers together, breathing a sigh of relief when she didn't pull away.

"That doesn't mean trouble and publicity won't court you," she continued. "When it does, because I'm with you, it'll rebound on me." She paused. "It's not just myself I'm worried about. It's Emily. I don't want to do anything that will catch Lee's attention."

"I thought he'd been quiet since that last crazy demand. He didn't even take up your offer to Skype with Emily."

"I'd like to keep it that way. I can't risk anything that gets him thinking about the custody agreement again. Em's been through too much already."

"I promise I won't let anything happen that could hurt you or Emily."

Maggie's tense gaze searched his face. She must have been slightly reassured by what she saw because her expression eased a bit. "I'm sure you'll do your best."

"So, you'll come to the gala evening." Jake started to relax, his mind already rushing ahead to how he could make the evening special.

"I need some time to think about it."

Her response stopped him in his tracks. He tamped down his impatience. "It's a few hours one evening. How bad could it be?"

"Maybe we could wait until another function, later in the season," she hedged.

Desperation rose, threatening to choke him. He searched frantically for a way to convince her. "There isn't another function like this unless we win the Cup. Even then, that won't be until June." He didn't want to wait that long.

"Then maybe we could attend one of the other team events. Something a little lower profile. Don't the wives and girlfriends get involved in the coat drive and the food drive?"

"Sure, and I'd love for you to be part of those, but the gala evening is special."

"Jake, please." Her imploring tone caught his attention.

He was pushing too hard again. Jumping to his feet, he paced as he tried to rein himself in. "You're worrying about something that may not happen. I understand why, but hiding from the world isn't the answer."

Maggie bristled. "That's not what I'm doing."

"Isn't it?"

"No. I don't see what's wrong with needing a little time to make sure I do the right thing for me and my daughter. I don't see what the rush is."

"I want to show you how important you are to me, damn it." He thrust his fingers through his hair, then stopped in front of her. "I may not be handling it the way you'd like, but I've never wanted to get serious with anyone before."

She lifted her chin. "You're important to me, too. I'm just asking for a few days."

"Okay," he said grudgingly. "Sure. A few days."

The walk back to his parents' house wasn't as lighthearted as earlier—no passionate stops en route. They returned to find Emily dozing on the sofa and Tracy yawning.

"Time to get you ladies home," he said.

Laden with leftovers, they got into his M-Class. They hadn't gone a mile before Tracy and Emily were asleep.

For most of the journey, he and Maggie were lost in their own thoughts. When she finally broke the silence, it was to confirm their plans for Saturday. They were all coming to watch him play, then Tracy would take Emily home so he and Maggie could have dinner.

His body began to hum with anticipation at the thought of the private, postdinner rendezvous they'd planned.

At the house, he carried a sleeping Emily inside. He

said good-night to Tracy, then grabbed Maggie's hand and pulled her back outside. As she half-closed the door behind her, he brought her into his arms for a hot kiss.

"Something to help your deliberations." He released her and climbed into his SUV.

As he drove off with a cheery wave, he saw Maggie touch her fingers to her lips, as if to keep his taste there. The hungry look in her eyes was encouraging. Enough to make him feel confident that things would work out as he'd hoped.

But as he drove home, that confidence began to melt away and was replaced by doubts.

Maggie's physical response wasn't an issue. He had enough evidence to prove she found him attractive, his touch pleasurable. Whether that was enough to make her step outside her comfort zone was something else altogether.

All the sparks in the world didn't matter a damn if she wasn't prepared to take their relationship to the next level. He understood her concerns, but he'd said he'd make sure nothing happened. Why couldn't that be enough for her to say yes?

He didn't need to hear the echo of Tru's voice to know this was another of those situations where he had to be patient and hold off the pressure. It went against his nature to sit around waiting for things to take their course, but he knew if he pushed too hard he'd push Maggie away completely. He had to trust that if he stepped back and gave her space she'd come around.

Jake pulled into his driveway and turned off the engine. As he took the keys out of the ignition, a worrying thought occurred to him. What if she never became comfortable enough to attend events by his side? He couldn't duck media coverage forever. He had responsibilities to his team, the fans and the community that couldn't be blown off. Sure, he could compromise on some things, but he couldn't give them all up.

He didn't want to give Maggie up, either.

There were some tough choices ahead for him. Damn it. Sometimes trying to be a good man and do the right thing sucked.

"WHAT SHOULD I do?"

Maggie looked at her sister sitting on the opposite sofa cradling a glass of wine. "I'm thrilled Jake wants our relationship to become more serious, but I'm also scared."

She touched her fingers to her throbbing lips, where his heady flavor lingered. "I care for him, but I want to take things slowly. I rushed into marriage with Lee. Perhaps if I'd waited, I would have found out what he was really like and saved myself a lot of heartache."

"True. But then you wouldn't have Emily, either. What's more, you wouldn't be over here. Nor had the opportunity to meet Jake."

Maggie pursed her lips. "Your point being?"

"You can't keep beating yourself up about the past. Mistakes or not, it is what it is. The only thing you have control over is what happens next."

"Which is why I want to do things properly this time."

"Isn't that what Jake's suggesting with the gala evening?"

"Don't get me wrong—it sounds like a great event. I

admit, I miss getting dressed up in a glitzy new gown and hot shoes. But it's not all glamour and fun. The media and paparazzi will be circling and swooping like vultures. One wrong step and they'll pounce."

Her stomach rolled at the thought of dealing with the fallout.

"Jake's never had to court publicity and he's never misbehaved to get coverage. Even with that thing in Tampa, he tried to minimize the fuss." Tracy shook her head. "He's crazy about you. He wants to show you off and brag about you being an item. Not because it makes him look good but because he's happy and proud to be with you."

"But there's so much at stake. I can't afford to let my guard down again. I'm scared that if I give in on this I'll step onto a slippery slope that can only end in disaster."

Tracy set her glass down. "It's one evening, Maggie. You've told Jake your concerns and he's promised he'll make sure everything goes smoothly. If worse comes to the worst and it all goes pear-shaped, you'll know not to trust him again."

"True." A spark of hope lit within her. "Maybe I could give the gala evening a go."

"You never know—this could be the start of something fabulous." Tracy's smile was broken up by a yawn. "You don't have to make a decision tonight. Sleep on it."

Maggie replayed both the evening's conversations while she got ready for bed. Thought about the worst that could happen and how she'd deal with it. Considered the best that could happen, too. Gradually, her mind became clear and she came to a decision.

She was tired of giving up the things she enjoyed, of pushing aside what she wanted, of letting the past rule her present. She was fed up of being cautious all the time because she was scared of what might happen. The gala evening was another step in reclaiming her life. The perfect way to brush away the past and clean the slate for a new future.

Maggie drifted off to sleep with a smile on her face, thinking about what she could wear to knock Jake's socks off.

Her optimism remained the next morning. Though it was wet and dreary, she felt as if the sun was shining brightly. She couldn't wait to tell Jake she'd changed her mind.

Hugging her happy secret to herself, she skipped downstairs to the kitchen to make a cup of tea. Then she sat at the kitchen table, scanning department store websites on her iPad to get some ideas for what she might wear.

Maggie was browsing the virtual shoe department at Neiman Marcus when a notification popped up on her screen announcing an email from her solicitor. She clicked through to the message, which said simply to call. Today, if possible.

Her heart sank. What problem had cropped up now? What was Lee up to?

She picked up the phone and dialed Samantha's number.

After exchanging greetings, her solicitor got to the

point. "Lee and Patty are bringing their wedding forward by six months to the week before Christmas. They've signed an exclusive deal with *Hello!* magazine to cover the buildup to the celebrations, as well as the wedding itself."

"I guess Patty's not worried about it being 'the wedding kiss of death.'"

"No matter how many marriages break up following a *Hello!* feature, every bride thinks it won't happen to them," Samantha said wryly.

"Myself included." Her wedding to Lee had been a *Hello!* exclusive, too. "I'm guessing you didn't call to discuss the details of their wedding."

"Patty wants Emily to be a bridesmaid. Lee is demanding Emily return to England immediately for dress fittings."

"Which will be photographed for the magazine feature." Anger churned her stomach. "We've been through this. Lee can't drag Emily back to England on a whim. Especially not when his real motive is to use her for his own PR game."

"I've already made that point to his lawyer. I also said Lee is being a tad disingenuous, given he hasn't contacted his daughter despite accepting our Skype alternative. There's been no comeback on that, but I wanted to warn you because the media circus around the wedding has already started."

"So there's nothing I can do but stick to the current game plan?"

"I'm afraid not. I'll keep you posted if things develop."

Tracy came into the kitchen as Maggie was boiling

the kettle for some fresh tea and commiserated with her over Lee's demands.

"I hope you won't let this affect your decision about the gala evening."

Trust her sister to zero in on the problem Maggie had been pondering. "I wonder if it's sensible to go. The wedding fuss probably won't make it over here, but can I risk it? Someone might see something, then make the connection and—"

"To hell with being sensible," Tracy interrupted. "Don't let this nonsense stop you from doing what's best for you. Not going would be dancing to Lee's tune again. Wouldn't you rather dance with your favorite hockey hunk?"

Wasn't that what Maggie had decided last night? She smiled. "No contest."

Tracy laid her hand on Maggie's shoulder. "Before you change your mind, call Jake and tell him."

"Actually, I think I'll wait and tell him in person, after dinner tonight. Then he can show his appreciation properly."

"I like your thinking." Tracy grinned.

"In the meantime, I need your help to find a fabulous dress and some killer shoes."

"I saw just the thing yesterday." Tracy typed an address into Maggie's iPad. "Check out these Louboutins."

Maggie sighed. "Perfect."

I'M AN IDIOT!

Jake tugged so hard the laces on his skates snapped.

Damn it. A bad sign.

He tamped down the superstitious twinge as the equipment guy tossed him a packet of spare laces. It wasn't bad luck, just bad thoughts. Mainly about his conversation with Maggie last night. He'd had nothing but bad thoughts since he'd opened his big mouth and stuck his size twelve in it.

"You ready?" Tru stood at the door.

"Sure." The extra practice should take his mind off last night's fiasco.

Walking down the corridor, Tru asked, "Will your fight with Maggie affect your play?"

"It was only a difference of opinion."

"Then how come you both looked upset?"

"Later," he said. "Now's not the time."

Tru nodded, then hit the ice.

Ike came up behind him, drinking a soda. "Can you keep your head after yesterday?"

Jeez, had everyone noticed? "I'm fine."

Ike shrugged. "Okay."

"Trust me." Jake skated out to join Tru.

Only everything wasn't fine. The *clack-clack* of his blades was choppy, out of sync. Another bad sign. He stopped sharply, sending up a spray of white.

Feel the ice.

He started skating again. Twice clockwise, twice counterclockwise.

Tru and Jake touched sticks then skated sprints across the rink. His muscles settled into a familiar rhythm. A whistle blast, and they switched to a one-touch passing drill. Then they fired pucks at Ike.

Jake's timing was off. His stickwork was bad. His shots were worse.

He skated to the boards and grabbed a water bottle, squirting water over his face and down his dry throat as the two brothers joined him.

Ike swore. "Get her out of your head. The team can't afford this crap."

"She's not in my head." Instantly, that's exactly where she was, wearing a kaleidoscope of expressions. Shock. Frustration. Disappointment.

He shook his head to clear it. "I'll be okay," he ground out.

"What happened yesterday?" Tru demanded. "Don't give me bull about a disagreement."

Jake sighed and filled them in on the conversation.

Tru's eyebrows spiked. "You're that serious about her?"

"For sure."

"Jeez. Next you'll be talking about the future." Ike's lip curled.

"Right. I can't even convince her to come to a public event with me to show the world we're a couple." Jake slammed the water bottle back on the boards.

He'd been prepared to put himself and his reputation out there to show his feelings for her. Was it so much to ask her to take a little leap of faith and do the same?

Ike adjusted his mask. "You've been sweet-talking women since kindergarten."

"Well, it didn't work this time." When it mattered most.

Tru tapped Jake's helmet with his glove. "Maybe

you only think it's what you want, what you *should* do instead of what you *want* to do."

"Run that by me again."

"Isn't this another part of your 'be a saint' kick?"

"I'm trying to live a better life." Jake glared at him. "Not earn a damn halo."

"I got you wanting to cut out the high-octane lifestyle, but this is the other extreme."

Ike nodded. "By the all-star break, you'll be talking about kids, a minivan and a spot on the PTA. Nuts." He skated off to his crease.

Jake turned to Tru. "You think I'm crazy, too?"

"No." There was understanding in Tru's eyes. "But you've only been dating a few weeks. Why the desperate need to make a statement about how serious you are about her?"

"Why wait? I already know all I need to about Maggie. You said it yourself. She's—" how to describe her without sounding like a sappy Hallmark card? "—perfect for me."

"No one's perfect, bro." Concern tinged the understanding.

"She's pretty damn close. I care for her. A lot. Want to be with her. A lot." He wanted her, period. "I'm not interested in being with anyone else, and the thought of spending the rest of my life with her doesn't scare the crap out of me."

Ike yelled across the rink for them to get their asses in gear.

Tru tapped his stick against Jake's pads. "She's not

perfect when she affects your play. Personal problems have no place on the ice."

His stomach dropped to his blades. "I'll handle it."

"Then do it. Fast. If you don't, your ice time will be cut." His friend's voice was serious. "This kind of thing costs teams championships. I know you don't want to let yourself or the guys down, but if you keep this up, you'll become a liability."

Jake set his jaw. "Consider it fixed."

He took off, skating at a furious pace, pushing to get his rhythm again. Forcing his body to feel right. When sweat streamed down his back, he stopped and grabbed a water bottle.

He drank, then poured water over his face. "I'm ready. Let's go again."

A muscle twitched in Tru's jaw. "Sure."

With gritty determination, Jake pushed aside the memory of last night's disagreement and what it meant for his relationship with Maggie. He'd deal with that later. For now, he had work to do.

CHAPTER FIFTEEN

MAGGIE STILL WASN'T in her seat.

Jake swore under his breath as he climbed over the boards for the start of the second period the following afternoon.

When he'd skated out for the beginning of the game and seen her sitting in his allocated seats with Emily and Tracy, his heart had jolted. Hope had soared when she'd smiled at him before the opening face-off. Everything would be okay.

Instantly, his skating had clicked back into sync.

His concentration had been absolute during a frenetic first period. He'd played out of his skin, blocking shots, intercepting passes, back checking and throwing his body around.

But as he'd headed off the ice for the first intermission, he'd seen her vacant seat and sick dread had filled him. He'd tried to convince himself there was a logical explanation. After all, Emily and Tracy had still been there, laughing and talking as normal.

Now the sight of the still-empty place hit his chest with the force of a slap shot, shaking his focus. What had gone wrong? Nothing had happened—a little chirping, but no fights, no big hits.

He adjusted the tape on his stick and tried to park

his concerns. He had a game to play. This was a division rival—points from them were prime. He shoved his mouth guard in, narrowed his gaze.

Focus.

It didn't work. His first shift sucked. As the period progressed, his play deteriorated and Max shortened his ice time.

Jake kept his head down and tightened his grip on his stick, but the ice had already tilted against him. When his mistimed pass was intercepted, resulting in a Penguins' goal at the end of the second, Max ripped him a new one, then benched him.

Being taken out of the game burned like acid in his gut. He'd never been benched before.

Never again, he vowed.

His mind steadied for a few minutes, but being out of the play made it hard to maintain focus. He couldn't stop his gaze from wandering toward that damn empty seat.

The clock ticked down slowly to the final horn. The game grew chippy and disjointed. Tempers frayed as nothing went the Cats' way—pucks took weird bounces, sticks broke at awkward moments, refs gave penalty after penalty.

All Jake could do was sit there, frustrated, unable to do a damn thing to right the mess he'd caused. No one spoke to him. Everyone's attention was fixed on rescuing the game. He wished he was somewhere else.

With two minutes to go, Max pulled Ike for an extra attacker. Vlad scored almost immediately, tying the game and bringing the Cats back to life.

Maggie reappeared a moment later. She ruffled Emily's hair before slumping into her seat. Her miserable expression told him whatever was wrong had nothing to do with him.

A switch flipped in his brain. As the problem wasn't him, he'd find a way to fix it.

Once this game was over.

"Come on, come on," he muttered, willing the puck up the ice.

Thankfully, JB delivered as the announcer called the last minute of play.

The arena erupted. Everyone leaped to their feet yelling and chanting.

Except Maggie, who stared out at the ice, oblivious to the jubilation around her.

Jake left the celebrating Cats and headed for the locker room. Ignoring the disgusted glare Ike shot him, he stripped off his sweaty gear and ducked into the shower.

Tru joined him, concern written all over his face. "Max is on the warpath."

Jake barely got back to his locker before the angry manager appeared. "I'm…"

Max slashed his hand through the air, interrupting Jake's apology. "I don't want to hear it. Words don't cut it—I want action. I need to be able to rely on you. You have one last chance, Bad Boy. Next screw up and you're a healthy scratch."

Jake's stomach lurched at the threat to sit him out completely. If he couldn't find a way to stop Maggie messing with his head, he'd have to give her up.

Time had just run out.

He toweled off, rubbing his skin nearly raw as he tried to figure out what the hell to do. He dressed slowly, his fingers fumbling with his shirt buttons. Though the room buzzed with the victory high, he couldn't get past how he'd let his teammates down. That wouldn't happen again. He clenched his jaw. More importantly, he wouldn't let Adam down.

His cell beeped with a text. He grabbed the phone, then tossed it aside with a snarl of disgust. Nick had been calling for weeks. Jake had told him he hadn't looked at the damn boxes, but the guy refused to let it go.

He deleted the message without reading it and grabbed his gear. "Cover for me, Tru. I want to avoid the postgame media call."

"Sure. Get out of here."

Jake slipped out of the locker room and headed for the family area, where Maggie stood waiting for him. Despite her carefully bland expression, her eyes were shadowed with emotional turmoil.

Her lips curved into a tentative half smile as he approached, making his heart lift.

"It's good to see you." He leaned down and pressed a swift, hard kiss to her lips.

Her heightened color was the only sign of how his kiss had affected her. "You don't think Emily would let me miss a game, do you?"

"Whatever the reason, I'm glad you came."

"Me, too." She cleared her throat. "We should talk."

Jake kept his tone deliberately light, even as his gut tightened. "No problem."

He slung an arm across her shoulders, taking comfort from the way she relaxed into his body rather than stiffening. They headed out toward the underground parking lot, where the team cars were warmed up, ready for their owners. Jake veered between optimism and pessimism about the reason she wanted to talk.

Damn, this relationship business was tough. He'd rather face Stemgarder any day.

Once they were in his SUV, he tackled the subject head-on. "What happened at the game?"

She bit her lip. "I'm sorry I missed so much of your play."

"That's okay. I sucked anyway." Jake maneuvered out of the arena and onto the busy streets. He knew he should tell her the problems it had caused him but he couldn't bring himself to admit it. "I was worried. Was there a problem?"

"You could say." Maggie sighed. "My solicitor called. Lee won't back off on his demands for Emily to go to England."

Irritation spiked as she explained about her ex's wedding and his demands. No wonder she'd been upset. Why couldn't the jerk leave Maggie and Emily alone?

"I know he's only insisting on these fittings because he needs the media coverage."

Jake frowned. "Why?"

"His contract is up for renewal at the end of the season and he's desperate for good publicity. After our divorce, the team threatened to get rid of him if he didn't get his act together. He thinks the wedding exclusive, especially the shots of Patty and Emily together, will present a nice family image and help his case."

"His demands are still impractical."

"I offered to send Emily's measurements and promised to get her there a few days early for a final fitting." Maggie grimaced. "As it is, Emily doesn't want to go to the wedding. Even if I can convince her to go, she'll hate having to wear such a fancy dress."

He fought to keep a straight face. *That's my girl!* "I guess your ex didn't like that."

"Lee's threatened to overturn his agreement for Emily to spend the year in the U.S. with me. He also wants joint custody." Her voice wavered. "Samantha doesn't think he'll succeed, but it'll be almost impossible to stop Lee from getting some form of shared custody."

"But you'll fight him?"

"I'll do what I can." She sighed. "Which brings me to the reason for our talk. I was going to tell you I'd come to the gala evening, but now I'm not sure."

Damn the jerk. "What difference does this make?"

"With all the publicity Lee's wedding will get, I think I should keep a low profile. The media will rake the past over enough as it is. Better if I don't fuel it further by being in the public eye myself."

"I don't get how attending a charity dinner would harm your position."

"In itself, it won't." She bit her lip. "But Lee will be desperate to convince everyone that he's the better parent and he'd love anything that would suggest I'm an unfit mother. I can't afford anything to go wrong. The merest whiff of trouble could do terrible damage."

"I know you've had bad experiences in the past, but you'll be with me. I promised nothing bad would happen and it won't. I won't let it."

"Still, it might be better if I avoided the evening altogether." She picked at a seam.

Something else was bothering her. She wouldn't meet his gaze.

Realization dawned. "You're worried he'll use our relationship to prove his point?"

"I'm sorry, but you have to admit, your reputation isn't exactly wholesome."

Her words sucker punched him. Jake's grip tightened on the steering wheel until his knuckles turned white. Unsure how to respond, he said nothing.

During the rest of the drive to the restaurant, the silence was heavy and tense.

He was staring down the tunnel of defeat, but he didn't want to let their relationship go. There had to be a way around this. A way to show Maggie she was wrong. About him, them, how good they could be together...everything. And in doing so, rescue his season.

Jake turned into the restaurant parking lot, pulled into a space and turned off the engine. An idea began to form in his mind.

"Maggie." He took her hand and interlaced his fingers with hers.

She turned to look at him. The hopeful spark in her eyes gave him courage.

"If you don't want to come to the gala evening,

I'll let it drop. But I think you're missing the perfect opportunity to fight back. After all, the best defense is offense."

"How do you mean?" She frowned.

"Preventing trouble is only half the battle. Instead of being afraid of the media, we need to use them to tell the story we want."

She tilted her head, considering. "How do we ensure they get the right message?"

"Simple. They know I usually fly solo when it comes to important team events." He squeezed her hand. "If I take you, it shows them I've changed far more effectively than anything I could say. Then we plant other key snippets of information with the journalists—about your role as a partner in your sister's business, how well-adjusted Emily is—and get some good PR shots." He smiled. "It's not salacious gossip, but it's better than schmaltzy wedding coverage."

She gave a slow nod. "It could work."

"What could go wrong?"

Maggie shot him a wry look.

He held up one hand in mock surrender. "Nothing will go wrong. Not on my shift."

"I really can't afford the slightest bit of bad publicity."

He tilted her chin so her gaze met his and hoped his sincerity was plain for her to see. "There won't be a bad word printed. I promise."

"You can't control what they write. It's too…"

He pressed a finger to her lips, stemming the flow. "Trust me."

Maggie studied him for what seemed like forever. He could see the mixed emotions in her eyes. She wanted to believe in him, but the past weighed heavily.

He wanted to press, but knew that would only push her away. "I believe this is the perfect play, but the decision is yours. I'll abide by your choice."

He forced himself to remain quiet. The erratic thump of his heart echoed in his ears.

Finally, she swallowed hard. "All right."

FLASHBULBS EXPLODED AROUND the open door of the stretch limo.

The butterflies that had been fluttering in Maggie's stomach throughout the drive to the event hotel started to dive-bomb as if they were dogfighting in *Top Gun*.

You can do this. For Emily.

She forced herself to slide forward and get out of the car. Noise bombarded her from all sides—the cheers of the waiting crowd, journalists firing questions and those bloody camera-toting vultures snapping away—a shock after the smooth quiet of the soundproofed car. Feeling exposed and vulnerable, she brushed her palms nervously down her silk dress and waited for Jake.

Her gaze flicked from side to side. It felt like everything was closing in on her. Her breath came in short bursts. Her chest ached as her heart lurched erratically.

The urge to bolt hit her. This wasn't what she'd wanted, what she'd signed up for. Why had she thought she enjoyed these events? Maybe that had changed as much as she had.

Then a warm hand settled in the small of her back.

A tall, solid body pressed against her side, providing strength and support. Soothing her panic.

"Panty hose or stockings?" Jake murmured in her ear, his breath feathering the side of her neck like a delicate caress.

She gave a startled laugh and shot him a look through her lashes to see if his question was serious.

He gave her a too-damn-sexy smile. Her pulse skittered at the gleam in his blue eyes. The underlying concern there warmed her heart and eased her tension; it was a clever distraction.

Determined he shouldn't have all the fun, Maggie brushed a light kiss to the ridge of his jaw. "Lace-edged hold ups."

His cough covered a strangled moan. "Wicked woman. You're killing me."

This time it was Maggie who smiled. The Louboutins with the silver buttons were worth every penny. As was the black cocktail dress, whose column of silver buttons ran from the deep-cut V in the middle of her back down to the hem that flirted with the backs of her knees.

Jake's fingers caught her chin and stole a sizzling kiss from her parted lips.

The fans went wild. More cameras flashed, capturing the moment, but the dance of Jake's tongue across her bottom lip proved another excellent distraction.

The waiting crowd began to chant his name. Slowly, he let her go. He caught her hand and pulled her with him to the cordoned-off area full of people in Ice Cats jerseys.

Once again, Jake's generosity with the fans impressed her. He chatted cheerfully with everyone, making each person feel special, and signed whatever they wanted. He even treated those fans who criticized him with respect and a dash of self-deprecating humor.

As a result, Maggie felt more relaxed about this event than any she'd attended with Lee. Perhaps this evening wouldn't be so bad after all—once they'd run the media gauntlet.

Still, when a Cats' staffer approached, asking her and Jake to head inside, she tensed.

"A few more minutes and the worst will be over," Jake said quietly. "Then we can focus on enjoying ourselves."

"At least until you have to put on your apron and serve dinner."

"They said we'd wear our sweaters, not an apron." He rolled his eyes when he saw her teasing smile. "Funny."

At the hotel entrance, they were stopped by a couple of TV reporters. Jake seemed to know Archie, a tall man, whose scarred face suggested he was a former player, and Lois, a painfully thin woman with a brittle smile. Archie's questions were mainly about hockey, particularly the recent rumors that some big NHL names were caught up in the internet pharmacy scandal.

Lois was more interested in Jake's social life. From her pointed questions, Maggie sensed the woman had more than a professional interest in Jake. She seemed put out when he made a show of putting his arm across Maggie's shoulders and pulling her close.

"So Bad Boy is finally getting serious?" The question dripped with cynicism.

"For sure." Jake launched into his preplanned spiel, adding the perfect touches of earnestness and romance.

Maggie's pulse tripped when Lois's assessing gaze zeroed in on her.

This was the one. If danger was to come from anyone, it was this hard-edged gossipmonger. She made a mental note to avoid Lois as much as possible.

After an approving look at Maggie's shoes, Lois flicked her gaze dismissively over the rest of her and turned her attention back to Jake. It was so blatant, Maggie bit back a laugh.

Thankfully, the Cats' staffer reappeared, disentangled them from Lois's talons and hurried them inside. There, he handed Maggie off to a colleague who would take her to join the other girlfriends and wives, before directing Jake to the booth where he'd have his session with the season-ticket holders.

"I'll come and find you as soon as I'm done." Jake dropped a quick kiss on her lips.

Maggie was touched that he cared enough to reassure her.

"I'll be fine." She smiled. "I'll be with familiar faces."

The Cats' women were far more down to earth and friendly than the football WAGs. Perhaps because these women didn't compete to be the most fashionable, or most photographed. Many were childhood sweethearts from the same small towns as their partners, and family oriented. A few were athletes, some had their own careers and others managed the charitable foundations set up by their husbands. They even treated Jenny like one of the gang. When she'd mentioned this to her friend, Jenny had explained that they didn't consider her a threat. They knew she didn't sleep with married men.

Maggie followed her chaperone into the anteroom set aside for the women. She was greeted warmly and teased about taking part in her first jersey auction. Jenny waved from across the room, where she handed out the special signed Cats jerseys that each woman would model during the auction.

"I didn't know you were coming." Maggie gave her friend a hug before slipping on the red Badoletti jersey.

"It was last minute." Jenny turned to show the name on the back of her jersey—Larocque. "The kid didn't want to go stag, so he asked nicely if I'd come with him."

"You've forgiven him for being a jerk early on?"

"Sure. Though I made him grovel repeatedly." She grinned. "Thing is, ever since he's been living with Jake and hanging around with the families, he's felt like a kid brother. One that needs an occasional cuff to the head."

Maggie laughed and helped Jenny hand out jerseys. When they were finished, they joined the others for a fortifying glass of champagne before heading into the ballroom.

The atmosphere there was less frenetic than outside. People chatted while music played in the background, accompanied by the clink of glasses. Waiters glided discreetly through the crowd, holding trays of canapés and drinks. Even the select group of media allowed inside was restrained.

She and Jenny circulated through the various entertainment stations set up beyond the dinner tables around the outside of the ballroom. Attendees could gamble alongside players in the special Ice Cats casino or compete against them in the multimedia area. There was also a small dance floor with a DJ playing golden oldies.

Jake appeared a few minutes before dinner was called and stole her away onto the dance floor to take advantage of a slow track. "The plan is going perfectly. They love you. They love us being here together, and the idea that you've 'tamed Bad Boy' has captured their imaginations. Should make great reading tomorrow. Your jerk of an ex won't be able to compete with this kind of good publicity."

Even as she savored the moments wrapped in his arms, Maggie's stomach tightened. She didn't want to tempt fate by calling this evening perfect. It was going well. Enough that she could imagine attending such events in the future with Jake—but she couldn't quite relax. Old habits died hard.

Dinner was a hoot. The players did a wonderful job of serving the dinners. There was a good-natured competition to see who could earn the most "tips" by serving with the greatest flourish. Ralinkov took the prize, hamming it up with his unique style that was part snooty butler, part flamboyant Spanish waiter.

By the time the auction started, most guests were in a relaxed state of mind. Judging by the many flushed faces, perhaps a little too relaxed. At least it eased the grip people had on their wallets as the bids for the jerseys skyrocketed.

The Cats' wives and girlfriends modeled the jerseys at the front of the ballroom as the auctioneer announced each lot with great gusto.

Maggie was pleased when Jake's jersey raised the second-highest amount, after the captain, Scotty Matthews. The winner was a walking, talking New Jersey cliché. From his shiny suit and slicked-back hair to his heavy gold jewelry and brash swagger, he'd have done well in a bit part on *The Sopranos*. He was even called Tony.

Unfortunately, he didn't seem to realize—or didn't want to—that Maggie wasn't part of the deal. She managed to duck his overly "helpful" hands when he tried to assist her in taking off the jersey. During the photos, she gritted her teeth and subtly swiped his meaty hand off her backside rather than cause a scene. When Jake had to leave them to continue with his host duties, Tony grabbed her arm and insisted she join him for a drink.

He didn't take her polite refusal well, tightening his grip and repeating his offer.

Maggie tried to shake him off and excuse herself, but he wouldn't take no for an answer. From the angry glint in his eye, things would turn nasty if she didn't get away from him. That was the last thing she needed, especially with so many photographers hovering nearby.

"I have to join Jake," she said frostily. "Enjoy the jersey and have a nice evening."

"I'm one of the Ice Cats' biggest sponsors." Tony's fingers bit into her arm. "When I tell you to have a drink with me, you do it and with a goddamn smile on your face."

Maggie wrenched her arm out of his clammy grasp. He tried to grab her again, but she jabbed her elbow back, hard, into his midsection. He tried again, this time sliding his arm around her waist. Maggie bumped him away with her hip, trying to create some space between them.

Unfortunately, he must have been drunker than she'd thought, because he tumbled backward, pinwheeling his arms like Wile E. Coyote after he'd run off a cliff. Unable to regain his balance, Tony fell backward into a waiter holding a tray of empty glasses. There was a large, resounding crash as the two men hit the ground.

The ballroom went silent.

Everyone stopped. Even the waitstaff stood and stared.

The strains of Michael Jackson's "Bad" echoed around the room until the DJ faded it out. Cameras whirred and flashed all around her.

"Bitch!" Tony spat, as he tried to disentangle his limbs from the waiter's.

Mortified, Maggie tried to step back, away from the scene, but her legs were frozen in place. Her skin crawled with the sensation of so many pairs of eyes watching her. Judging.

The walls seemed to close in on her. The air was dense—it was hard to draw breath.

Here and there murmurs started. No one moved. They were determined not to miss a moment of gossip. She sensed their disgust and disdain.

Tears pricked her eyes, but she refused to let them spill.

The DJ neatly segued into "Thriller," encouraging everyone to get on the dance floor, but he couldn't drown out Tony's vile stream of abuse.

Tru and Ike appeared and grabbed Tony's arms, hauling him to his feet. When he tried to lunge at Maggie, they restrained him and started to haul him away.

She needed to get out of here. Get some air.

Turning, she stumbled to a stop when she saw Lois and the cameraman recording everything. The smugly satisfied smile on the reporter's face made Maggie's stomach roll.

"Beat it, Lois." Jenny stepped in front of the reporter and blocked the camera lens with her hand. "There's no story here."

Lois started to argue, but Jenny leaned forward and said something to her that Maggie couldn't hear. The other woman paled, then nodded to her cameraman. She flounced off, but not before deliberately snapping a picture on her smart phone. No doubt she was already tweeting about what had happened.

Jenny wrapped a comforting arm around Maggie's waist. "Are you okay?"

Maggie nodded dumbly, unable to force words through her constricted throat.

"Come on. I'm sure you could do with a stiff drink after being pawed by Tony. All that money and not a nickel's worth of class."

Jenny's calm support soothed Maggie's ragged nerves. She allowed herself to be steered away toward the ballroom doors.

Her heart stuttered when Jake appeared before her, his expression thunderous, his jaw grimly set. She wasn't scared; his rage wasn't aimed at her. He'd never hurt her. No, her concern was about what would happen next if she didn't stop him.

She reached out and laid a hand on his arm. "It's all right. Tru and Ike have Tony under control. Let them deal with him."

"Did that bastard hurt you?" Worry mixed with the fury blazing in his blue eyes as they raked over her, inspecting her from head to toe. His hand cupped her chin gently. His thumb caressed her cheek, then her lips.

"I'm fine. Just a little shaken. Nothing a glass of wine can't fix."

"Yeah, well, he's going to learn never to lay his hands on my woman again."

Her gut twisted. "Jake, don't. It's not worth it. He's not worth it."

But it was like he didn't hear her plea. He stormed across to where his friends still held the raging man. Maggie didn't hear what he growled at Tony, only the threatening tone.

Tony's response was crystal clear. "Get your cheap

piece of ass under control, Bad Boy, or you'll be the one paying the price."

Jake's fist ploughed into Tony's face.

Bone crunched, blood spurted.

A camera flash exploded.

The perfect evening had become a perfect nightmare.

CHAPTER SIXTEEN

MAGGIE'S SILENCE WAS a hell of a lot more painful than his bruised knuckles.

For the first time in his life, Jake hadn't a clue what to say to make this nightmare situation right. Charm wouldn't bail him out of the mess he'd created.

His gut burned. After all his assurances, he'd blown it.

He just wasn't cut out to be a good man. He'd been whistling in the wind to think he could change. Hadn't tonight been proof of that? He'd done the very thing Maggie had been afraid of. Worse, he'd done it in full view of the media and every idiot with a cell phone and a Twitter account.

The pictures had probably already hit the internet. By tomorrow, every sports blog, podcast and talk show would have commented on the details. The nonsports media would get in on the act, too, happy to take another pop at hockey's violence.

Everything he'd been trying to do for the past few months had blown up in one hotheaded moment. Thing was, given a do over, he couldn't swear he'd have done anything different. That's who he was. No one got away with bullying on his watch.

Unfortunately, Maggie would suffer the consequences, no matter how justified Jake's actions were or how much that jackass had deserved the broken nose. He looked across the limo at her, pressed as close to the far door as she could. Her head was turned away, staring out of the tinted window, though he doubted she saw anything of the landscape flashing past.

Jake reached out to touch her but pulled his hand back at the last second. He wanted to bridge the gap, but he wasn't sure how. The distance between them felt broader than the width of the limo.

The familiar building silhouettes told him they weren't far from Tracy's house. He didn't want Maggie to leave the car with this situation unresolved, but where did he even start?

With the basics. But how? With his reputation…

The germ of an idea occurred. Getting the attention of the media was about the only thing his reputation was good for, so why didn't he use it to tackle the problem head-on?

The more he thought about it, the more he knew it was the only way to rescue the situation. His stomach churned at what he'd have to do, what it would cost him, but he owed Maggie nothing less.

Before he did anything, he'd have to get her approval. For that, he'd have to get her to talk to him. Time to bridge that gap.

"I'm sorry," he said quietly.

For several moments, she didn't respond. He hunched his shoulders against the feeling of inadequacy that crept into his body.

Slowly, she turned to face him. "I told you to leave him alone."

"I know. I lost my temper. But no woman should be treated that way, let alone my woman."

"A noble sentiment." Her lip curled. "This was exactly what I was afraid of and why I didn't want to come tonight. You promised nothing would happen. I should have known better." Her short laugh scraped already raw nerves. "I did know better."

Feeling lower than a slug and knowing he'd earned every damning word, he forced himself to keep quiet until she'd said her piece.

"It was bad enough that I knocked Tony to the ground," she continued. "Your macho behavior compounded the damage."

"I couldn't let him get away with what he did."

"Tru and Ike had it under control," she snapped. "I begged you not to get involved. But even though I'd shared my concerns with you, you waded in. Now instead of an unfortunate accident, there's one heck of a juicy story out there. Lee will be thrilled. He couldn't have planned this better himself."

Each stinging word was like a well-aimed dart. "I'll speak to the media and—"

"Please don't," she said coolly. "You've done enough."

"But I can spin the story so they see it's my fault and nothing to do with you."

"Really? After you went to such lengths to tell them we're together and serious about each other, they'll drop me from all the stories." She arched an eyebrow. "I don't think so."

"I can't just sit on my hands and let you suffer."

"Too bloody late. Anyway, I'm sure the Ice Cats would prefer if you said nothing."

"I don't give a rat's ass what they think. I bet they'll back me one hundred percent. If they don't, then I won't be part of an organization that condones sponsors abusing women and…"

He swore when he caught her surprised expression. "Your jerk of an ex wanted you to put up with grab handing so you didn't upset the team?"

"Lee felt I should do whatever it took to keep the sponsors happy," she said crisply, though she dropped her gaze.

"Even for him, that's a new low." Jake grimaced. "What kills me is that you think I'm as bad as he is."

"You don't help your case when you do stuff like tonight." Her tone softened slightly.

"You're right." He sighed. "At least, let me try to fix this."

When she started to shake her head, he cut her off. "Look, it's already as bad as it can be. But it's still only a local story. Maybe I can ensure it doesn't get to the U.K. Or, if it does, make it all about a dumb hockey player from New Jersey." There was no question he fit that bill. "If it doesn't work, you're no worse off. What have you got to lose?"

"My daughter. My life over here. Everything I've worked so hard for over the past few months." Her voice cracked on the last word.

Her anguish sliced through him like a freshly sharpened blade on clean ice. History was repeating itself. He hadn't paid enough attention to Adam when it mattered, had put himself first. Now he'd done the same to Maggie.

This time, though, he had a chance to do something to make the situation right.

If she'd let him.

"Give me a couple of days. Let me try to minimize the damage." He paused, uncertain what else to say to convince her. "Please."

Maggie stared out the window, saying nothing.

The limo turned smoothly into Tracy's drive. Time had run out.

Desperate, he made one last play. "It's up to you. I'll do whatever you think is best."

She turned, her eyes widening. "You're backing off?"

"You have too much at stake for me to try to railroad you."

She thought for a few moments. "All right. Give it your best shot."

Relief rushed through him. It was a start. "Thank you."

His mind was already turning over a list of who to contact first. The journalists who covered the Cats. The big guys like Dreger and McKenzie at TSN, whose stories would be retweeted, as well as the key hockey bloggers.

Maggie's voice, barely above a whisper, interrupted

his thoughts. "If it doesn't work…" Her words faded, as if she didn't want to finish the sentence.

She didn't need to.

"It will. I'll make sure of it. Trust me one more time."

But as the limo pulled to a stop, doubts danced at the edges of his brain. Maggie's future, Emily's future—hell, his own future—was in his hands. What if he couldn't fix this? What if he was too late? How could he live with himself if he failed someone he cared about again?

"CREDIT WHERE CREDIT'S due. Jake's lived up to his promise."

Jenny shot a triumphant look at Tracy, making Maggie smile.

The women were meeting for lunch at Tracy's house, having decided Maggie should lie low until they'd seen the full extent of the coverage of the gala-evening fiasco. Jenny had brought takeout and was spreading containers across the kitchen table while Maggie laid out plates and cutlery and Tracy made hot drinks to ward off the chill of the gray day.

Maggie wasn't sure she could eat anything. She was trying to put on a cheerful front, though her stomach had been in knots for the past couple of days. Her nerves were pretty much shot. She'd barely slept and she jumped whenever the phone rang.

Every time she turned around, she was assailed by stories of that night. She and Jake had been plastered over every magazine, website and chat show. While most of the stories had focused on Jake, they'd all included a particularly unflattering picture of Maggie, with Tony sprawled at her feet.

It hadn't helped that she and Jake hadn't seen each other at all since that night. They'd opted for a low profile, too. Though they'd spoken often on the phone, it wasn't the same as being with him. Aside from missing him, she'd come to realize how much of a presence he'd become in her life. How much she enjoyed that presence.

Jenny took the cover off a plastic salad bowl and split the contents between three plates. "Jake's done everything he can to deflect attention from Maggie."

"I give him kudos for punching out that tosser, Tony." Tracy held her hands up in mock surrender. "Jake's certainly put himself about, appearing on podcasts, talk radio and phone-conference roundtables with journalists."

Jake's determination to fix the problem, along with the huge personal sacrifice he was making for her and Emily, had melted Maggie's heart. Other than Tracy, no one had ever cared enough for her to put their reputation, their soul, on the line. Not her parents, not her so-called friends back home and certainly not Lee.

Tracy interrupted Maggie's thoughts, calling her and Jenny to sit and eat.

Jenny stabbed her grilled chicken breast with relish. "I hear the Cats told Tony that they appreciate his support, but his money isn't worth that kind of behavior."

Maggie nodded. "Not only did the team stand behind Jake one hundred percent, they also stood up for me. Tony backed down pretty quickly."

"Rumor has it Tony tried to switch allegiance to the other hockey teams in the area, but they wanted nothing to do with him." Tracy grinned. "That'll teach him."

Maggie pushed her food around her plate. "Why do I feel like it's been too easy? That trouble's waiting round the corner, ready to ambush me?"

"Past experience," Tracy said softly. "You haven't had an easy ride of it, sis. If anyone has earned the right to be cynical about the media, it's you."

"Perhaps I deserved it. I used to chase column inches myself." Maggie laid her fork down, giving up all pretense of trying to eat.

"Maybe in the early days, but not during your divorce. It still infuriates me how Lee's behavior was downplayed, just because he was a well-known football star." Her sister jabbed a carrot stick into the bowl of hummus.

"This time, everyone's on your side." Jenny sent her a reassuring look. "I know we still haven't seen what's in the weeklies, but the coverage has been favorable elsewhere. Jake's indignation over Tony trying to paw you played well on all the gossip sites."

"True," Maggie admitted. "But I won't relax until I see what the bestselling mags back home, like *Coffee Break* and *Chit Chat,* say."

"They're out tomorrow, right?"

She nodded. "With the time difference, we'll get our first glimpse of what's in their next issues tonight on their websites. If we make it through this week's edi-

tion relatively unscathed, we should be okay. If not…"
She broke off, not wanting to put it into words.

"I'm sure it'll be fine." Tracy laid a hand on her arm.
"It'd be different if you'd had a go at someone they
know, like that Russian billionaire who owns Chelsea."

"I suppose so."

"From tomorrow, things will go back to normal."
Jenny raised her coffee cup in a salute.

"Not really. Samantha has received a formal demand
from Lee to change the custody arrangements. That'll
be very hard to fight."

"If he's so determined to change the rules, you
should be, too."

Maggie tilted her head, considering. "How do I do
that?"

"Apply for residency and move here permanently."

"I'll second that." Tracy nodded her approval.

"I'd love to, but if Lee gets shared custody, Em's life
would be totally disrupted. She'd be pulled from pil-
lar to post every few weeks. Assuming he'd even give
permission."

Tracy pursed her lips. "I can't see him giving an
inch."

"Perhaps you could make it worth his while," Jenny
mused.

"How?"

"Offer to take Emily back to England during school
holidays. In between, they can Skype, like you suggested before. He gets regular contact and quality time
without disrupting Emily too much."

Maggie's stomach twisted. "I don't want her staying

with him. Even with Patty there to run interference, I don't trust him."

"Won't shared custody mean she has to stay with him whether you like it or not? This way, you dictate the terms."

"I suppose so," she admitted reluctantly. "I'll check that out with Samantha."

"By then, you and Jake will be a settled, steady couple, so he'll help keep Lee in line."

Her heart thunked heavily. Once. Twice.

"Settled? Steady?" She forced the words out of her suddenly numb lips. "I've only just left my marriage behind. I'm not sure I'm ready to leap into another serious relationship."

Even as she spoke, her mind began playing with the idea. Would it be so bad?

"One thing's beyond doubt," Tracy said. "Jake's a far better man than Lee ever was."

"Yes!" Jenny pumped the air with her fist. "We've converted your cynical sister."

Tracy rolled her eyes. "I'll still hang, draw and quarter him if he hurts Maggie."

"Don't worry. If that happens—which it won't— I'll help you."

"You're jumping the gun." Maggie shook her head. "We're nowhere near that stage."

Jenny waved her hand dismissively. "Sure you are. For a start, Jake's in love with you."

This time, Maggie couldn't force out a sound.

In love with her? He couldn't be. Could he?

310 A PERFECT DISTRACTION

As if she'd heard the silent question, Tracy nodded. "The guy's in love with you."

Maggie stared wide-eyed at her sister and her friend as their words tumbled around her brain. "How can you tell?"

"He's settling down, looking to build a future with you. Inviting you to the gala evening was proof of his commitment," Jenny said. "He's never been prepared to do that before. He's always preferred hot-and-cold-running bed partners rather than one special woman."

Memories of how that event had turned out brought Maggie back to reality with a jolt. "The gala evening was a disaster."

"True, but he's worked hard to make things right," Tracy said. "Why bother if he isn't in love with you?"

"It's obvious." Jenny nodded. "Just as it's obvious you're in love with him."

"I'm not…" The automatic denial died on Maggie's lips.

Was she in love with Jake?

Something clicked inside, like the final piece of a jigsaw puzzle sliding into place. The rush of sensations and feelings made her light-headed. Warmth, happiness—this was right. Tension, worry—could she trust herself to know what was right? Iciness, fear—was she making another mistake?

Yet in the midst of the maelstrom, there was a core of certainty. It grew with each passing second, corralling and calming the swirling emotions, until there was only the steady glow of assurance. Her heart gave a joyous skip, then pounded.

I love Jake.

She touched trembling fingers to her mouth, to keep the words from bursting out. They couldn't be contained.

"I love Jake." The wonder in her hushed voice made Jenny smile mistily.

"It's worked out perfectly. Two of my favorite people will be together and you can stay here in New Jersey."

Maggie tried to ignore the frisson of unease that slithered down her spine. There was no such thing as perfect. "It's a long way from being settled."

"I know." The mist faded from Jenny's expression. "But it's a great start and the future looks promising. You can be levelheaded and realistic, but I'll keep hoping everything will turn out as I predict."

With Jenny's words, Maggie realized that alongside the steady flame of love burning inside her was another, smaller glow. One that had been missing for so long she could barely recall when it had last been alight.

Hope.

"HOLD UP, BAD BOY."

Jake stopped at the urgency in the trainer's voice. "What's up, Steve?"

The guy jogged toward him. "Coach said to remind you to give your sample for the drug test after tonight's game."

He frowned. "Again? I only gave one ten days ago."

"Just passing on a message." Steve shrugged. "The league's been edgy ever since investigators started naming names in that internet pharmacy case. Some big sports stars have been accused of buying steroids from the site. It's only a matter of time before they name an NHL player."

"I don't get it." Jake shook his head. "That junk can seriously damage your health."

"Not to mention your career. At least you're not one of those idiots."

"Damn straight."

"Anyway, don't forget." The trainer started to walk away, then turned back. "Oh, and the media's desperate to get at you, but we're holding them off."

"I appreciate the heads-up. Perhaps Charlie Sheen will do me a favor and go crazy again." Jake stalked into the empty locker room.

He tossed his bag on the floor and slumped by his locker, rolling his shoulders to relieve the tightness. The past few days had been rough.

He'd been dogged by journalists at home, at his parents' and at practice. His cell was permanently diverted to voice mail. It was great that his version of events was getting out there, but it was taking its toll on him. Not just personally but also on the ice.

Luckily, the Cats hadn't had a game until tonight, so his poor play had only been during practice. He needed desperately to be back to normal, and fast.

To cap it all, he hadn't seen Maggie since the gala evening, and it was killing him. Their brief phone conversations weren't nearly enough. Something had changed between them. He sensed it in the way she spoke, her tone of voice. Jake hoped it meant she'd forgiven him. A warm glow filled him, wrapping around his heart. Images danced through his head—golden-hued happy pictures that resonated in his soul.

Maybe some good had come of this crap with Tony—not that he'd thank the jerk.

Jake touched his fingers to his lips, recalling her taste from their last kiss. Reliving the feel of her mouth beneath his. Her body in his arms.

He puffed out a frustrated breath. He had to find a way to see Maggie after the game.

Voices echoed in the corridor outside the locker room. Jake straightened, trying to pull it together. He had a game to prepare for.

Not just any game, either. Though the season wasn't halfway through, a win tonight against the second-place Flyers would widen the gap between them, putting the Cats firmly in control of their division. Two points closer to securing a play-off berth. Two points closer to lifting the Stanley Cup.

Several teammates entered laughing. When they saw him, they came to an abrupt stop.

Unease crept down his spine. "What's going on?"

Juergen and Vlad exchanged uncomfortable looks while Larocque headed for his locker, avoiding Jake's gaze.

The creeping turned to a stampede. "Fellas?"

The Russian swore. "Have you seen the latest pieces from the U.K. about Maggie?"

"I haven't had a chance—they only came out late last night. Why?"

Juergen said quietly, "You should take a look."

His stomach nosedived to his Nikes. "It's that bad?"

"They regurgitated every piece of salacious gossip about her, going back to when she was single." Juergen pulled out his phone, tapped in some details then turned it to show Jake. "Check this out."

"It's a blonde dancing on a table." A hot blonde in a low-cut top, micromini and skyscraper heels that showed off her fabulous legs.

"It's Maggie."

"You're kidding." He laughed, but it sounded hollow. The Swede shook his head, his serious expression confirming this was no joke. Jake studied the picture again, but could only find superficial similarities with the woman he knew. "No way."

"Maggie Hayden—her maiden name—was an über 'It Girl.'" Vlad's tone was apologetic. "The press nicknamed her 'The Divine Miss H,' and she had more tabloid coverage than Posh Spice."

Maggie hadn't been exaggerating when she'd said any hint of trouble could be used against her. His gut twisted. He'd downplayed her concerns, brushed them aside. His arrogant assumption that he knew better was going to cost Maggie dear. "That was a long time ago. A lot has changed since then."

"Not what the media are saying." Juergen shifted uncomfortably. "It gets worse. There's no mention of the story you've been pushing."

Jake blinked. "Nothing?"

"Nothing about why you punched Tony, only that you brawled with a team's major sponsor. Apparently, you're proof that she's still hanging out with the wrong kind of guy."

"They also mentioned Tampa," JB added miserably. It really was that bad.

"See for yourself on the 'net," Juergen suggested.

Pushing out of the locker room, Jake stalked down the corridor to the operations director's office. "Can I borrow your computer, Tom?"

"Sure, Bad Boy. Help yourself. I've got to check a problem with one of the Zambonis."

It took Google less than a second to prove the guys were right. The photo of Tony lying sprawled at Maggie's feet was splashed across every publication, alongside pictures of him laying Tony out. For extra color, they'd added a plethora of stories and pictures from her past and his.

Meanwhile, her jerk ex-husband had expressed his "shock and disbelief" and his "heartfelt concern" for his beloved daughter, while vowing to wrest custody from Maggie. Mentions of Lee's abusive behavior were brushed over in favor of descriptions of his "happy new life" and upcoming nuptials.

Jake slowly got to his feet. His body ached almost as badly as it had in those early days after the accident.

This was all his fault. Maggie had tried to warn him but he'd been too wrapped up in his own needs to listen.

Didn't that have an uncomfortably familiar ring to it?

Now Maggie and Emily would pay the price. Just as Adam had.

Once again, Jake had been too damn sure of himself. Arrogantly assuming he could put everything right.

What a joke. All he'd done was make things worse.

His selfishness had almost certainly cost Maggie custody of her daughter. Bile burned his throat.

He trudged back to the locker room, oblivious to the game preparations around him. As he suited up, questions bounced through his mind, like pucks on soft ice.

What could he do to fix things?

Haven't you done enough already?

He could…

No.

Jake pulled himself up short. That was how he'd got them all into this mess.

He was no closer to figuring out what to do by game time.

Jake tried to concentrate on his play. He pushed through shift after shift, but even the adrenaline of a spirited ice battle couldn't dull the nauseous edge to his tension. Though Maggie wasn't in the stands, he couldn't stop his gaze from flicking to where she usually sat.

The Ice Cats played a solid first period and went back to the locker room a goal up.

As the coaches outlined tactics for the second, Jake's mind strayed. Images of Maggie whirled through his brain. The uptight woman in the drab outfit and sensible shoes from their first meeting morphed into the sexy babe in that red suit with the killer heels. Then a smiling Maggie danced tantalizingly through his mind in a variety of outfits with strategically placed buttons before becoming the pouting blonde wild child with the barely there clothes.

A shroud of gloom settled about his taut shoulders.

By the time he hit the ice again, Jake's nerves were jumpy, his concentration shaky. He gritted his teeth and tried to clear his mind.

It didn't work. He barely made it through his shift.

Jake climbed back over the boards and slumped on the bench. As he waited for play to resume, he looked up at the Jumbotron. Instead of the rah-rah images pumped out by the arena, those damn pictures of Maggie cycled through his brain. They were joined by still more: Emily's pale face as Maggie fanned the smoke from the burned bacon; Emily's fear as she handed him the broken banister knob.

Dizzy with the mental kaleidoscope, Jake tightened his hold on the boards. It didn't help.

Snapshots of Adam flashed through his brain. His friend's white-knuckled grip on the steering wheel, followed by Adam's changing expressions as he went from cheerful to depressed and back again. The car veering into oncoming traffic, swerving to avoid bright headlights, overcompensating to slide onto the gravel shoulder, then over the edge and down an embankment. Finally, Adam hanging upside down in the rolled, wrecked car, his body contorted grotesquely, his eyes staring sightlessly into the night as blue lights flickered across his pale face.

The ref blew his whistle, disrupting the mental display. It didn't stop the simple message from echoing in his head and sending a dagger through his heart.

You will never be good enough for Maggie.

Jake didn't want to listen, but he couldn't ignore the nagging inner voice. Especially when he knew the damn thing was right. He would never be a good man, no matter how hard he tried. He'd been a fool to think that changing his life, his reputation, would be enough. He should have known better. Hell, he *had* known better.

A shout sent him back onto the ice. He barely knew where he was or what he was doing. Opposing players drove forward as he tried to keep pace. The puck bounced over his stick as he attempted a poke check. Momentum carried him away from the play instead of toward it.

Three on one. He couldn't get back. *Skate, damn it!*

It was no good. He was too late.

The smack of graphite on rubber. The red flash of the goal light. Boos from the crowd.

Frustration. Desperation. Despair.

He dropped his head and skated back to the bench. He'd let the team down.

Unacceptable.

A heavy hand slapped his shoulder. Max. "You're sitting the rest of the game, Bad Boy."

As his teammates struggled to right the situation he'd caused, Jake knew he had to do the same. He owed it to them. To Adam. To himself.

The only thing he could control was what he could deliver on the ice. As long as he was focused, he could guarantee success. From now on, hockey had to be the only thing on his mind and in his heart. Winning the Cup had to come first. He clenched his fist in his glove and pounded it on the board in front of him.

As for Maggie, he wouldn't be responsible for wrecking her life any further. The best damn thing he could do for her was to stay as far away as possible. His soul ached at the thought of what he'd lose, yet he knew he had no choice. He cared too much for her.

Jake stared out at the ice, his mind oblivious to the frenetic action taking place before him.

There was only one solution.

The pain of what he had to do radiated from his heart until it felt like all his nerve endings were aflame. He bowed his head, resting it on his glove and ruthlessly forced his brain to clamp down on the agony. When he lifted his head finally, he was resolute.

The time had come to make the ultimate sacrifice.

CHAPTER SEVENTEEN

"JAKE WAS A bloody liability tonight."

Maggie couldn't disagree with Tracy's verdict. The guilt that had squeezed her chest every time the cameras had focused on him, his expression thunderous, got worse. His bad play had been because of her.

Jenny nodded, her expression glum. "I'm not surprised he was benched—his turnover led to the Flyers' game-winning goal."

The three women were curled up in comfortable chairs in front of the TV, each cradling a mug of hot chocolate. Maggie's mobile phone lay on the coffee table between them, next to a crumb-covered dessert plate with one brownie remaining.

The commentators on the postgame show blamed Jake for the loss and speculated about the distraction caused by "recent events in his personal life."

Maggie groaned. "I thought my day couldn't get any worse."

The nightmare had actually started last night. The weeklies back home had been more vicious than she'd expected. Each sneering commentary had been a bruising blow.

Then this morning, Samantha had phoned. Lee was making good on his threat to wrest custody from her.

Her solicitor had reassured her that the same law which kept Lee in Emily's life, ensured Maggie couldn't be excluded either, but she faced a tough fight. One the media would relish.

Things had gone downhill from there. Work had been impossible. Maggie had spent the day making statements to the media—damage control that felt like a finger in a leaking levee.

Now as the hands on the mantel clock edged toward eleven, Maggie's body ached with exhaustion and worry. She'd known how events would unfold as a result of the awful publicity, but she'd underestimated the toll it would take on her.

To cap it all, her phone had been ominously silent.

As it was game day, Jake had been tied up with the morning skate. But he'd promised to phone her. They'd agreed she shouldn't attend the game, given the media fuss, but he'd sworn he couldn't get through the day without hearing her voice. Yet he still hadn't rung.

His silence couldn't be good.

"I'm sure there's a good explanation." The hint of uncertainty in Jenny's tone wasn't reassuring.

"He's probably decided I'm not worth the bother." She couldn't blame him; she'd never been good enough for Lee, either.

Tracy snorted. "After everything he's done over the past few days, why would he suddenly change his mind about you?"

"Because it hasn't made a scrap of difference."

Jenny shook her head. "Jake will be as frustrated as you are."

The mantel clock chimed. Eleven-thirty.

Her phone remained silent.

"If that's true, why hasn't he called, or even texted?"

"I guarantee Jake hasn't changed his mind about you." Jenny eyed the sole remaining brownie wistfully, then pushed the plate away. "He thinks you're perfect."

A chill went through Maggie. "I keep telling you, there's no such thing. I'm not perfect."

"All right, he thinks you're perfect *for him*. He won't walk away because your situation is too challenging."

Maggie wished she had her friend's confidence. "We'll see."

Jenny rose, stifling a yawn and hugged Maggie. "If you haven't heard from him by morning, I'll go to his house and beat some sense into him."

Once Jenny had gone, the sisters tidied up the kitchen.

"I can't believe Jake will let you down." Tracy wiped the counter.

"I hope you're right."

"I know I am. This rubbish will die down. Your solicitor will sort Lee out. Life will return to normal. You and Emily will get residency." Tracy grinned. "You'll live close by, maybe even with Jake, and everything will be perfect."

There was that bloody word again. *Perfect.*

Maggie knew better than to count on everything working out. Still, that little flicker of hope hadn't been extinguished yet. Maybe this time would be different.

When Tracy went to bed soon after, Maggie returned to the living room. The clock marked midnight. As each chime echoed through the quiet house, a dark pre-scient feeling hovered over her like a gathering storm cloud.

"Enough." She grabbed her mobile and dialed.

No answer.

When it clicked through to voice mail, she hung up and tried again. Still no answer. This time she left a message asking him to call.

After ten minutes, she tried again. When she still had no joy, she called Tru.

"Hey, Maggie. What's up?" His cautious tone sent an uneasy shiver down her spine.

She bit her lip. Whatever was wrong, she had to know. "I've been trying to reach Jake but keeping get-ting his voice mail."

"Uh…he didn't feel well and left."

So Jake didn't want to speak to her.

"I see." She tried to sound calm, though she was close to shattering.

"We're sharing a ride to practice tomorrow. Can I give him a message?"

Unwilling to appear needy, she declined. She snapped her phone shut. She wanted to toss the bloody thing against the wall, but switched it off and laid it on the table before heading upstairs to bed. That way, she wouldn't spend all night waiting for the phone to ring and dying inside when it didn't.

After a restless night, during which she'd slept only fitfully, Maggie made herself wait until she'd seen Emily off to school before turning the phone back on.

No missed calls.

"Nothing?" Tracy stood in the doorway.

Maggie shook her head, unable to speak past the lump in her throat.

"Go over there."

"I will, later. He has practice shortly, and I have work to do."

"Don't worry about work. I'll cover for you."

"Thanks, but I'll face him in my own time. On my terms." Maggie hugged her sister, then went upstairs.

She deserved better than Jake's silence. Had the right to the truth, delivered in person. If their relationship was over, so be it. Her heart ached, but she stiffened her resolve. Better to know than to cower with dread. She was stronger than that.

Squaring her shoulders, she switched on her computer.

Maggie worked until the early afternoon, skipping lunch because she couldn't face food. Unable to focus, she did routine tasks that required little thought. Ibuprofen kept her throbbing temples from becoming a full-fledged headache.

By two, she'd had enough.

Arriving at Jake's house, Maggie was surprised to see the reporters had gone. Another juicy story must have broken.

There was no answer when she rang the doorbell.

She checked her watch. He should have returned from practice by now. Should she leave or let herself in? Not prepared to let him keep avoiding her, she used her spare key to open the front door.

The house was dark and still. His training bag lay next to the stairs.

Jake was here?

She called out, but there was no response. With growing apprehension, she realized where he'd be.

Maggie walked into the darkened den. As her hand reached for the light switch, a rough voice stopped her short.

"I'm honored. It's the paparazzi's darling—The Divine Miss H."

"MAKER'S MARK. ROCKS." Jake held up his glass. "Want one?"

Maggie pursed her lips. "It's a little early for booze."

"Whatever."

"I'll get some tea." The hurt in her brown eyes sent a fiery arrow into his gut.

His hungry gaze followed her out of the room.

What the hell was wrong with him? All he had to do was tell Maggie it was over. No need to be a jackass. Yet the harsh words had spewed from his mouth like lava from a volcano.

Why? He'd never had a problem closing out a relationship before. Usually glad to end things, he was always civil and able to move on without a backward glance. His heart had never caught the way it did every time he thought about a future without Maggie. He drained the glass and poured another.

With the glass halfway to his lips, he stilled. The problem with booze was it didn't numb you quickly enough. Before you got to the happy oblivion it promised, you had to go through a nasty phase of total clarity and truth.

This was his moment of clarity. His truth was simple. He hadn't been in love with those other women.

He was in love with Maggie.

A bubble of pure happiness welled up inside him.

Even as he savored the feeling, another truth hit, and damn if it wasn't as cold and hard as the crystal tumbler he drank from.

That didn't change anything.

Pain speared his chest, bursting the bubble and leaving shards of ice in its place. Time to head for oblivion.

To love.

Jake raised his glass in a mock toast, then tossed back the drink. Amber liquid burned its way down his throat.

Love sucked.

Maggie returned and perched on edge of the sofa, cradling her mug. "You haven't been to practice?"

"Nope."

"What about JB?"

"He's out."

"What's going on, Jake?"

He hadn't expected her to tackle him head-on. "What?"

"I'm not an idiot. One minute, you're desperate to show the world we're serious about each other. The next, you won't answer my calls."

That, ladies and gentlemen, sums up the sorry state of Jake Badoletti's life.

Damn, his glass was empty. He poured another drink.

"You saw the U.K. coverage." Her words were a statement, not a question.

"Yeah."

"You assured me your plan would work."

"I was wrong." About so many things. About getting a second chance. About being able to change.

About deserving a woman like Maggie.

Her silence was damning. Finally she said, "That's it?"

He shrugged, unable to share his thoughts.

"What happened to standing by me? Fighting with me?"

This conversation was killing him. He downed his drink. The bourbon soured his stomach but he didn't care. "I need to focus on hockey right now."

"I don't see how the two things are related."

"You watched the game?"

She nodded.

"You, me, this situation is a huge distraction I can't afford."

"You're blaming your poor play on me?" She looked incredulous.

"I told you, I need to focus." That line sounded as tired as he felt.

"So you'll play better if we stop seeing each other?"

She made him sound like a temperamental child. She didn't understand how much he'd agonized over his decision. The gut-wrenching torment that decision was causing.

"Yes." He swallowed hard to shift the tightness in

his throat, then forced the damning words out of his mouth. "I'm not interested in you anymore."

"Really? Could have fooled me." The wobble in her voice belied her cool expression.

"I don't mean physically." No way could he deny the attraction that sizzled between them. "It's complicated."

"Try me." Her words were clipped. "I deserve the truth, Jake."

A glint of copper caught his eye. Adam's lucky penny lay on the table. The broken chain—Jake had ripped it off after the game—was reproachful.

She was right. He owed her the truth.

Jake reached past the internal turmoil, slowly being numbed by bourbon, and grabbed onto a festering kernel of self-disgust. "It's not you, it's me."

Maggie arched an eyebrow, her distress stark in her eyes. "A stupid cliché is the best you can do?"

He shot her a frustrated look, which she met squarely.

"Why don't you just admit it?" Her voice broke on the final word. She cleared her throat. "I'm not good enough for you."

His heart contracted at the irony. "*I'm* a liability to *you*."

"Right." Her lips twisted.

He started to reach out to her, wanting to take her in his arms and comfort her. He dropped his hand. He couldn't let his feelings for Maggie derail him. This was too important. Drawing on a strength of will honed by years of professional sport, he channeled the emotions roiling inside.

"Without me in your life, this will blow over." Jake

inhaled a raspy breath. "I'm already responsible for ruining one life. I won't have yours on my conscience, too."

"You're talking about Adam?" she asked softly.

"He was a good man who didn't get the chance to live the life he deserved. Adam died too damn young and I...didn't." His voice caught. "I let him down."

"How?" There was no censure, just curiosity. "I thought he was driving.... His mistakes caused the accident."

"He was." His mind went back to that night. Relived each heart-stopping moment. "But something wasn't right." He visualized the sheen of sweat on Adam's skin, the tremor in his hands. His friend's wild laugh echoed in his ears. "Hadn't been for weeks."

He explained about Adam's erratic behavior. "I deliberately avoided the problem, made excuses instead of confronting him. His weird actions that night were the last straw. I planned to tackle him about it after..." He drained his glass, welcoming the fiery burn as punishment for his guilt. "I never got the chance."

"I'm sorry. I understand your pain." Her gentle voice soothed him.

For a moment, he reveled in its warmth. Then he remembered what he had to do and rolled his shoulders to shake off the mantle of comfort.

"What happened made me realize I wasn't proud of the person I'd become, so I tried to change. I'm determined to be the best player I can. Nothing, no one, can get in the way of that. I owe it to my parents and my team. I owe it to myself." He met her steady dark gaze. "I owe it to Adam."

"What about me?"

Hell, yes. He owed it to Maggie, too. "I'm the wrong guy for you."

"In what way?"

Before he could speak, Maggie let out a choked laugh. "Never mind. You think I'm not capable of knowing what's best for me." Beneath the bitter words, anguish shimmered.

"You don't understand…"

His words trailed off miserably, as he realized he'd skated into a trap.

"I let myself fall in love with you." Her voice broke. "I thought you were different."

His heart twisted as a tear trailed down her cheek.

She was in love with him? "I'm nothing like your ex."

"Yet, like him, you've always known better." Her watery smile was sad. "I won't have my life dictated to me by any man. I need someone who believes in me the way I believe in him."

She paused, probably waiting for him to reassure her.

The words wouldn't come. Better to let her leave angry, disappointed, than to hurt her anymore.

"I thought as much." Maggie rose and walked slowly to the door. "Good luck."

It sounded like goodbye.

The pain that seared through him was crippling. Jake poured another shot—a double—but knew bourbon couldn't soften the edge of his misery.

He'd done what he had to. He and Maggie were finished. No more worries, no more distractions. He could focus on winning the Cup.

He slammed the glass down, shattering it. A puddle of amber liquid spread over the table, then dripped to the floor. The fumes made his stomach rebel.

Maggie was better off without him. If only he could find a way to convince himself that he was better off without her.

RAGE. FRUSTRATION. HURT.

The tumult of emotions coursing through Maggie kept her going through the drive home. Once inside the house, her knees gave out and she slid to the floor.

She had no idea how long she sat there, slumped against the door. Cold seeped through her clothes, chilling her to the bone, but she hadn't the will to move. Numbness gradually replaced pain.

She'd been a fool to hope that what they'd shared would be enough to overcome any problems. A sad laugh escaped her dry lips. Wrong again.

"What's wrong, Mummy?" Emily's voice pushed aside Maggie's self-pity.

Averting her face, she tried to compose her expression. Perhaps Emily wouldn't notice the misery shadowing her mother's eyes.

No such luck. Emily knelt beside her. "Did you fight with Mr. Jake?"

There was no point lying; she'd find out soon enough. "Yes."

"But you're still going to marry him, right?"

Shocked, Maggie blurted out, "Married? Why would you think that?"

"Everyone's been talking about it since Thanksgiving. How you're 'in love'—" Emily rolled her eyes "—and you'll get engaged soon."

Maggie didn't know whether to laugh or cry. "We won't. From now on, I won't be seeing Mr. Jake at all."

Emily's face fell. "You're not friends anymore?"

"No."

Her daughter was silent for a moment. "When I fall out with my friends, you tell me to make up with them."

Hoist by her own petard. "Sometimes, you can't do that. Especially if they hurt you."

"Like Daddy did?"

Maggie nodded, her throat tight.

"Mr. Jake didn't hurt you like Daddy." Disbelief rang in Emily's tone. Maggie's wasn't the only heart he'd wormed his way into.

"No, sweetie. He'd never do that."

"Then why can't you make up?"

How could she explain? She didn't want to bad-mouth Jake, but she needed Emily to understand this couldn't be resolved. "We don't get along anymore."

"You don't like each other?"

"Not really." Like? No. Love? Unfortunately, yes.

"Doesn't Mr. Jake like me?"

Maggie's heart squeezed. She hugged her daughter. "Of course he does. Even though we're not together anymore, you'll always be special to him."

"Maybe you'll change your minds."

"We won't." Maggie's tone was gentle but firm.

Emily tilted her head. "Does this mean we have to go home?"

Maggie deliberately hadn't mentioned the forthcoming custody battle. There was no point upsetting Emily until the situation was clearer.

"Do you want to go back to England?" she asked cautiously.

"Nope. I want to live here. Can we?"

"We'll see."

"Okay. Can I watch *The Aristocats?*"

She'd barely nodded before Emily ran to the living room and started the DVD.

Maggie got to her feet slowly and went to stand at the living room door.

Emily turned. "It'll be okay, Mummy."

Her daughter's innocent words tore through the numbness, exposing the raw emotions.

Choking back the tears, Maggie dashed into the kitchen and almost ran into Tracy.

Her sister handed her a glass of wine. "I figured you could use a sympathetic ear."

The last vestiges of Maggie's control vanished. Tears spilled over as she slumped into a chair. The whole miserable story flooded out.

"It's déjà vu. I'm so stupid," Maggie said brokenly.

"You're not. Jake's not Lee."

"Breaking up with me for my own good is no different to Lee running my life." She dashed a tear from her cheek. "Falling in love with Jake was another foolish mistake."

"No, it wasn't. Jake's the idiot. Who sacrifices a lifetime of happiness with the most wonderful woman he'll ever meet for the possibility of a moment of glory?"

Maggie sniffed. "You're biased."

"Sure, but it's still the truth," Tracy huffed. "Jake's thrown away the one person who could help him see that he's a good man. He's so wrapped up in guilt about what happened to Adam, he's lost sight of the kind of bloke he is. Jake said it himself—he thinks he doesn't deserve you. Dumping you is just another way for him to protect you."

"But that's crazy."

"Bless him, he's a man. They always go for the quickest solution to a problem. Jake blames himself for what's happening to you, so to put that right fast he's removing himself from your life."

"Instead of standing beside me and weathering the storm."

Tracy shrugged. "I said the quickest way, not the best."

It made a strange kind of sense. "So what do I do now?"

"You carry on with your life." Tracy covered Maggie's hand with hers. "The media fuss will die down. Someone else will grab the headlines. Jake's play won't improve because he'll still be thinking about you and he'll realize he hasn't chosen the best solution after all."

"What if he doesn't?" The hollow feeling inside threatened to overwhelm her.

"You'll survive. It won't be easy and it'll hurt like

hell, but you've come through worse." Tracy smiled reassuringly. "I have faith in you."

In other words, there wasn't a bloody thing Maggie could do but wait. And hope.

CHAPTER EIGHTEEN

"MAN, I'M GLAD that road trip is done."

Jake dragged his case across the airport parking lot to Tru's SUV.

They'd been away for five days and played three grueling games, losing all of them in overtime. Tonight's loss had been the worst, as they'd been up by two goals going into the final period. To add insult to injury, JB had been knocked out. Fearing a concussion, doctors had kept the kid in the Nashville hospital overnight.

Jake's play hadn't been bad enough to get scratched, but not as good as it needed to be, either. As hard as he'd tried, he hadn't regained his focus. Maggie was his last thought at night and his first on waking. Plus, countless times in between.

There had been some tough moments on the trip, too: the woman with dark, curly hair who'd sat behind their bench in DC; the little girl in Nashville who'd called him Mr. Jake.

Cutting Maggie out of his life hadn't helped him play better. It had made him ache to the depths of his soul. The road trip had reinforced what he'd realized the night of their fight—he might be the wrong man for Maggie, but she was the perfect woman for him.

He loved her. Missed her. Wanted to be with her. Wanted a future with her.

The knowledge that he couldn't have any of that sliced through his heart like a blade through fresh ice.

"At least we have a couple of days before the next game." Tru unlocked his Range Rover.

Jake tossed his case in the back. "And time for twelve hours' shut-eye before tomorrow's practice."

"You gonna be okay?" Tru shot him the same concerned look he'd been giving Jake ever since he'd spilled his hungover guts about what had happened.

"Yeah."

"Okay. But if you need…"

"Thanks."

Tru backed off and started the engine.

Jake leaned his head back and stared out the window. He couldn't talk about it. The pain was still too great. Besides, nothing anyone could say would help.

The rest of the journey passed in silence.

As they pulled up to Jake's house, he saw the lights were on. Though he tried not to get his hopes up, his heart leaped.

"Good luck." Tru jabbed his shoulder.

Jake nodded, his throat tight. He got out of the car and gathered his gear. Then he inhaled deeply and walked to the front steps.

Tru's window rolled down. "Pick me up for practice?"

"Sure." He kept his gaze fixed firmly ahead.

Jake pushed the door open as his friend pulled away.

"Hello, jackass." Jenny stalked toward him. "Someone needs to set you straight."

"Do we have to do this now?" He dropped his case. "It's God-knows-what time, and I passed exhausted somewhere over Kentucky."

"Too bad."

Jake rotated his aching shoulders. "Why now? We could have spoken while I was away."

"I know how distractions affect your game."

Her words knocked the wind out of him.

He closed his eyes briefly. "I'm not doing this out here."

Jenny followed him into the living room, her boots clicking on the hardwood floor.

He slumped onto a sofa. "Help yourself to a drink."

She cuffed his head, then sat next to him. "That's for hurting Maggie."

"I screwed up." Jake scrubbed his hand across his jaw. "I wish I could put this right, but I can't."

"Why not?"

"I'm not good enough for her."

"Don't make me hit you again." Her expression softened. "None of this will make up for Adam's death. Or bring him back."

"I know. But it's not fair that I lived when he didn't. There's a lot of truth in that saying 'only the good die young.'"

"Adam wasn't a saint, Jake."

"He was a better person than me." His voice sounded hollow. His eyes burned. "Bad Boy by name, Bad Boy by nature."

"You're more than a nickname." She threw her arms up in frustration. "You're a good friend, teammate, mentor and son. You're honest, loyal, generous and kind."

"I sound like a damn dog."

"Better than the devil you think you are. What makes someone a good person is what's inside here." She patted her chest.

"What's inside for damn sure isn't good enough."

"The hell it isn't. Everyone who knows you believes in you. Isn't it time you believed in yourself?"

"I don't know if I can," he whispered brokenly.

She hugged him and rose. "Think about this…Maggie fell for you. Not your nickname, not your reputation. She thought you were worthy of her love. I do, too. Seems like the only person you need to convince is yourself."

Long after Jenny had left, Jake sat staring into space. He wanted desperately to believe what she'd said, but how could he? He'd let Adam down. He'd let Maggie down.

No. Better he stuck to his guns and focused on the one thing he could do right. Play hockey. Because he was damned if he'd let anyone else down.

TIME WAS NOT the great healer everyone claimed.

Rain hammered the windows, making Maggie shiver and cradle her mug of tea tightly. She sat on the sofa, snug in a thick sweater, soft jogging bottoms and fleecy socks. Emily was at Amy's and Tracy was at a meeting, leaving Maggie alone in the too-quiet house.

The dreary afternoon reflected her feelings. It had only been a week, but she didn't feel the slightest bit better. Each moment that passed without hearing from Jake killed what little hope she had. She told herself it was for the best. If he couldn't believe in her, in himself, in the two of them together, then their relationship wasn't worth anything.

That didn't keep her from missing him.

Work had kept her busy, but as most of their projects were for the Ice Cats, it had been impossible to keep her mind off Jake. Even the new business pitch to the local NBA team had involved going to the arena they shared with the Cats. Thankfully, the hockey team was away, so she hadn't had to worry about bumping into Jake. But the familiar loop of videos playing outside had stolen her breath. Especially the one featuring Jake.

With his ice-blue gaze fixed on her, his growled challenge, "Are you ready for me?" had struck at her core.

"The problem is," she muttered, "you weren't ready for me."

She'd scanned the internet daily, pathetically eager for information about him. His stats hadn't improved. Clearly, ending their relationship hadn't helped his play, but would Jake recognize that?

Maggie sipped her cooling tea. As Tracy had predicted, the media fuss had blown over almost as quickly as it had started. Lee had gone surprisingly quiet, too. Rumors that he might be traded during the upcoming transfer window made her nervous—he didn't respond well to uncertainty.

She bit back a yawn. Sleep had been elusive. When she'd finally succumbed, her dreams had been filled with endless replays of that conversation in Jake's den. Each time they reached the critical moment, where she awaited his reassurance, she would jolt awake with wet cheeks and an aching heart.

The phone rang, interrupting her thoughts. She let the answering machine kick in.

"Umm...hello. This is Patty. I...uh...wanted to speak to Maggie."

Why on earth would Lee's fiancée be calling her? As Maggie listened to the stumbling message, sympathy rose in her. Patty sounded upset, stressed.

Maggie jumped up and grabbed the receiver. "Hello." The silence on the other end made her uneasy. "Are you okay?"

"I'm fine." Patty released an audibly shaky breath.

"Are you sure?"

"I'm...nothing's broken."

She swore. "He hit you."

"It was a misunderstanding."

"No, it wasn't," Maggie said firmly. "This is how it starts. A misunderstanding, followed by a tearful apology and a promise never to do it again. Trust me, he won't keep that promise." Her healed arm twinged as if to emphasize the point.

"This is different. He loves me."

Patty's naive insistence sounded painfully familiar. "Even so, he will hit you again."

"But he's promised to go into an anger-management program."

Maggie knew then she'd never convince Patty that Lee wouldn't change. She softened her tone. "Good."

"The team insisted. This is his last chance. I'll work with him. We'll find coping strategies together."

If the club dumped Lee, Patty's life would become hellish. "Good luck with that."

Maggie wished she could save Patty from the pain to come but knew the younger woman would cling to her delusions until it was too late.

As if she'd read Maggie's mind, Patty's tone changed abruptly. "I don't expect you to understand. If you'd supported him instead of attacking him, he wouldn't be in this situation. And I wouldn't have to sort out the mess you created."

Maggie's spine stiffened, all sympathy gone. "I presume you called me for a reason."

"I want to offer you a deal."

"Excuse me?" That was the last thing she'd expected.

"We both need something from each other, and I've figured out a way for us to get it."

"Go on."

"There's a good chance Lee will be called up for the England squad next week. If he does, he'll be back in favor with his club and that'll ease his mind over the transfer."

"What does that have to do with me? I can't influence his selection."

"Lee can't afford any bad press while the England manager is making up his mind. He also needs to play his best game this weekend. I don't want him to have any distractions."

Not another bloody athlete with distraction problems.

"I still don't see how that affects me."

"The custody battle is winding him up."

Maggie gritted her teeth. "I won't give him full custody."

"I'm not asking you to. I want Lee to drop his challenge and give you permission to stay in America permanently."

Shock made Maggie's knees unsteady. She sank back onto the sofa. "But you were the one pushing for happy families."

"I've changed my mind."

"Why?" Maggie couldn't believe it.

"I'm pregnant."

"Oh." Unsure how to respond, she said simply, "Congratulations."

"Thanks." Patty's tone was smug. "Everything's coming together perfectly."

Maggie winced. She hoped the other woman wouldn't be forced to eat her words. "What do you get out of this deal?"

"Lee doesn't see Emily again."

How Maggie wanted that. "But, by law, he'll have to keep his visitation rights."

"I think, between us, we can make sure he doesn't use them."

Maggie didn't want to look a gift horse in the mouth, but it sounded too good to be true.

"One more thing." Patty paused. "Once Lee's child support ends, Emily has no further financial claim on him. I want my children to be his sole inheritors."

Guaranteeing Emily's custody was worth more than every penny of Lee's money. "You have a deal."

"Great. This is a time-sensitive offer. The paperwork must be completed and signed by close of play Thursday, so Lee can focus on his game on Saturday."

Maggie had two days. "You're sure you can get Lee to agree to the terms?"

"He's really sorry about what he did and is desperate to make up for it. Plus, he'll be thrilled about our baby. He'll agree to whatever I ask. I've had our lawyer prepare the necessary documents, so they can be sent straight over to your solicitor."

"I'll fly to England tomorrow."

Tracy walked in as Maggie hung up. "Is everything okay?"

"I'm afraid to say yes, in case I jinx it." She filled her sister in on Patty's call. "It seems too easy."

"Most people wouldn't call giving up Emily's rights to Lee's millions easy."

"She'll have enough in her trust to go to university or do whatever she wants."

"Then everything's fine." Tracy grinned.

Maggie sighed. "I won't relax until it's all signed, sealed and delivered."

"I don't blame you. Still, if this comes off, your problems are solved and you can focus on getting that residency."

When Maggie didn't respond, Tracy looked concerned. "You haven't changed your mind because of the situation with Jake?"

Maggie shook her head. "There's nothing for me back home. What's more, I won't let my mistake with Jake dictate my life. The best thing for me and Emily is to build on what we have here."

"I'll let the comment about your 'mistake' slide because we have more important things to sort out." Tracy arched an eyebrow pointedly. "Like a flight to England."

"Can you check what's available with the airlines while I talk to my solicitor?"

"Sure."

As Maggie ran upstairs to the office, she allowed a touch of excitement to seep into her body. Patty's deal would secure Emily's future.

It might help Maggie with Jake, too. Once the custody issue had been dealt with, he couldn't use that excuse for why he shouldn't be in her life.

But would it be enough to convince him they should be together?

"HIT THE SHOWERS, everyone." Max's voice rang out around the rink.

Jake headed off the ice with his teammates. Practice was better today—his rhythm was finally returning, but damn it was slow. At least he wasn't passing like a rookie anymore.

Max stopped him outside the locker room. "When you're done, I need to see you in my office, Bad Boy."

"Sure. What's up?"

The coach shook his head, his expression grim.

Baffled by Max's behavior, Jake showered and changed, then headed down the corridor. His heart gave a heavy thud when he saw who else was in the coach's office. Phillip Hannah, the Cats' general manager, sat behind the desk, while the medic and head trainer leaned against the filing cabinets. They all looked somber.

This was bad. Real bad.

Two men in dark suits entered behind him. One was tall and thin, with fair hair. The other was stocky and bald. The hard look they gave him as they closed the door was unsettling.

He nodded at them.

No reaction. Not a twitch. What was their problem?

"Have a seat, Bad Boy." The GM's usual friendliness was missing.

Tension tightened Jake's shoulders. He sat.

"These gentlemen are from the district attorney's office. They're investigating a serious allegation that's been made against you."

"What kind of allegation?"

The bald suit spoke. "We have information that leads us to believe you purchased illegal performance-enhancing drugs."

The tension whooshed out of him. "If you'd seen me play recently, you'd know I don't take steroids." Their faces didn't crack. Jake frowned. "I'm clean. The tests will prove that."

"They do." The team medic looked apologetic. "We've taken additional random samples since this surfaced."

His stomach rolled. How long had he been under suspicion? "What evidence do you have on me?"

"Proof that you purchased drugs from an internet pharmacy." The tall suit looked smug.

"That's crap." He clenched his fists. "Someone's lying."

"The pharmacy recorded their transactions," the man said coolly. "All drugs supplied were logged, dates and quantities as well as credit-card details. You're on their list."

This couldn't be happening. "Impossible. I've never, ever juiced up." He looked desperately to his coach and the other staff. "You guys know me better than that."

Max nodded. "The Ice Cats stand behind you one hundred percent."

Before Jake could breathe a sigh of relief, Phillip said, "Unfortunately, until this is cleared up, we have to follow League rules and keep you off the ice."

"I'm suspended?" Jake's voice came out scratchy and raw.

"Your hearing is tomorrow afternoon, at 4:00 p.m. at NHL headquarters." The bald suit's lip curled. "Bring a lawyer."

CHAPTER NINETEEN

"I CAN'T BELIEVE it's really happening."

Maggie slipped her passport into her handbag, then sat at the kitchen table. "The custody papers have been approved by both solicitors."

"By this time tomorrow, it will all be over." Tracy raised a mug in salute.

"As soon as it's ratified by the court, Emily and I will apply for residency."

"Great. We'll also formalize the partnership agreement."

"You don't have to do that," Maggie said softly.

"You're already doing the job—you should reap the benefits. Besides, I love the thought of the two of us working together and succeeding in a venture we've created and grown."

"*You've* created and grown."

"Your hard work these past few months has helped make us what we are. So be graceful and accept that you're stuck with me."

Maggie grinned. "Thank you."

Her sister's riposte was interrupted by the doorbell.

A few moments later, Jenny rushed into the kitchen. "Have you heard about Bad Boy?"

From her friend's pale face, it was serious.

"Is Jake hurt?" Maggie's heart squeezed.

"They're accusing him of being the big NHL name in that internet-pharmacy scandal." Jenny dropped into a seat. "He's been suspended."

"Jake would never take steroids."

"I know. But apparently they have Jake's name and credit-card information on several orders."

Though the evidence sounded damning, Maggie knew it couldn't be true. "I don't care. Jake's innocent."

"The Cats are standing by him, but the League's hands are tied. With steroids being such a hot topic, they need to know how many hockey players are involved."

"He won't even allow anesthetic when he's stitched up. Why would he take steroids?" Maggie shook her head. "It doesn't add up."

"There's huge pressure to stay healthy, heal quickly and keep playing," Tracy offered. "Plus, the game has got so fast and the margin for error is small."

"You have an inside track, Jenny," Maggie said. "You must have heard rumors about players using."

"Sure, but never anything about Jake."

"Then who? Anyone on the Ice Cats?"

"No..." Her hesitation suggested she knew something but was loath to share it.

"You can trust us."

"It's not about trust. It's...difficult." Jenny sighed. "In the months before Adam's death, I heard speculation that he might be juicing."

Despite her friend's reluctance, Maggie sensed they were on the right path. "Go on."

"Some players always try to cut corners. Especially if they're not really good enough. Adam didn't have Jake's natural skill and he often struggled to perform."

"His stats *were* unusually good in the weeks before he died. He could have had some 'extra help.'" Tracy used air quotes.

"All athletes go through fluky spells." Maggie hated what this would do to Jake if it was true. "Were there any other signs?"

"His erratic behavior," Jenny said slowly.

"Had he bulked up? Did he have skin problems?"

"Maybe. But if Adam was using, why don't the investigators have his name?"

"They may have ignored him because he's dead."

"Perhaps he didn't use that internet pharmacy," Tracy suggested.

An idea occurred to Maggie. One that made horrible sense. "What if he used the pharmacy but didn't use his own name? What if he used Jake's information as a cover?"

"He wouldn't do that to his closest friend." Jenny's words lacked conviction.

"Why? Because he was such a great bloke?" She was tired of hearing about how wonderful Adam was. "If he took steroids, he'd have been desperate to hide it, and Jake would be a perfect cover."

The more she thought about it, the more she knew it was the answer. "If we could prove what Adam did, we could clear Jake's name."

"Jake's hearing is this afternoon," Tracy said. "There isn't enough time to find proof."

"Without concrete evidence, convincing anyone Adam's guilty will be impossible." Jenny looked apologetic.

There had to be a way. "What about Adam's roommate, Nick? He'd know."

"If he did, he'd have said so by now."

"Unless he was trying to protect himself." Maggie blew out a frustrated breath. "Can you get hold of him?"

"Give me a few minutes to make some calls."

Her friend pulled out her phone and began dialing. Within minutes, she had Nick's number. She put the call on speaker when he answered.

They exchanged greetings, then Jenny got to the point. "Was Adam using PEDs?"

The silence vibrated with tension.

"Jake's career is on the line here, Nick. He doesn't deserve to be punished for something we both know he didn't do."

Still, he said nothing.

Exasperated, Jenny swore. "Look, I don't care if you were using, too. Just tell me the truth about Adam."

Finally, Nick said quietly, "We both tried them. But when they didn't work, I quit. I begged Adam to stop, but he kept upping the dose. Then he started stacking, using multiple steroids at once."

"Why didn't you tell someone? Get him help."

"I couldn't risk it, in case they suspected I'd taken them, too."

Doing nothing had cost Adam his life and almost killed Jake, Maggie thought bitterly.

"Why didn't you say anything after the accident?" Jenny's voice was calm despite her disgusted expression.

"I thought they'd figure it out when they examined his body. When they didn't, I let the secret be buried with him. You know, I've been trying to reach Jake since they raided that internet pharmacy, but he won't return my calls."

Nick's whining grated on Maggie's nerves.

"Do you have information that will help Jake?" Jenny asked.

When he didn't reply, she spoke through gritted teeth. "If you don't tell me, I'll go to the NHL and you'll be implicated."

He swore. "Adam used a credit card in Jake's name to buy the drugs."

Maggie felt both relieved and sick. Jake's friend had set him up.

"Do you have proof?" Jenny demanded.

"It's in those boxes that Jake has."

Both Maggie and Tracy were on their feet before Jenny had hung up.

"Do you still have the key Jake gave you?" Tracy grabbed the car keys.

"Yes, but we can't just go into his house and open them without his permission."

"Call and ask him."

"He might refuse," Jenny warned. "Jake won't want to tarnish Adam's memory, even to save himself."

"Without his permission, the investigators may not allow the evidence," Tracy added.

Maggie's heart sank. The very traits that convinced her Jake was innocent might seal his guilt. The kitchen clock ticked loudly, emphasizing the passing time.

"Stuff it." She thumped the table. "Let's find the papers first, then worry about the rest of it later."

"What about your flight?" Tracy tapped her watch. "We've only got a few hours before you have to leave."

"Jake can't wait." Maggie didn't hesitate. "I'm packed and ready to go. So the sooner we get going, the sooner we get this done."

"All right," Tracy said. "I'll drive."

Her sister broke the speed limits getting to Jake's house, but no one complained. Once inside, they rushed down into the basement. The boxes were in the same place the delivery guy had dumped them on the day Jake had moved in.

They went through the boxes one at a time, checking each one meticulously, then resealing it and moving it across to the other side of the basement.

An hour passed, then two. The pile of unopened boxes diminished steadily, but they didn't find what they needed. The silence in the basement grew tense as the minutes ticked by, broken only by the rustle of paper and the jarring rip of packing tape.

Finally, there was only one box left.

Maggie took a deep breath as she sliced through the tape. The evidence had to be in here.

On the surface, it contained memorabilia and albums of press cuttings. Pucks, folded game-worn jerseys, programs and photos.

Her shoulders slumped as she stacked the items carefully beside her.

Time to admit defeat.

Lifting out a promotional bobblehead doll, she noticed the bottom of the box wasn't lined with packing paper like the others. Curious, she pulled out a thick plastic folder filled with documents.

Her heart jolted.

With shaking fingers she opened the folder. Even before she'd finished reading the top page, she knew she'd hit the jackpot.

"A credit card receipt from the internet pharmacy in Jake's name, but with Adam's address. And the card itself." She flipped it over. "This isn't Jake's signature. We have to get this to Jake's hearing."

Jenny dusted her hands on her jeans and got to her feet. "My boss is out of town and I don't have any meetings this afternoon." She was the personal assistant to a local media mogul. "If we leave now, we should just make it."

Tracy looked at her watch and grimaced. "You'll have to go without me. I need to be there when Emily gets home from school." She turned to Maggie. "You have just enough time to get home before the driver arrives to pick you up."

Maggie had a tough choice to make. If she missed the plane, she'd miss tomorrow's meeting and lose her deal with Patty. She had no wiggle room. It was that meeting or nothing.

On the other hand, this was her chance to prove to

Jake that she believed in him, even if he didn't believe in himself.

Newark Airport or the NHL headquarters in Manhattan?

"I'll get the evidence there in time," Jenny promised.

Maggie had no choice. There was only one answer.

Much as she wanted to follow her heart, this time her daughter came first.

THREE FORTY-FIVE.

The minute hand inched forward. The illuminated NHL logo in the reception of the League's headquarters seemed to pulse with the same frequency as Jake's heart.

He ran a finger under his too-tight collar. The damn thing was choking him. This already felt like the longest day of his life, and it wasn't anywhere near over. His parents and Aunt Karina had dropped by the house earlier to show their support.

"We'll show them you're not a jerkie."

"Junkie." He'd managed a half smile for Tru's mom.

"Junkie, jerkie. It's the same, no?"

"Either way, you're not a cheat," his mom had said, straightening his tie. Their unquestioning belief in his innocence had touched him deeply.

As had the many supportive texts, tweets and emails from teammates and other players, referees, commentators, journalists and fans. The Cats and the NHL Players' Association had issued statements backing Jake and vowing to clear his name.

The one voice he'd wanted to hear was Maggie's.

But his phone had remained silent. Despite what had happened between them, he knew she wouldn't believe this crap about him. That he needed her reassurance only reinforced the mistake he'd made.

Rotating his tense shoulders, he steeled himself for the meeting ahead. How had he ended up in this mess? It was like one of those thrillers where the hero knows he's innocent, but everyone else thinks he's guilty. Only the chances of a happy ending in Jake's case were zero.

Now Phillip Hannah and Max sat alongside the NHLPA lawyer and Ike, the union rep, waiting to be called into the meeting. They were clock-watching, too—the team was flying to Boston later. Jake knew, barring a miracle, he wouldn't be joining them.

He got to his feet, needing to move. He paced the corridor, past the monitors that covered the walls, showing classic games. The steel-gray and white decor, inspired by blades and ice, felt stark and unforgiving.

At the far end was an alcove containing a huge crystal slab etched with an image of the Stanley Cup. On the walls behind were plaques engraved with the names of those who'd won it. If this crazy situation wasn't resolved, he'd never get the chance to see his name up there.

Or to honor Adam.

"Mr. Badoletti, they're ready for you in the executive boardroom."

The walk back to the reception area was the hardest of his life. Each step taking him closer to the end of his career.

"It'll be fine." Ike squeezed his shoulder.

Jake would have joked about his friend's uncharacteristic optimism, only his throat was too tight. He nodded and followed Ike into the conference room.

The NHL commissioner, a short, gnome-faced man with thinning dark hair greeted them before sitting at the head of the long table. To his right were the other League officials and the suits from the previous day. All looked grim.

Jake sat opposite the suits. Ike and Max flanked him and were joined by their GM and the lawyer.

The commissioner restated the League's position on banned substances before handing over to the bald suit. But before he could speak, a commotion of raised voices sounded outside. The door burst open, and a woman with long, blond hair rushed in, with the receptionist hot on her heels.

Jake was shocked. What was Jenny doing here?

"I said you couldn't be disturbed, but she got away from me." The receptionist glared at Jenny.

"I have crucial evidence and I won't leave until I've presented it." Jenny walked to Jake's side of the table, clearly marking herself as one of his team.

His head reeled as if he'd been high sticked even as a spark of hope lit within him. What evidence could she have?

"I'll deal with this." The commissioner nodded to the receptionist. Once she'd gone, he said, "I don't know who you are, but this is an important meeting."

His patronizing tone made Jake grind his teeth. He was about to leap to Jenny's defense, but she shook her head at him.

"I am fully aware of the gravity of this meeting. I wouldn't have insisted on being here otherwise." Her voice was calm and professional, despite her casual outfit. "My name is Jenny Martin and I represent Making Your Move. They're employed by the Ice Cats to look after Jake Badoletti."

"That's true." Phillip Hannah nodded, though he looked as bemused as Jake felt.

"I don't understand the relevance." The commissioner frowned.

"Following Mr. Badoletti's move from Chicago, there were a number of unopened storage boxes in his basement. He asked Making Your Move to sort through them on his behalf and organize their contents."

What was she talking about? Which bo— A lightbulb flashed in his brain. Adam's things. There was evidence in those boxes?

He'd barely processed that thought when Jenny dropped her bombshell.

"In one, we discovered papers pertinent to this case." She slapped a folder on the table. "This contains proof that Adam Stewart took out a credit card in Jake Badoletti's name and used that card to order steroids from the internet pharmacy."

The room erupted as everyone began to speak at once. Neither of the suits looked smug now.

Jake swallowed the bile that rose. Adam was responsible for this?

The commissioner called for quiet. "This will need to be checked out."

"Be my guest." She slid the folder down the table

toward him. "Before I go, I'd like a moment with Mr. Badoletti."

The commissioner nodded.

Still shell-shocked by what she'd revealed, Jake rose and joined her. Once in the corridor, Jenny said, "Let's get away from that room."

As if she knew he needed a few moments to process what he'd heard, she walked silently by his side until they reached the alcove with the etched Stanley Cup.

Jake stared at the holy grail of hockey, recalling his earlier guilt. Emotions swirled inside him. Relief at knowing the truth warred with sadness and disappointment. Jenny's information explained Adam's strange behavior that last night, but not why his friend had framed him.

He threw his head back and glared at the ceiling. "How could you betray me like that?"

No answer. No rumble of thunder nor lightning bolt—the lights didn't even blink.

Typical.

Anger erupted. For all his sins, Jake would never stab a friend in the back. Hell, he wouldn't do that to an enemy. Adam may have seemed like a good man, but he hadn't understood the meaning of friendship or loyalty.

Jenny touched his arm. "Adam wasn't a saint, but he wasn't the devil, either. Like the rest of us, he was a human being with flaws who made some bad decisions."

"How can you defend him? His 'bad decisions' nearly cost me my life and my career."

"He paid a pretty high price himself."

Her soft words cut through his rage. She was right. Adam had paid the ultimate price.

Jenny had been right about Adam all along. Hell, everyone who cared for him had said the same thing but he hadn't been able to see it. Until now.

Saint, sinner…sinner, saint. It wasn't that simple, that black-and-white. If it wasn't that simple for Adam, then maybe it wasn't for Jake, either.

Maybe he wasn't the devil he thought he was. Maybe there was a good man inside Jake Badoletti after all. That was something to think about. At least, once today was done.

"This nightmare will soon be over," he said. "I can't thank you enough."

"I know you're still reeling and you've got to get back into the meeting. But before I go, there's something you should know."

What else could she possibly throw at him? "Go on."

"Maggie never doubted you." Jenny forced him to meet her steady gaze. "She was determined to do something. She pushed to find the truth."

Jenny explained what they'd done. "Maggie risked missing the meeting that would have guaranteed sole custody of Emily because she wouldn't give up on you."

She reached up and kissed his cheek. "Think about that, Bad Boy."

The realization of what Maggie had been prepared to sacrifice for him was humbling. All because she believed in him. Even after he'd pushed her away, her faith in him hadn't wavered. She'd seen beyond his reputation, beyond his nickname, beyond his own self-doubt. She'd seen the man he wanted to be.

The man he was.

The fist that had gripped his heart since the accident loosened. He blew out a shuddering breath and with it went the anxiety and guilt of the past eleven months. The self-recrimination and the self-doubt. With it, too, went his anger toward Adam. For what he'd done—taking the drugs and framing Jake. For what he hadn't done—believed in their friendship enough to ask for help.

And, Jake was finally able to admit, for dying.

Adam's death had been the wake-up call Jake had needed. His own survival had been a chance to put things right. What Jake hadn't understood until now was that with everything his friend had lost when he'd died, Adam had lost the chance to put things right, too.

As he walked back down the corridor to the conference room, Jake realized this was another wake-up call. A chance for a do over. One he intended to seize with both hands.

He'd still do everything he could to win the Stanley Cup and raise it in Adam's honor. But he also planned to do something else his friend had never got the chance to do—live a life that was long, happy and free from regrets.

A life that, assuming he could get her to agree, would include Maggie and Emily.

His pace quickened as his mind buzzed with renewed purpose. He had a lot of work to do. Starting today.

Starting now.

Jake opened the door to the conference room. "If we're done here, I have some things I need to take care of."

"WOULD YOU LIKE breakfast?"

Maggie smiled at the flight attendant. "Tea and a bacon sandwich would be lovely."

She was exhausted. Unable to sleep, she'd been too restless to read or watch a movie. Hopefully, adrenaline and caffeine would keep her going until she was on the plane home.

The lack of phone service on the plane had left too much time to think and worry—about Jake, her upcoming meeting with Lee then Jake again.

Had Jenny arrived in time? Had the information been enough?

Would Lee actually sign the papers? Could this finally be the end of it?

How had Jake reacted when he'd learned about Maggie's help?

She'd deliberately pushed aside thoughts of the future. There'd be plenty of time for that on the return journey, once she'd seen how everything played out.

Maggie stirred her tea. The time hadn't been wasted. She'd sorted out her jumbled feelings about her past and decided finally to stop beating herself up about loving a celebrity lifestyle. Who wouldn't enjoy going to glamorous events, meeting household names, wearing designer fashions and receiving special service—like an upgrade to upper class when the woman at the Virgin Atlantic check-in had recognized her?

Sure there was a downside—the lack of privacy, the paparazzi, the gossip media. But like the calories in her bacon sandwich, that was the price you paid.

"More tea?" the stewardess asked. "This will be the last round before we land."

"No, thanks."

"We'll be starting our descent shortly, so if you want to beat the rush for the bathroom, I'd nip in now."

"Good idea." Maggie stood and got her carry-on bag down from the overhead locker.

The problem, she reflected as she got changed, wasn't the lifestyle but her lack of self-belief. Her mistaken fear that enjoying those things would somehow turn her back into meek Margaret and she'd make the same mistakes that had hurt Emily.

"I'll never be meek Margaret again," she told her reflection. And while she'd probably make mistakes, she'd never do anything to hurt her daughter.

Maggie had finally embraced the person she really was.

"Ladies and gentlemen…"

At the pilot's announcement, Maggie buttoned the jacket on her red suit. She'd brought it deliberately because it had marked a turning point in her blossoming self-confidence and her relationship with Jake. She hoped it would mark a turning point in her future.

Somehow the suit gave her extra strength, as if Jake was with her. She could almost feel the warmth of his hand against her back as she returned to her seat. The whisper of his breath against her neck as she fastened her seat belt.

Instead of making her more vulnerable, having the right man by her side made her stronger. Jake was the right man. She knew that to the depths of her soul.

But how did she convince him?

The jolt of the plane landing broke into her thoughts.

Once inside the terminal, Maggie switched on her phone. Her heart lifted as she listened to Emily's voice mail—her version of a hockey chant.

"Let's go, Mummy! Go, Mummy, go!"

Tracy added her good luck wishes but said nothing about what had happened at NHL headquarters.

Scrolling through her texts, Maggie found one from Jenny. A smiley face.

Jake's name had been cleared. Relief filled her, but she was left with unanswered questions. How had he reacted? What did this mean for the future?

Maggie shook her head. She couldn't fret about that now. She had a meeting to get to.

As she didn't have luggage, Maggie breezed through the formalities. The prebooked driver was waiting in arrivals, holding up a sign with her name.

Despite the rush-hour traffic, the journey passed quickly. As neither side had wanted to risk a media presence, Samantha had suggested using a neutral office facility near the airport.

When Maggie arrived, her solicitor was already there. They hugged, laughing over their coordinating outfits; Samantha wore a stunning red tweed suit and the same black patent Chanel shoes as Maggie.

"The meeting shouldn't take long." Samantha led the way into the conference room and chose seats on one side of the long table. She opened her red-leather briefcase and laid out folders. "Everything has been agreed in principle, so all we need are the signatures."

Maggie poured them coffee. "You think it'll go that smoothly?"

"Sadly, no. Lee is bound to make a last-minute power play to soothe his ego. But I won't let him derail things." She gave Maggie a firm look. "Don't let him get to you."

Maggie squared her shoulders. "I won't."

"Good. Now, before they get here, we should go through the amendments."

They took their seats and bent their heads over the folders. The phone rang as they finished, announcing that Lee and Patty had arrived with their lawyer.

Maggie's heart thumped heavily. "Showtime."

Samantha rubbed her hands together, her smile predatory. "I'm looking forward to finishing that weasel off."

The door opened and Patty came into the room, alone.

It was like looking in the mirror ten years ago. Maggie shouldn't have been shocked by the changes to the young soap star, but she was. Patty's once-dark hair was now blond. The plum-and-gold leather Versace suit was low cut, with a micromini that barely covered her bum, while the six-inch heels of the matching Prada peep toes made Maggie's calves ache.

"Lee's on the phone. He'll be here shortly." Concern tinged Patty's smile.

When the door opened again, Maggie tensed, but the

familiar dread at seeing Lee never appeared. Though her stomach knotted nervously, she felt calm, strong. Ready to deal with whatever Lee threw at her.

As ever, her ex made a grand entrance, talking loudly on his mobile while barking out orders to the lawyer scurrying behind. He stalked to the table, stopping behind Patty's chair. He unbuttoned his Armani jacket, then shot his cuffs, fiddling deliberately with his Rolex before resting his hands on Patty's shoulders.

Maggie recognized the pose. She recalled the bite of his fingers into her skin, an admonition to do as she was told. It felt good to be free of him.

Once again, she was surprised. He no longer scared her. Lee seemed smaller, slighter than she remembered. His skin was pasty, and his hair had been carefully slicked back over the beginnings of a bald patch that he must curse every morning.

Compared to Jake, her ex definitely came up short.

"You look terrible, Margaret." He cast a pitying look over her. "Your hair, that suit. Positively middle-aged."

What a jerk. Instead of shriveling inside, Maggie restrained her urge to laugh. His opinion couldn't have mattered less. "Shall we get on with the meeting?"

His eyes narrowed. "We'll start when I'm ready."

"Well, get a move on." Maggie tapped her watch. "I have a plane to catch."

He clenched his jaw. "How dare—"

"Lee has to get back to the training ground, too," Patty interceded quickly. "He has a big game on Saturday."

"Ah, yes." Maggie couldn't resist tweaking the tiger's

tail. Especially now she knew his teeth couldn't harm her. "You're hoping to impress the England manager. Good luck with that."

Lee glared at her, then sat.

"Before you both sign, I'll outline the terms of the agreement so there is absolutely no misunderstanding," Samantha said smoothly. "Maggie retains full custody and is free to take Emily to the U.S. permanently. Lee's visitation rights remain unchanged."

Maggie and Patty exchanged knowing looks. Those visits would never happen.

"Child support continues until Emily is nineteen. Finally, any future attempts to challenge this agreement will be dealt with under New Jersey state law. If that's clear, you may sign the papers." Samantha passed Maggie her Montblanc fountain pen and showed her where to sign.

Lee pulled out a gold Cross Townsend.

Maggie held her breath. She wouldn't rest easy until the ink was dry.

He touched the pen to the paper, then stopped. He smiled maliciously as he put the pen down. "I won't pay child support for a child I have nothing to do with."

Samantha didn't blink. "By law, you have no choice."

"Then chase me for payment through the New Jersey courts."

"It doesn't work that way."

"Lee, darling…" Patty began, but stopped when he speared her with a blazing glare.

Maggie didn't care about the money, but she was fed up with Lee's silly games. She wouldn't let him mess her around again. "Stop being childish and sign the damn papers."

Lee surged to his feet, fist clenched. "You stupid bitch."

Samantha leaped up, throwing her arm protectively in front of Maggie.

Lee's solicitor sputtered as Patty pleaded for calm.

Maggie's heart pounded but she wasn't scared of him anymore. "Sit down and shut up."

"How dare you speak to me like that?"

Maggie rolled her eyes. "Quite easily. Your bully-boy tactics bore me. Now, either you sign those papers or I'm calling a press conference. I don't think your team will be too impressed when they hear my story."

Patty gasped. "But you promised."

Samantha sat, a smile playing around her lips.

"I'll keep my end of the bargain if Lee does." Maggie laid her phone on the table, then crossed her arms. "He has two minutes, or my first call will be to the *Daily Mail*."

Lee's solicitor murmured furiously. After a couple of tense moments, Lee slashed his signature across the papers, then tossed them across the table.

"Patty, we're leaving. Now." He stormed out.

Patty jumped up and rushed after him, shooting an annoyed look at Maggie over her shoulder. Lee's solicitor gathered his papers and followed, closing the door behind him.

Maggie slumped back in her chair, letting out a heavy breath.

"Well done." Samantha laughed. "I think you've seen the last of Lee."

"I hope Patty will be okay. This deal wouldn't have happened without her. I hate to think she'll bear the brunt of his fury."

"She's made her bed—it's up to her to choose if she really wants to lie in it." Samantha touched Maggie's arm before putting the folders in her briefcase. "Go home, hug Emily for me and enjoy your new life."

Giddy with happiness and relief, Maggie grinned. "Thank you. I will."

Adrenaline kept Maggie going until she got onto the plane. As she got to her seat, her knees suddenly went weak and she sank into the seat.

"Can I get you a drink?" the flight attendant asked.

"Definitely champagne."

The woman smiled politely as she passed a champagne flute. Probably thought that was what Maggie always drank. She didn't care. She was celebrating.

Once the plane took off, Maggie fell asleep. She didn't wake until it was time to land. Thankfully, a driver was waiting for her in arrivals, and they were soon in the car, heading for the turnpike.

Maggie stared out of the window at the familiar landmarks. A sense of homecoming filled her heart. She couldn't wait to see Emily and Tracy.

She couldn't wait to see Jake, either. She was tired of waiting for him to realize what they had together was special. Time to stop allowing the past to deny them the chance of a wonderful future. Maggie let her head drop back and closed her eyes. She fell asleep planning what she'd say to him.

She woke as the car stopped. It took a moment to realize the Victorian they'd stopped in front of wasn't Tracy's. Her heart jolted. She started to tell the driver he'd made a mistake, but the words died in her throat as Jake stepped forward and opened the door.

"Welcome home, Maggie."

CHAPTER TWENTY

MAGGIE STARED AT Jake's hand as he offered to help her out of the car, but didn't move.

His smile wavered. "Do you want Chuck to take you to Tracy's house?"

The uncertainty in his expression cut through the shock that had immobilized her.

"No, that's okay. I'll stay." She put her hand in his, savoring the warmth and strength of his grip. "For now."

"Thank you." Jake touched his lips to her fingers, sending a tingle through her, then released her. "Go on in. I'll get your bag."

As she climbed the steps, Jake took her carry-on from the driver and palmed him a tip.

Maggie paced the entrance hall. This had to be a good sign, didn't it? He wouldn't bring her here to tell her they had no future. Would he?

Jake closed the front door and put her bag at the foot of the stairs. The scene had a cozy familiarity to it, as if they'd done it a hundred times before. *Wishful thinking.*

"I should let Tracy know I'm here." She unbuttoned her coat. "When I called her from the airport, I said I wouldn't be long."

"She knows."

Maggie arched an eyebrow. "My sister let you kidnap me?"

Jake massaged the back of his neck. "She wanted to help an idiot man apologize."

Her pulse skipped. "I see."

The conversation died to awkward silence as they stood, trying to read each other.

"Why don't you make yourself comfortable and I'll make you some tea?"

"All right." She laid her coat over the banister.

Heat flared in his eyes as he saw her red suit, giving her a boost of confidence she didn't know she needed. Suddenly, she felt in control again.

"I'll wait in the den."

Jake nodded. "I won't be long."

She walked down the hall, putting an extra swing in her hips.

In the den, her confidence faltered. Memories of their last conversation…argument…disaster flashed through her mind. Hopefully, they'd exorcise that specter shortly.

She turned on table lamps to brighten the room in the fading afternoon light. Deliberately, she sat in Jake's leather armchair, kicked off her shoes and curled her legs under her.

Jake entered a few minutes later and handed her a mug of tea. She smiled—he'd made it just as she liked it.

He sat on the sofa, resting his elbows on his thighs and staring into the steaming mug he cradled in his hands as if it held the meaning of the universe.

Maggie sipped her tea and waited.

"Jenny told me what you did. How you believed in me." He exhaled heavily and looked up, meeting her gaze. "Thank you doesn't seem enough."

"You were innocent. It was only a matter of time before they uncovered the truth."

"How much would it have damaged me, my integrity, in the meantime? The suspicion would never have gone away. People would have always questioned whether there was any truth in the story."

"Not the people who know you."

"Maybe." Jake shrugged. "Anyway, thanks to you, I don't have to worry about that. My career and reputation are safe."

"What happens next?"

"The investigators verify the information, but that shouldn't take long."

"Good. The sooner you can put it behind you, the better. Then you can focus on playing hockey and winning the Cup." *And me,* she added silently.

"Yeah." His voice resonated with unspoken emotion.

He must be thinking of his friend. "I'm sorry about Adam."

His shoulders hunched, as if he was bracing himself against the painful knowledge of his friend's betrayal. "Me, too."

"I don't suppose the investigators will do anything with the evidence against him."

"There's no point." He put his mug on the table. "But Adam's parents want to make the story public."

Her eyes widened. "They do?"

"I spoke to them after the hearing. I thought they should hear about Adam from me." He scrubbed his hand over his jaw. "They felt terrible about Adam's deceit, but they were also relieved to have an explanation for his death."

She felt sorry for them. "Maybe it'll help them heal."

Jake smiled. "We're setting up the Adam Stewart Foundation, to provide education about the dangers of steroids and support people caught up with them. If we prevent even one athlete from following that path, it'll mean Adam's life wasn't wasted."

Maggie wasn't surprised Jake had found a way to honor his friend despite Adam's betrayal. Jake was a good man. If only he could see the truth about himself.

"This mess with Adam opened my eyes." He leaned forward. "Made me realize my old high-octane life didn't make me a bad person. Just as all Adam's noble deeds didn't make him a saint." He tapped his chest. "What's in here is what's really important."

Maybe Adam had done him a favor after all. Happiness filled her. Still, uncertainty remained. He'd said nothing about what that meant for her or their relationship.

"Do you plan to go back to your old life?" Her heart gave a heavy thump as she waited for his answer.

He shook his head. "I don't want that anymore. At least, not all the time. I wouldn't mind the occasional party or high-profile event."

He waited for her reaction, his gaze intent.

"That's a lesson we both learned." She smiled and

shared her thoughts from the plane. "It's not the life that makes the woman or man, but the other way round."

"So you'd be happy to accompany me to another function? I'd like another shot at showing everyone how serious I am about you."

Her smile faded. Not quite the result she'd hoped for. "I thought you said there wasn't another big event until June."

"There isn't. But, if you agree, this one will be special."

"I don't understand." She frowned.

"It would be our wedding. I'd like you to marry me."

Her heart slammed against her ribs. "M-marry?"

He took the cup out of her hands and twined their fingers. "You're perfect for me."

"Hardly." Her old insecurities rose, threatening to choke her. "I won't change, Jake. Not for you. Not for anyone."

"I don't want you to."

She searched his eyes. Could she trust the message that glowed in the brilliant blue depths? "You don't?"

"I love you, Maggie, just as you are."

She'd heard of time standing still but had never experienced it until now. "Oh."

"I'd hoped for a little more enthusiasm."

Happiness exploded within her. "Wow."

"Better." He grinned.

"Are you sure? There will always be issues and people desperate for a story. What happens the next time things go belly-up and we're splashed across the media?"

"Nothing can hurt us if we deal with things together. We make a good team. If we're honest and trust each other, we can handle anything anyone throws at us." Jake's earnest expression was as convincing as his words.

Doubt lingered. "Even if it distracts you from your play?"

He looked chagrined. "My insecurities hampered my play. I didn't trust what was in my heart. You helped me believe in myself again. Gave me the strength to be the man and player I want to be. I know you don't like hockey, but…"

Maggie laid her finger over his lips. "I love you just as you are."

When he started to speak, she shook her head. "Hockey's not bad. Just don't expect me to keep quiet when someone hurts you."

"Same goes." His tongue licked the length of her finger, sending heat spiraling through her. "You didn't answer my question. Will you marry me?"

"Yes, please," she breathed, as his mouth covered the pulse point of her wrist.

"How about raising a hockey team of our own?" His lips trailed along her arm, lingering at the inside of her elbow.

She gasped as desire pooled deep within. "Well, maybe a top line."

"And a defensive pair."

"That's five children!"

He laughed and took her in his arms. "I believe in big families."

"We'll see," she managed, before his mouth covered hers.

His kisses were still convincing. And delicious.

When he finally lifted his head, he asked, "Do you think Emily will be okay with this?"

"Trust me, she'll be thrilled."

"I nearly forgot." He pulled an old red box out of his pocket and flipped open the lid. "This was my grandmother's ring. If you don't like it, we can get another one, but I thought it would be perfect for you."

This time, the word didn't make her wince. As he slipped the ring onto her finger, she smiled, then pulled his head to hers. "You're right...it's perfect."

EPILOGUE

"Last minute of play in the period."

The sound of 18,000 people on their feet, cheering, clapping and stomping, almost drowned out the announcer's voice. Maggie had never experienced anything like the excitement inside the arena.

Beside her, Emily jumped up and down as Jenny and Tracy screamed themselves hoarse. Gio high-fived everyone around him while Tina and Aunt Karina hugged tearfully.

The volume exploded as the crowd counted down the final twenty seconds of the game.

Maggie joined in, though her throat tightened, stealing her voice as her Jake flew over the boards with Tru at his side. There was no way Minnesota could get three goals in the time left, but Jake's expression was as intense for the final face-off as it had been for the first.

With five seconds to go, helmets, sticks and gloves were tossed to the ice as the victorious Ice Cats began to celebrate. Jake leaped in the air, fist pumped, then bear-hugged Tru. They both raced across to join the swarm of screaming, laughing, hugging players surrounding Ike. JB jumped into the mass like a body-surfer at a concert.

The sheer joy in their faces made Maggie well up.

Her heart ached momentarily for their defeated opposition, who stood heads hanging or sat slumped on
the ice. It had been a tough series, each game decided
by one goal. The teams had alternated victories, finally
needing the seventh game to break the deadlock. She
knew what it had cost Jake to get to this point, how
he'd played his heart out. She couldn't imagine going
through all that and facing the agony of coming up one
game, one goal, short.

"Mummy, look!" Emily shouted.

Maggie's gaze swung to the glass to see Jake blow-
ing kisses to her.

I love you, he mouthed.

Her tears spilled over.

Tracy and Jenny hugged Maggie, laughing and teasing.

As the teams' traditional handshake line started, a
steward collected Jake's family and friends and guided
them to the Zamboni entrance, where they could watch
the Cup ceremony before joining the players on the ice.

Once the Cup was on its stand, the NHL commissioner began to speak. A chorus of boos rang out.
Those boos turned to cheers as he handed Scotty Matthews, the Ice Cats' captain, the huge silver chalice. The
crowd went wild as Scotty raised the Cup over his head.

Maggie hadn't thought she could get any more emotional, but when the captain passed the Cup to Jake, the
tears started again. Her heart swelled with pride and
joy as she saw the man she loved realizing the dream
he'd had since he'd first strapped on skates.

Before he passed the trophy to Tru, Jake looked up to the rafters and bobbed the Cup in tribute to Adam.

Her Bad Boy truly was a good man.

A SHORT TIME later, Maggie stood beside Jake as he answered commentator Mike "Doc" Emrick's questions.

Battered and bruised, sweat poured down his face and clung to that awful play-off beard Jake had insisted on growing. It didn't hide his new array of scars.

How she loved this man. Her warrior.

She couldn't wait for their wedding, next week after the NHL award ceremony. She and Emily had already moved into Jake's house.

It seemed a long time since she'd arrived in New Jersey, wondering what her new life would bring. Even in her wildest dreams she couldn't have imagined how it had turned out, from her partnership with Tracy in Making Your Move to her very own Bad Boy.

As Jake would say—perfect.

"Last question, then I'll let you carry on with your celebrations," the commentator said. "What of the future? You've already said you'll be back with the Cats next season, ready to make another run for the Cup. What else do you hope for?"

Jake grinned, then winked at Maggie. "A baby."

* * * * *

LARGER-PRINT BOOKS!
GET 2 FREE LARGER-PRINT NOVELS PLUS
2 FREE GIFTS!

H HARLEQUIN®

super romance®

More Story...More Romance

ReaderService.com

Manage your account online!

- Review your order history
- Manage your payments
- Update your address

**We've designed
the Harlequin® Reader Service
website just for you.**

Enjoy all the features!

- Reader excerpts from any series
- Respond to mailings and
  special monthly offers
- Discover new series available to you
- Browse the Bonus Bucks catalog
- Share your feedback

Visit us at:
ReaderService.com

RS13